BOOK ONE OF

THE SHROUD SOLUTION

A SUSPENSE NOVEL

K. BRUCE MACKENZIE

The Shroud Solution
A Suspense Novel
©2020 K. Bruce Mackenzie

All rights reserved.

Books may be purchased in quantity and/or special sales by contacting the author or publisher at *BruceMackenzieAuthor.com*.

Published by

BruceMackenzieAuthor.com

Book Design: Nick Zelinger, NZ Graphics
Book Consultant: Judith Briles, The Book Shepherd

ISBN: 978-1-7334007-0-1 (Hardcover)
ISBN: 978-1-7334007-1-8 (Paperback)
ISBN: 978-1-7334007-2-5 (eBook)
ISBN: 978-1-7334007-3-2 (Audio)
LCCN: 2019918830

First Edition

Printed in USA

To the Memory of My Mother and Father
Who Worked Tirelessly To Provide Me With a Strong Education
Florence and Malcolm Mackenzie

PART ONE

THE ASSIGNMENT

CHICAGO, ILLINOIS
WEDNESDAY, APRIL 11, 2001
11:22 A.M.

He stood at the observation window of the nursery at the maternity ward looking at the newborns with a satisfied expression. He appeared to be a proud new father.

In reality, he was an assassin searching for his target.

Code name Cobra, he knew this would be the most difficult and most important assignment of his career. He received the contract only this past Monday evening and at first, he refused to accept it. Never had he been given a target like this. But, when he was told the background and what the survival of the target would mean, he gladly accepted the challenge. And, what an enormous challenge it was.

In the past, he had been given weeks, sometimes months, to prepare. He had the time to study his targets, their schedules, habits, and idiosyncrasies. He had the time to plan the location, the time, and the method of assassination. False identities, disguises, and—most important—his escape were all meticulously planned and developed.

Not this time.

He was given only two days to develop his plan, formulate his identity, travel to Chicago, study the surroundings and, finally, to execute his target and make his escape. There was no leeway; there was no tomorrow; there was no room for error. Failure was unacceptable.

The future of millions of people depended upon him.

Before his departure, he colored his hair with gray highlights, glued on a fake mustache to match the photo of one of his American passports, and selected a plain gold wedding band from his large collection of jewelry. With his dark complexion, he appeared to have recently returned from a family vacation in the tropics. He wore

3

a navy blue traditional American business suit with a white shirt and a solid dark blue tie.

He blended in perfectly.

He arrived at O'Hare International Airport on an early morning flight and took a taxi to the Park Ridge Sheraton. Satisfied after observing the lobby traffic for ten minutes from a comfortable armchair, he took another taxi to the Northwestern commuter train station. Standing on the platform amongst the crowd in the brisk morning air, he carefully observed all the surrounding people. He waited only a short time for the next train to downtown, confident he was not being followed or eyed with suspicion.

Less than thirty minutes later, he joined the throngs of bustling commuters streaming through the downtown Northwestern Station. It was a typical overcast damp Chicago April morning, which accentuated the smell and taste of automobile and bus exhaust. As he walked the three blocks from the Northwestern Station to the Union Station, he noticed how few people spoke as they hastened to their workplaces. They were oblivious to the blaring of car horns and the shrill police whistles as traffic was directed through the busy intersections.

After surveying his surroundings, he boarded a taxi and had the driver take him to the Drake Hotel on North Michigan Avenue. After entering the hotel, he watched the taxi depart and then walked two blocks to the Ritz Carlton Hotel at Water Tower Place. He checked in under the name of William Dodd, paid cash for the room and retrieved a package that had been left for him by a delivery service. He allowed a bellman to show him to his room, giving him an average unmemorable tip. After closing and locking the door behind the departing bellman, he opened the package. Satisfied with its contents, which included a backpack, he hung the uniform in the closet and put the rest of the items in a dresser drawer.

After exiting the hotel via the Michigan Avenue entrance, he walked the four blocks to Chicago Metropolitan Hospital. As he stood on the sidewalk across the street, he studied the gray granite exterior and paid close attention to the emergency exit door on the ground level at the west end of the massive fourteen-story building. He had previously accessed the floor plans of the eighty-year old structure on his computer and knew exactly where he needed to go.

Satisfied, he crossed the street and entered the hospital, walking purposefully past the information and security desk toward the elevator bank. One of the receptionists called out, "Sir, you need to sign in and get a visitor pass."

"Oh, I'm sorry, I went outside for a walk," he replied. Reaching in his suit coat pocket, he produced a hospital visitor badge, which had been left for him in the package, and clipped it to his lapel. He smiled at her as he added, "I'm sorry, I almost forgot."

Cobra continued to the elevators and rode up to the maternity ward on the fourth floor. Breathing in the sterile antiseptic air, he walked past the nurse's office and approached the large glass viewing windows. Glancing at the two couples looking at their babies through the large viewing windows, he wondered if either of them might be the parents of his target.

He distanced himself from the doting parents and proceeded to count the number of bassinets. There were thirty-seven, with twenty-six being occupied. He assumed the other eleven babies were in the rooms with their mothers. Disappointed, he observed the bassinets were not labeled with the names of the occupants but rather with a hospital code. Unfortunately, this could prevent him from identifying his specific target unless he could locate the occupancy chart. Glancing at his watch, he noted that it was nearly noon. He had enough time.

He observed several large racks of metal shelving lining the far wall, containing towels, bed linens, and both plastic and cloth diapers.

There were also several cabinets lining the wall. He watched as a nurse came into the room, went straight to one of the cabinets and pulled out a pair of latex gloves, putting them on her hands. As he began to formulate his plan, a sinister smile momentarily crept across his face. Had someone seen it, they would have felt a chill sweep over their body. But he was too smart and too experienced to let body language give him away. His warm smile quickly returned, and he once again appeared to be the ecstatic father of a newborn baby.

He looked up, observed the ceiling tiles and counted the sprinkler heads. He allowed a brief smile. Continuing to watch the nurses at work, he waited patiently until one opened the door to the large storage room located at the back of the nursery. Once again, the sinister smile briefly darkened his face. Everything was exactly as he had hoped.

Realizing he had been there for nearly an hour, he walked toward the end of the hallway, passing a door to the nursery. He casually tried to turn the knob. As he expected, the door was locked, but it was a lock he could easily pick. Continuing to the end of the hallway, he opened the door to the emergency stairway and stepped through to the landing. As he closed the door, no alarm sounded, and his shoulders relaxed. Everything was fitting into place.

A moment later he descended to the main floor and entered the lobby. Again, there was no alarm. As he walked past the security desk, one of the guards stopped him and said, "Sir, what were you doing in the emergency stairwell?"

Giving his warmest smile, the assassin responded, "I thought I'd get some exercise by walking down the stairs."

"Didn't you see the signs saying hospital personnel only?"

"I'm sorry, I didn't notice them. It won't happen again."

"That's okay, no problem. Do you want to turn in your badge?"

"No, I'm just going out for a walk and to grab a bite to eat. I'll be back in a while." He smiled at the guard and glanced at the information sign. Visiting hours were 9:00 a.m. to 8:30 p.m. Leaving the hospital, Cobra grinned as he strode away. This was not going to be as difficult as he had thought. Almost everything he might need was in that storage room or on the shelves.

Back at the hotel, he went to the gift shop and bought three packs of cigarettes and a lighter. He also asked the clerk for six books of matches and where he might purchase duct tape. He was directed to the sundry shop where he made his purchase, then went to the coffee shop. After a light snack he went straight to his room, checked that no one had entered during his absence and stripped naked.

After a long hot shower, he turned the water to cold and stood in the icy spray for a full thirty seconds. Refreshed, he admired himself in the mirror as he dried off. He was tall, six feet three, with a lean muscular body. His dark hair was cut close in an American style and the gray tint made him look older than his thirty-three years. His face was handsome when he smiled, which he did only when he had to. Running his fingers over the scars from the two bullet wounds in his chest, he thought about the mistakes he had made early in his career and his vow to never let that happen again. He kept himself in shape with daily exercise and he was an excellent athlete, having mastered physical skills that would keep him alive. His advanced military training earned him commendations for martial arts, marksmanship, and close order weaponry.

In short, Cobra was a highly-trained, highly-skilled killing machine with neither compassion nor remorse.

———

After peacefully sleeping for several hours, he retrieved the uniform and the other items that had been left for him at the hotel that morning and placed them in his backpack. Before he left his room, he wiped down every surface, handle, and doorknob he had touched. As he walked back to the hospital through the crisp air, he contemplated his assignment, preparing himself for possible multiple kills.

The sun was setting as he clipped the visitor pass to his lapel while climbing the steps to the main entrance of the hospital. This time the security guards barely took notice of him and did not comment on the backpack as he walked past them to the elevator bank. Instead of taking an elevator up to the fourth-floor nursery, he went down to the cafeteria. He had two and a half hours to occupy and he was hungry. Cobra didn't leave anything to chance. He did not want to be one of the last visitors to walk past the security guards—the last one in their memories.

He took his time eating, watching the other diners as he slowly ate a slightly stale roast beef sandwich. When his watch read 7:50, it was time to play the role of the proud new father and visit the nursery. This time, there was one couple and three single men admiring their babies as Cobra entered the observation area. He nodded and flashed a brief smile as he walked to the end of the viewing windows. One of the men appeared to be a young doctor as he was dressed in hospital scrubs and had a stethoscope around his neck.

Cobra gazed at one of the sleeping babies while watching the reduced nursing staff from the corner of his eye. By 8:20, the other visitors had departed, and he quietly walked to the emergency stairs. As he passed the door to the nursery, he again tried to turn the handle.

It was still locked. It didn't matter.

He entered the stairway landing to prepare himself for the long wait. After climbing the stairs to the first landing, he sat against the wall in a strategic location where he could observe the stairs leading up as well as those leading down. Mostly he relied on his hearing. If he heard someone coming down the stairs, he would silently walk down ahead of them until they exited. Likewise, if someone was coming up, he would climb until they left the stairwell.

He had another seven hours to wait.

CHICAGO, ILLINOIS
THURSDAY, APRIL 12, 2001
3:31 A.M.

Finally, it was time.

The assassin took off his business suit and put on the black pants and matching black button-down collared shirt. White lettering spelled out "Reliable Plumbing Company" on the shirt pocket. He changed shoes, putting on a pair of soft-soled shoes and then clipped on the contractor's pass from his bag. After stuffing his discarded clothes into his bag, he fastened the tool belt around his waist. Satisfied, he left the stairwell and silently walked out into the nursery viewing area.

As expected, it was empty.

He easily picked the lock to the door and eased into the dimly lit nursery. There were only two female nurses in the next room, doing paperwork at their desks. He anticipated a larger staff. They would not be obstacles for long.

He silently walked to the storage room door, entered and retrieved the step stool he had observed that afternoon. Cobra placed the stool under one of the sprinkler heads, climbed up and gave out an intentional cough. Every action he made had a purpose.

The nurses rushed into the room. The first one through the door demanded, "Who are you? What are you doing here?"

"I'm sorry, I didn't mean to startle you," he replied, flashing a warm smile. "I was called at this ungodly hour to repair the sprinkler system in the newborn nursery."

"I wasn't told anything about this. How did you get in?" she snarled. The younger nurse stood by her side.

"They let me in the door over there." He turned and pointed to the door with the lock he had just picked. Again, he gave her a warm smile. She seemed to relax for a moment, then scowled at him. "No one is allowed in here without my knowledge and approval, especially in the middle of the night. Let me see your work order," she demanded.

"Of course," he politely responded as he climbed off the stool. Reaching in his back pocket, he pulled out some papers and held them out to her in his right hand. As she moved toward him in the dim light, he could observe her a little better. She was young, about thirty years of age. Her auburn hair fell around a strikingly pretty face.

He focused on her eyes, so he was unable to size up the rest of her. If she made a sudden retreating move, he was ready to spring at her and her eyes would give away her intention before her body would. The younger nurse remained silent but appeared concerned.

As she moved forward to reach for the work order, he made his move. With the quickness of a striking serpent, his left hand lashed out and grabbed her throat. He drew her body into his, turned her sideways and wrapped his right arm around her head. He gave a quick jerk to her head, snapping her delicate neck. As she went limp, Cobra dropped her body to the floor.

The younger nurse clasped her hands to her mouth, eyes wide with horror. Before she could utter a sound, he grabbed her by her hair and yanked her head up. He gave a hard chop to her throat, crushing her windpipe. After letting her crumble to the floor, he felt for a pulse in both bodies.

Satisfied they were both dead, he dragged the bodies into the storage room and dropped them at the far end where they could not be seen. He found the two oxygen tanks he had seen earlier and wheeled them out into the dimly lit nursery, placing one at each end of the room.

After glancing at the rows of bassinets, he rushed to the nurse's office and searched for a list of the babies' names.

Nothing.

Quickly and silently, he went to work. Gathering a bundle of cloth diapers from the storage racks, Cobra set about lifting the ceiling tile at one of the sprinkler heads. Wrapping a cloth diaper around the sprinkler head he tied it with the duct tape. He quickly did this with each of the sprinkler heads in the main nursery room, storage room, and each of the supply closets, constantly on the alert for the arrival of any hospital staff.

He was familiar with this type of fire prevention system. The main valve had a tamper alarm which, if activated, would send an alarm directly to both the fire department and the security desk. There were zone valves located above the ceiling grids, also protected by tamper alarms and there were smoke detectors located in several locations in the nursery and each of the supply closets and the storage room. He disabled them.

He knew he could not deactivate the entire system, so he had to temporarily immobilize it. The sprinkler heads would be activated when heat melted the temperature-sensitive link at the sprinkler head. The diapers around the sprinkler heads would delay the activation. Once the system was activated, the diapers would contain the spray, resulting in ineffective dripping of the water to the floor.

Cobra went to the metal shelving racks and moved one of them to the center of the nursery. The bottom shelves held linens while the upper shelves stored towels, cloth diapers, and baby blankets. He went to the storage room, gathered all the bottles of alcohol and placed them on a cart. Rolling the cart out to the nursery he heard, for the first time, the sounds of whimpering and soft gentle moans coming from the bassinets. He paused for a few seconds as he thought about what he was about to do.

He had no room for weakness.

He went to the supply cabinet, removed all the boxes of latex gloves, opened them and spread them over the linens on the bottom shelf. Then he opened the bottles of alcohol and poured them over the linens. He went back to the two other metal shelves laden with linens, towels, blankets and diapers and moved them out to the ends of the room next to the oxygen tanks, repeating the procedure of spreading latex gloves over the linens and dousing them with alcohol. Constantly listening for any unusual sounds, he hurried to the nursing station in the next room and locked both doors leading to the outside corridor. He then slid a desk in front of each door, making entrance difficult.

Once again, he rifled through the papers stacked on the desks and searched through the desk drawers.

No list.

Disappointed, but resolved, the assassin hastened back to the nursery. He surveyed his work. Satisfied, he removed his uniform and again put on his business suit. Now, it was time for the final part.

He unwrapped all three packs of cigarettes and removed four or five cigarettes from each pack, throwing them on the floor. He then opened three packs of matches, placing one on each of the three alcohol-soaked linens on the three shelves. He took out three cigarettes and lit them altogether, taking several puffs of each one to get the tobacco burning. He slid a burning cigarette back in each pack, the burning end facing out. He started at the shelves at the end of the room furthest from the door and quickly placed the pack next to the open book of matches. He rushed to the center shelf and then the shelf nearest the door, repeating the procedure.

Now that the time-delayed fuses were set, he opened the valves of the oxygen tanks, slowly spreading gas into the nursery. He grabbed his bag and left the nursery, locking the door behind him as he hurried to the stairwell and silently ran down the stairs. Passing the main floor, he descended one more floor to the exit door to the outside and easily disabled the alarm connection.

As he left the building, he glanced at his watch and was pleased to note that the entire operation took only eleven minutes.

He hastened back to the hotel and caught a cab for the Northwestern Station. After the cab drove away, he changed direction and walked the three blocks to the Union Station. As he walked up the steps to the station, through the crisp early morning air he heard the distant wailing of sirens.

He smiled briefly as he proceeded to the departure area and the six o'clock train to Milwaukee.

Throughout the hospital, the speaker system emitted three loud chimes followed by the announcement: *"Mr. McRoberts, fourth floor, Pod A. I repeat, Mr. McRoberts, fourth floor, Pod A. I repeat again, Mr. McRoberts, fourth floor, Pod A."*

A young doctor on the fifth floor, just finishing his tedious twelve-hour shift, froze as the chimes and the message were repeated two more times. All the hospital staff knew this to be the coded message that the fire alarm system had been set off. His body chilled as he realized this was the location of the newborn nursery.

He rushed down the nearest stairway and ran toward the nursery. He coughed as he reached the smoky hallway with the viewing windows. Dark black smoke poured out from under the door to the nurse's station.

Where were the three on-duty nurses?

He reached the viewing windows, coughing in the hot pungent fumes. Looking through the windows, his heart stopped as he saw flames shooting up through thick black smoke. He ran back to the nursing station door. It was locked. He stepped back and kicked at the door with all his strength. It didn't budge. He tried two more times, then ran down the hallway to the nursery door. Locked.

Oh my God. Those poor babies can't survive that smoke and fire.

Through the viewing window, he could barely see the deadly flames through the thick black smoke caused by the burning latex. When he kicked in the door, he was met by a surge of flames that engulfed his entire body.

Within seconds, he was dead.

―――――――

It was an uneventful ninety-minute train ride to the downtown Milwaukee station.

Cobra took a taxi to the InterContinental Hotel, waited a moment until it departed, and walked five blocks to the Grand Avenue Mall. He boarded another taxi and had the driver take him to Sensenbrenner Hall at Marquette University. Walking to 9th Street, he hailed another taxi and had the driver take him to the airport. Using a different identity, he purchased a one-way coach ticket to Detroit where he would again change identities and make his way home. He felt comfortable that he had covered his tracks.

As he approached his gate, he saw large crowds gathered around the television monitors watching the CNN news channel. He saw anger on several shocked faces and tears on others.

Joining the gathering, he quizzed a female viewer, "What happened?"

Visibly shaken, she replied, "There was a horrible fire in a hospital in Chicago and thirty-seven newborn babies and five hospital staff were killed. They say it was arson." Sniffling through her sobs, she continued, "What kind of person could do such a thing? Why?"

Cobra wondered who the other three staff members were.

He would have been extremely perplexed had he known there were four other assassins in the hospital at the time of the fire.

PART TWO

THE BEGINNING

FOUR YEARS EARLIER

FLIGHT 6853
ROME TO EDINBURGH
TUESDAY, JUNE 24, 1997

The British Airways flight left Rome at 1:40 in the afternoon, bound for Birmingham and then on to Edinburgh. The two men sitting in seats 7A and 7B talked quietly. Their kind elderly faces exuded a peacefulness not often seen in the first-class section. The flight attendants normally had to cater to the egos of celebrities, business icons, or the wealthy. These two men were different; they didn't want cocktails, just a simple glass of wine for each. When the flight attendants served the meal, these two passengers simply requested whatever was easiest for the attendants to serve.

They did, however, gather the attention of the other passengers, particularly those who were Italian. It wasn't often that one had the opportunity to take an airline flight with two cardinals of the Catholic church. Dressed in their black cassocks with red trim and scarlet band cinctures, they each displayed a large pectoral cross and wore a red zucchetto. They were very noticeable.

"Oleg, you've been a lifelong friend of His Holiness and his closest confidant. You grew up together in Poland. Do you think he will listen to you when you explain our project?" asked the silver-haired cardinal, speaking Italian with a German accent.

"Oh, Loleck will listen. Whether he will see it our way is a different matter. We would be asking so much of him. He would have to circumvent a lot of church doctrine." After a contemplative pause, Oleg softly continued, "Giuseppe, it will pain me to put him through so much consternation. He has had so much tragedy in his life, but this project is critical, and Pope John Paul II is probably the strongest Pope in history."

"I know his mother died when he was young and that you saved his life in a streetcar accident," replied the silver-haired cardinal. "Tell me about your youth with our Pope. It had to have been be terribly difficult growing up in Poland during the war."

"His Holiness is three years older than I and our fathers were in the army together. Loleck's father became a tailor and my father became a baker in Wadowice. Our town had about ten thousand people at that time, eight thousand Catholics and two thousand Jews. Everyone in our town called His Holiness by his nickname, Loleck, instead of his given name of Karol."

"So, you were best friends with our Pope as a youth?"

"Yes, Loleck was liked by everyone, but he spent most of his time with his father. They lived in a one-room apartment behind the church and my family lived in two rooms attached to our bakery. His father, who was also named Karol, was a strict disciplinarian and, fortunately, Loleck was an excellent student and athlete. Like I said, he spent most of his time at home, studying religion, poetry, and theater. He had a passion for all three."

Taking a small sip of wine, Oleg continued, "I was a close friend, but his best friend was Jerzy Kluger. Jerzy and I spent many an afternoon sitting in the Wojtyla kitchen, next to the coal stove, listening to Loleck's father tell stories about ancient Greece and Rome, and, of course, Poland. We, in turn, would spend time with the Kluger family. They were rich by our standards. They had a six-room apartment overlooking the town square and we would go there and listen to music performed by a string quartet. At first, the Klugers had difficulty accepting us. They were Jews and we were strict Catholics. In those days, many Catholics were prejudiced toward the Jews, Loleck being the exception. He became a good friend to the entire Kluger family."

Giuseppe asked, "I believe that is the same Kluger who assisted the Pope in extending diplomatic recognition to Israel back in 1993?"

"Yes, that relationship has lasted over sixty years."

"As has yours, Oleg."

"Yes, it has been a wonderful relationship. He went into the priesthood, studying at an underground seminary in Krakow during the war and I joined him about a year later. All the seminaries were closed by the occupying Nazis, so we had to study in secret at night while we worked in a chemical plant during the day."

"What became of his father during this time?" asked Giuseppe.

"He died in early 1941, so he was never able to see his dream fulfilled of having his son go into the priesthood. Loleck had a sad childhood. First his mother died and then his older brother Edmund died when Loleck was twelve.

"I had forgotten that. Remind me, how did his brother die?" Giuseppe inquired.

"He died of scarlet fever when he was only twenty-six years old. He was a physician and caught the disease from one of his patients." Oleg paused, reflecting on the past, then quietly said, "That is why his Holiness is now so reflective. He understands pain and suffering. It seems as though they have followed him around his entire life." Oleg bowed his head and added, "I am blessed to have him as my friend and mentor; he is like a brother to me. I must admit that I love him more than life itself and would do anything for him."

After several minutes of silence and changing the subject, Giuseppe whispered, "Oleg, I'm afraid that if the project is successful, there will be many people who would not want to see the baby survive."

"I also have that same concern, Giuseppe. But my biggest fear is that if the project is not successful, then the world may not long survive. We have an important meeting tomorrow at the institute, and I would like to take a short nap. Now let us have no more talk of this on the airplane, there are too many ears present. We can discuss it further when we get to Edinburgh."

Cardinal Aleksandr Jaropelk, known as Oleg to his close friends, did not know just how true his words were. He also did not take notice of the passenger sitting in seat 2C.

The passenger had a dark complexion and thick curly black hair. He was wearing casual slacks with a short sleeve shirt revealing thick black arm hair. He appeared to be sleeping throughout most of the flight, listening to music on his headphones.

Close inspection would reveal these were not the airline-provided headphones and they were not plugged into the outlet on the armrest. They were plugged into a pocket-size amplifier/recorder, from which another wire led to a highly sensitive directional microphone. The passenger had a blanket draped over his lap so no one could observe the audio interception device or the directional microphone, which was placed under his left arm and was aimed directly at seats 7A and 7B.

It was early evening when the two cardinals retrieved their bags and took a taxi to their hotel, The Scotsman, in Edinburgh. It was a plain granite building, only because it was the former headquarters of Scotland's leading newspaper and had been transformed into one of its better hotels. Oleg and Giuseppe were surprised with its grand marble staircase and stained-glass windows where the senior staff of the old newspaper had once walked.

After checking in, they went to their rooms to freshen up, agreeing to meet in the hotel restaurant for dinner at 7:30. At the airport and now again at the hotel, they were the object of interest by many of the nearby people and the subject of conversation of most of those.

Even with seventeen percent of the population, the Catholic church was not particularly strong in Scotland. The fires of the religious wars of the seventeenth century still burned brightly in the hearts of many Scots as the animosity toward the Church had been passed down through generations. Many, if not most, of the eighty-five thousand Catholics were Catholics in name only. The people of Scotland were not used to seeing cardinals in their midst and most did not even recognize them as being cardinals.

One man in the crowd did recognize them. The dark-complexioned man with thick curly black hair stood at the far side of the lobby and casually watched them as they checked in.

At dinner, the cardinals each ordered the same menu items, after receiving recommendations from their waiter. They chatted over a haggis appetizer, leeks soup, a greens salad and an angus beef filet mignon, cooked medium rare. The food at the Vatican was excellent, but angus beef was a rare treat. They had the waiter select a bottle of merlot, which they sipped before and during dinner.

"Oleg, you've done all of the research on this project, tell me about our meeting tomorrow."

"Well, my friend, in anticipation of this discussion, I brought some information with me on the Roslin Institute." He reached in his pocket and removed his handwritten notes. "It was established in 1993 and named after the local village. It's a wholly owned, but independent institute of the Biotechnology and Biological Research Council. Its predecessors, however, go back to 1919 when they were linked to animal genetics research at the University of Edinburgh. In 1993 it was transformed from traditional farm animal research to research of modern biotechnology to farm and other animals."

Cardinal Jaropelk paused to enjoy several bites of his filet before continuing his reading. "They apparently have more than three hundred on staff plus students and visiting scientists who work in molecular and cell biology, quantitative genetics, endocrinology, development biology, animal behavior and nutrition."

With a dash of humor, Giuseppe commented, "I have no idea what that all means, but it sounds very impressive. With such a large, highly skilled staff, where do they get their money?"

Searching through his notes, Oleg found what he was looking for, and continued reading. "Roslin Institute has a very large annual budget and receives additional funding from a variety of different sources, including governmental, industrial and private." After taking several more bites of his delicious steak, Oleg observed, "We know they have experimented with animal genetics and it is possible the next step might be human genetics. That as you know, Joseph, is exactly why we are here. Tomorrow we will meet with Dr. Graham and Dr. Wilmut."

"Tell me about them, Oleg."

Again, looking at his notes, Oleg responded, "Dr. Duncan Graham is the director and chief executive of the Roslin Institute and is an honorary professor of genetics at the University of Edinburgh. He was trained first in agriculture and then in genetics. He's in charge of the entire institute."

Pausing to find the biography of Dr. Wilmut, he continued, "Dr. Wilmut is fifty-three years old and was born in England. He led the team that cloned Dolly the sheep in July of last year. In 1995 he led a team that created live lambs, Megan and Morag, from embryo-derived cells that had been cultured in the laboratory for several weeks. This was the first time that live animals had been derived from cultured cells. The next step was the creation of Dolly. Dolly was the first animal cloned from a cell taken from an adult animal. Prior to this, biologists thought that the cells in our bodies were fixed in their roles. The creation of Dolly from a mammary gland cell of a six-year old sheep showed that this was not the case."

"How did they come to name the cloned sheep Dolly?" Giuseppe inquired.

"I read that they named her after an American singer named Dolly Parton. Why, I don't know."

"Well, now that they have cloned a sheep, I wonder what the next step is."

"As you know, Giuseppe, that is exactly what we are here to find out."

The two cardinals returned to their dining, savoring their succulent steaks in silence. After finishing their dessert of fresh berries bathed in a marsala sabayon sauce, the cardinals sipped their wine, chatting idly.

Getting back to the topic of their trip, Giuseppe asked, "Are we going to see Archbishop O'Brien?"

"No, for his own safety I did not want to get him involved. I had him set up our meeting at the institute tomorrow, but that is the extent of it. He was somewhat taken aback that we could not meet with him and was curious as to why we wanted to meet with the scientists. God forgive me, but I had to be untruthful."

"What did you tell him?"

"I simply told him that His Holiness is concerned about where this scientific breakthrough is headed, and he wanted us to meet with the head of the institute. Dr. Graham is a large contributor to the church and Archbishop O'Brien knows him well. I instructed him that this meeting was to be held in the strictest of confidence."

Glancing at his watch, Cardinal Jaropelk yawned. "Between the long day of traveling and the excellent dinner and wine, I am exhausted." As they got up and left their table, most of the diners watched the two men of the Church.

One diner did not watch; he was seated with his back to them several tables away. As the cardinals left and all eyes were upon them, he deftly tucked the directional microphone into his coat pocket, along with the recorder to which it had been attached.

25

After several minutes, the man with the thick dark curly hair also left the dining room and headed to his room. He was anxious to listen to the recording and to report the conversation to his superiors.

EDINBURGH, SCOTLAND
WEDNESDAY, JUNE 25, 1997
9:00 A.M.

The black Bentley from the Roslin Institute arrived at precisely the appointed time to pick up the two cardinals in front of their hotel. They had been standing by the entrance in the cool misty morning air for several minutes.

The driver introduced himself as Angus MacGregor and told them he worked for the Roslin Institute as head of security. Appearing to be in his early thirties, he was a large man, about six feet six inches tall. He appeared to weigh a solid two hundred and fifty pounds and to be in excellent physical condition. His warm smile made the cardinals feel comfortable, but as he opened the back door for them his steely blue eyes quickly glanced about, looking for anything out of the ordinary.

"I am not a Catholic; how do I address you two gentlemen?" he asked the two cardinals as he got behind the wheel on the right side of the Bentley.

Oleg sat back and sunk into the soft leather upholstery and with a warm smile brightening his face, responded, "You can call me Cardinal Aleksandr or by my nickname, Oleg. This is my colleague, Cardinal Giuseppe."

"We have some extra time before your meeting with the director at 10:00. Would you like a quick tour of our city?"

"That would be wonderful," answered Giuseppe. "We've never been to Edinburgh."

Angus drove a short distance to Edinburgh Castle and gave them a brief history of the enormous fortress. After several minutes he drove them down the Royal Mile past St. Giles Cathedral to Holyrood House. "Now, this is truly a castle. It was home to the kings and queens of the sixteenth and seventeenth centuries."

The cardinals were fascinated to learn that the Royal Family stayed at Holyrood during their annual summer visit to Edinburgh.

Leaving the old part of the city, Angus drove south through quaint residential neighborhoods. Oleg noticed that Angus had stopped his tour directing and was concentrating fully on his driving. He thought this a little odd since the traffic was light and Angus must be well familiar with the roads.

It was nearing ten o'clock, the time of their appointment, when Angus announced that he was making a slight detour to fill the car with petrol. Oleg was again curious as to why Angus would make this detour when they must be only a few minutes from their destination. Angus took his time filling the car with petrol and then departed for the clinic.

"Do you gentlemen ever travel with security?" Angus inquired.

"No, we don't. Why do you ask?"

"I'm simply curious."

Driving down a two-lane quiet country road, Angus turned the Bentley into the driveway of the Roslin Institute. Passing the security building on the right, they approached the security gate.

As a uniformed guard approached the car, Angus stepped out and the guard held a small device up to his eyes. Looking at the reading on the device the guard nodded his approval and then peered into the back seat of the Bentley. After a few quiet words with Angus, the guard again looked into the back seat and welcomed the visitors to the Roslin Institute.

"Angus, if you don't mind my asking, what was that about?" Giuseppe inquired.

"We have very tight security here at the institute. There are some who would like to pirate our research and there are others who would like to stop our research. I won't go into all of the security measures, but suffice it to say, they are extensive," replied Angus.

They drove past the security gate a short distance to the entrance to the headquarters building. Angus got out of the car and stepped back to the rear door, holding it open for the two representatives of the Vatican.

"I'll escort you to the director's office," Angus stated as he held open the front door of the building for them. Oleg observed that the building was plain and sterile in appearance, but the grounds were well manicured and appeared to be extensive.

After they approached the metal detectors, Oleg noticed there were several security cameras mounted on the lobby walls as well as in the elevator. It took several minutes to get cleared, as the cardinals were wearing metal crosses. The security guard was forced to run a hand-held metal detector over the two guests. He apologized profusely and was politely informed by the cardinals that this was a common occurrence.

Exiting on the top floor of the three-story building, they again went through a metal detector with the same results and proceeded to an office door at the far end of the corridor. Again, Angus held the door open for the visitors. After entering the reception area, they were greeted by the director's secretary, introduced by Angus as Mrs. Morrison.

Glancing at her watch, Mrs. Morrison commented, "The director has been waiting for you for ten minutes, I'll see you in."

"That was my fault," Angus declared. There was no sign of remorse in either his voice or his mannerisms; this was simply a matter of fact statement.

Mrs. Morrison looked up at him with raised eyebrows.

As they entered the spacious cherrywood-paneled office, Dr. Graham, joined by another man, came around from behind his desk to greet them. "Cardinals, it is a pleasure to receive you both. I'm Duncan Graham. Please be seated," he said in a crisp matter-of-fact tone as he directed them to the seating area.

There were six upholstered wingback chairs surrounding a round table forming a conversation area in the middle of the office. At the far end of the office, Oleg noticed a large formal conference table with twelve leather chairs.

"May I offer you some tea?" Without waiting for an answer, Mrs. Morrison had already poured tea at a nearby serving credenza and set four cups on the table. Without further prompting she excused herself and left the office, closing the door behind her.

"Gentlemen, how may I help you?"

"Please Dr. Graham, call me Oleg and my colleague, Giuseppe. It is our pleasure to meet you." Facing the other man, "And, you must be Dr. Wilmut."

Dr. Graham responded, "Actually, Dr. Wilmut is out of the country on business. This is Dr. Wilmut's top assistant, Ian McKinney. Dr. McKinney has worked closely with Dr. Wilmut on the Dolly Project. I assume that is why you came all the way from the Vatican to meet with us, to make certain that our scientific breakthrough is not going to lead to the cloning of humans."

Giuseppe quickly responded, "I must say, Dr. Graham, you certainly are direct. Yes, that is one reason we are here to talk to you."

Satisfied, Dr. Graham leaned back. "Cardinal Giuseppe," he

challenged, "You have an Italian name, yet you speak English with a German accent?"

Oleg interjected, "Allow me to explain. Oleg is short for Aleksandr. My full name is Aleksandr Jaropelk and Giuseppe's the nickname I have given my associate here. His full name is Joseph Ratzinger and you are correct, he is a German."

Cardinal Ratzinger added, "Oleg thinks that someday, heaven forbid, I may become Pope and that I would have a much better chance having an Italian nickname. He means this, of course, in jest."

Cardinal Jaropelk added, "My colleague is too modest. He is high on the list to become Dean of the College of Cardinals someday."

"That is most impressive." Before Dr. Graham could continue, his telephone suddenly rang.

The cardinals didn't know it, but Mrs. Morrison had strict orders not to interrupt during a meeting unless it was an emergency. He walked over to his desk. "Excuse me for a moment, gentlemen." Picking up the phone, he curtly said, "Yes?" Dr. Graham listened for a moment, then interjected, "Any idea who? Keep me apprised."

As Dr. Graham was listening and talking, Oleg watched him closely. He could tell this was a man with a strong personality who was accustomed to having his directions carried out promptly and correctly. In his midfifties with brown thinning hair and an expensive business suit, he seemed to have a polite, pleasant personality. Still, there was a sternness to him that fit his position.

Ending the short telephone call, Dr. Graham rejoined his guests. "I must admit that because of your comment, Cardinal Jaropelk, I am curious. Please, let's get to your reason for this visit."

Oleg began the conversation. "His Holiness, and the entire College of Cardinals are very concerned about the direction of modern genetic science." With a somewhat knowing look on his face, Dr. Graham started to interject.

As he held up his hand to silence Dr. Graham, Oleg continued, "I will come directly to the point. You have successfully cloned a sheep and there is grave concern that your next step will be to clone a human being. Is it possible to clone a human being? And, if it is, what is your position on this matter?"

Dr. Graham had anticipated this question. "You are very direct and to the point. I appreciate that. I, too, will be direct. First, you tell me that Cardinal Ratzinger is in line to become Dean of the College of Cardinals and someday possibly Pope. Why is it that you, Cardinal Jaropelk, appear to be leading this inquiry?"

"Dr. Graham," Cardinal Ratzinger interjected before Oleg could respond, "It is true that I am at a higher level at the Vatican than my colleague. However, you should understand that Cardinal Jaropelk is the closest friend and confidant to His Holiness. They grew up together and His Holiness will listen to whatever Oleg has to say."

"Thank you, I understand," Dr. Graham responded. "Now, in answer to your question, we absolutely have no intention whatsoever to attempt to clone a human being. We believe this would be carrying genetic science too far. However, I think you should understand where we think these discoveries will lead us."

Pausing for several sips of tea, Dr. Graham sat back with his arms crossed. "A clone is merely the name for a group of organisms or other living matter with exactly the same genetic material. Genetic material consists of genes, the parts of cells that determine the characteristics of living things. Gentlemen, there are countless clones that exist today."

Cardinal Jaropelk's eyes widened as he turned to his colleague, Giuseppe, and saw him suck in his breath.

Duncan Graham paused and Ian McKinney remained silent with a knowing smile.

Graham continued, "There are many examples of clones that exist in nature. In human beings and other higher animals, clones form naturally in the form of identical twins. Single-celled organisms, including bacteria, protozoa and yeast, produce genetically identical offspring through asexual reproduction. These offspring are considered clones because they develop from only one parent. Plants can also reproduce asexually through a process called vegetative propagation. A piece of root or stem can generate a new plant that is genetically identical to the donor plant. Vegetative propagation helps people obtain plant clones with desired traits. For example, a farmer or breeder will use this technique to develop apples with a unique flavor or roses with a certain color." Dr. Graham paused again to take several more sips of his tea before continuing.

"The term cloning refers to three distinctly different procedures, each with different goals. It is unfortunate that the first thing people think about when they hear the word 'clone' is a Hollywood movie with the creation of human monsters or an army of superhuman soldiers. The reality is quite different."

He paused to observe their reaction. He noticed that Cardinal Ratzinger bristled when he used the term "human beings and other higher animals." He decided to leave that topic alone. He had the cardinal's attention and he didn't want to waste time by diverting onto another subject.

"As I said, there are three different types of cloning. The first is embryo cloning and is a medical technique that produces monozygotic or identical twins or triplets. It duplicates the same process that nature uses. One or more cells are removed from a fertilized embryo and are encouraged to develop into one or more duplicate embryos. Thus, twins or triplets are formed with identical DNA. This has been done for many years on various species of animals, but there has not been any experimentation on humans, to our knowledge."

Both cardinals leaned forward as they listened to the lecture.

Dr. Graham continued, "The second type of cloning is adult DNA cloning, also known as reproductive cloning. It is a technique that produces a duplicate of an existing animal. The DNA from an ovum is removed and replaced with the DNA from a cell removed from an adult animal. Then, the fertilized ovum, now called a pre-embryo, is implanted in a womb and allowed to develop in a new animal. This is how Dolly was created. The third type is called therapeutic cloning and is also known as biomedical cloning. This is a procedure whose initial stages are identical to adult DNA cloning. However, the stem cells are removed from the pre-embryo with the intent of producing tissue or an entire organ to be transplanted back into the person who supplied the DNA. The pre-embryo dies in the process. In the future, this procedure could produce a healthy copy of a sick person's tissue or organs for transplant and could be greatly superior to relying on organ transplants from other people."

"Why would this procedure be better than organ transplants?" Oleg inquired.

"There are several reasons," Dr. Graham responded. "First, the supply would be unlimited; there would be no waiting lists. Second, the tissue or organ would have the sick person's original DNA so the patient would not have to take immunosuppressant drugs for the rest of his or her life. Further, this would mean little or no danger of organ rejection."

Getting up to refill his cup of tea, Dr. Graham kept speaking. "This is the direction that genetic research is going, gentlemen, not in the cloning of humans. There simply is no reason to clone humans. What would we achieve? There is enough research to be done in biomedical cloning to keep us all busy for decades. We want to develop the procedures for creating new organs to extend man's healthy lifespan, not create man. That is God's work, not ours."

Both cardinals shifted uneasily in their chairs at this last statement.

"Before I finish with the scientific aspects of cloning and move on to the moral aspects, I will answer your previous question. Yes, it will someday be possible to clone a human being." Dr. Graham paused to let this statement sink in. "However, the science has not progressed anywhere near the point where this is possible. In the case of Dolly, a cell was taken from the mammary tissue of a mature six-year-old sheep and was fused with a sheep ovum which had its nucleus removed. The 'fertilized' cell was then stimulated with an electric pulse."

He paused for dramatic effect. "Now, listen closely, gentlemen … we made two hundred and seventy-seven attempts at cell fusion. Of those, only twenty-nine began to divide. These were all implanted in ewes. Of these, thirteen became pregnant, but there was only one birth—Dolly."

Again, pausing for several sips of tea, he continued, "What I'm trying to tell you is, this science is in its infancy. We don't know what the ramifications of Dolly will be. Will Dolly be fertile and able to produce offspring? We just don't know. Also, cells seem to have an internal clock that causes them to die off after a normal life. Since Dolly was conceived from a six-year-old cell, does that mean her life expectancy will be reduced from eleven years to five years? Does the cloning process create random errors in the expression of individual genes? The egg must have its genes reprogrammed in minutes or hours during the cloning process. Ova normally take years to ripen naturally in ovaries. What will these effects be? Again, we just don't know. Our understanding of reproductive cloning, at this time, is just too meager to even contemplate research into human cloning."

With this pause, both cardinals, along with Dr. McKinney at the request of Dr. Graham, got up and refilled their teacups. This gave Cardinal Jaropelk an opportunity to briefly study Dr. McKinney. While standing next to him, the cardinal observed that he was considerably taller than himself. He thought him to be a handsome man, with wavy sandy-colored hair. But he seemed very dour. Dr. McKinney had yet to say a word during the entire meeting.

"Gentlemen," Dr. Graham continued, once everyone was again seated, "I've given you the basics of the scientific aspects of the cloning procedure. Now let me tell you exactly where this institute and where I personally stand on the moral aspects of this science. There are several arguments both for and against human cloning. Believe me, we have heard and discussed them all. Allow me to recite just a few of the arguments against cloning." His voice became stern, but still friendly, as he leaned forward and put his elbows on the table with his chin resting on his clenched fists. His piercing eyes stared first at Cardinal Ratzinger and then at Cardinal Jaropelk.

"Cloning could produce abnormal humans; they may be disabled or become disabled later in life. Such problems have occurred in other cloned animals and there is no reason to think this might not happen in humans. Large-scale cloning could deplete genetic diversity and it is diversity that drives evolution and adaptation. Cloning could result in the introduction of defects into the human gene pool. Cloning could lead to the creation of genetically engineered groups of people designed for specific purposes, such as warfare or even slavery. Cloning could lead to an attempt to alter the human race according to an arbitrary standard. Cloning is unsafe because there are too many unknown factors that could adversely affect the offspring. A clone could have a diminished sense of value. A clone could have fewer rights than other people. Clones could be used as an organ incubator for organ transplants. Cloning could destroy the traditional concept of family."

He paused and added, "Cloning is against God's will and some aspects of science should be off limits." Graham stood and firmly stated, "Gentlemen, I believe in all of these arguments against human cloning and I stand here to tell you the Roslin Institute will not be involved in any way with this aspect of genetic science."

Dr. Graham paused to let this last statement take effect. He broke the silence with a warm smile as he sat back down in his chair, stating, "Gentlemen, I hope that answers your questions and trust that this will make His Holiness feel secure in the direction that the Roslin Institute intends to proceed."

Cardinal Ratzinger's eyes were fixed on his partner as Oleg rubbed his jaw while gazing down. Finally, Oleg broke the silence and announced, "Dr. Graham, Cardinal Ratzinger and I greatly appreciate your extremely informative lecture and I am certain that His Holiness and the entire College of Cardinals, for that matter, will be more than satisfied with your direction. However, I have several questions."

"What can I answer for you?" the director responded.

Oleg swallowed and pressed his lips together. "You said that it is possible to clone a human being. Would it be possible to clone a human being from a sample of blood?"

"Yes, of course," replied Dr. Graham.

"Is it possible to clone a human being from a sample of blood that is two thousand years old?"

The room was silent until Dr. Graham softly said, "Where are you going with this, Cardinal Jaropelk?" Then he added, looking directly at Giuseppe, "And Cardinal Ratzinger?"

His entire demeanor had changed from being friendly and courteous to being serious and stern.

Taking note of this, Oleg replied, "Dr. Graham, we are here on a fact-finding mission, nothing more at this point. And we would like yours and Dr. McKinney's assurances that what I am about to ask you will stay strictly among us."

Softly, after receiving the assurances from both doctors, Oleg continued, "I would like to know if it is possible to clone our Lord Jesus Christ from the Shroud of Turin."

Graham shot up out of his chair and slammed the palms of his hands on the table, shouting, "No, it is not possible! Not only is it impossible, it would be wrong. Not only would it be wrong, it would be unholy!" He sat back down, gathering his composure.

Ian McKinney stiffened in response to Duncan Graham's outburst.

After a moment, Dr. Graham seemed to force himself to calm down. He said, "Gentlemen, I think this meeting may last a little longer than I had anticipated." He pushed the button on his intercom and said, "Mrs. Morrison, would you please cancel my appointments for the afternoon and have some lunch brought up for the four of us. Also, would you alert Angus that our visitors will not be returning to their hotel until later in the afternoon. Thank you."

"Gentlemen," Dr. Graham stated, "lunch will be soon be served. I suggest we suspend this conversation and wash up. My washroom is over there." He nodded at a closed door at the rear of his expansive office.

After each of the four men had used the facilities, they gathered at the seating area. Shortly, there was a soft knock on the office door. The door to the office opened and Mrs. Morrison ushered in the institute's chef with lunch for the director, Dr. McKinney, and the two cardinals.

As he watched the chef roll the serving cart over to the conference table and set up the lunches, Graham offered, "Gentlemen, please follow me while we take a break from our conversation and enjoy some good Scottish food. Let's see what we have here."

Taking the lids off the several platters of food, he exclaimed with delight, "We have some freshly caught grilled river salmon surrounded by boiled petite potatoes. Over here we have some quail stuffed with haggis, smothered with what looks like a berry sauce. Oh, and yes, we have here my favorite, French onion soup."

After pausing and looking at his guests, he remarked, "This soup and their wines are the only good things to come out of that wretched country." This brought modest laughter from his guests.

Oleg responded, "I cannot comment on your statement, Dr. Graham. However, I certainly agree with you on their soup and wines. I might also add their bread and cheese. If I may ask, how did lunch arrive so quickly?"

"Please, Oleg, let's cease the formalities; call me Duncan. And the same applies to you Joseph, or Giuseppe. I think I will stay with Joseph, if it's all the same to you."

"Whatever you wish, Duncan. I answer to both."

"In answer to your question, we have lunch prepared daily for our entire staff. What you are about to eat is from our executive menu."

As they dined for the next forty minutes, the conversation ranged from the excellent quality of their lunch to the Catholic Church in Scotland and to the Scottish movement for independence. There was purposely no further talk of cloning or the Shroud of Turin. They talked about the Pope and Oleg related stories of his childhood with Karol Wojtyla.

Dr. Graham asked Cardinal Ratzinger about his youth and his rise through the ranks of the Vatican. After their dining was completed, Dr. Graham stated, "Gentlemen, will you excuse Ian and me for about five minutes? We need to meet with one of my employees. Make yourselves comfortable; we shall return shortly."

"Who are we meeting with?" asked Ian McKinney as they left the director's office.

"We're meeting with your brother-in-law," responded Duncan Graham, "and I want the topic of this conversation to remain between us." They hurriedly walked down the hall to the office of Angus MacGregor.

Graham rapped on the door and then immediately entered, followed by McKinney. Angus started to rise, but sat back down when Dr. Graham instructed, "Sit down, Angus. Let's hear about your drive to the institute this morning with the two cardinals."

Ian had a puzzled look as he waited for the conversation to begin. Angus sat down with his burly arms folded across his desk.

"I picked them up promptly at 9:00 a.m. They were waiting outside for me. It certainly wasn't difficult to spot them, being dressed in their Church garments and all. We had some extra time, so I drove up to the castle and spent about ten minutes there while I gave them a little history. Then we drove down to Holyrood while I continued acting as a tour guide. After about five minutes at Holyrood we turned around to head up Cannongate to South Bridge and the drive to the institute. As we turned around at Holyrood, I noticed a light blue Opel Corsa parked facing us and the driver had his right hand up covering his face. I didn't think much of it at the time because I wasn't concentrating on looking for things out of the ordinary. Shortly after we reached Clerk Street, I noticed what appeared to be the same vehicle following us two spaces back."

Angus paused, taking several large swallows of the bottled water that he always carried with him. "I continued driving at a normal speed, observing this guy. On two different occasions, the autos between us made turns off the A-701 and he pulled over to the left to allow another auto to come between us. It was nearing your 10:00 appointment time and I decided to try and learn a little more. So, I made a slight detour by turning left onto Captain's Road and drove about five blocks to a filling station, got out and filled the tank with petrol, even though it was nearly full. I pretended not to be watching, but as he drove by, I got a glimpse of the driver."

"And what did you observe?" asked the director.

"There were no passengers, just the driver. He had very dark hair, he was probably Mediterranean, possibly Middle Eastern. We left the petrol station and came straight here. He continued to follow us, and as we drove into our entry, he continued on past."

"That was good, Angus. Were you able to make any other observations?"

"Yes, it was a rental car, so this guy was not local. If I had to guess, he was a foreigner."

"Very good," replied the director. "He will most likely be following you when you leave here. Act like there is nothing unusual and that you don't spot him. Take the cardinals directly back to their hotel and drop them off. I expect they will be leaving tomorrow, and this matter will be closed."

"Should I offer to take them to the airport tomorrow?" Angus inquired.

"No, absolutely not," Duncan commanded. "Our business with the good cardinals will be over in a short time and this matter will be over as well. I do not want anyone to receive the impression that we have had more than a cursory conversation with these gentlemen. And, Ian, I needn't remind you that this entire matter goes no further."

"Of course, Duncan," Ian quickly responded.

They returned to the director's office and found the cardinals seated in the wingback chairs where they had sat before lunch.

Dr. Graham spoke first. "Now then, my dear cardinals, this idea of yours is not only preposterous and unthinkable, it is impossible. I happen to know a little about the Shroud of Turin."

Duncan watched the two cardinals exchange glances. Apparently, they had anticipated his objection though perhaps not his vehemence.

"I would be happy to hear of your knowledge of the Shroud as long as you will allow me to interject some facts as I know them to be," Oleg offered.

"Of course," Graham conceded as he momentarily gazed downward and struggled to regain his composure. He drew in a deep breath.

"Now, as I was saying," Dr. Graham lectured, "It is my understanding the Shroud of Turin has been proven to be a hoax and a forgery. I know the authenticity of the Shroud has been the subject of heated debate for decades, but even the Pope declared it to be fraudulent."

"That is true," Oleg responded. "However, there have been many developments since the studies done in 1988 on which His Holiness based his opinion."

Dr. Graham looked straight into the eyes of Cardinal Jaropelk and then Cardinal Ratzinger.

"Gentlemen, for purposes of this discussion, I don't care if the Shroud is authentic or not. It doesn't make any difference. Any blood samples that may—and I emphasize the word may—be on the Shroud are far too old, have been tainted by hundreds of people handling the Shroud over the centuries and are totally useless. So, even if I were inclined to attempt your fiasco of an idea, it would be totally impossible." He turned to Ian McKinney for confirmation.

"The DNA not only has to be intact, but it has to be untainted in order to be useful," McKinney offered.

Ian nodded his head and softly affirmed, "Totally impossible!" He then emphasized this statement by saying, "Both now and in the future."

Cardinal Jaropelk's shoulders slumped.

Dr. Graham broke the strained silence. "Gentlemen, I know you've come a long way. You are obviously experts on the Shroud, and I would like to learn more about it from your perspective. How about you, Ian?"

Dr. McKinney responded, somewhat sheepishly, "Frankly, gentlemen, my knowledge of the Shroud of Turin is very limited. But, yes, I definitely would like to learn more."

Oleg responded with a relieved smile, "I will be delighted to relate the history of the Shroud and tell you why I am absolutely convinced it is authentic."

The director interjected, "Would you cardinals also be kind enough to explain to me why you would undertake such a monumental and history-changing endeavor, if it were possible?"

Oleg glanced at Joseph, who nodded his approval. "We will give you our reasons," replied Oleg, "but first let's discuss the Shroud."

All four sat back in their chairs, making themselves comfortable.

Oleg began, "The Shroud is one of Christianity's most sacred and most disputed relics. It is a piece of linen about four and a half meters long and a little over one meter wide. It has the front and rear image of a tall, bearded man bearing the marks of crucifixion on the front of the Shroud. Its first recorded appearance was in France in about 1300, where it belonged to the Charny family who guarded it in the French village of Lirey. In 1453, it was purchased by Ludovico of Savoy and was guarded in the village of Chambery in the Sainte Chapelle. There was a fire in 1532 and a corner of the Shroud was scorched. The Shroud had been folded into forty-eight layers and stored in a silver urn, so the fire left a symmetrical burn mark. The Chambery Clare nuns performed some restoration work by sewing on some thirty patches of various sizes. They also sewed on a backing to the entire Shroud in order to give it better support. This is important to remember, as I will explain later."

Both Dr. Graham and Dr. McKinney quietly listened without expression.

Oleg continued, "In 1587, Emanuele Filiberto carried the Shroud to Turin where it was kept, first, in the cathedral and since 1964, in the Guarini Chapel. In 1983, the exiled King Umberto II gave the possession to His Holiness, the Pope. Since then, the Bishop of Turin has been its custodian. For more than six hundred years, there has been heated debate over the origin of the image and whether or not it is the burial cloth of Jesus Christ. On the night of April 4 of this year there was a fire in the Guarini Chapel, where the Shroud was kept in a bulletproof glass case. A quick-thinking fireman broke the glass with an ax and saved the Shroud. There is strong evidence that the fire was intentionally set. Right now, the bishop is keeping the Shroud in the Cathedral of St. John the Baptist, where he plans on building a totally secure and fireproof storage facility for the relic."

Dr. Graham interjected, "I understand that one of the many arguments against its authenticity is the huge gap of nearly thirteen hundred years where there is no recorded evidence of the existence of the Shroud. Wouldn't there be some evidence of such an important Christian relic?" inquired the director, his hands raised with his palms up.

"That is an excellent question," responded Oleg with increased excitement. "Allow me to tell you what we believe its early history to be. Pollen samples taken from the Shroud reveal that it has been in Palestine and Turkey as well as northern Europe. We believe that Christ's burial cloth was taken by early Christians and kept in obscurity for safety reasons. There is a legend that the disciple Thaddeus took a cloth with the miraculous imprint of Christ's face to Edessa in about 40 AD. The legend has it that he stored it in a wall during the persecutions of 57 AD and that it was forgotten until its discovery during the siege of the city in 525. Reportedly, it was kept in Edessa until 944 and then in Constantinople until its disappearance in 1204. There was a pilgrim's account in 570 of a reference to 'the cloth which was over the head of Jesus' kept in a cave on the Jordan River.'

Oleg paused to formulate his thoughts. "In 670, there was another account of a pilgrim having seen the Shroud of Christ exhibited in a church in Jerusalem. There was a reference in the apocryphal second century 'Gospel of the Hebrew' that Jesus gave his Shroud to the servant of the priest and there was a statement by St. Nino in the fourth century that the burial linen was first held by Pilate's wife and then by St. Luke, who 'put it in a place known only to himself.' There is, of course, no way of verifying any of the stories. We tend to believe that the actual Shroud was safely kept in secrecy by early Christians during the persecutions and that its existence was forgotten for over five hundred years. This could easily have happened as its guardians may well have perished in the persecutions. We believe it ended up at the church in Constantinople where it first appears on the lists of relics in 1093 as 'the linens found in the tomb after the resurrection.' In 1203, a French soldier with the crusaders camped in Constantinople and noted that a church there exhibited Christ's burial cloth and that 'his figure could be plainly seen.' It is very likely that this cloth and the Shroud of Turin are one in the same. This is further supported by the fact that there have been no other shrouds mentioned having a full body imprint and by the existence, on the Shroud of Turin, of pollen from the Constantinople region."

Oleg knew that he had everyone's rapt attention with his history lesson. "In 1204, the crusaders sacked the city of Constantinople and carried off many relics looted from churches and monasteries of the East. The theory has been put forth that the Turin Shroud was kept and secretly worshipped by the Knights Templars between 1204 and 1314 and then passed on to a French knight, Geoffrey de Charny. Another theory put forth has it that the Shroud was brought to Besancon from Constantinople by a crusader captain in 1207. So, you see, Dr. Graham, the existence of the Shroud prior to 1300 is entirely feasible and explainable. Early Christians would not have kept records of its existence because they would not have wanted to endanger its existence during the persecutions."

"Fascinating!" replied the director. "I believe your supposition of its early history could be valid. However, it does not prove that this was the burial cloth of Jesus."

"You are absolutely correct, Duncan," Oleg responded, and then added, "I don't believe that it's possible to ever prove that it is the actual burial cloth of Christ, unless ..." He let his sentence end.

The director gave him a serious stare and sternly said, "And that is impossible, as we discussed."

Ian McKinney interjected, "Tell us about the image. What is it and how did it get onto the linen cloth?"

"I will be delighted, but, before I do, I'd like to point out some interesting aspects of the Byzantine possession of the Shroud. There are several pieces of artwork of the Byzantine era, beginning in the early 500s that show remarkable congruence to the image on the Shroud. Several professors at an American university are presently doing research on the matter. As an example, there is an icon of Christ in St. Catherine's Monastery at Mt. Sinai that shows many points of congruence. The same holds true with the coin of Justinian II struck in the late 600s. It appears that by the early 500s, the Shroud image was becoming the prototype for most depictions of Jesus Christ."

"Very interesting," commented the director.

Oleg continued, "In response to your question, Dr. McKinney, the Shroud is sepia or yellow in color and contains the image of a man in a rust color. The image is identical with the Biblical account of the scourging and crucifixion of Jesus and lacks the sharp outline and vivid color of a painting. The majority opinion up until the 1930s was that it was a medieval painting. It was exhibited in 1931 and a set of photographs was taken that led to great controversy. The photographic negatives were found to present a stronger image with perfectly proportioned features. The image was found to be anatomically perfect down to the smallest detail. The characteristic features of rigor mortis, wounds, and blood flows provided conclusive evidence that the image was formed by direct or indirect contact with a corpse, and not painted on or scorched on by a hot statue. The body was that of an adult male, about five feet eleven inches in height, with a beard, mustache, and long hair falling to the shoulders. He has been described as a man 'of a physical type found in modern times among Sephardic Jews and noble Arabs.'" Oleg paused to take a sip of tea.

Oleg's eyes sparkled with excitement as he continued. "Death had occurred several hours prior to the deposition of the corpse, which was laid out on half of the Shroud with the other half being drawn over the head in order to cover the body. It was clear to the inspecting scientists that the cloth was in contact with the body for at least several hours, but not more than two or three days, assuming that decomposition was progressing at a normal rate. Doctors described the body as being frozen in an attitude of death while hanging by the arms. The rib cage is abnormally expanded and the large pectoral muscles are enlarged and drawn up toward the collarbone. This is consistent with a slow death by hanging during which the victim must raise his body by exertion of the legs in order to exhale. The feet were positioned with the left placed on the instep of the right with a single nail impaling both.

"The greatest interest was in the wounds. Forensic pathologists described them as being flawless and unable to be faked, with each wound having bled in a manner corresponding to the nature of the injury. There are a number of facial wounds, including swelling of both eyebrows, a torn right eyelid, large swelling below the right eye, a swollen nose, a bruise on the right cheek and large swelling in the left cheek and left side of the chin. The body has countless marks of a severe flogging estimated at between sixty and one hundred and twenty lashes. These contusions are found on both sides of the body from the shoulders to the calves, with only the arms spared. Superimposed on the flogging marks on the right shoulder and left scapular region are two broad excoriated areas, considered to have resulted from friction or pressure from a flat surface, as from carrying the crossbar or writhing on the cross. Also, there are contusions on both knees and on the left kneecap, as from repeated falls. The crucifixion wounds are seen in the blood flows from the wrists and feet. The Shroud shows the nail wounds to be in the wrists, not in the palms as traditionally depicted in art. This is important because studies have shown nailing at the point of the Shroud image, between the bones of the wrist, allowed the body weight to be supported, whereas the palm would tear away from the nail under the body weight."

Again, pausing for tea, Oleg continued, "The forensic pathologists further observed that the median nerve located in the wrists would invariably be injured by the nail, causing the thumb to retract into the palm. Neither thumb is visible on the Shroud, the assumption being that their position in the palm was retained by rigor mortis. The angles of the blood flows from the wrists were roughly fifty-five degrees and sixty-five degrees, which establishes the crucifixion position. The difference in angles is due to the slightly different positions assumed by the body on the cross and is seen as having been necessary in order to breathe or an attempt to relieve the pain in the wrists. The median nerve is sensory and injuries to it are excruciatingly painful."

Oleg paused, waiting for a verbal reaction. There was none. McKinney and Graham remained silent.

The cardinal acknowledged, "Before you ask, I know the pathology I just described would have described any crucifixion victim. However, there is more."

Graham's attention increased as he awaited Oleg's next words.

"Around the circumference of the entire upper head are at least thirty blood flows from spike wounds, exhibiting the same realism as those on the wrists and feet. Between the fifth and sixth ribs on the right side of the body is an oval puncture wound with blood flowing down from the wound and onto the lower back, indicating a second outflow after the body was moved to a horizontal position. All authorities agreed that this wound was inflicted after death. What you must remember is that the crown of thorns and piercing the side of the body were particular to the death of Jesus and were not a common practice."

The director somberly remarked, "It is amazing that pathologists could discern all of this from their study."

Joseph commented, for the first time in a while, "One of the experts studying the Shroud remarked that 'The Shroud of Turin is either the most awesome and instructive relic of Jesus Christ in existence, or it is the most ingenious, most unbelievably clever, product of the human mind and hand on record. It is one or the other, there is no middle ground.' I agree with him. It is either real or the most elaborate hoax in history."

Oleg had the rapt attention of both scientists as he continued.

"Direct examination of the Shroud began in 1969 through 1973 with the appointment of an eleven-member Turin commission. Five of the members were scientists. A much more detailed examination took place by a group of American scientists in 1978 through 1981. This examination yielded identifications of pollen from forty-nine species of plants, with thirteen being exclusive to the Negev and Dead Sea areas. Others were from the southwestern Turkey/northern Syria and the Istanbul areas, with a few coming from northern Europe. The linen is a three-to-one herringbone twill, a common weave in antiquity and was hand-spun and hand-loomed."

48

Oleg paused and looked at both scientists. "This is very important because after 1200 AD, most European thread was spun on a wheel. They conducted twelve tests confirming the existence of blood on the Shroud and they found no significant traces of pigments, dyes, stains, or chemicals. It was thus determined that the image was not painted, printed, or otherwise artificially imposed on the cloth. There are far more scientific results from this examination, but the conclusion was that the Shroud was used to wrap a corpse, and the image is the result of some form of interaction between body and cloth and does not derive from the use of paint, powder, acid, or other materials that could have been used to create an image on the cloth."

Oleg paused for a sip of tea but mostly for effect.

"In short, Dr. McKinney, no one knows how the image got onto the cloth. There have been many theories put forth. Once past the disproven theories that the Shroud is a hoax, the most widely accepted Jesus theory is that with the resurrection came an enormous blast of energy that left the imprint of the body on the Shroud. I might have failed to mention that the pathologists found the blood on the Shroud preceded the creation of the image."

Oleg intended for this bit of information to have a somber effect. It did.

"My dear cardinal," the director stated with an understanding smile, "Everything you say is plausible and makes sense to me. But, what about the carbon dating and the fact that His Holiness has decreed that the Shroud of Turin is not authentic?"

"Dr. Graham, I am delighted to answer this question. First, you must realize how and when the carbon dating was done. The carbon dating was done in 1988 and it was performed on one small patch from a controversial part of the Shroud. I say controversial because this part of the Shroud had some restoration performed in the sixteenth century and this 'invisible' darning could have affected the radiocarbon dating results. A series of pictures of one of the samples used for the dating was recently sent to three independent textile experts without telling them that the samples were taken from the Shroud. All three experts recognized a different weaving on one side of the sample. According to Beta Analytic, the largest provider of radiocarbon dating in the world, a mixture of sixty percent of material from the sixteenth century, with forty percent of material from the first century would result in a thirteenth century dating. We intend to have this testing pursued further, but it does offer the potential that the carbon dating was in error. Now, I don't mean the carbon dating itself was performed incorrectly, but the single sample taken should be called into question.

"Oddly enough, the original protocol, developed by a large panel of experts prior to the radiocarbon dating, was changed. Instead of taking samples from several locations on the Shroud and presenting them to seven different laboratories, only one sample was taken and provided to only three laboratories. Of equal importance, these three laboratories did not perform any chemical analyses on the linen sample. A detailed chemical composition was never determined. Had it been, it may well have shown the there was a mixture of threads from different centuries in the sample."

"Why not simply do another radiocarbon dating?" inquired Dr. McKinney.

"There are a number of reasons, doctor," Oleg replied. "There needs to be a lot more testing of many areas before going to that expensive and very public procedure. I might also add that in 1995 the Russian scholar Dmitri Kouznetsov concluded that the 1532 fire had modified the present radiocarbon amount in the Shroud, altering its dating."

"What is the Biblical record of the Shroud?" inquired Dr. Graham.

Cardinal Ratzinger responded to this question.

"The Gospels of Matthew, Mark, Luke, and John all convey the information that Jesus' burial was hasty and incomplete because of the approaching Sabbath. All four reference that Joseph of Aramathea requested permission from Pontius Pilot to receive the body for a private burial and all four describe the body as being wrapped in a clean white linen cloth. According to John, Joseph of Arimathea and a follower, Nicodemus, bathed the body with a mixture of myrrh and aloes and wrapped it in the white linen. The wounds on the Shroud image are identical to the wounds described in the four Gospels."

Dr. McKinney had a puzzled look and appeared to be about to speak, when Duncan stood up.

"Cardinals," Duncan Graham said with a warm smile, "this has truly been a pleasure and has indeed been quite informative. I must say, based on what you have told me, I am inclined to admit that the Shroud of Turin may well be authentic. I am truly sorry that I cannot be of more assistance to you and His Holiness. I hope you are not too disappointed and that you understand."

Joseph winced and a flush crept across Oleg's face.

Dr. Graham slowly sat back down in his chair and looked straight into Oleg's eyes. With an incredulous look, he exclaimed, "Does the Pope even know you're here?!"

Oleg quietly responded, "No, he doesn't, and we'd appreciate it if it could remain that way."

After what seemed like several minutes, the director responded, "Of course, this entire meeting will remain among us. Gentlemen, how about some liquid refreshments before we continue? I think we may be here for a while longer. What would you like—tea, coffee, water, soda?"

The cardinals placed their order and the director said, "Ian, how about you?" Dr. McKinney was deep in thought and didn't hear the question.

"Ian?" Duncan asked a little louder.

Ian's head snapped up and he quickly responded, "I'm sorry. I'm an agnostic and I'm a little amazed by all of this. I'll have water."

"Before I give the order to Mrs. Morrison," Duncan said, "what are your return arrangements, and can we help in any way?"

"We are on a return flight tomorrow morning at 11:00 a.m. on British Airways. Thank you, we are set."

The four sat back down and made small talk for a few minutes until Mrs. Morrison came in with the refreshments.

Dr. Graham began the next round of discussions, his tone blunt and straightforward.

"Okay, tell me why. Why are you really here? What are you really trying to accomplish, and why are you doing this behind the Pope's back? Gentlemen, I don't mean to sound harsh, but you come here at the request of my archbishop, occupy virtually my entire day, want me to participate in an outlandish scheme that is unethical at best, and unholy, at worst. You present yourselves as emissaries of His Holiness the Pope, and now you tell me that he doesn't even know you are here. I believe you owe me an explanation."

Oleg sat quietly, looking down at his lap. He lifted his head and looked straight into the director's eyes. "Yes, we do owe you an explanation and I am happy to give it to you. We did not advise His Holiness of this project because we honestly did not anticipate that it would be feasible. There was no point in alarming him over a potential project that promised very little chance of success. If the project had proven possible, we would have gone back to him and presented all of the facts so that he might make an informed decision as to whether or not to proceed."

Oleg turned to Joseph to observe his reaction.

Cardinal Ratzinger nodded his approval.

Oleg continued, "We know some Texas researchers reportedly did a DNA study of supposed Shroud bloodstains. The validity of the samples that they used is in question and their results have not been officially recognized. Nevertheless, they found that the blood on the Shroud is from a male human, but that it is so old and degraded that few DNA segments were found. This eliminated any possibility of cloning.

"Other DNA experts have stated there has been so much contamination of the Shroud over the centuries, having been handled by perhaps thousands of people, that no DNA testing could possibly be accurate. So, you see, Dr. Graham, we thought your response would be what it was, but we had to make certain. This project is far too important to not pursue all avenues. Also, we never represented we were emissaries of His Holiness. We merely presented our credentials and asked about the feasibility of the project. You assumed the rest."

Dr. Graham nodded in resigned agreement. "You're right."

"Now, as to why we would consider undertaking such a monumental project, the answer is simple, yet very complex. Simply put, we believe mankind is rapidly heading toward self-destruction and it is imminent. We believe the only way this can be altered is with the return of Jesus Christ and for him to alter the course of mankind."

"Well, that's certainly a bold statement," Dr. Graham exclaimed. "And that's certainly a bold solution on your part. What gives you the right to play God? The last time I looked, God sent His Son down to save mankind. Don't you think He would do it again, if He felt it was necessary?"

"We don't believe we can take that chance and we believe, if it were possible, it may be our calling here on Earth to make it happen. We feel we are being called by God, if you will, to plant the seed of our Lord's second coming."

"Please forgive me if I sound cynical, but isn't that a little presumptuous on your part?" the director asked with some intended cynicism.

"We would be but the weavers. God would sew the final product together as He sees fit," Oleg responded.

Graham questioned, "Okay, let's assume for the moment that you have been called upon to put this impossible project together. Why do you think we are on the path to self-destruction?"

Oleg again glanced at Joseph and received an affirmative nod.

"I won't dwell on the rapid decline of morality, contraception being taught in the schools in many countries, the overabundance of pornography in movies, on television, and in advertising. The decline of the family, which has been the backbone of civilization for thousands of years, the insatiable greed of many of the captains of industry looking out solely for themselves and no longer for their employees or the public, politicians stealing money from the public, the adulation of false gods in the form of professional athletes and movie stars who don't possess one-tenth of the positive qualities of the teacher in the classroom or the policeman or fireman working hard for his community. As the addictions to drugs, alcohol, and pornography increase, there is a corresponding decline of Christianity. This is both Catholic and Protestant, particularly in Europe where the churches and cathedrals are virtually empty. There are tens of thousands of babies killed each year as a form of birth control, not to mention by ethnic cleansing."

Oleg paused to take a deep breath. He was getting worked up and he obviously felt very strongly about these issues.

"Ah, 'ethnic cleansing,' a new term for mass murder, a term that has become acceptable with the press and with the television commentators. I thought that the world might have seen the last of genocide with the holocaust, but no, now it's become commonplace."

Oleg took a sip of his lemonade, then continued.

"Worldwide, there are corrupt politicians who lie and steal. There was an American president, twenty-five years ago, who had to leave office because he constantly lied to cover up a staff indiscretion. And now there is an American president being impeached for lying under oath and for his personal misconduct. But that's nothing compared to the killing. It's the killing that scares us the most. Let me ask you, Dr. Graham and Dr. McKinney, how many people do you think have been killed because of warfare this century?"

Leaning in, the director thought for a moment and then responded, "Well, there were probably twenty million alone in World War II, so I would guess about twenty-five or thirty million."

"What's your guess, Dr. McKinney?"

"I would estimate about the same as Duncan, maybe a couple of million more."

They both looked at Oleg, anxiously awaiting his response.

Oleg slowed down and took several sips of his lemonade, relishing the expectant look on both of their faces.

"Get ready, gentlemen, you weren't even close. There have been nearly *one hundred and eighty million deaths* due to warfare in this century. To put that into perspective, that is the equivalent of every man, woman, and child living today in Italy, France, and the United Kingdom."

He paused to let this sink in before he continued.

"And now, we are seeing hate groups springing up all over the globe with the indiscriminate killing of women and children in order to make a political or religious statement. *Muslim fundamentalists* is the new catch phrase for murderers and terrorists. You have ten countries with nuclear weapons capabilities with an eleventh—Iraq—getting close. Gentlemen, it is only a matter of time before some madman sets off a nuclear device leading to nuclear holocaust. You want to know why we are willing to take the chance of playing God? Well, that is the reason, Dr. Graham, to save mankind. This is not an ego thing with us. We simply believe that we are being called on to plant the seed to save mankind."

"Well, you certainly are passionate and make a fascinating argument. If this project were at all possible, I would be inclined to further discuss the matter. But, unfortunately—or fortunately as the case may be—it is not. You have given me much to think about and I want to extend an invitation to both of you to call on me if ever I may be of assistance on any matter whatsoever." He chuckled. "With the exception of the cloning of Jesus, of course."

Abruptly standing, signaling the end of the meeting, the director warmly shook hands with both cardinals, and went to his intercom.

"Mrs. Morrison, would you please have Angus come in right away."

A moment later, Mrs. Morrison admitted Angus MacGregor.

Angus greeted them. "Gentlemen, I will be delighted to take you to your hotel, just follow me."

Before they turned to the door, there was a round of thanks and goodbyes followed by Oleg's reminder of the secrecy of the meeting.

It was nearly four o'clock when they left the institute.

———

Angus exited the institute, turning right onto the narrow two-lane country road. Almost immediately, he noticed that the same light blue Opel Corsa was again following him. He paid little further attention as he drove the cardinals back to their hotel. They were very quiet on the drive back, not offering any conversation either to Angus or to each other. Angus sensed the mood and did not attempt to engage them in conversation.

After dropping them off at their hotel and bidding them a safe journey back to Rome, he turned the Bentley around and headed back to the institute. He drove straight past the Opel Corsa and this time got a good look at the driver.

He's definitely from the Middle East, Angus thought to himself.

His thoughts were interrupted by the ringing of his cell phone. Looking at caller ID, he recognized the cell phone number of his brother-in-law.

"Are you alone?"

"Yes," Angus responded.

"Can you meet me tonight at my cottage?"

Angus replied that he could be available, and they agreed to meet at 6:00.

After hanging up, Angus called his wife Kathleen and told her he would not be home for dinner due to company business.

Seated in the dining room of the hotel that evening, the cardinals did not carry on much of a conversation. They chatted idly, each deep in thought, as they ate a light dinner.

At one point, Joseph asked Oleg if he was disappointed. Oleg gave a barely perceptible nod of his head.

Sitting two tables away, the dark-haired man with the directional microphone could not pick up an answer.

EDINBURGH, SCOTLAND
THURSDAY, JUNE 26, 1997
9:02 A.M.

Despite the heavy morning traffic, the cab ride to the airport took less than an hour on this unusually warm and sunny day. Neither of the cardinals was in a talkative mood during breakfast nor on the ride to the airport. They arrived early, so there were few people in line at the British Airways check-in counter. After checking their bags, they walked to the security area, where they once again had to submit to a more thorough search because of the metal they wore.

As they left the security area, Oleg's head lowered, and his shoulders slumped as they took the long walk to the departure gate. When they reached their boarding area, they collapsed onto two seats at the far end of the seating area where they were alone.

Joseph was the first to share his thoughts. "Oleg, I learned much from our meeting with the scientists, and I feel more comfortable with where this new science is going." After a reflective pause, he added, "As long as it's in the hands of people like Dr. Graham."

"Giuseppe, I agree with you but I'm disappointed," Oleg muttered as he stared down at his hands. "The idea of bringing back our Savior to save mankind was foolish. We've dreamt the impossible and we've been two foolish old men." After a moment he added, "Going through the extensive security reminds me of why we are here. It is unfortunate we live in a world that is so troubled that we need security of this nature. We tried, my dear friend, we tried. Now we have no choice but to go home and pray for guidance. What else can we do?"

Cardinal Ratzinger leaned over and replied, "I suppose all we can do is to urge His Holiness to continue to reach out to all the people of the world as he has been doing."

"I fully agree with you, Giuseppe. I'm afraid there is nothing else we can do."

They sat quietly, deep in thought, as the boarding area began to fill up with passengers traveling to Rome. It was nearing 10:00 and it had been quiet for nearly ten minutes.

"Oleg, did you hear that?" Joseph gasped.

"No, what?" questioned his colleague.

"There was an announcement. Listen. Maybe it will be announced again."

They waited anxiously for another moment, Oleg wondering what Joseph had heard. Then the announcement came again.

"Paging Giuseppe Oleg; paging Giuseppe Oleg. Please pick up a courtesy phone. Mr. Giuseppe Oleg, please pick up a courtesy phone."

Oleg's eyes narrowed as he gave a questioning look to Joseph. Joseph shrugged in return as he slowly got up from his seat and led the way to the counter to get directions to the nearest courtesy phone. As they approached the phone, Oleg again gave a questioning look to Joseph.

"You go ahead and answer it," Joseph murmured.

"Hello?" Oleg spoke into the receiver, his tone hesitant.

"I need to be certain who this is," responded the voice on the other end of the line.

"This is Cardinal…" Oleg paused, then questioned, "Who is this speaking?"

"Please, I must be certain. Let me ask you a couple of questions. When I am certain that you are who you say you are, then I will reveal my identity."

Oleg was quiet for a moment, pondering this cryptic phone call, then reluctantly said, "All right, go ahead."

"What did you have for lunch yesterday?"

Perplexed, Oleg replied, "Salmon and some quail."

"And did you have anything to drink in the afternoon?"

"Yes, I had a glass of lemonade."

There was a brief silence before the voice on the other end responded in a relieved tone, "Cardinal Jaropelk, this is Ian McKinney." Before Oleg could reply, McKinney hurriedly cut in, "And please don't say my name out loud."

"All right, what is this about?"

"I would like to meet with you and Cardinal Ratzinger. I have some questions for you and some ideas which you may find of interest."

"But we're about to board our plane," Oleg stated.

"I understand that. However, I think it would be in your best interests to delay your departure and spend another day in our fair country. I can assure you, it will not be time wasted."

"Please, tell me, what is this about?"

"I will tell you everything in person, but not on the phone. I suggest you return to the ticket counter and exchange your tickets for tomorrow. Your luggage will already have been sent through, but we will supply you with whatever you require for your extra day in Edinburgh. Then, walk out to the passenger pick-up area and we will be waiting for you in the same car you rode in yesterday. And, please, talk to your colleague very quietly about this matter. We believe someone may be listening to your conversations."

Oleg relayed the conversation to Joseph, and they pondered what to do. They were perplexed, but curious about what Dr. McKinney wanted to discuss.

It took only a moment for them to realize they had to meet with the scientist. If they didn't, they would always wonder what this had been about. As they turned around and started walking back to the main terminal, each had a bewildered look on his face.

So did the man with the black curly hair who was standing on the other side of the seating area watching them.

As the cardinals waited in the lengthy line, they quietly discussed the call from Dr. McKinney and their sudden change of plans. Once again, they failed to notice the dark-haired man standing nearby wearing earphones and holding a jacket in his arms. They also failed to notice his sudden departure from the line and his hurried exit from the terminal.

Angus did not.

"Ian, I think that's the man that followed us yesterday," Angus exclaimed, nodding toward the dark-haired man racing to the parking lot.

"What are you going to do? We can't have this connected in any way to the institute.

After a momentary pause, Angus reached for his cell phone and quickly dialed a number. As soon as there was a response, he crisply ordered, "It's me, I need your immediate help. I'm about to leave the airport in the Bentley and I think I'm going to be followed, probably by a light blue Opel Corsa. I need you to intercept the tail. Bring the Hummer, and I think you may have to play rough. I want you to find out as much as you can about him, who he is and where he's from. Let's think about how we're going to do this."

Angus paused, formulating a plan. "I'm going to drive south into the Pentland Hills. I'll take the A-720 to Lanark Road. About two miles to the south, there's a sign directing you to the Harlaw reservoir and the village of Balerno. Go south on this single lane country road. About a mile down this road, there's a small cut-off dirt road. Wait there for us. I'll ring you up when I'm a few minutes away. Start driving slowly toward the reservoir. I'll come up behind you and pass you, so pull over as much as you can to let me by. When this guy tries to pass you, take care of him. I'll drive on, I can't be associated with your accident. Like I said, find out everything you can. My guess is, he has a cell phone. Get it and we can find out who he's been contacting. I don't want the police involved in this in any way, and I certainly don't want our friend going to the police. So, you know what you may have to do. If someone happens by, show them your credentials and ask them to move along. Whatever happens, make it fast and make it thorough. Don't leave any signs behind. Call me when it's done. And—this is important—there can be no connection to the institute. Yes, there will be some extra for you on this one. Any questions? Good. I'll ring you within an hour."

Fifteen minutes later, the cardinals approached the Bentley. Angus got out, greeted them, and ushered them into the back seat.

"Welcome, gentlemen," Ian said as he turned around to face them. "I'll be very blunt. I believe there's a possibility I can accomplish what you were hoping could be done. I have a lot of questions for you and there is a lot to talk about. But first, we're going to go on a little drive and then we'll proceed to my home where we can discuss everything in private. Angus has a little business that requires his attention, so I suggest you sit back and relax."

Joseph gasped and his eyes widened. Oleg stiffened as his mouth dropped open. It was several moments before Oleg started to say something, but Ian cut him off, saying that Angus had to concentrate on his driving. Turning away, Oleg sat back and looked out the window.

Less than thirty minutes later, Oleg noticed they had left the highway and got on the A-70 heading south. He observed, after several more minutes, that Angus was quietly speaking on his cell phone just before he turned left onto a one-lane country road.

In the quaint countryside, the only sign of life was the sheep grazing in the fields behind the hedgerows and stone walls that separated the fields. He didn't see any farmhouses and there was no other traffic on the road.

Angus mumbled a few words into the cell phone and then disconnected. He looked over at Ian and gave an almost imperceptible nod. While driving, Angus was constantly looking at the rearview mirror, so much so that Oleg turned around and looked over his shoulder to see what he was watching. That's when he saw there was, indeed, another car on this quiet country road, about two hundred yards behind them. Joseph noticed what was happening and he, too, turned around to see what Angus was watching. They both had concerned expressions, but neither said a word. After another moment, Oleg noticed they were rapidly approaching another vehicle, and a strange looking one at that. It reminded him of a military vehicle. It was moving slowly and as Angus approached, the driver pulled over as far to the left as possible as Angus drove by.

Angus picked up his speed and after several minutes he slowed down as they entered a small village. Once through the village, Oleg observed they had returned to the same road, the A-70. They headed in the direction from where they had come and were soon heading toward the airport.

Oleg could no longer contain himself. "Would you please tell us what is going on? It appears that we're on our way back toward the airport."

Angus glanced over at Ian and received a small nod of approval. He was about to speak when his cell phone rang. He quickly answered it, saying only, "Give me the details." After listening for several minutes, he said, "Call me when you find out. Good job!" Looking over at his brother-in-law, he added, "Let's go to your home, Ian."

Ian slightly turned his head and said to the cardinals, "Gentlemen, I promise I will explain everything as soon as we arrive at my home. We'll be there in about twenty minutes. Meanwhile, I assure you that you are safe."

Joseph thought this to be an odd comment. He turned to Oleg with his mouth slightly open but said nothing.

———

Shortly before noon, they arrived at Ian's country cottage on the northern outskirts of the village of Broxburn, six miles west of the Edinburgh Airport. As Angus drove into Ian's driveway, Joseph remarked about the quaintness of the cottage and the peacefulness of the surrounding fields and rolling hills.

Ian had purchased the cottage in 1991, shortly after he started with the institute. The nearby residents knew Dr. McKinney to be an extremely private person who kept to himself when he was home, which wasn't often as he worked long hours.

Angus had Ian move his Land Rover from his garage and park it in front of the cottage while Angus drove the Bentley into the garage, out of site. The four men went into the house where they were greeted by the effervescent MacDuff. Duffy, as Ian called him, was a West Highland terrier, white as new-fallen snow, and totally loyal to Ian.

Angus announced, "I'm driving into town to purchase food for lunch, dinner, and tomorrow's breakfast." He also took orders from the cardinals for toiletries and sleepwear. "I'll be gone about an hour and we can begin our discussion when I return.

Angus took the Land Rover, and instead of driving straight to town, he parked the car behind the local pub and walked across the fields to a place where he could observe Ian's cottage without being seen. He sat in the field for nearly thirty minutes, until he was satisfied there was no unusual traffic around the cottage.

Meanwhile, Ian showed his guests to his study and told them to make themselves comfortable while he made some fresh lemonade. The study was his pride and joy. It was large, almost four hundred square feet, and the bookshelves covering the upper portion of three of the four walls were filled with books, mostly scientific. The lower portion was all cabinetry containing shelving and countless file drawers. Ian had collected an enormous amount of scientific papers and articles and they were all filed by topic. No matter how obscure, few had been discarded.

He had a large desk with the latest in computer equipment and a small pipe stand holding four different pipes. Along one wall, there was a comfortable sofa and his favorite piece of furniture, a large soft leather recliner chair. He had a television, which was rarely turned on, and his stereo system was top of the line. His typical evening was spent sitting in his chair, listening to classical music, preferably Beethoven, and reading while smoking one of his pipes. Before retiring at night, usually at eleven o'clock, he would take a long walk, no matter what the weather, with his dog and a glass of single malt scotch whisky.

Ian had resigned himself to a life of bachelorhood. His true loves were his work, his dog, his cottage, and his Scottish heritage. He had one sister, Kathleen, who was married to Angus MacGregor. Both of his parents were deceased.

The townspeople seldom saw him, unless they were out for a late evening stroll themselves. Occasionally, he would walk into the village on a Saturday night and stop at the pub for a bite to eat and a glass of ale.

After settling in, the cardinals had the opportunity to observe and study Dr. McKinney. He had been a quiet spectator during yesterday's meeting and had rarely spoken. Oleg thought his personality certainly fit the stereotype of a scientist, in that he appeared to be somewhat shy and was soft-spoken. His statement that he was an agnostic or an atheist was not surprising.

What was surprising was his forcefulness in taking command of the situation this morning. His appearance was not that of the stereo-typical scientist. He was tall—Oleg guessed him to be about six feet three inches—and he appeared to have a lean muscular body. He obviously didn't spend all his time in the lab; somehow, he was getting exercise to keep fit.

Oleg studied his face, noticing the blue eyes, the sandy reddish-colored wavy hair that was cut to a normal length, and his ruddy complexion. Oleg noticed he did not smile, and he constantly had a serious look on his face. He didn't laugh and his eyes did not have a sparkle to them. He didn't appear to be unhappy, but he certainly was not joyful. There was little warmth.

Oleg didn't dislike him, but he didn't think there was much depth to him. He thought Dr. McKinney would be a difficult person to get to know.

It was nearly two o'clock when Angus returned with his purchases. After having received a short call on his cell phone, he made lunch for Ian and the cardinals.

After eating, they sat down in the study to talk. Ian began, "Gentlemen, it is imperative that we be forthright, and I would like to begin with several questions."

"Excuse me, Dr. McKinney, but Cardinal Ratzinger and I have questions of you. We have no idea why you brought us here and why you told us that we are safe. This implied it may not have been the case. I believe you owe us some answers." Oleg used his formal name to add emphasis to what he had said. "Dr. McKinney," he continued, "I can assure you that both Cardinal Ratzinger and I want a forthright conversation."

"I will explain, Oleg, but I need to be certain that I understand some things you said yesterday," Ian replied, returning to the familiar. "You mentioned that women bathed the body of Jesus with myrrh and aloes."

As his face reddened, Joseph exclaimed, "Yes, according to the gospel of John, that is what happened."

Ian continued, "You also mentioned yesterday that one of the theories on how the image was transferred onto the Shroud was through a blast of energy. Would you care to elaborate?"

"Yes, of course. The most prevalent theory is the resurrection came with an enormous blast of energy that left the imprint of the body on the linen," Joseph replied, becoming more relaxed.

"Is this what you cardinals believe?"

Oleg quickly responded, "Definitely! It is the only theory that makes sense. A resurrection would certainly require a huge amount of energy to bring life back to a dead body and then raising that body to another dimension. What are you getting at?"

Ian reflected for a moment, then responded, "If what you say is true, this energy could have solidified the aloes and if the aloes had been in contact with the blood, then the blood, along with its DNA, might have been preserved."

The cardinals were stunned by this statement. Joseph was the first to offer a rebuttal. "Wouldn't this have come up during all the examinations and testing?"

"Not unless they did specific tests for the existence of solidified oils on the Shroud. Did they?"

After a thoughtful pause, Oleg responded, "Not to my knowledge. But what does this mean to you, Dr. McKinney?"

"It means that, if what you say is accurate, there is a possibility that we could extract an intact sample of the DNA and cloning could be possible." The cardinals sat stone silent as Ian McKinney's words sank in. They watched as Ian casually lit his pipe.

Angus, who had sat quietly throughout the conversation, interjected, "Ian, before you discuss this further, I think you should all know about some events of yesterday and this morning." The cardinals were still speechless and simply stared at Angus without uttering a sound.

Clearing his throat, Angus looked directly at the cardinals and continued, "We were followed yesterday when I drove you to the institute and again when I drove you back to your hotel. I managed to get a look at the driver. He came out of the airport this morning just before you did and while we were waiting for you to change your airline tickets, he got his car and he followed us out of the airport. I had him intercepted this morning on a deserted country road and we were able to learn quite a bit about him."

Ian knew about this, but the cardinals were stunned.

Angus continued, "He had a directional microphone with him that fed to a tape recorder. Gentlemen, he was on your flight to Edinburgh; he followed you all the way from Rome. Not only did he follow you, but he likely recorded your conversations on the airplane, at dinner your first night here, and again last night after our meeting."

Oleg glanced at Joseph, then turned to Angus and quizzed him, "Who is he and why was he following us?"

Angus looked down at his lap and cleared his throat. "The question is who was he, not who is he."

Oleg's mouth dropped open at this and Joseph exhaled a deep breath.

"He met with a fatal traffic accident this morning," Angus declared. "At this moment we don't know who he was, other than he carried an Israeli passport. Does the name Saul Wexler mean anything to either of you?"

Unable to speak, both cardinals shook their heads.

Oleg noticed his incredulous look as Ian questioned, "Mossad?"

"I don't think so. This bloke was far too careless for them. His identity is being checked from his fingerprints as we speak." Angus paused for a moment, then added, "He had a cell phone and we have experts who are trying to trace any calls he made within the past ten days."

"When will you know something?" Ian asked.

"Most likely this evening. The tapes are being brought to me later this afternoon. I think he was acting alone; there were no signs of an accomplice. But, just to be safe, I'm going to stay here with you tonight. As to why he was following you, I think that is obvious. You probably discussed your cloning concept during your conversations and he probably has that on tape. I'll know more when I listen to the tapes. The important question should be: Who was he working for and how much did he relay to his superiors before he met his unfortunate demise?"

The cardinals were stunned. This was an incredible turn of events. Not only was the cloning now a possibility, but their plan might be known by other people. "This is too much to fathom," Joseph said. "And, who is checking on his identity, the institute?"

"No!" Angus shouted. "The director knows nothing of this, nor will he. I have contacts in the intelligence agencies. We'll leave it at that." Changing subjects, Angus urged, "Ian, why don't you continue."

Ian cautioned, "If you decide to pursue this venture, the institute will not be involved in any manner whatsoever. And furthermore, no one at the institute must ever know about it."

Joseph interjected, "This is too much to comprehend. Let's get back to the cloning. If I understand correctly, you are saying there is a possibility that the oils used to bathe the body of Jesus could have been solidified with the resurrection and if they had been mixed with his blood, that his DNA might have been preserved and a cloning could be possible."

"That is precisely what I am saying."

"Well, it seems to me," Cardinal Ratzinger added, "there would have to be tests done on the Shroud to determine if any solidified oils exist." No one spoke as they absorbed the gravity of what Joseph had said.

Ian slowly nodded his head.

Joseph thought for a moment, then continued, "Let's assume that the Shroud could be made available for this testing, who would do the testing and what would be involved?"

Ian had already thought this out. "I would do the testing myself. The equipment needed is small and the procedure would take but a few days. As far as location, it could be done almost anywhere. If there are any solidified oils, I would take samples and then put them through extensive testing to determine if they, indeed, did contain any blood samples. If they did, then further tests would be performed to determine if there was any DNA and to determine if it was intact and had been preserved."

Ian anticipated the next question. Before it was asked, he declared, "The entire procedure would take several weeks, and a laboratory with the proper equipment would have to be located. Since your scheme may now be known, this procedure would have to be done with the utmost security. It absolutely could not be done at the institute."

"But where could it be done?" Oleg asked.

"I suggest that we first examine the Shroud before we get overly concerned about the next step."

Angus interjected, "Ian, why don't you and I take Duffy for a walk and let the cardinals discuss this matter privately." Ian concurred.

Shortly after Ian and Angus left the cottage, Oleg pensively said, "Guiseppe, I know this is sudden, but I think we should move forward."

"It's so secretive. Do you think we can trust these men?"

Oleg measured his response, "We were foolish, Guiseppe, to think that a major research facility like the Roslin Institute would entertain a project like this. It would have to be secretive." He frowned before adding, "We just didn't think ahead. As far as Ian is concerned, there's something about him that I like. There's an underlying sadness or loneliness to him, but I think he's an honest man."

"But, Oleg, he's an atheist. He even told us that."

"I know, but there's something about him that intrigues me. Did you happen to see this photograph?" Oleg walked to the bookshelves across the room where there were some photographs displayed. They were mostly of family scenes, probably of his parents, but there were several of Ian standing atop barren mountain tops with mountains and valleys in the background.

"This man obviously loves rugged nature. Perhaps, that's his way of communicating with God. I tell you, Guiseppe, this man has a hidden spirituality to him. He reminds me of a younger Loleck. There's a kindness to him but I also sense that he has been deeply hurt. Loleck sought comfort in his faith, and I think Ian has found comfort in science and in nature. I trust him and I think we should propose to His Holiness that we allow him to do the testing."

Cardinal Ratzinger agreed, although it was with some reluctance on his part.

When Ian and Angus returned, Oleg announced, "Guiseppe and I will talk to John Paul II and see if he will even allow this first step. But we have reservations and many questions." Everyone was quiet as they digested what was happening.

Angus suggested, "Perhaps you two might want to rest before we have a late supper and further discussions."

They agreed and Ian showed them to their rooms as Angus brought out some toiletries and sleepwear he had purchased for them. It was late afternoon when they lay down in their beds to take much needed naps.

The cardinals awoke after several hours and met in Giuseppe's room to discuss the day's events and to plan a course of action. Joseph confessed, "I want to proceed, but I have so many questions. This plan has so much uncertainty."

"How can Ian perform these tests while working for the institute? Where could they find a secure laboratory and what would be the costs involved? What role does Angus have, and most important, what does Ian want out of this?"

They walked out to the study and joined Ian, Angus, and the ever-present Duffy. Ian was having a glass of Macallan, while Angus was drinking from a bottle of water. Angus, too, enjoyed a "wee dram" as he called it, but he considered himself to be on duty and didn't want to compromise his attention or awareness.

"Ah, good evening," Ian said, as the cardinals entered the room. Without standing, he motioned for them to sit down on the sofa. "Would you care for a bit of our favorite beverage?"

Before they could respond, Angus got up from his chair and said, "I think I'll take a short walk and then fix us something to eat. I bought some beef pies at the butcher shop and they look superb." Without waiting for a response, he walked out the back door and proceeded to quietly walk around the cottage, oberving the surroundings.

Oleg responded, "Ian, I believe I will have a taste of your whisky, it's been a long time. We don't drink much alcohol and when we do, it's usually wine with dinner. How about you, Giuseppe, won't you join me?"

Cardinal Ratzinger thought for a moment, then replied, "Why not, as they say, 'when in Rome.' I'm not certain that I've ever tasted your national drink." This brought forth a little laughter from the others and served to lighten the atmosphere.

Ian had just prepared their drinks and was handing them to the cardinals when Angus appeared. "It's a quiet night," Angus stated, looking directly at Ian with a satisfied smile. He went to the kitchen to prepare their supper, informing them he would return momentarily after putting their meals in the oven.

Ian and the cardinals didn't hear Angus's cell phone ring while he was in the kitchen. He was on the phone for more than five minutes.

Oleg took a sip of his whisky, gave a slight shudder, and then remarked, "It is quite tasty … and smooth, I might add. What kind is it, not that I would have heard of it?"

"It's Macallan 18. It's as good as you can get, that's reasonably affordable. It's my favorite."

Cardinal Ratzinger changed the topic. "Ian, we've decided to approach His Holiness and tell him of the entire plan. We don't know what his response will be. We'll be asking him to break the laws of the Church and to authorize a secret operation that would be unthinkable to most people on Earth and certainly to most Christians. Nevertheless, we will talk to him and try to convince him that we should at least determine if the concept is feasible. If not feasible, it would put the concept to rest forever."

There was a tone of finality in the way he spoke. "If His Holiness agrees, we can arrange to have you examine the Shroud in Turin in complete privacy and security. As far as the laboratory tests, we think it would be best to have them performed at the Vatican. You could be our guests and we could arrange to have all the equipment necessary for your testing. This would be the most secure location."

He paused for a moment. "Dr. McKinney," he purposely returned to the formal title to emphasize what he was about to ask. "You would have to leave your work at the Roslin Institute for several weeks. Would this not jeopardize your employment?"

Ian leaned forward and affirmed. "Both Angus and I have accumulated nearly ten weeks of vacation time and would simply use some of that. As far as setting up the laboratory in the Vatican, that would certainly be secure, but do you have a totally private area that could serve as an aseptic laboratory?"

Oleg responded, "Dr. McKinney, what do you know of the Vatican?"

"Only that the Pope lives and works there."

"Allow me to enlighten you," Oleg replied. "Vatican City is actually the smallest state in the world as it consists of just over a hundred acres and it is totally enclosed within stone walls. It's located within the city of Rome, and it is so small that not all its essential services fit within its walls. In fact, the Vatican possesses more territory outside of its walls than within."

Oleg paused and took a sip of his Scotch whisky. "There are only about four hundred and fifty citizens, and half of them represent the Church abroad. An additional three hundred people from other countries reside there temporarily. The city-state consists of one-third buildings, one-third tiny squares and courtyards and one-third gardens. All in all, there are over ten thousand rooms, so I don't believe finding a suitable location for your work would be difficult."

"I wasn't aware of that," Ian responded with widening eyes.

Oleg took another sip of whisky, then continued, "Wait till you see St. Peter's; you will be amazed. It's the largest cathedral in the world and covers an area of forty-four thousand square meters." Oleg's voice increased in volume and his gestures became more animated as he described his home. "And you won't believe the museum," he exclaimed. "It's the largest single fresco museum in the world with over four hundred thousand feet of space."

"I wasn't aware there was a museum. Is it open to the public?" Ian inquired.

"Parts are, as are parts of the library, which houses over eight hundred thousand books including nearly one hundred thousand ancient manuscripts."

"That is impressive!" Ian marveled.

"Words cannot begin to describe the Vatican. The collection of art treasures is the largest in the world. Hopefully, you will be able to see it soon, with the Pope's blessing."

Joseph interjected, "Aleksandr is a wonderful tour guide, but can we get back to the situation at hand?" He gave a knowing smile to Oleg and inquired, "Ian, what would the costs for this project be and what are you looking to achieve?"

Ian smiled and replied, "I anticipated your question and I've spent some time considering this while you gentlemen were resting. The first phase, which would be the testing of the preserved blood samples, would not be too costly, approximately twenty thousand British pounds for equipment and materials. Angus and I would like to receive some compensation for this work, say ten thousand pounds for the three weeks of work. This, of course, assumes that we find solidified oils on the Shroud. Should we not find any, and the project is abandoned, then the trip to Turin and the ability to examine the Shroud will be all the compensation we would want."

Joseph responded, "That certainly seems reasonable." After a thoughtful pause, he challenged, "Ian, why are you doing this?"

Ian asked the cardinals if they would like their drinks refreshed. After both declined, he went to his cherrywood bar and poured himself another Macallan. He took a sip and let the smooth liquid relax his body.

"Gentlemen, as you know, I'm not a religious man. I guess you would say that I'm an agnostic. It's not that I don't believe that Jesus was the Son of God, I just don't know. It seems so unrealistic and far-fetched to me that this supreme being would send His son down to Earth, and have him heal the sick, restore sight to the blind and raise the dead. And after he's killed, he somehow gets resurrected and rises to heaven. In my world of science, that's just not possible. But I will say that your description of the Shroud and your conclusions as to how the image got onto the Shroud are captivating. I'm trying to open my mind to any possibility but, you must understand, it is extremely difficult. I say this only because I want to be totally truthful with you. I would be doing this strictly for the benefit of science, not for your reasons of saving mankind."

"I see," Oleg sighed. "And Ian, I understand. But what do you want from this? Assume for the moment that you do find oils on the Shroud, that they are solidified, that they do contain the blood of Jesus, that the DNA is intact, and that His Holiness would give his blessings to the entire project. What would the project look like? How would you proceed, and what compensation would you want?"

"Those are a lot of assumptions, Oleg. It's extremely doubtful that all these things would occur. However, should they happen, Angus and I would have to leave the employ of the Roslin Institute and proceed on our own."

Oleg started to ask a question, but Ian cut him off. "Angus would come with me for security purposes and would be an absolute necessity." Oleg nodded, as the question he was about to ask was answered.

"Neither of us would be able to return to the institute, so we would be forsaking our careers. We would expect to be compensated accordingly. As far as building a laboratory to perfect the cloning and finding the proper host mother, this would also be quite costly. This is all supposition, so I have not even thought about preparing a realistic budget, but suffice it to say, the cost would run in the millions of pounds." Ian looked at both cardinals for a reaction.

Cardinal Ratzinger softly said, "That could be arranged." There were several moments of total silence, as all four men digested what had been said and what the future might hold in store for them. Angus broke the silence by stating that dinner was ready and suggesting they adjourn to the dining area where they could enjoy the meat pies and continue their conversation.

Angus sat them at the table and placed the steaming hot, brown-crusted beef pies in front of them. The cardinals breathed in the rich aroma. "When will you approach the Pope and when do you think you'll receive his answer?" Ian asked after he took a bite of his meal.

Oleg thought for a moment before replying, "We'll talk to him shortly after our return. Umm, this is delicious. I must say, Scottish food is more impressive than what I had imagined." After taking several more bites, he continued, "Regarding when he'll respond to us, I don't know. If it's an absolute no, we'll know immediately. I anticipate he will want to think about it and pray over it and that he would respond within a week. How would you like us to contact you to let you know his response?"

Angus silently contemplated the question. "I don't want to use the telephone service. Why don't you write a letter to Ian at the institute saying how much you enjoyed meeting him? Write virtually the same letter to Dr. Graham at the same time. If the Pope gives his blessing to examining the Shroud, end the letter by telling Ian you would hope to see him again someday. Mention in the letter that you enjoy traveling and that your next trip will be somewhere—you decide the place—on a certain date. That will be the date that we will meet you in Turin. How does that sound, Ian?"

"That's fine. However, allow a couple of weeks to procure the instruments that we'll need for the examination and for both of us to arrange our vacation schedules."

Angus then added, "Any further contact will be by telephone, but only after we install encryption machines on both ends. I assume you have a private line at the Vatican."

Both Oleg and Giuseppe nodded affirmatively. "Should this project require any further travel on your part, you will have to dress as civilians and travel under assumed names. I can arrange the false passports should the project move forward."

"Is this all necessary?" Cardinal Ratzinger questioned.

"Yes, I'm afraid it is," Angus assured him. "I received some information about our friend who was following you. The tape was brought to me while you were resting."

All three heads perked up as they eagerly waited to hear what Angus was about to say.

"His real name was Shakar al Harith and he was a Syrian associated with an international terrorist group. As I mentioned earlier, he traveled with an Israeli passport under the name of Saul Wexler. It is easier to travel throughout Europe with an Israeli passport than with a passport from Syria."

The cardinals listened attentively, as did Ian.

"He followed you and was on your flight to Edinburgh. He recorded your conversations on the flight and both of your dinner conversations. Unfortunately, on the airplane you talked about a project and how some people might not want the baby to survive. At dinner you talked about the Roslin Institute and about cloning."

The cardinals were stunned.

Angus added, "It doesn't take a genius to figure out that you came to Edinburgh to talk to the Roslin Institute about the cloning of a human. How much else they assume is pure conjecture."

Joseph had a dazed look as he stammered, "What do you mean, 'they'? I thought he was alone."

Angus quickly responded, "He made several phone calls, all to the same number in Damascus. The calls cannot be traced any further than that. All of the calls were nearly thirty minutes in length, so we must assume he played the recordings to whoever was on the other end of the call."

Oleg and Joseph silently gaped at each other. Angus continued, "So, you see, gentlemen, from here on, security is essential. Like you said on the airplane, Joseph, there may be people who would not want to see the baby survive."

"I said that?" Joseph gasped as his shoulders tightened.

"Yes, I listened to your words," Angus replied.

They finished eating in silence until Angus stated, "If the Pope agrees to the examination, I repeat, you are to advise us of the date you want to meet in Turin. This will be done by stating that you are once again traveling and leaving on a certain date. We'll meet you at the Cathedral in Turin at eight o'clock on the morning of that date. We'll be dressed as tourists and we can make arrangements to bring our equipment to the location of the Shroud at that time. Does everyone understand, and is everyone in agreement?"

The four finished their meals in silence, each harboring his own thoughts and fears.

Ian and the cardinals went back to the study where Ian went to his stereo system and put on a CD of Beethoven's fourth piano concerto, his favorite.

Angus finished cleaning up after the meal and entered the study. "Gentlemen, it's been a long eventful day. Unless there are any other items you wish to discuss, I suggest we retire for the night."

Looking at the two cardinals, Angus joked, "I say that because you two are sitting on what will be my bed tonight." As the cardinals immediately got up, they realized Angus was speaking in jest and each emitted a slight laugh.

Ian refilled his glass of whisky and announced, "This is when I take my nightly stroll with Duffy. Oleg and Joseph, I bid you both good night."

Angus walked up to Ian and whispered in his ear. After a short pause, Ian stated, "On second thought, I think I'll skip the walk tonight and just take Duffy out to the backyard."

EDINBURGH, SCOTLAND
FRIDAY, JUNE 27, 1997
7:51 A.M.

Ian drove the cardinals to the airport in his Land Rover while Angus concentrated on watching the surrounding traffic. After they dropped the cardinals off and said their goodbyes, Ian drove to the far end of the terminal and dropped Angus off.

After walking back to the British Airways ticket area, Angus spotted the cardinals nearing the front of the check-in line. He went to the security area, showed his credentials to pass through security, and began casually walking to the gate for the flight to Rome. After buying a newspaper, he walked to the seating area at the first gate, sat down and opened the paper, discreetly watching the surrounding people.

When the cardinals walked past, he waited several minutes, again watching all the people in the terminal, looking for anything out of the ordinary. Once the cardinals reached their gate and made themselves comfortable in the seating area, Angus sat down across the terminal from them and ostensibly began reading his newspaper.

He sat there for over an hour, until the cardinals boarded the plane for their flight back to Rome.

Angus did not observe anything or anyone out of the ordinary as he carefully looked at every passenger as they boarded. He waited until the plane pulled away from the gate before he went to the parking garage to find Ian.

Finding the Land Rover, he climbed in the passenger side and observed that Ian was writing down a list of items and numbers on a pad of paper. "What have you been doing for the past hour and a half?" he inquired.

"Well, I thought I would make a list of the material, along with the costs, that we would need for the first phase of the examination. That was very basic, so I did the same for the items we would need for the testing of the blood samples. Meanwhile, I believe we should learn as much as possible about this shroud."

"You're being quite optimistic, aren't you?" Angus questioned. "I don't give this scheme much of a chance of success."

Ian was driving out of the parking garage when he replied, "You just never know."

They reached the exit, Ian paid the attendant and they drove out of the airport grounds before Ian continued, "Speaking of never knowing, what happened to our friend Abdul, or whatever his name was?"

Angus chuckled and replied, "His name was Shakar. The Hummer forced him off the road and his car overturned. My friend went to him and pulled him out of the car. He had a broken arm and was already in some pain. He was hesitant to tell my friend who he worked for, but my friend convinced him very quickly. It's amazing what a little pressure applied to a broken arm will do to loosen up someone's tongue."

Ian winced at the thought. Angus went on, "He told my friend his real name, where he lived, and who he worked for. Apparently, he was instructed to follow the cardinals, eavesdrop on their conversations and report to his superiors in Damascus."

Ian asked, "But how would anyone know what the cardinals were planning even before they left Rome?"

"That's a good question; we may never know the answer. But, obviously, someone knew something of the good cardinals' plan. Anyway, my friend was convinced that Shakar told him everything he knew. He had to twist his arm a little bit, so to speak. Then he twisted his neck a little bit. Now, our friend Shakar will live happily ever after with all those virgins up in heaven. It's a pity that these Arabs don't know how to drive on these lonely Scottish country roads. My friend scraped the Hummer's paint off the rental car and made sure there were no signs of another vehicle at the site. He took his fingerprints and gathered together his directional microphone, recorder, and cell phone. He also made an imprint of his hotel room key. Then he drove into Balerno, stopped at a pay phone and called the police, reporting an accident on the Harlow Reservoir Road. He went immediately to the hotel and searched his room and his belongings. He left nothing that would lead the police to believe that our Arab friend was anything other than what he appeared to be."

"Well, that certainly appears to be nice and tidy. Won't his superiors suspect something when they learn of his demise?"

"I'm sure they will, but we can't be concerned. The police will attempt to contact the next of kin through his Israeli passport. When they learn it was a fake passport, they will have no alternative but to eventually cremate the body that was left from this unfortunate auto accident. So, I doubt that his superiors will ever learn of his fate."

They drove back to Ian's cottage where Angus retrieved the Bentley from the garage and they both drove separately to the institute, arriving in the late morning.

The cardinals arrived in Rome in the late afternoon, having not spoken one word about their trip, their meetings, their plan, or their upcoming talk with the Pope. They had learned their lesson well. They retrieved their bags and called for a driver to the Vatican, arriving in time for supper.

After dining, Oleg went to the Pope's secretary and requested an appointment with His Holiness. Oleg met with him often, so this was nothing unusual. The secretary inquired as to how much time he would need and was mildly surprised when Oleg informed him that he would need an hour and that Cardinal Ratzinger would be joining them.

The next available appointment time was Monday afternoon.

THE VATICAN
MONDAY, JUNE 30, 1997
3:00 P.M.

The Pope's personal secretary, Antonio, admitted the two cardinals to the papal apartments on the third floor of the Apostolic Palace. He led them through several rooms until they reached the Pope's private study. After knocking softly, he opened the door for the cardinals.

Pope John Paul II stood and greeted his guests, an unusual gesture for anyone other than these two. This Pope relied heavily on Joseph Ratzinger when it came to business and papal matters, while Aleksandr Jaropelk was the Pope's closest personal friend and confidant.

John Paul flashed a warm welcoming smile as he grasped Joseph's hand in both of his. The tenderness and love that was exuded from the gesture brought a feeling of joy and contentment to the cardinal. "Joseph, it is good to see you, you look well."

"Thank you, Your Holiness, I am well," he responded, realizing how much he loved and admired this man.

John Paul turned to his lifelong friend, looked deep into his eyes, then gave him a warm hug. "It has been several weeks since I've seen you, Oleg. That is too long, I have missed you."

"It is I who have missed you, Loleck. You are looking well, though somewhat tired. I grow weary of having to tell you to slow down; it never does any good. I guess it's just not your nature."

"Then why don't you cease," John Paul quipped, emitting a slight chuckle.

"I guess it's just not your nature to quit badgering me," Oleg retorted. "So, we just have to put up with each other." The two usually started their greeting with this loving banter.

John Paul quickly changed to a somber mood and said, "Oleg, you are here on serious business; you have a very pensive look to you." He could often read Oleg's thoughts and could always recognize his moods. "Come, let us sit and you can tell me what it is that requires an hour of your Pope's time." His eyes twinkled as he said this.

John Paul ushered his two cardinals to a large sofa located close to the window, while he sat in a large chair facing them. There were several windows in the Pope's study, but this was "the" window. Of all the twelve thousand windows in the Vatican, this was the most famous. Nearly every Sunday at noon for centuries, the sitting Pope has appeared at the window and said the Angelus together with the faithful gathered in St. Peter's Square below.

Focusing on Oleg, he beamed. "Tell me what it is that's on your mind, my dear friend."

Oleg had thought through this conversation countless times over the past months. "Loleck, we have had many serious conversations over the past fifty years, but this is the most important conversation we will ever have." He paused to let these words sink in.

John Paul's smile faded as he stared intently into Oleg's eyes. Joseph noted that the Pope sat up a little straighter in his chair. Oleg continued, "Loleck, I want you to have an open mind as you listen to what we're about to tell you. And, please, let me finish before you comment."

After a moment of silence, John Paul responded, "My dear friend, of course I will listen to what you say, as I always have. I can see this is going to be quite difficult for you. I honor and I respect that."

He got up and slowly walked to a credenza located between two of the windows on the wall to his right. He reached for a pitcher placed on a tray, slowly turned to his visitors and said, "I'm going to have a glass of cold lemonade, would you care to join me?"

Both Joseph and Aleksandr started to get up from their sofa when John Paul quickly said, "No, please sit; I will serve you." After bringing them each a full glass of lemonade, John Paul sat down in his chair, took several swallows of the refreshing liquid and put his glass down on the table next to him.

As he raised his right arm and gently motioned for Oleg to continue, he softly said, "Please, my dear friend, tell me what it is that is of such magnitude."

Oleg took several swallows of lemonade and began, "Loleck, we fear for mankind. The violence, the killing, the bombings, the warfare have convinced us that mankind is on a rapid road to self-destruction. And, we think this self-destruction is not only imminent, but could happen within our lifetimes. If ever there has been a time for God to send his son back to Earth, that time is now." John Paul nodded his agreement but said nothing.

Oleg looked to Joseph and Joseph proceeded to outline the current moral problems which existed in the world today. When he told the Pope about the hundred and eighty million war deaths in the century, John Paul appeared to be about to question the number but sat back and remained silent.

Oleg then described their trip to Scotland and their meeting with Dr. Graham and Dr. McKinney. When he told John Paul about the idea of cloning Jesus from the Shroud of Turin and that he had inquired about the feasibility of such a project, John Paul swallowed hard and rose from his chair. He turned his back on Oleg and went to his window and looked out at St. Peter's Square where he had blessed so many millions of people over the years. He remained there, silently, for several moments.

He turned back to the cardinals, looked piercingly at Oleg, and said, "And what did this Dr. Graham think of your preposterous idea?"

Slightly taken aback by John Paul's choice of words, Oleg responded, "He said that it was impossible to do and that even if it could be done, he and his institute would have nothing to do with it."

John Paul raised his eyes and returned to his chair and sat down. He looked first at Joseph and then at Oleg. "There's more, isn't there?"

Oleg nodded and softly said, "Yes, Loleck, there is more. There is a lot more."

He proceeded to tell the Pope about the phone call from Dr. McKinney at the airport and the drive to Dr. McKinney's cottage. He purposely left out the part about being followed on the plane, on the way to and from the Roslin Institute and on their drive from the airport. There was no need to complicate the situation. He related the conversations with Dr. McKinney and Angus MacGregor in detail. Nearly an hour had passed when Oleg finished his description of their trip and all the conversations.

"Loleck, I know this project sounds preposterous, but we both feel that God is calling us to plant the seed to save mankind. I keep thinking about the war dead in this century. Loleck, that's the equivalent of every man, woman, and child living today in Italy, France, England, and the entire UK. With the rise of radical Islam, it is only a matter of time before we see nuclear holocaust."

"I'm afraid you may be right, but this is not the way to prevent it." John Paul paused, then added, "I still find it difficult to believe your figure of one hundred and eighty million war dead. Where did you get these figures?"

Oleg reached into his briefcase he had brought with him and had set on the floor. He brought out some papers and handed them to John Paul. "These are the figures and, unfortunately, they are accurate."

John Paul took them and read.

TWENTIETH CENTURY ATTROCITIES

DEATH TOLL	EVENT	DATES
50,000,000	Second World War (some overlap w/Stalin; includes Sino-Japanese War and Holocaust)	1937-1945
48,250,000	China: Mao Zedong's regime (includes famine)	1949-1976
20,000,000	USSR: Stalin's regime (incl. WW2-era atrocities)	1924-1953
15,000,000	First World War (incl. Armenian massacres)	1914-1918
8,800,000	Russian Civil War	1918-1921
4,000,000	China: Warlord & Nationalist Era	1917-1937
3,000,000	Congo Free State	1900-1908

DEATH TOLL	EVENT	DATES
2,800,000	Korean War	1950-1953
2,700,000	2nd Indochina War (incl. Laos & Cambodia)	1960-1975
2,500,000	Chinese Civil War	1945-1949
2,100,000	German Expulsions after WW2	1945-1947
1,900,000	Second Sudanese Civil War	1983
1,700,000	Congolese Civil War	1997-
1,650,000	Cambodia: Khmer Rouge Regime	1975-1977
1,400,000	Ethiopian Civil Wars	1962-1992
1,250,000	Mexican Revolution	1910-1920
1,250,000	East Pakistan Massacres	1971
1,000,000	Iran-Iraq War	1980-1988
1,000,000	Nigeria: Biafran Revolt	1967-1970
800,000	Mozambique Civil War	1976-1992
800,000	Rwandan Massacres	1994
650,000	French-Algerian War	1954-1962
600,000	First Indochina War	1945-1954
500,000	India-Pakistan Partition	1947
500,000	Indonesia: Massacre of Communists	1965-1967
500,000	Angolan Civil War	1975-1974
500,000	First Sudanese Civil War	1955-1972
500,000	Decline of Amazonian Indians	1900-1997
365,000	Spanish Civil War	1936-1936
350,000	Somalia Civil War	1991-
Unknown	North Korea: Communist Regime	1948-

John Paul studied the figures for several minutes without saying a word. Joseph and Oleg watched him apprehensively, trying to discern a reaction.

"This is astonishing," John Paul exclaimed. "But not as astonishing as your solution to the problem. Do you realize what you're asking me to condone?"

Before either cardinal could respond, John Paul chastised them. "You're not just asking me to condone it, you're asking me to sponsor it, and to fund it." In a much softer voice, he continued, "And to hide it." He paused for a moment. "You're asking too much of me, Oleg. And, you don't even know if it's feasible."

Oleg sensed a glimmer of hope with this last statement. He was careful to mask it. "Loleck, why don't we find out if it is possible. There is very little cost, it won't take much time and there would be no harm in finding out if there is any preserved blood with viable DNA on the Shroud. If there is none, the subject will never again come up, not now or in the future."

There was silence, then Oleg continued, "If the tests are negative, no one in future generations will ever again come up with this idea." He looked deeply into John Paul's eyes and said, "If there are any future generations."

His comment was not lost on John Paul, who was pensive for a minute, then said, "And if there is preserved blood with viable DNA on the Shroud?"

"Then you will have to make a monumental decision," Oleg responded. He paused for a moment, then continued, "But, let's find out. We have nothing to lose, and at least we'll know for certain."

The Pope rose from his chair, turned and again walked to his window and looked out over the square. He didn't speak for several minutes.

Even though his back was turned, Oleg knew he was deep in thought. There was no more for Oleg to say and Joseph, who had been quiet throughout most of the meeting, was not about to start a conversation.

Finally, John Paul turned and walked back to his chair and sat down. Oleg knew what he was going to say, and he was elated. But, another part of him was saddened by the burden he had placed on the shoulders of this peaceful and wonderful man.

John Paul looked up at the two cardinals and said with resignation, "I will pray on this. I go to Castel Gandolfo on Thursday morning. Let's meet on Wednesday and I will give you my answer. Arrange a time with Antonio on your way out. I must go to my chapel now."

The Pope had his own personal chapel in his apartments and Oleg knew he spent several hours each day alone in prayer. Oleg knew this was his only solitude and he needed this special time to reflect on the many burdens that were thrust upon him and the many critical decisions he had to make every day. John Paul II had confided to Oleg that these hours of prayer were when he felt as close to God as he had ever felt.

"And Oleg," he said as they were leaving, "why don't you design a detailed plan of where, when, and how you would set up your lab in the event you do find blood on the Shroud."

Oleg nodded without saying a word. John Paul quietly added, "Just in case I am foolish enough to allow you to move forward with this insane idea of yours. And, Joseph," John Paul quipped, "I trust that next time we meet, you will be able to speak at least several words." His eyes again twinkled as his lips formed a slight smile.

The tension relieved, Cardinal Joseph Ratzinger and Cardinal Aleksandr Jaropelk left the personal apartments of Pope John Paul II.

Antonio created a time slot of one half-hour at 2:30 on Wednesday to again meet with His Holiness.

As they left the area and proceeded to their own offices and their own duties, Oleg suggested, "Let's meet in my office after dinner and discuss details of the plan. Loleck's last comment, when he teased you, has eased my concern about the hardship we're placing on him."

DAMASCUS, SYRIA
TUESDAY, JULY 1, 1997
10:11 A.M.

The six dark-bearded Shia men, dressed in their traditional keffiyehs sat at a plain rectangular table in a nondescript room in the outskirts of the city. They had just listened to the recorded conversations that had been phoned to their leader.

The leader, sitting at the head of the table, spoke first, "As you can hear, the reception is not very clear. The two men talking are cardinals from the Vatican. I've listened to the conversation several times and I don't know what to think. It appears they are talking about cloning a human being and this Roslin Institute cloned a sheep last year. That's all we know until I hear from al Harith. Now, let's move on to more urgent matters."

THE VATICAN
TUESDAY, JULY 1, 1997
1:18 P.M.

Oleg and Joseph had met for several hours the previous night, but they required more time to finalize the details of the testing. Each spent the morning attending to his regular duties and again met in Joseph's office after lunch. They prepared a written report and because of the nature of the report, they had to type it themselves.

"Do you think His Holiness will approve of the testing?" Joseph inquired.

"Yes, I suppose he will, Giuseppe."

"You don't seem to be very enthusiastic, Oleg."

"I'm sorry. I'm excited with the prospect of determining if the project is feasible, but I am saddened with the prospect of placing such an enormous burden on the shoulders of my dear friend." Oleg was pensive. "If there is, indeed, preserved blood on the Shroud and if the DNA is intact, then he will have to make an extremely difficult decision. As the most important man in the world, he is already faced with having to make enormous decisions, almost daily. I hate to thrust such a burden on him."

"I understand your feelings, Oleg. But, don't lose sight of the fact that what we may be able to do could be saving mankind."

"You're correct, as usual, my friend. I will endeavor to keep this matter in perspective."

TEL AVIV, ISRAEL
TUESDAY, JULY 1, 1997
4:58 P.M.

"Gentlemen," Mossad Director Danny Yatom began, "Yesterday, we learned of a situation and we're not quite sure of what to make of it. An Arab operative name Shakar al Harith was killed last Friday in an automobile accident outside of Edinburgh, Scotland. We were able to intercept bits and pieces of several cell phone calls he made to his contact in Damascus. He had a fake Israeli passport and traveled as Saul Wexler. When the Scottish police contacted our government authorities to locate the next of kin, they were informed that it was a fake passport. They were stymied and had to cremate the body and close their file.

"We, of course, were aware of Mr. al Harith and monitored his travels. He was a minor agent and not very skilled. His superiors must have thought that having an Israeli passport would make travel easier. Viper, I want you to go to Edinburgh and find out what you can. The phone calls he made indicated he was following several cardinals from the Vatican and mentioned a Dr. McKinney with the Roslin Institute. We don't know the connection, but he may have been on to something and we need to know what it was."

"What is the Roslin Institute?" Viper asked as he leaned forward.

"It's legitimate; it's a major research facility. They were in the news last year for cloning a sheep. What's interesting is that we suspect al Harith's death may not have been an accident. I can't imagine that a research facility would be responsible. I also can't imagine what the connection is between a research facility, an Arab agent, and the Vatican. Anything that is of interest to the Arabs is of interest to us. Right now, this is low priority, but you never know what it may turn into. Fox, we will keep you in reserve in case Viper's cover gets blown. Viper, you're off to Edinburgh tomorrow."

"Danny, why are we getting involved in this?" Fox asked.

"I realize surveillance is not your area of expertise, but I don't know where this may lead." He added, "If it leads anywhere. However, if there has been a killing of an Islamist agent, this could develop into the need for your skills. And, if that happens, I want you two involved from the beginning."

THE VATICAN
WEDNESDAY, JULY 2, 1997
2:30 P.M.

Once again, Antonio ushered Cardinal Ratzinger and Cardinal Jaropelk into the private apartments of Pope John Paul II. Once again, as they entered his study, he was standing by his favorite window, staring out over St. Peter's Square.

Without turning to face his guests, he said to them, "Please, sit down and make yourselves comfortable."

The cardinals sat down on the sofa and anxiously waited for John Paul to turn around and begin the meeting. Even without seeing his face, Oleg felt the consternation that John Paul was experiencing. Not a word was spoken for several moments.

Finally, he turned around, walked to his chair and sat down. Looking directly at Oleg, he said, "My friends, I have decided to allow you to conduct the tests on the Shroud."

Both Oleg and Joseph let out a deep breath. Neither uttered a word. "The initial test will be to determine if there is, indeed, blood present in solidified oils. And, if there is, you are to conduct tests to determine if there is intact DNA present in the blood."

Both cardinals silently nodded their heads.

The Pope continued, "I want these tests conducted in the utmost secrecy. If word gets out, I will immediately stop the testing and the program will be totally abandoned. Am I making myself absolutely clear?"

"Yes, Loleck, you are making yourself clear," Oleg replied.

"Your Holiness, I understand completely," Joseph added.

John Paul continued, "Furthermore, I want you to understand. If you do find blood and if there is DNA that is intact, I have no intention of proceeding with this cloning fiasco. Is that understood?" Before they could answer, he said, "My hope is that these tests will prove to be negative and this concept will never again be brought up, not now, and not in future generations."

Oleg softly said, "If there are future generations."

"Oleg, you made this comment two days ago. Do you think your Pope is getting so senile that you need to repeat yourself?" John Paul smiled. "Or, are you getting so senile that you don't remember?" His eyes twinkled as he teased his best friend. "Now, let me see your report."

Joseph handed him the report and sat back down. Oleg crossed and uncrossed his legs several times while John Paul read and then reread the six-page report. Finally, John Paul conceded, "Very well, I will make sure the funds are made available to you from my personal accounts. When do you plan on starting?"

Joseph quickly responded, "Immediately, Your Holiness."

"Then I will look forward to our next meeting and to learning the results. Now, if you will excuse me, I want to pray about this." John Paul ushered them to the door.

As they left, they heard the Pope tell Antonio to cancel any remaining appointments he had, and that he was not to be disturbed for the remainder of the afternoon.

The cardinals agreed to meet again after dinner and write the letters to Ian McKinney and Dr. Graham.

After it was completed, the McKinney letter read:

Dear Dr. McKinney,

Cardinal Ratzinger and I sincerely enjoyed meeting you recently and appreciate the opportunity to have learned of your work. Our only regret is that we did not have the opportunity to spend more time in your beautiful country. I do not get the opportunity to travel very often, however, I am taking a short holiday on July 22 of this year to visit some old friends. I hope to see you again someday.

Sincerely,

Cardinal Aleksandr Jaropelk

"Well, that's certainly a short letter you wrote," Joseph remarked to Oleg after they sat down again in Joseph's office.

"It is as we discussed," Oleg replied. "He knows that he and Angus are to meet us at the cathedral at 8:00 a.m. We'll send this Federal Express, so there's no chance of it being intercepted. I have already contacted Cardinal Saldarini and we are to meet with him the day after tomorrow to make the arrangements for the Shroud's availability for testing. He knows nothing else, nor will he.

"I will arrange for him to take a well-deserved vacation for two weeks to see his relatives beginning that very day—July 22, which is a Tuesday. We will arrive on Monday the twenty-first to make sure that all arrangements are satisfactory."

DAMASCUS, SYRIA
THURSDAY, JULY 3, 1997
4:12 P.M.

The same six men sat around the same table just as they had six days earlier. The leader announced, "Our friend Shakar al Harith is dead." After silencing the room, he continued, "He was in a car accident in Scotland. The police easily discovered he was traveling with a fake Israeli passport."

After listening to the discussion for several minutes, the leader looked at the man seated to his right and announced, "Salam, I want you to go to Edinburgh and present yourself as a cousin of al Harith. I want you to obtain a copy of the police report and learn as much as possible. Use one of your fake passports. The cardinals may have left. If so, I want you to go to Rome, find the cardinals and see what you can learn."

"May I ask, have you notified The Director?"

"You know I don't have direct contact with him. I notified Hassan Nasrallah. He's my superior and it's up to him if he wants to contact The Director."

EDINBURGH, SCOTLAND
WEDNESDAY, JULY 9, 1997
6:25 P.M.

The two striking young ladies sat at a quiet table at the back of their favorite restaurant. After they were served their pints of ale, Shannon began, "So, Laura, tell me what's new with you. We missed our Wednesday dinner for the past two weeks, so we have some catching up to do."

"There's not really much new: my parents are fine; my job is good; my social life is nonexistent; and I'm three weeks older than when we last met."

"No new male suitors?"

Laura displayed a wide grin and chuckled. "Everyone who comes on to me is either twenty-five years old and hoping to get lucky or they're fifty years old with a disappearing wedding ring."

After a thoughtful pause, she added, "I don't think there are many eligible bachelors left in Scotland who are in their midthirties."

"Tell me about it. You don't have that many years on me, girl," Shannon quipped.

"Shannon, you're only twenty-seven and I just turned thirty-three. I'd say that's a lot of years."

"I'm sure the right man will come along and you'll have a wonderful marriage."

Laura gazed past her friend and with a slight smile, murmured, "No, I have no prospects for marriage and certainly no prospects for motherhood. I've accepted my fate." She looked down at her folded hands and mumbled, "I had that opportunity, but it didn't work out."

"Laura, I've asked you several times to tell me about him, but you've always replied with a 'someday I will'. Well, I think that someday is now."

Laura sighed as her shoulders slumped. After a long exhale she conceded, "All right, I'll tell you about him. But first, I need something stronger than this ale." She perked up and signaled their waiter. "Bring us each four shots of whisky and a glass of water."

After drinking two of the shots and deliberating for several minutes, she recounted, "It's been, gosh, over five years now."

Shannon drank two of her shots, shuddered, and leaned forward with her elbows on the table and her chin on her clenched hands.

"I loved Brian. He had a great personality and was well-liked by everyone. He was handsome, and humorous, and had a good job with a promising career as a construction manager. Everything was wonderful. He was everything that a girl from a lower middle-class background could possibly hope for. We dated for almost two years when we became engaged." She thoughtfully added, "He was my first lover. I wanted to save myself for the 'perfect man'. Well, he wasn't so perfect."

"So, you waited until you were engaged?" Shannon exclaimed.

"Yes, and that's when he started changing. He became more demanding and more self-centered. It felt like that's all he wanted."

"And how was it for you, Laura?"

She reached for a shot glass, shrugged and gulped it down. "I feel like I'm in the confession booth, Shannon." After a reflective pause, she revealed, "I enjoyed our physical relationship, but I began to wonder why he enjoyed it so much more than I did. I never seemed to feel the completion that he obviously felt. On a lot of weekends, instead of going out, he wanted me to cook dinner for him at his apartment. I started to feel like I was becoming like my mother."

"What do you mean?" Shannon asked.

"All I remember growing up was my mother constantly catering to my father and always taking care of his needs and his demands. I felt like I was falling into a trap."

"So, you broke the engagement?"

"Yes. It was the hardest thing I've ever done."

"How did he take it?"

"I prepared so much for different responses: grief, anger, disbelief, defensiveness. But I didn't prepare myself for what he showed."

"What was that?"

"Indifference." She paused and reflected. "We returned to his flat after having a light dinner on a Friday night. He wanted to immediately get into bed, but I told him I had something very important to discuss. Finally, he realized I was serious because I stood with my arms crossed and wouldn't move. He barely listened as I told him that I'd been having serious questions about our future. When I told him that I didn't want to marry him, he suddenly paid attention. I was crying when I took off my engagement ring and handed it to him."

"What did he do?"

"He took it and asked me if I was certain about this. I put my arms around his neck and buried my head against his chest and sobbed that I was. Shannon, he didn't even lift his arms to comfort me. I left his flat and drove home to my parents' house. I never heard from him again."

"Laura, that had to be so hard to do."

"It was, but what was even more difficult was hearing my parents' reaction. I was still crying when I got home. When I told them what I did, my father was furious. He screamed at me that I had just ruined my life as well as his. When I told him that all Brian cared about was selfish sex, his response was that there was nothing wrong with that because he would provide me with a comfortable life. My mother idn't say a word in my defense. Within two weeks, I moved out and got my own small flat."

"Oh my gosh, that had to be so terrible. Do you have any regrets?"

"Absolutely not," Laura exclaimed. Even though I had to get a second job to make ends meet, leaving him was the best thing I ever did. And, it was time for me to move away from my parents. After a few months my relationship with my parents became stronger than it ever was."

"Did you ever see him again?"

"I ran into him a couple of times at social functions over the next several years, but he didn't speak to me. He got married after a few years and divorced about a year later." Laura raised her chin up and pronounced, "Some friends told me his wife left him after he hit her on several occasions."

"Well, girl, you certainly got lucky there. Have you had any relationships since then?"

"It wasn't luck, Shannon, I followed my instincts. And, yes, I've been in several relationships since then but nothing serious. And I certainly didn't let them get too physical."

Shannon's eyes widened as she gasped, "Are you telling me you haven't had sex in over five years?"

"I haven't. It just doesn't make sense to me to give away my body without giving away my heart. I haven't met anyone yet that I would trust with my heart."

"Like I said earlier, I'm sure the right one will come along someday," Shannon pronounced.

"Maybe, but I really don't care very much. I'd rather be single with some lonely nights than married and unhappy," Laura exclaimed as she downed her last shot. "Speaking of not caring and of middle-aged men, my boss is going away for a holiday," Laura effused.

"Really? Dr. McKinney is actually taking a vacation?"

"Yes, he's going away for at least several weeks," Laura responded.
"Where's he going?"

"He didn't say. But it will certainly relieve the stuffy atmosphere around the office."

TURIN, ITALY
TUESDAY, JULY 22, 1997
8:07 A.M.

Several weeks prior, Oleg had met with Cardinal Saldarini, the Cardinal of Turin, and had made arrangements for the Shroud to be examined and to have some minor tests performed. Oleg had also informed his fellow cardinal that it might be necessary to transport the Shroud to the Vatican for further testing.

Cardinal Saldarini was obviously very concerned. However, after receiving a short phone call from Pope John Paul II, his concerns were put to rest. The Pope informed him that he was personally having some testing done and that this testing was to be held in strict confidence and would not be made public.

Giovanni Saldarini arranged for the Shroud to be brought out from its temporary storage and displayed on a long worktable that had been previously used for the examination of the Shroud. The Cathedral of St. John the Baptist was to be closed for several days, both to the public and the clergy, with exception of Cardinals Ratzinger and Jaropelk, their two visitors, and a team of cathedral guards.

Oleg and Joseph warmly greeted Ian McKinney and Angus MacGregor as they entered the cathedral. After receiving assurances from the cardinals that these were the expected guests, the guards locked the doors and escorted the four of them to a large, high-ceiling, brightly lit basement room where the Shroud was mounted on a large board and set up horizontally against the wall. The room had previously been remodeled with white painted drywall on the walls, ceiling tiles and bright fluorescent ceiling fixtures and tiled floors. A large worktable had been placed in the center of the room

Ian and Angus were surprised by the cleanliness of the room as they breathed in the aseptic air. Oleg explained that an air filtration system had been installed and that the room had been modernized for the previous testing of the Shroud.

Ian moved quickly ahead of the others to view the relic and as he stood and silently looked at the Shroud, a feeling of awe crept over him. "It's quite inspirational, isn't it, Ian?" Oleg commented. Ian did not respond.

"Where is your equipment?" Joseph asked, breaking the trance.

"Yes. Yes, I'm sorry, this is quite amazing," Ian replied. "The equipment is in our hotel room in two large metal cases. We didn't want to bring them in the taxi. We thought they might draw attention."

"Very wise," Oleg responded. "I'll have one of the guards drive Angus to your hotel and retrieve the cases. Meanwhile, you can begin your preparations. Please remember that the sanctity and preservation of the Shroud are of the utmost importance."

Ian remained mesmerized by the Shroud and simply muttered, "Yes, by all means. I can see that." After a pause, he repeated, "This is quite amazing." He turned to Cardinal Jaropelk and softly said, "Oleg, if these tests prove to be positive, I may have more questions of you than you have of me." He returned to staring at the Shroud and after a moment, muttered, "Yes, quite amazing."

Oleg and Joseph glanced at each other. Oleg smiled and asked, "Even more amazing than Dolly the sheep?" Ian didn't respond. He didn't have to.

Oleg looked again at Giuseppe and quietly said, "You are not the first person to be deeply affected by the Shroud, Ian. It is certainly nothing to be ashamed of."

He paused to allow Ian to digest what he had said, then continued, "Just think, this is the two-thousand-year-old burial cloth for the Son of God and his image was imprinted onto the cloth by a blast of energy as he was resurrected into heaven."

Ian didn't respond—he was transfixed by the image on the Shroud. After a moment, Oleg said, "Ian, I, too, could look at it all day, but shouldn't you start to examine it?"

"Yes." he softly responded. "Yes, of course."

"But, Ian," Oleg replied with a humorous smile, "you have to forget about the theological implications of the Shroud and concentrate on the scientific aspects of this piece of cloth that you are testing. It is a piece of linen, nothing more, and you are here simply to perform tests on it."

Ian broke out of his trance, looked at the cardinal and slowly began to smile. Joseph also broke into a sly grin and soon the three were joined in soft laughter.

"All right, your point is made. For a moment, I lost sight of why I'm here."

About twenty minutes later, Angus returned with the equipment cases and opened them up. The cardinals watched, not having any idea of what it all was. Angus removed an item that resembled a small radio and quickly walked around the room, scanning for any listening devices. Apparently satisfied, he explained he was merely taking a precaution.

Joseph asked, "Oleg and I are going to go up to the cathedral, do you have any idea how long your testing will take?"

"All I'm looking for is the existence of solidified oils. If I find any, I merely have to check the samples for blood. That is all I can accomplish here. It's not very exciting, so please, attend to whatever duties you might have. If I find something, I'll call you immediately."

"Before we leave, Giuseppe and I would like to know how you test for the existence of solidified oils?"

Ian walked to the cases and removed a handheld piece of equipment that resembled a hair dryer and lifted it up. "I will slowly move this scanner over the entire Shroud. It will detect any solid substances on the material. Angus and I will first divide the entire Shroud into one-inch squares with this red string. As the scanner detects a solid object, we will note its location on a chart."

Giuseppe questioned, "It seems like this will take quite some time?"

"Not as much as you would think. We will simply hammer these looped nails onto the display board in one-inch intervals around the entire perimeter of the Shroud. Then we will thread the string through the eyelets. By my calculations, this will result in over seven thousand squares. We'll number the squares from one to one hundred and seventy-one lengthwise and we'll letter the squares from A to Z, then, use double letters for the remaining seventeen inches of the width. When we detect any significant solid substance, we will note that on our chart, which we have already prepared. When the scanning is completed, we will use this high-power microscope to examine any solid substances that are detected."

"How long do you think this will take?" Oleg inquired.

Ian reflected. "If it takes one minute to measure and install each of the four hundred and twenty nails, there is slightly more than seven hours of total work. Allowing for some downtime for refreshments, lunch, and other necessary functions, I would hope that the two of us could have this phase completed, with the string wound through the nails by the end of the day. Like I said, it won't be terribly exciting to watch. It will be more interesting tomorrow when we begin to scan the Shroud."

The cardinals were impressed with the simplicity of the procedure and said so as they prepared to leave. "We'll return with lunch in several hours. Meanwhile, we'll have water and lemonade brought to you. The washrooms are down this hallway to your right," Oleg informed them. "Oh yes, and I hope you understand that the four guards must remain here throughout the entire procedure."

Ian responded that he was perfectly fine with them being here.

"None of them speak a word of English, so they will not understand what we are saying." Oleg informed them.

It was nearly six-thirty in the evening when Ian and Angus finished threading the string through the last of the eyelets and stood back and surveyed their work. Looking at the Shroud in its horizontal position from several feet away, they could no longer see the front and back images of the man on the cloth as they were covered by the red string.

"It's been a long tedious day and Angus and I are hungry. You don't suppose there's a restaurant in this city that has a supply of good single malt, do you?" Ian asked the cardinals.

Joseph smiled at Oleg, and turned to Ian and replied, "This is a country of wine with some beer. However, I think several of the better restaurants may be able to satisfy your needs, although I doubt they would serve your Macallan."

Ian looked a little saddened by the prospect of not having his favorite "wee dram" in the evening.

"However," Joseph continued as he reached into a leather satchel he was carrying, "I did come across this in Rome." He pulled out a bottle of Macallan 21.

Ian broke into a bright smile and exclaimed, "Bless you, Cardinal Joseph. You are a wonderful man."

"No, bless you, Ian and Angus. And bless this endeavor," Oleg stated. "We will need all of God's blessings should your testing be positive tomorrow. Now, we're going to one of the finest restaurants in Turin and we might even join you in one of your 'wee drams' if you will allow us."

"Of course, my friends, I would be proud to have you join me drinking the water of life."

Sixty minutes later, the four were seated at a table enjoying a fabulous Italian dinner. Each course was better than the previous one. The restaurant owner graciously provided glasses, ice and water for the Scotch whisky as they each enjoyed sipping the smooth liquid.

The conversation was light, and they purposely did not discuss the project. Angus constantly surveyed the other diners looking for any sign of unusual interest in their party.

Joseph changed the topic of conversation and asked Ian, "You referred earlier to this as the 'water of life.' My understanding is that the Latin term 'acqua vitae,' meaning 'water of life' referred to our Italian wine."

"Aye," Ian exclaimed. "You are correct, Joseph. However, in the old Gaelic language, water of life is spelled *uisge beatha* and pronounced 'ooskie bayha.' When so many Scots went to America in the late 1700s, the term became shortened to the present name *whisky*."

Giuseppe commented, "Well, that is fascinating. I commend you on your national drink and your knowledge of its history."

After dinner, the driver took Ian and Angus back to their hotel and drove the cardinals to the Bishop's rectory where they were staying. Again, nothing was said about their project except that they had a big day in front of them tomorrow.

DAMASCUS, SYRIA
WEDNESDAY, JULY 23, 1997
7:08 P.M.

The leader addressed his four cohorts, "Salam spent ten days in Edinburgh." The leader shrugged his shoulders as he added, "He didn't learn much. The police report showed al Harith died in an automobile accident. The cardinals had already returned to Rome, so he never saw them. And, he didn't see anything suspicious about McKinney. So, I sent him off to Rome. He learned that the cardinals went to Turin, Italy, together yesterday. I sent him there this morning. If he doesn't learn anything there, I'll bring him home."

TURIN, ITALY
WEDNESDAY, JULY 23, 1997
8:04 A.M.

Standing at the entrance of the cathedral, the cardinals anxiously awaited the arrival of Ian and Angus. The four of them immediately went to the basement room where the Shroud rested, just as they had left it the previous evening.

Because the image could not be seen, unless he stood looking down upon it, Ian had lessened his awe and regained his scientific excitement. He quickly went to the equipment cases, grasped the scanner and went to work.

He noticed that the cardinals were attentively watching, so he explained, "I'll start at the top left of the Shroud at 1-A and proceed across the first row to 1-QQ, then double back from row 2-QQ to 2-A. This will start with the feet of the frontal view."

Angus held the computer printout of the coordinates for the cardinals to see.

Ian continued, "If the scanner detects a solid particle, Angus will record it on his chart.

After nearly ninety minutes, the scanner had yet to detect any solid particles. When Ian noticed their worried looks, he cautioned, "Don't be too concerned. We have yet to reach the image on the Shroud."

Finally, the scanner detected a solid particle at 11-U. The cardinals jumped out of their chairs and rushed to the Shroud to see what it was.

"Relax—don't get excited. It's nothing you can see, and it could be anything," Ian explained. "Hundreds of our coordinates will likely test positive."

The cardinals, after peering at the little one-inch square, realized there was, indeed, nothing to see. They went back to their chairs, knowing this was going to be a long tedious process.

Ian observed their disappointment and did a quick calculation in his head. "Gentlemen, it has taken ninety minutes to scan four hundred and fifty-one squares. That's about twelve seconds per square. At this pace, it will take a long time to complete the scanning."

The reaction was predictable, each cardinal let out a deep breath as they fully comprehended just how long this testing was going to take.

"Is there any way to make the process faster?" Joseph asked.

"No, there really isn't, Joseph. Like I said, it takes about twelve seconds to adequately scan each square and there are more than seventy-three hundred squares. That's more than twenty-four hours, or three days after we account for lunch and other downtime."

"Do you need to scan all of the squares?" asked Oleg. As soon as he said it, he realized how foolish the question was.

Ian sensed his regret about asking the question and replied, "I'm sure you agree with me, Oleg. We have just this one opportunity to test the Shroud and we must be totally thorough."

Oleg nodded his agreement.

"For scheduling purposes, once the scanning is done, how long will it take to determine if there is blood in the solid particles?" Joseph inquired.

"Well, let's calculate that. Let's assume there are two thousand positive squares and it takes thirty seconds to determine if the solid particles are, in fact, solidified oils. Then, you have one thousand minutes or nearly seventeen hours of work. Again, with rest stops, that's another three days. I can determine if there's blood in the particles at the same time we determine exactly what the solid particles are. That's as much as we can do here. We would have to set up a more thorough laboratory to determine if there is any preserved DNA in the blood samples. So, gentlemen, it appears that we will be working here for another week."

Everyone was quiet for a moment as they digested the time schedule.

Ian broke the silence. "Well, I must get along with my testing."

Ian took the scanner, went back to the Shroud and continued his work. "11-V," he called out almost immediately. He continued scanning the remainder of row eleven, then dropped down to row twelve and came back. After about eight minutes he called out 12-W, followed immediately with 12-V, 12-U, and 12-T. There was an excitement in the room as Ian continued to call out squares over the next several hours.

After completing row 31, Ian stopped and said, "I'm hungry; let's pause for lunch." He stretched, then walked slowly to a sofa at the far end of the room and sank into the soft cushions. Oleg had lunch brought in for themselves and the guards.

An idea came to Ian. "Angus, every time I get to the middle of the Shroud, I have to stop and walk around to the other side to continue. I'm going to change the procedure. I'll scan rows thirty-two through fifty-eight, A through V. Then I'll move to the other side of the table and do W through QQ. When we finish row fifty-eight, we'll end for the day," he exclaimed.

"That will certainly save some time," Angus agreed.

Oleg added, "And that will make it easier on you, my friend." Ian nodded appreciatively and continued eating his pasta salad.

By midafternoon, Ian had completed row fifty-eight A through V and decided to take a break. Oleg suggested they go upstairs and take a quick tour of the cathedral. Neither Ian nor Angus had ever been inside a Roman Catholic cathedral and were amazed by its opulence and grandeur. Ian inquired, "Tell me, Oleg, when was the cathedral built?"

"It was constructed from 1491 through 1498," replied Oleg.

"Well, it's certainly a beautiful structure. Forgive my boldness, my friend, but when the people were so poor in those days, why did your church build such opulent and expensive structures?"

Oleg was thoughtful for a moment and then responded, "That is an excellent question. I can best answer it by saying that the Church of five hundred years ago was considerably different from the Church of today. Five hundred years ago, several popes had children, they raised armies, and amassed considerable wealth. The cathedral was the center of activity in the city and was attended daily by most people. I suppose that the people needed the magnificence of the physical church because their lives did not have as much purpose as they do today. They relied on the Church for everything from friendships to salvation."

Angus asked, "Wasn't the wealth of the church, compared to the poverty of the people, one of the main reasons for the reformation?"

Oleg nodded his head and, with a resigned look on his face, replied, "I suppose there is some truth to that." Everyone was quiet for several moments.

Ian looked at the high ceiling of the cathedral, then glanced at his watch and broke the silence by stating, "Well, let's get back to work. It's almost four o'clock and we have several hours of work yet to do this afternoon."

It was nearly six o'clock when Ian finished scanning the remainder of rows thirty-one through fifty-eight. By his calculations he had scanned twenty-four hundred and ninety-four squares. "How many positives did we have, Angus?"

"Six hundred and nine, to be exact," Angus answered.

Ian walked over to Angus and looked at the chart with the positive squares. He took a quick glance at it and immediately looked up at Angus with a slight smile.

Angus was about to say something when Ian quickly interjected, "Let's complete tomorrow's testing and then see if there is a pattern. Meanwhile, I've been on my feet all day and I'm tired."

Joseph smiled and said, "I have just the answer. Let's have another fine Italian dinner and a 'wee dram' as you call it."

"That's a wonderful idea, Joseph," Ian quipped.

As they left the room, the guards locked up behind them, just as a new shift came to replace them. Cardinal Jaropelk informed the guards they would return in the morning.

TEL AVIV, ISRAEL
WEDNESDAY, JULY 24, 1997
7:21 A.M.

"Fox," Director Yatom said after he called him into his office, "Shai contacted us last night and told us this Dr. McKinney and the head of security for the Roslin Institute left yesterday for Turin, Italy. He's certain his cover is intact, but I'm sending you there today to find out what's going on.

"We have also learned that the same two cardinals from the Vatican also left for Turin late yesterday. Fox, I want to know what this is about. It's starting to intrigue me."

TURIN, ITALY
THURSDAY, JULY 24, 1997
8:08 A.M.

As soon as the guards admitted Ian, Angus, and the two cardinals to the basement testing room Ian got right to work.

Angus suggested, "Ian, would it make it easier to test the entire side of the Shroud from rows fifty-nine to one hundred seventy-one, A through V and then complete the remaining side tomorrow?"

Ian thoughtfully replied to his suggestion, "No, let's continue the same way. I want to see how this pattern develops." Having said this, Ian began scanning.

The morning ended as they paused for lunch, with Ian having scanned almost fourteen hundred more squares. He had now completed row 110, A through V.

While eating their lunch of individual pizzas, Ian asked Angus to see the chart. He looked at it for a moment and a look of satisfaction appeared on his face. Angus knew that look, which said *just as I thought*.

"Should we continue with the testing?" Angus asked, knowing immediately that it was not a smart question.

Ian replied, "Yes, by all means. We'll scan the entire Shroud."

Joseph was the first to interject, asking, "Why would you stop testing? What did you find?"

"We're detecting a pattern. I want to finish today's work, and then I'll be reasonably certain. We can discuss the findings at the end of the workday."

The cardinals appeared satisfied, but their curiosity was heightened. After an hour, they excused themselves and said they were going upstairs to the cathedral to pray for the success of the testing.

It was nearly four-thirty in the afternoon when Ian completed the remainder of rows fifty-nine through one hundred-and-ten. "Let's do another ten or fifteen rows in their entirety, Angus. It should only take about another two hours. I'm anxious to see the pattern."

"I agree," he responded.

Ian completed the next fifteen rows at 6:20, took off his latex gloves, put the scanner back in its case, and went to look at the chart. He studied it for a moment, then walked over to where the cardinals were eagerly waiting for an explanation.

"Gentlemen, look at this." He showed the computerized chart with its grid system, squares that had tested positive filled with Xs. "What do you see?"

They each looked intently at the chart for a moment.

Oleg excitedly announced, "It's almost the same shape as the image on the Shroud. Does this mean …."

Before he could finish, Ian interjected, "Yes, I'm optimistic and excited this could mean the solids that have been detected could be solidified oils. We won't know until I conduct those tests the day after tomorrow. I want to caution you, just because the solids have the same pattern as the image, they could be anything. However, it certainly is a positive sign."

There was an excitement in the air as they left the cathedral and climbed into the waiting automobile to take them to their dinner.

The early evening remained hot and humid and there were still quite a few people in the piazza looking in the shops or gazing at the cathedral.

Angus observed there were several tourists who were taking pictures. He also noticed that one man appeared to be taking pictures of them.

TURIN, ITALY
FRIDAY, JULY 25, 1997
8:11 A.M.

They began the day just as they had the previous three. Ian and the cardinals were visibly excited as Ian began the scanning.

Oleg noticed Angus was more somber. He didn't comment.

Lunch was served shortly after noon. Ian completed row 171, A through V, and was already scanning the remaining half of the top part of the Shroud. He stood back and looked at the maze of red string that crisscrossed the Shroud. "A few more hours and we'll be completed," he said as he went to look at the chart. "Anything different with the pattern, Angus?" he inquired.

"No. It's the same pattern."

"Excellent!" Ian effused, as he picked up the chart and glanced at it.

At precisely 4:25 p.m., Ian finished the scanning of the Shroud. He again looked at the chart and asked Angus, "Do you know how many squares tested positive?"

Angus looked at his notes and responded, "There are precisely eighteen hundred and sixty-seven squares that have tested positive. All but eighty-nine are within the image and these are spread randomly across the Shroud."

Ian picked up the chart, studied it for a brief moment, then exclaimed, "Oleg, Joseph, come look at this!" The cardinals rushed over to view the chart. What they saw amazed and excited both of them.

The pattern on the chart revealed almost an exact replica of both the front and back images on the Shroud.

Joseph took a deep breath while Oleg shuddered, as if he felt a chill go over his entire body.

Ian watched their reactions, then told them, "I'll caution you both, don't get overly excited. We don't know what the solid materials are. They could be anything." He paused for a few seconds, and continued, "But, it certainly is promising, isn't it?"

Ian sat down to relax. "Tomorrow we'll learn a bit more about what we have here," he stated.

———

As they left the cathedral, Angus felt a sense of unease. He couldn't explain it, but he sensed there was something evil in the area.

As the driver held the door open for the cardinals, Angus stood against the car and again surveyed the crowd. There were only about forty people in the piazza in front of the cathedral, many of whom were women and children.

He studied the faces and the dress of the men. Nothing suspicious or out of the ordinary stood out. All the men appeared to be local and he didn't see anyone who looked like the "tourist" who had appeared to be taking their picture yesterday evening. But Angus knew he could well be in any of the shops that lined the street across the piazza watching them.

Indeed, he was.

———

The cardinals were energized and talked animatedly throughout dinner. Ian, too, showed his excitement. Angus, on the other hand, was somber and pensive. He barely talked. He was obviously deep in thought as he frequently looked around the restaurant.

Ian noticed this but said nothing. Finally, as dessert was being served, Ian leaned over and whispered in Angus's ear, "Do we need to talk?" Angus looked at Ian and nodded.

Ian didn't speak as he hurriedly ate his dessert. The cardinals noted his change of mood and fell silent as they, too, ate their desserts more quickly.

After the four had climbed into their waiting car, Ian asked, "Angus, can we talk here?"

"No, let's go back to the cathedral." Oleg gave the instructions in Italian to their driver, who was also one of the guards. Not a word was said during the ten-minute drive back.

When they arrived, one of the guards let them into the cathedral and escorted them to the basement testing room. There were two guards posted at the top of the stairs and two more standing at the locked door to the room. After admitting them to the room, the guards locked the door behind them and stood by the door.

Oleg started to speak, but Angus motioned for him to be silent. Angus went to one of his equipment cases, took out the scanner and once again swept the entire room for listening devices. Satisfied the room was still secure, he put the equipment away and turned to face Ian and the cardinals.

"I think we're being watched." The cardinals were shocked, while Ian had suspected this was what Angus was going to tell them.

"What did you see?" Ian asked.

"Not much. Last evening, when we left, there were some tourists taking pictures of the cathedral and one man looked like he was taking pictures of us. I looked more closely this evening but didn't see anything suspicious."

"Well, that probably was merely a tourist taking a picture of Oleg and myself. It happens quite frequently." Ian looked at Angus and, without saying a word, gave him an inquiring look.

"I didn't see anything tonight when we left, but I had the feeling we were being watched."

"What do you want to do?" asked Ian.

"I'd like to finish our work and leave here as soon as possible." he pronounced with pursed lips. "I'm not comfortable here without the ability to obtain rapid backup assistance."

It had been many years since Ian had seen Angus so troubled.

"I have an idea," Angus proposed. "Why do we have to examine all of the positive squares here? If we find solidified oils and they do contain blood, we could take the Shroud to the Vatican and continue the testing where it is secure. Why not first examine those areas where you suspect that Jesus bled and if they test positive, we can pack up and leave?"

Ian pondered for a moment, and concluded, "All right, that makes sense. Let's do that. Where would those areas most likely be?" he asked the cardinals.

Joseph replied, "Christ was scourged all over his body, so there would have been bleeding over his entire body. But the body was cleansed after removal from the cross." He thought for a moment and continued, "The heaviest concentrations of blood would have been on the wrists, the feet, the forehead area and, of course, the piercing under the ribs on his right side. If there was additional bleeding after the body was cleansed, these would be the most likely places."

"All right," Ian said, "let's start with those areas tomorrow. If they test positive, let's go to your Vatican and continue our work. Oleg, would you make the arrangements in the event we want to depart quickly."

"I will, and I'm also going to request that we increase the security." Everyone was comfortable with the new plan.

Oleg made several quick telephone calls and they left the testing room for the car ride to their hotel and a much-needed night of sleep.

From the dark shadows across the piazza, two separate pairs of eyes were watching them, each unaware of the other.

TURIN, ITALY
SATURDAY, JULY 26, 1997
8:14 A.M.

As they did the previous mornings, the guards admitted the four men into the basement testing area. The mood was different today. The tedious work of the past four days was over and there was a feeling of excitement in the room.

Ian immediately got started as Angus again searched the room for listening devices. There were none.

"Oleg and Joseph, where would you like me to begin?" Ian asked.

Joseph quickly responded, "Try the head area; let's start at the top."

Ian noticed a quizzical look on Angus's face. "Were you about to say something?"

"No, proceed. You are the scientist," Angus replied.

Ian looked at the chart, took the microscope and placed it over seventy-eight-S and examined the square. Oleg and Giuseppe each held their breath as they waited for Ian to announce his findings. After nearly a minute, Ian moved the equipment over to seventy-eight-T and examined that square for another minute.

"I have some good news," Ian stoically announced. "It appears as though the solid material could be solidified oils, but there is no sign of blood. We had positive results in the next seven rows. I'll examine those squares and let you know if I find anything different."

After nearly forty-five agonizing minutes without speaking, Ian removed the equipment, looked at the cardinals and said, "There are no signs of blood anywhere on the facial area."

Ian looked at Oleg and saw a look of disappointment. He saw Joseph appearing equally depressed. Realizing that today might be the culmination of months of their planning and dreaming, Ian stated, "Don't get too depressed, we have a long way to go."

He glanced at Angus and saw a questioning look on his face. He simply said, "Angus?"

"Now, I'm not an expert on this matter, but it seems to me if the body was cleansed after death, the most likely area where bleeding would continue might be the wrists. Perhaps that is where we should be concentrating our search."

Ian nodded thoughtfully and said, "Yes, I believe you might be right, Angus. Very good." He thought for a moment, then said to the cardinals, "Gentlemen, you know the Shroud far better than I. Where were the wrists on the image?"

They couldn't see the image on the Shroud, as it was nearly concealed by the red string, but they each knew the position of the image.

Oleg responded, "The wrists were placed one on top of the other on the center of the body. That would put them at the lower abdomen."

Ian again studied the chart for a moment and then took the equipment directly to thirty-nine-R. There were nine squares in row thirty-nine that tested positive for solids. He examined all nine and then went to row forty, where eight squares had tested positive.

It took more than an hour to examine fifty-eight squares in rows thirty-nine through forty-five that had tested positive. Ian removed the equipment and went over to the table near the cardinals and opened a bottle of water. He took several swallows, shook his head and announced that there was no sign of blood.

K. BRUCE MACKENZIE

After several more swallows of water, he excused himself and left the room. Ian didn't want the cardinals to see his disappointment as he walked down the hall to the bathroom. After a few minutes, he returned.

"Angus, let's get moving, we have a lot of work yet to do." He took the equipment and examined the nine positive squares in row forty-six. Everyone knew that the results were negative by his continued silence. At row forty-seven, his body stiffened slightly as he stared intently into the apparatus, spending almost two full minutes.

"We have blood on forty-seven-S."

The cardinals immediately jumped up from the couch and rushed over to Ian, apparently forgetting there was nothing they could see. Angus marked the chart.

"Forty-seven-T is positive," Ian announced. "And so is forty-seven-U. The blood in all three squares appears to be trapped within solidified oils."

After another hour, Ian had examined an additional fifty-three squares and had located blood in nineteen of them. He removed the equipment, stood back and said, "Well, I think we can go to the next phase, gentlemen. Let's go to the security of the Vatican. Oleg, what are the arrangements?"

Oleg beamed. "I'll make the telephone call and the transport truck will be waiting for us at the back of the cathedral in two hours to pack up the Shroud. The security guards will do the packing and we'll be joined for the drive to Rome by a large additional security force."

"Do we have ten minutes to test another ten squares?" asked Ian.

"Well, yes, I suppose so. But why?" asked Oleg.

"I'm curious about the location of the piercing. Look at the chart and tell me where you think it is."

Oleg looked at the chart for a moment and responded, "I would guess that it is around fifty-nine-BB."

120

Ian quickly retrieved the equipment, went to the Shroud and placed it on fifty-nine-BB. Thirty seconds later, he exclaimed, "It's there!" He then examined fifty-nine-AA, fifty-nine-Z and fifty-nine-Y. They were all positive.

He picked up the equipment with a satisfied smile on his face and gave it to Angus to pack. The guards began to pack the Shroud in its storage container while Angus finished packing Ian's equipment.

Angus announced, "Ian, why don't you have one of the guards take you back to our hotel so you can check out and gather our belongings. I think I'll have a look around the piazza. I'd like to go out through a rear exit so I won't be seen. Ian, wait for twenty minutes before you leave the cathedral. I want to be in position to observe anyone who might be watching."

Joseph escorted him upstairs and they walked to a rear door. "Are you concerned?" Joseph fretted.

"Yes, I am. I hope I'm wrong, but I sense that we've been watched for the past several days. I'm going to look around the piazza. I'll be back in about an hour." Angus left the cathedral and began walking, circling the piazza, a block away, until he ended up at far side of the square.

Angus located a spot where he could readily observe the activities taking place on the piazza but could not easily be seen. After a few minutes, Ian emerged from the cathedral with a guard and climbed into the waiting car. Immediately afterward, the two cardinals and another guard exited the cathedral and climbed into a second waiting car.

Angus observed a man standing about a hundred feet away in the shadows of a storefront taking pictures of the men as they departed.

The man looked much like the "tourist" he saw several days ago taking pictures.

Angus started to walk toward him when he noticed a second man on the far side of the piazza who was also taking pictures of Ian and the cardinals. Oddly, after the cardinals departed, he turned around and looked to be taking pictures of the "tourist."

Angus ducked into a shop and continued to watch the men through the window. The "tourist" was unaware he was having his picture taken by the second man. Angus was about to confront them when he thought better of it. He took out his camera, walked outside and began taking photos of both men. He thought it might be better to try and identify the men rather than to confront them.

He decided to wait and watch the "tourist" and the second man. He was relieved when they each remained in the piazza. As long as they stayed there, they could not know that a truck had just parked behind the cathedral and the Shroud was being loaded. Thirty-seven minutes later, the cardinals returned to the cathedral after gathering their belongings. Thankfully, they left their belongings in the car, so the two observers were not tipped off that they might be leaving.

Angus made a mental note to have everyone equipped with cell phones to avoid just such a mistake. The "tourist" and the other observer were intently watching the cardinals enter the cathedral when Ian returned in the second car. They remained in their positions after Ian entered the cathedral.

Angus watched them for another five minutes and then audibly muttered to himself, "Why not?" He moved to a position in the piazza where he was in a direct line with the two men and then walked directly toward the "tourist," watching the second man as he briskly strode forward.

He was only about twenty feet away when the "tourist" looked up and saw Angus almost upon him. Angus nearly chuckled out loud at his startled reaction. In the next brief seconds, he determined the "tourist" was of Middle Eastern descent and was not very professional. Angus could already smell his pungent body odor and his sour breath as he looked at his yellow decayed teeth. His appearance reminded Angus of their "friend" back in Edinburgh and wondered if there was a connection.

Angus strode right past the panic-stricken man without saying a word. He continued walking directly toward the second man who was standing in the shadows about a hundred feet away. As he purposely approached him, the man didn't move a muscle and displayed no reaction as his eyes bored directly at Angus.

This one is certainly more professional, Angus thought.

As he got closer, Angus was surprised by this man's appearance. He was taller than the "tourist," appearing to be several inches over six feet in height. He was older, probably in his early to midfifties, and was deeply tanned. He had blond hair that was just starting to gray and he appeared to be in excellent physical shape. Angus watched his hands to make certain that he didn't reach for a weapon. This was a major concern, as Angus was unarmed.

The man didn't move as Angus approached. When Angus was only several feet away, the man said with a slight accent, "Can I help you?"

Momentarily taken aback, Angus quickly responded, "No, I was simply curious about you and your friend."

The man scoffed, "I can assure you, that idiot is no friend of mine." He turned and started to walk away. "But you might be, Agent MacGregor."

As the man continued walking away, Angus was dumbfounded by his comment. He realized that he would have ample time to think about it, so he turned and walked directly to the main entrance of the cathedral and rapped on the door for admittance.

"That was a long hour," Joseph commented. "We're ready to leave. Did you see anything?"

"Just a couple of acquaintances," Angus responded. Joseph was about to ask for details when Oleg and Ian came upstairs.

Oleg urged them to join them in leaving by the back door to the awaiting cars. "We can talk on the drive to Rome," he said. "We'll have plenty of time."

"How far is Rome?" Ian inquired.

"It's seven hundred kilometers, or about four hundred and forty miles. We should arrive sometime around midnight," Oleg offered.

THE VATICAN
SUNDAY, JULY 27, 1997
12:16 A.M.

The caravan, consisting of the truck carrying the Shroud, the van with the two cardinals, Ian, Angus, and the driver, and four additional cars with four guards in each car finally arrived at the Vatican after an eight-hour drive. Despite the tedious but uneventful drive, Angus remained constantly alert.

Oleg and Joseph directed the guards to unload the Shroud and to take it to a basement room in the Papal Palace, where they set it up on a large display table, just as they had in Turin. After the guards secured the room, Oleg showed the guards to their quarters while Joseph escorted Ian and Angus to their rooms. As Joseph was leaving, Ian gave him a handwritten list of the items they would require for the additional testing. They bid good night to each other and retired for a much-needed night of sleep.

It was shortly after nine a.m. when Oleg and Joseph completed celebrating mass. They went to the rooms of Ian and Angus and escorted them to breakfast. While dining, they discussed the items necessary for the testing. Ian informed them where they could obtain the needed items and that they should be able to have them delivered within three days. Meanwhile, Ian would continue to test all the positive squares for solidified oils containing blood.

"Gentlemen, will we have the opportunity to meet the Pope?" Ian asked of the cardinals.

"His Holiness spends most of the season at the summer palace at Gandolfo. However, he is returning on Thursday specifically to meet both of you and to discuss the project," Oleg responded. "Meanwhile, I suggest we spend the remainder of the day touring the Vatican museums."

Before leaving on the tour, Angus inquired about the possibility of transmitting some digital photos to Scotland. Oleg took him to the Vatican printing press building where he had the photos transmitted to his contact at MI-6. He enclosed a written request to attempt to identify the two men in the pictures. Being Sunday, he did not anticipate receiving a response until the next day.

THE VATICAN
WEDNESDAY, JULY 30, 1997
6:12 P.M.

Ian and Angus had spent all day Monday and Tuesday testing for solidified oils and for the presence of blood. After testing all the positive squares, Ian surveyed the results. Of the seventy-five hundred and thirty-three squares on the Shroud, eighteen hundred and sixty-seven tested positive for solids. Of these, one hundred and thirty-one tested positive for solidified oils containing blood.

Ian had spent most of Wednesday lifting the one hundred and thirty-one samples of blood, placing each one in a separate Petri dish which were then labeled and refrigerated.

"Well," Ian exclaimed, "that's all we can do until the laboratory equipment arrives."

"When will that be?" asked Angus.

"Oleg tells me it will be tomorrow afternoon. It will take us a full day to unpack and set up the equipment. So, hopefully, we can begin testing on Saturday. I have a feeling that the good cardinals will not allow us to work on Sunday, so it will be Monday before we have the results. After that, one way or another, I can go home to McDuff and you can go home to Kathleen."

Ian paused and clasped Angus's hand. With grateful eyes, he exclaimed, "By the way, thank you for being here with me. And thank you for having Kathleen watch Duffy for me."

"Ian, you know I owe you my life. I'll be by your side for as long as this project lasts."

Separately, they each wondered just how long that might be. Angus broke the silence. "Ian, I haven't had the right opportunity to tell you this, but it appears this project is known by at least two different groups." Ian, as always, was completely composed and displayed little reaction.

Angus described in detail his venture out to the piazza in Turin and his brief conversation with the "other" man. "That telephone call I took earlier was from my contact at MI-6. They don't know who the 'tourist' was. They suspect he was a minor Muslim operative who could be working for any number of Middle East organizations. They don't think he was very high up in rank and, based on his reaction when I appeared before him, I agree.

"It turns out they think the other man could possibly be an assassin with the Israeli Mossad. They're not completely certain because they've never seen photos of him, and his age has been reported to be anywhere from the early forties to the midfifties. But, my picture fits one of the descriptions of him. Apparently, he can change his identity and appearance and he is responsible for many significant assassinations around the world over the past two decades. That's all they know."

"What do you make of this?" Ian asked, for the first time showing some genuine concern.

"I think our Arab friend from Edinburgh reported in enough information that it piqued the interest of his superiors. When they found out he's living happily ever after with all those virgins, they sent another one to Turin to watch us. Fortunately, this one was equally inept."

"That explains the Arab, but what about this killer from the Mossad?"

"I'm guessing that the Mossad got wind of something happening, probably through a contact with the Arab group, and they sent their guy to see what this was all about. He wasn't there to kill anyone; he was there to observe. If he had wanted to kill either of us, we wouldn't be here now."

"But why send a killer to just watch?" Ian asked.

Reluctantly, Angus responded after taking several swallows from his bottled water. "That's a good question. Probably because they felt he might be called upon to use his skills, maybe to stop this project. I think one thing is for certain. This guy is a trained professional. He has been able to keep his identity secret for decades and he's smart. I'm sure it didn't take much for him to figure out what we're up to."

Ian thought for a moment and then said, "I'm glad we're safely behind these protected walls of the Vatican."

Angus nodded. He wasn't so sure the walls offered all that much protection.

"On a happier note," Ian continued, "while you were out taking your telephone call, Oleg informed me that we have a meeting with the Pope tomorrow morning."

"Now, that will interesting," Angus replied. "What do we call him and aren't we supposed to kiss his ring or something like that?"

Ian gave out a slight laugh and replied, "I'm quite certain Oleg and Joseph will instruct us how to act."

They were interrupted by a knock on the door. One of the three guards stationed at the door asked a question of the visitor in Italian. He received his answer, then unlocked and opened the door for Oleg and Joseph. Oleg asked about their progress for the day and Ian brought the cardinals up-to-date, omitting any mention of the men on the piazza.

Joseph was holding a brown paper bag, walked up to Ian and said with a gleam in his eye, "Look what I found in the Vatican commissary." He lifted out a bottle of Macallan whisky.

"Cardinal Ratzinger, if you keep doing this for me, I may have to become a Catholic." They all laughed.

Oleg added, with a big smile, "If he keeps smuggling Scotch whisky into the Vatican, he may have to become a Protestant." Now the laughter was uproarious.

Angus glanced over at the three guards to see if there was a reaction. There was none.

THE VATICAN
THURSDAY, JULY 31, 1997
9:57 A.M.

The two cardinals escorted Ian and Angus to the Pope's apartments and were promptly met by Antonio. He took them to John Paul's study, softly rapped on the door and admitted them for their papal meeting.

As he entered, Ian quickly observed the antique furnishings and artwork in the room. Then he focused on John Paul II, who remained seated in his large comfortable chair. Ian had been coached by Oleg and he promptly walked up to the Pope, who extended his hand to Ian.

"Your Holiness, it is an honor. Please allow me to introduce…" Before he could finish, John Paul got up and took a step toward Angus.

"You must be Angus, the brother-in-law and security expert. And you must be Dr. Ian McKinney." It was very unusual for the Pope to extend himself in this manner.

"Please be seated," John Paul said, noting Oleg and Joseph's shock. He then added, "Gentlemen, we're here to discuss the viability of a monumental and historical project. I think we can dispense with the formalities."

Ian was immediately in awe of his kindness and his gentle nature. *This man has an aura about him*, Ian thought.

Angus didn't say a word.

John Paul continued, "It is my understanding that you have discovered a significant amount of solidified oils on the Shroud and that you have also determined that there is some amount of blood contained in the oils."

"Yes." Ian's voice was soft but firm.

John Paul continued, "Oleg and Joseph tell me that the next step will be to determine if the blood contains viable DNA."

Oleg nodded.

"I must tell you that I sincerely hope and pray that it does not." No one spoke. "I say this because I do not want to look at the disappointment on the face of my dearest friend, when I have to tell him this experimentation can go no further. I say this because to continue would be unholy, and I would be placing myself above the Lord. I am a mere mortal and I cannot be more than that."

Ian glanced at both Oleg and Joseph and saw the disappointment on their faces.

John Paul noted their anguish and said, "I promised Oleg and Joseph that you could perform your tests to determine if there is DNA in the blood. I won't retract that promise. You gentlemen may proceed. It is not with my blessing and it is certainly not with my hope for success."

The four were relieved, but Ian was extremely concerned about the Pope's negative attitude. He said nothing, but his facial expression said that he understood.

John Paul added, "When do you expect to have your testing completed?"

"By Monday or Tuesday, assuming the equipment arrives today," Ian quickly answered.

"Good, go about your work," John Paul said. "We will meet again after you have completed your testing. I will pray for you, Dr. Ian McKinney, but not for your success."

Ian and Angus went to their lab and spent the rest of the day preparing for the arrival of the equipment. They had everything in order when the equipment arrived and was brought to the lab in the late afternoon. Ian checked the inventory and he and Angus began unpacking, always under the watchful eyes of the ever-present guards.

They were nearly finished when Oleg and Joseph arrived to see how they were doing and to take them to dinner. Ian informed them everything was in order and he fully expected to have all the equipment set up and ready to start testing by late the next day.

Angus informed Oleg that included with the scientific equipment was an encryption machine. They took it to Oleg's office, where Angus set it up and showed Oleg how to use it. "It's a simple concept," he told Oleg. "Anyone listening without the machine will simply hear a garbled conversation. When we return to Edinburgh, I'll set up a duplicate machine at Ian's cottage and we can have absolutely secure conversations."

"Is this necessary?" Oleg questioned.

"It's not only necessary, it's imperative," Angus asserted. "Your project has, unfortunately, brought you into a different world than what you are used to. There are some dangerous people out there who are concerned about what we are doing. Oleg, I noticed that you didn't mention anything about these matters to the Pope."

"No, he has enough on his mind. There's no need to worry him further at this point. If you and Ian find viable DNA, I will tell him everything before he makes his decision."

"It sounded this morning like he had already made his decision."

"Perhaps. Let's go get Ian and Giuseppe and have some dinner." Then he whispered, "And perhaps a wee dram."

THE VATICAN
FRIDAY, AUGUST 1, 1997
11:58 A.M.

Ian and Angus had spent the morning setting up and testing the equipment when Oleg and Joseph came to the lab to escort them to lunch. While dining, Oleg noticed that Ian was deep in thought and did not participate in their idle conversation. "Is everything all right, Ian? You seem to be rather pensive."

Ian was quiet for a moment, then responded, "Oleg, I'd like to talk to you and get your opinion on some matters."

"Of course, my friend, I'm always available to you. When would you like to meet?"

"Well, we'll be finished setting up and testing the new equipment by late afternoon."

"Fine, I'll come get you at the lab at, say, four o'clock. We'll go to my office where we can talk." Oleg turned to Angus and asked, "Angus, will you be all right for several hours?"

Before he could reply, Joseph interjected, "Angus, why don't I give you a tour of the Vatican grounds while they are occupied."

"I would like that," Angus responded.

As Oleg escorted them back to the lab, he had a knowing smile on his face.

It was nearly four o'clock when Oleg and Ian were comfortably seated in Oleg's spacious office. The young priest who served as Oleg's secretary brought them a pitcher of lemonade and then silently left the office, closing the door behind him.

Sensing that Ian was hesitant to start the conversation, Oleg began, "Ian, I've known you now for more than five weeks. I want you to know that I've developed a high regard and respect for you, both as a scientist and as a person. No matter what happens with our project, I want you to know that I consider you a friend. We've been through a lot together in a short period of time."

"Thank you, Oleg." He took a swallow of lemonade as he gathered his thoughts. "Oleg, I'm a scientist. My entire life I've studied and been trained to believe there is a scientific or mathematical answer for every question in nature. There's a scientific solution for every problem. We may not know that answer or solution, but it's waiting there to be discovered."

He paused to gather his thoughts. "Now, I'm not so sure. I'm confronted with the possibility that I am discovering the proof that an event actually happened that is scientifically impossible. Oleg, I discovered solidified oils that were rubbed on the corpse of a man who was killed two thousand years ago. And, now we find there's blood trapped in those oils, and it could be 'live' blood. The only way this could have happened was by a huge surge of energy, and that could be a resurrection. And, that's impossible!"

"Is it?"

"Yes, it is. Once a man is dead, he can't come back to life. It's scientifically impossible."

"Ah, there I agree with you, Ian. It is scientifically impossible."

Ian looked up with a surprised expression. After a thoughtful pause, Oleg repeated, "It is scientifically impossible, Ian, but it is not spiritually impossible. And it did happen. Jesus was not merely a man."

"Maybe he really didn't die on the cross. Maybe his followers took him down before he died," Ian exclaimed.

"No, my friend, there were too many witnesses, including his accusers and executioners. They made sure he was dead. They even put a spear into his side and likely pierced his heart, just to make sure. I say, likely, because John saw, and wrote, that the piercing produced blood and water. The water would have come from his heart. As an aside, except for John, none of his male followers were there."

"They weren't?" Ian asked in surprise. "Where were they? Why weren't they there?"

"They were in hiding. They were cowering in disbelief, afraid to come out. You must understand, Ian, they thought Jesus was the Son of God; he had told them that on many occasions. They couldn't understand how God could let His son die. They waited for Jesus to perform one of his miracles they had seen countless times. If he were the Son of God, surely he could stop this mistake, this travesty. But he didn't. He didn't defend himself at all. They were hoping all the way up until his scourging, his whipping, that he would do something. Then, in their own minds, they came to the realization that he was not who he said he was. He couldn't be. Otherwise, he would have stopped this brutal scourging. He was whipped nearly forty times."

Oleg paused to slow down; he felt he was getting too excited. "Now, these weren't like the whippings that your English seamen received, several hundred years ago, for some infraction. Your sailors would receive twenty lashes with a leather whip that would bruise and even cut the skin. Jesus received over a hundred lashes with whips that had nails and pieces of bone imbedded in the ends of the whips. These tore his flesh apart to the point where he was a bloody, pulverized mass of torn flesh. Most men would have died from shock or loss of blood at that time. His disciples saw this, and they couldn't bear it. Not so much because of the pain that they saw him going through, but because they were a selfish, self-centered lot, and they were thinking of themselves.

"They were thinking of their own disillusionment and worried about what they were going to do with their lives because they had wasted all this time, and given up so much, to follow this 'fraud.' No, they didn't take him down from the cross early. They had no reason to, and they couldn't have gotten away with it, even if they wanted to. Only John was there to watch, and that was as much to watch over Jesus' mother, Mary, and report back to the others, as it was to pay respects to the dying Jesus. And, they didn't make up stories about this event either. They were disheartened and even angry that they had been fooled by this man, this fraud. He wasn't the Son of God; he couldn't be. The Son of God was immortal, he couldn't die. He wouldn't let himself die. And, this Jesus guy allowed himself to be tortured, allowed himself to die."

"I didn't realize all this," Ian said after letting it all sink in.

"My friend, let me tell you about these men, these apostles, as we call them." Oleg poured more lemonade for each of them, and then went on. "There were twelve original apostles and several more joined the ranks after the resurrection. They were simple, mostly uneducated men, most being fishermen, with several tax collectors. But they all shared one thing in common. Do you know what that was, Ian?"

"I suppose that they were all followers of Jesus." he answered.

"No, Ian, except for Judas, they were all tortured and persecuted, and all but one, or maybe two, died horrible deaths. Peter was crucified upside down. His brother, Andrew, was also crucified. You know St. Andrew, Ian. He's your patron saint of Scotland. John was tortured several times, including being boiled in oil. However, he miraculously survived and eventually died a natural death.

"John's brother, James the Great, was beheaded. Matthew may have died a natural death, but most accounts have him being stabbed to death. Matthew's brother, James the Less, was stoned to death. Philip was also crucified upside down and Bartholomew was skinned alive and then beheaded. Thomas was stabbed to death. Simon and Jude Thaddaeus were martyred together. They were both being stoned when a man ran up to Simon and ran a spear through him and then a group of thugs fell on Jude Thaddaeus and cut him into pieces. And, of course, there was Judas, who betrayed Jesus. He went insane over what he had done and hanged himself."

"You said that several others joined their ranks. Did they die violently, too?" Ian asked.

"Yes, Matthias was an early follower of Jesus, but he wasn't thought of as one of the original twelve. After the resurrection, he replaced Judas and he was later stoned to death. Stephen and Paul were not believers until they were confronted by Jesus well after the resurrection. Stephen was also stoned to death and Paul was beheaded. That was the fate of the twelve original apostles and the three newcomers. Of course, these deaths occurred over a lot of years as these men were highly successful in spreading the new religion."

"I always thought of St. Paul as being one of the original disciples," Ian said.

"That's a common misconception," Oleg replied. "Paul was a sinful man in his early years and either took part in or gave his tacit approval of the martyrdom of St. Stephen as he was stoned to death. Shortly after that he was confronted by the resurrected Jesus, became baptized, and began his missions. Many people think of him as one of the original twelve because he accomplished so much and was so instrumental in the development of the early Church. Anyway, I'm getting away from the point I'm trying to make."

"Yes, you were talking about their violent deaths," Ian stated.

"Ian, I want to ask you an extremely important question. But first, try to imagine what the apostles felt when Jesus died on the cross. They were in severe depression and were totally bewildered by his death. They had dispersed and were in hiding, fearing for their very lives. Everything Jesus had taught them was now subject to question because they thought he had lied to them about being the Messiah, the Son of God. Then, suddenly, they abandoned their occupations, their friends and, in some cases, their wives and families. They left everything behind and traveled the known world to spread the message that Jesus was the Messiah, that he truly was the Son of God.

"Now, Ian, here's the important part. They did this knowing they were facing certain death, and not just death, but ridicule and torture and painful deaths. Why did they do this, Ian? What could have made them all—not just one or two, but every single one of them—face certain horrifying deaths to spread the word?"

Oleg had become excited and his voice had risen as he asked this last question. He sat back, took several swallows of lemonade and looked at Ian for an answer.

Ian was silent, so Oleg continued, "I'll tell you why. Because they saw Jesus. They saw him in the flesh, and he told each of them what he wanted them to do. They saw and touched the resurrected Jesus and were now fully convinced that he indeed was the Son of God. They certainly didn't go out on their missions and to certain death over a concept. They saw Jesus! It's the only possible explanation."

Oleg's speech had again risen in volume. He sat back and quietly said, "Ian, I want you to think about that. You're an extremely intelligent man. Try and come up with another explanation. I'll listen to it, but I don't think there's any other valid explanation."

Again, Ian was silent as he was deep in thought. "I will think about that, I truly will," he replied.

"Ian, I know what you're going through. You're a scientist. You use deductive reasoning in all your thought processes. Now, I want you to open your mind for a moment. Assume what I have said is true, that Jesus was the Son of God, and God sent him down to teach us His word. Assume he was put to death to pay for the sins of mankind and that he was resurrected. The energy from the resurrection left his image on his burial cloth and solidified the oils on his body and captured some of his blood. If this is all true, then there is a higher power somewhere out there that has power greater than our imaginations can even begin to conceive. Christians call this power God. Other religions call Him by other names. It doesn't matter. What does matter is that with God, with this higher power, anything is possible, absolutely anything!"

After a moment of deep reflection, Ian softly responded, "I understand what you're saying, Oleg. It just goes against all of the laws of science that I've lived by for my entire life."

"No! It does not!" Oleg exploded.

Stunned by Oleg's forceful rebuke, Ian started to respond.

Oleg continued, "The laws of science exist. They are proven; they are real. You must go back to the beginning of time. God created everything! Therefore, He created science and the laws of science. It didn't just happen that there are billions of suns out there with probably billions of planets. It didn't just happen that this planet Earth that we live on is home to an amazingly complex and phenomenal animal named man. God made man in His own image. He also created all forms of life that developed and evolved. But they didn't evolve into mankind. Our bodies are too complex, too intricate, too amazing to have had that happen. Your science is real, Ian. It is accurate. But you need to open your mind to the fact that this higher power oversaw the entire process and that with Him, anything is possible, anything."

Ian was unresponsive for several moments. "I've got a lot to think about."

"Yes, you do, and I know it's not easy. It's difficult to imagine. But, Ian, you're coming to your own conclusions through your deductive reasoning, and it's because of the Shroud. You're concluding there actually was a resurrection, and if there was a resurrection, then Jesus was divine. And if Jesus was divine, then there is a God. It all fits, Ian. It's out there for you to find, so go find it."

THE VATICAN
SATURDAY, AUGUST 2, 1997
7:17 A.M.

Ian and Angus began their work earlier than normal, with the analysis of the one hundred and thirty-one Petri dishes containing solidified oils and blood samples.

Ian's enthusiasm was equaled only by his excitement during those final days before the birth of Dolly. He had a restless night's sleep, with his mind going over his conversation with Oleg and all its ramifications. Combined with his great anticipation of today's work, he only managed a few hours of fitful sleep. Today's testing was not difficult. They merely had to remove the blood samples from the solidified oils and run the samples through a series of tests to determine if the DNA was intact. Then they had to run further tests to determine if the DNA was complete. Partial DNA, which would be the likely result, would be useless.

Ian decided to test only twenty of the samples. If the DNA was intact and complete, they could move forward, should the Pope give his blessing. They would need all the remaining samples for the actual cloning. Ian had informed Oleg and Joseph that they would know by early afternoon if the DNA was intact.

The cardinals arrived at the lab shortly before noon, excited to learn the results. "Have you gotten any results yet?" Joseph asked with obvious excitement.

"No, not yet," Ian replied. "We submitted sample number one before nine o'clock this morning and just finished entering number twenty a few minutes ago. It should take about four hours to get the results back from the computer on each sample. So, we should get a reading on number one in less than an hour. Then we'll get a reading every ten minutes on the next samples."

"Would you like to go get some lunch?" Oleg inquired.

"No, we need to stay here and watch the equipment and monitor the computer for results," Ian responded. "But we would sure like something to eat."

Joseph responded, "I'll call and have lunch brought down to us. We'll wait with you for the results."

Their lunch arrived after fifteen minutes and the four of them ate silently, anxiously awaiting the first results. They would soon receive the results of more than a month of planning and testing, and of more than twelve months of dreaming for Cardinals Jaropelk and Ratzinger. Very few words were spoken as they anxiously waited.

At precisely one-thirteen p.m., the computer announced that the analysis of sample one was complete and almost immediately the printer was activated. Ian rushed to the printer and nervously waited for the sheet to be ejected. It seemed like an eternity for the printing to be completed; in actuality, it was only about twenty seconds. Ian grabbed the sheet and began reading.

Angus and the cardinals sat on the edge of their chairs, looking at Ian's face for any positive sign. Ian displayed nothing. He finished reading and set the paper down.

He shivered as he slowly walked over to Oleg and quietly said, "The DNA is intact."

Oleg immediately stood up, clasped Ian's hand and exclaimed, "Praise God!" Ian stared into Oleg's eyes and a smile slowly crossed his face as he held the cardinal's hand with both of his for a moment.

"Let's not get too excited. Remember, the DNA must be complete. If it's not complete, it's of no use; it's totally worthless. It'll take the computer another forty-eight hours to complete the analysis and tell us if the DNA is complete." He anticipated the next question and quickly said, "But, it's certainly a good sign; I'm cautiously optimistic."

The four of them were still all smiles when the computer announced the arrival of sample two. When the printing was finished, Ian picked it up, studied it for a moment and said, "The DNA is intact. Just for your information, we took the samples from different parts of the image. Number one is from the ankle and number two is from the left wrist."

By five o'clock, they'd received the results from all twenty samples, recorded their findings and replaced the samples in the refrigerator.

All twenty samples contained intact DNA.

Oleg asked, "If you're certain we'll have the results by this time Monday, I'll set up a meeting with His Holiness for Tuesday." Ian nodded affirmatively. Oleg continued, "Good, I have some ideas about how we might spend the next two days. We have mass tomorrow morning at St. Peter's Basilica, and you are welcome to attend."

Ian thought for a moment and then replied, "Certainly. I've never seen a Catholic mass and to see it at St. Peter's would be a rare opportunity. What do you think, Angus?"

"Absolutely. It will be a pleasure," Angus responded.

"After mass, Giuseppe and I will give you a personal tour of the Sistine Chapel. At noon, His Holiness will appear at the window of his private study to say the Angelus together with several thousand of the faithful gathered in St. Peter's Square. After that, we'll take you into the city to see ancient Rome. On Monday, while we wait for the results, Giuseppe will continue your education with a tour of the Basilica and the catacombs below."

"That sounds wonderful," Ian responded. "Do you know what sounds wonderful right now? A wee dram, some dinner and a good night's sleep. I did not sleep well last night."

Oleg gave him a knowing look and said, "I can imagine."

THE VATICAN
SUNDAY, AUGUST 3, 1997
8:09 A.M.

"How did you sleep?" Oleg inquired of Ian as they sat down for breakfast.

"Like a newborn baby," Ian replied.

"That's good. You've been working hard and you've had a lot on your mind." Changing topics, he said to both Ian and Angus, "Mass will be in Italian, so you won't understand a word of it, and it will last about an hour and a half. You will be sitting with us, so Giuseppe and I will be able to explain it to you. We'll also be there to poke you in the ribs, should you fall asleep," Oleg jested.

After the long mass was completed, Ian stared at the surroundings in awe. The Basilica was certainly the most beautiful building he had ever seen. He found the mass to be exceedingly structured and boring, despite the amazing surroundings. Being spoken in Italian didn't help. It appeared that everyone was simply repeating exactly what they were supposed to say. There was no happiness, no joy in the service. If one chose to believe in God, was it a prerequisite to attend these services that seem so mechanical? He made a mental note to talk to Oleg about it.

As they made their exit from St. Peter's Basilica and strolled a short distance to the Sistine Chapel, Oleg gave them a brief history of the structure. "It was constructed between 1475 and 1483 by Pope Sixtus IV and the chapel was named for him."

When they entered the structure, both Ian and Angus were overwhelmed. They stood in awe of the sixty-foot high walls and the ceiling which were completely covered with magnificent frescoes. Look at the ceiling," Ian exclaimed. "It's incredible."

After spending a full hour with their private tour, Angus exclaimed, "This is the most amazing thing I have ever seen!"

After a moment, Ian mumbled, "Magnificent, absolutely magnificent."

It was nearing twelve o'clock noon, as the cardinals ushered their two guests out to St. Peter's Square to hear the Pope deliver the *Angelus*.

"The *Angelus* is a devotion in memory of the Annunciation," Joseph instructed. Ian and Angus looked bewildered, so Joseph further explained, "The Annunciation was the announcement by the Angel Gabriel to the Virgin Mary of the incarnation of Christ."

"His Holiness delivers this short devotion every Sunday at noon, except Easter, to the faithful gathered about us," Oleg added.

After listening to the *Angelus* and as the crowd dispersed, Oleg informed his guests they had a driver waiting and they would drive into the city, have some lunch, and see some of the sites of ancient Rome.

It was shortly after one o'clock when they sat down at one of the sidewalk cafés on the small piazza in front of the Pantheon. While they enjoyed their lunch, Oleg told them of its history.

After lunch and a tour, their driver drove them to the Colosseum. As they approached the massive structure, Oleg explained its history and how it was built by Jewish prisoners brought to Rome after the conquest of Jerusalem in 70 AD.

"Is this where Christians were fed to the lions?" Angus inquired during their tour.

"That was thought to be the case," Oleg responded, "but there is no strong evidence this was the site of the martyrdoms. Remember, the killing of the early Christians was largely done under Nero, and Nero died before the Colosseum was built. There probably were some Christians martyred in the structure having been killed by wild animals, but most of the thousands of Christian killings were done in other locations designed specifically for that type of cruel amusement."

They spent several hours walking through the ruins of the ancient Roman Forum as Oleg explained the history of the buildings and the magnificence of Rome two thousand years ago. Both Ian and Angus had studied Roman history in school years earlier, but to see the ruins of the ancient civilization was incredible to them. They were mesmerized by Oleg as he related the ancient history of Rome. He was obviously a serious student of the ancient culture and the two Scotsmen gained further respect for this very learned man.

As they were leaving the Forum, Oleg said, "It's been a long day and tomorrow we have, what could be a monumental day for all of us. Before we go have dinner, I want to show you one more ancient ruin."

They returned to their car and the driver drove them a short distance to what looked like a large park. After leaving the car, they walked out onto the grassy area and Oleg once again acted as a tour director.

"This is the Circus Maximus. The Roman chariot races were held here. If you saw the movie *Ben Hur*, this is where the great chariot race scene supposedly took place. Across the way you see the Palatine Hill, which was the site of the imperial palaces. It was the center of ancient Rome for centuries."

It was late afternoon after a full day of touring. "Well, enough of Roman history," Oleg pronounced. "Giuseppe and I are going to take you to our favorite restaurant in all of Rome."

A short time later, they arrived and were graciously greeted by the owner who personally seated them in a private room on the second floor of his family business. After they were seated, he brought them several bottles and announced in halting English, "I have for you one of our finest wines." He set the bottle on the table and said, "And I have a special gift for you." He handed them a bottle of Macallan 21. Ian was taken aback as he looked at Cardinal Ratzinger, who had a pleasant smile on his face.

"Joseph, you continue to surprise me. I am overwhelmed by your kindness." Ian murmured.

"Ian, I am overwhelmed by your scientific knowledge and by your fascination with our Shroud. I might add, I am also overwhelmed by your willingness to contemplate a nonscientific approach to some of the mysteries of life. I think God is shining His light upon you."

Ian was silent and contemplative for a moment and then softly responded, "Thank you, I appreciate that, Joseph."

They spent nearly two hours savoring the family-style dinner as they discussed Roman history while they drank wine and a good amount of the Macallan. Not a word was said about their reason for being in Rome. The long day ended with both Ian and Angus immediately falling asleep in their beds. They didn't have time to think about the importance of what might occur the next day.

And, because of the excitement of the day, nobody realized that they had been watched by several professional assassins throughout the day.

THE VATICAN
MONDAY, AUGUST 4, 1997
8:22 A.M.

Ian awoke, well rested, and after showering, immediately went to the lab to make certain all was well. The computers continued to run the lengthy analysis of the DNA, which was a good sign. He still estimated that it would be late afternoon or early evening before the analysis was complete. There was nothing more to do except wait. The computers were performing their job and the guards were protecting the Shroud and Ian's testing.

He left the lab and joined Angus and the cardinals for breakfast.

"Oleg, you mentioned earlier about taking us on a private tour of St. Peter's," Ian said while lifting a forkful of scramble eggs.

"Yes, we'd love to show you our pride and joy. When do you need to return to the lab?"

"We'll have most of the day free. I'd like to be back in the lab by late afternoon," Ian replied.

"Excellent. As soon as we're finished eating, we'll start the tour," Oleg replied. "It was very crowded yesterday for mass. We'll have the entire facility to ourselves all morning until it opens to the public."

"That would be wonderful," Ian replied, rubbing his chin.

Oleg noticed his consternation, "Do you have a question, Ian?"

"I do, Oleg. Can we talk for a few minutes before we start the tour?"

"Certainly we can. Let's take a walk. Giuseppe, why don't you and Angus catch up with us in twenty minutes or so?" After they entered one of the gardens, Oleg coaxed, "What is it that's on your mind, my friend?"

Raking his hand through his hair, Ian queried, "The Mass yesterday. It seemed so methodical, so dry. It appeared that everyone was just repeating the words by memory. There was no enthusiasm."

Oleg was silent as he reflected.

"I apologize if I offended you," Ian offered.

"No, no, there's nothing to be sorry about. I'm thinking how I should word this because you haven't had many religious services in your past to use as a comparison. I'll simply say this. The Protestant services you may have attended were linked to the Bible. The minister or pastor would give a sermon based on scripture or Biblical teachings. The congregation would largely be there to hear his message. If people didn't like his message, they could simply change churches or stop attending.

"It's different with the Catholic Church. Catholics attend Mass because of the ritual. Even though it's the same each day, we find comfort because of that. Our rituals, our services, go back nearly two thousand years. It doesn't matter which cathedral or church we attend; they are the same to us. Catholics take comfort and find God in our rituals and traditions even more than in the message the priest delivers." He added, "That's not too dissimilar from the Jewish religion. Their services and traditions go back several thousand years more."

"But, aren't you losing a lot of people because the service is so rote? It's my understanding that the number of people that attend Mass has diminished substantially, particularly in Europe."

"Ian, you are correct," the cardinal conceded. "It is a growing problem that is frequently discussed at the highest levels of the Church."

Oleg was deep in thought as they silently strolled through the garden. "Ian, I'm going to tell you something from deep in my heart. As you discover your spirituality, I don't believe it matters what church you attend. People should go where they are most comfortable, where they can experience God and realize there is a higher power than themselves and act accordingly."

Oleg again paused to gather his words. "Ian, I believe people don't have to go to church to believe in God. I think people can go to a seashore or a mountaintop and experience God in their own way. I'm at odds with the teachings of my own Church in this thinking," Oleg confessed. "When I tell Joseph this, he thinks I'm mentally unstable." They both laughed.

"Seriously, Ian, if you just look around you, you will see God everywhere. Look at all these trees and flowers. When I look at them, I see the beauty and wonder of God. Why do you love to go to your beautiful Scottish mountains? Ian, what do you see there that is so attractive to you? I'm guessing you find your hiking to be peaceful and wondrous."

Ian looked around and nodded his head just as he saw Angus approaching with Cardinal Ratzinger.

As they walked across the square, Cardinal Ratzinger began explaining the history of the Basilica. "Let's start at the beginning. Sometime between sixty-four and sixty-seven AD, Peter was martyred in Nero's Circus, at the foot of Vatican Hill, and entombed in a nearby burial ground. Reputedly, he was crucified upside down. His tomb is the reason that the Vatican exists. The city that you see around you was created to defend the tomb and the church that rose above it."

When they finally departed, it was shortly after four in the afternoon. Ian and Angus could not believe that the time had passed so quickly. Except for a short lunch break, they spent the entire day receiving an explanation of every sculpture and every painting in the Basilica.

"This is the most magnificent structure I have ever seen," Angus stated as they departed through the middle of the five huge brass entrance doors.

"It is unbelievable," Ian added.

Oleg broke the spell as he said, "I don't mean to end your euphoria, Ian, but do you think perhaps we should pay a visit to the lab?"

"Yes, I suppose we should," Ian quietly replied as he backed away from the Basilica, looking up at its grandeur. "Yes, yes, we should do that," he repeated as he regained his composure.

They walked back to the Papal Palace and immediately went to the basement lab. Ian quickly went to the computers and observed the progress. "It's a long process, but it's nearing the end. I'd guess that in another three hours, we'll have the results of the first sample."

Oleg suggested they go to their rooms, rest for a couple of hours, have dinner, and then return to the lab. His suggestion was welcomed by the others.

They ate their dinner quickly and quietly as they each were deep in thought. Soon they would know if the DNA was intact. The culmination of months of planning by the cardinals was near.

Soon Ian would know if his hard work and scientific exploration would lead to the possibility of cloning and a monumental scientific achievement, or if it was the end of a fruitless effort with cloning being an impossibility.

No one spoke a word as the guards admitted them to the lab. Ian again walked quickly to the computer to see if the analysis had been completed.

"Not yet," he exclaimed. "It should be soon. We'll just have to wait."

They sat down and talked quietly, mostly about their tour of ancient Rome and St. Peter's Basilica. It took their mind off the pending results. They were talking about some of the world-famous people who had visited the Basilica over the centuries when the computer signaled that the analysis of the first sample was completed.

Oleg, Joseph, and Angus were startled as they looked at Ian.

They didn't speak.

They barely breathed as Ian rushed to the computer. He punched some directions on the keyboard and, in a few seconds, the printer started. After what seemed like an eternity, the first page came off the printer, followed by seven more pages in rapid succession.

Ian picked up the first page, read it, and put it down. He looked over at the others with no discernable expression on his face. He picked up the second page and continued reading. The cardinals were feeling both excitement and trepidation as they nervously watched Ian for some reaction.

He gave none.

After he finished reading the second page, he put it down and slowly walked back to where the others were seated and sat down. He sank into his chair as the others were sitting on the edge of their chairs.

He looked at Oleg and softly said, "It's intact."

Everyone was silent, as the implications of what Ian told them began to sink in.

Suddenly, the computer signaled that the analysis of the second sample was completed.

With glazed eyes, Ian slowly stood up and ran his hands through his hair. He shook his head and stepped to the computer and ordered a printed copy of the results. As soon as the first page was printed, he quickly grabbed it and scanned the results.

He looked over at the others and exclaimed, "Sample two is intact!"

This time there was more excitement. Every five minutes for the next hour and a half, the results came in from another sample. Finally, all twenty samples had been analyzed and all twenty samples contained intact DNA.

Oleg broke the silence. "Well, tomorrow we meet with His Holiness at ten o'clock to discuss our findings." With his lips pressed together, he hesitated, "I will say a prayer that my good friend, Loleck, will have an open mind. Let's retire for the night; I am exhausted."

THE VATICAN
TUESDAY, AUGUST 5, 1997
9:59 A.M.

Antonio ushered the four men into the Pope's private study. John Paul II was seated in his favorite chair. This time he did not rise to greet them.

Oleg immediately walked to him, took his hand and kissed his ring. Joseph did the same while Ian and Angus stood still, not certain what to do. John Paul recognized their consternation and graciously said, "Please sit down, gentlemen and make yourselves comfortable."

John Paul stared at his lifelong friend. Oleg looked down for a moment and didn't say a word. Joseph looked straight into the eyes of the Pope, as did Ian and Angus.

As Oleg lifted his head to look at his lifelong friend, he started to speak.

John Paul cut him off by lifting his right hand and said, "I can see from your expression, my friend, that the results are positive."

"Yes, Loleck, they are. The DNA of our Lord Jesus Christ is intact."

"I was afraid of that," the Pope replied as he sat back in his chair and stared off into space. "Now, I have to disappoint you and you will not like my decision."

Hearing this, no one spoke.

Suddenly, Ian stood up and took a step toward Pope John Paul II and said, "Your Holiness, before you announce your decision, I would like to tell you several things I think are important for you to know." John Paul nodded his assent.

The others had no idea what Ian was about to say and looked perplexed.

John Paul glanced at Oleg and saw his surprise.

Ian continued, "First, I want you to know, whatever your decision is, Angus and I will abide by it. Should you decide this project should proceed no further, then we will completely abandon our work, and no one will ever learn of the testing of the Shroud."

"Thank you. You are men of honor," the Pope demurred.

"Second," Ian continued, "over the past several weeks, Oleg and I have grown to be good friends. I entered this project nearly six weeks ago as an atheist, or at least an agnostic. I'm a scientist. I have no room for religion in my world. But seeing the Shroud, learning its history and seeing the image of the man on the Shroud has caused me to look at my world in a different manner.

"Now, I don't know what to think. Part of me says this image conforms exactly to what Jesus was supposed to have looked like and to have experienced. If the image was transferred to the burial cloth, I'm convinced, from what I have seen and from what I have studied, this could only have happened from an enormous burst of energy. If this energy was from the resurrection of the man on the Shroud, then he had to be divine because no one in the history of mankind has ever been resurrected."

He hesitated. "And, if this is true, then Jesus was divine, which means there really is a God."

John Paul looked at him and tilted his head to one side.

Ian proclaimed, "The other part of me, the scientist part of me, says all of this is impossible. It could not have happened. There has to be a valid explanation for the image on the Shroud."

Ian paused for a moment and then confessed, "Your Holiness, if the Shroud can do this to me, an atheist, what will it do to the millions of others who aren't sure of what to believe. I keep saying to myself, Ian, if there is a supreme being up there who has the power to send himself down to Earth, to live and then die, and resurrect himself, then anything is possible.

"And, all my laws of science have no meaning as they relate to God. I ask you, is it possible that God intended for the DNA of Jesus to remain intact for two thousand years until my science could make something happen with it? Is it possible for God to have implanted this plan into the minds of Cardinal Jaropelk and Cardinal Ratzinger? Is it possible that God wants His son Jesus Christ to return and this is His method?"

John Paul looked at Ian, and for the first time in decades, he was speechless.

Ian conceded, "I don't know the answers to these questions, but I've sure wondered about them over the past days."

Again, no one spoke. Oleg leaned forward and stared at Ian as he placed his hand over his heart.

Angus looked proudly at his brother-in-law and slowly nodded his head with an understanding smile. Cardinal Ratzinger looked at the Pope and contemplated the profound words that Ian had spoken. Ian broke the silence and added, "There's one more thing, Your Holiness."

The silence was heavy.

"We've been followed, and we've been watched during this testing."

John Paul looked up with a surprised look on his face.

"Angus, tell us everything that has happened in this regard," Ian directed.

Angus proceeded to relate the incident in Edinburgh, how the cardinals were followed from Rome to Edinburgh, to the Roslin Institute and to the airport. He told them how this man not only followed them but was listening to and recording their conversations. He told John Paul about the "accident" and that the man who had followed them was a minor operative for a radical Middle East organization. He told him about the second Arab watching them in Turin and about the assassin from the Israeli Mossad watching both them and the Arab.

"Your Holiness," Angus fretted, "if you decide to authorize us to continue this project, as I hope you will, it is imperative that it be done with the utmost of secrecy and with tight security."

Again, the room fell silent.

John Paul stood up and slowly walked to his favorite window and looked out upon St. Peter's Square. He stood there, with his back to the other four men.

Finally, he turned around and looked at each of his four guests and declared, "I will think and pray about this, but I need time. Oleg and Joseph, have Antonio set up a meeting for late next month; make it on a Friday. I will meet with you six weeks from this Friday and I will give you my decision at that time.

"Meanwhile, Dr. McKinney, please dismantle the lab, secure all of the samples here at the Vatican. Joseph, please see to that. And, Oleg, please return the Shroud to its rightful home as soon as possible. Ian and Angus, I suggest you return to your country and resume your lives. I greatly appreciate your honesty and integrity, and I am sorry that I will probably have to disappoint you. However, I am delighted that this experience has opened your scientific eyes to the wondrous things that God can achieve. Ian, you are one of these wondrous achievements. I will pray for you and for your continued appreciation of what God is revealing to you. Please go in peace and go in safety."

The Pope got up, went to Ian and warmly shook his hand, then turned to Angus and did the same. As he ushered them out from his study, he put his arm around Ian's shoulder and quietly said to him, "There really is a God, Dr. McKinney. He has revealed himself to you. Go seek Him in your own way. When you find Him, Ian, your life will be blessed."

As they left the Pope's apartments, Oleg said, "Let's go to my office and make our plans."

TEL AVIV, ISRAEL
THURSDAY, AUGUST 7, 1997
8:02 A.M.

Director Yatom brought Viper into his office. "Fox reports the same two cardinals from the Vatican met for five days in Turin with your two friends from the Roslin Institute. He lost them on Saturday the twenty-sixth but picked them up again in Rome several days later. Now, here's what's interesting. When they were in Turin, they met every day at the Cathedral of St. John the Baptist. They spent every day inside the cathedral, which was closed to the public.

"What would they be doing inside a cathedral for five days?" Viper questioned.

"We don't know. But of even greater interest is that Fox found another minor Arab agent watching them the entire time. This guy wasn't very good because he was easily spotted by the Scottish security man. Unfortunately, so was Fox, so he's now off the assignment.

"However, he had the foresight to go to Rome and he learned after several days that the cardinals and your Scottish friends spent the next ten days at the Vatican. The Scots went back to Edinburgh yesterday. You are on a flight to Edinburgh tomorrow afternoon to see what you can find out. I have no idea what's going on, but it concerns me."

ROSLIN, SCOTLAND
THURSDAY, AUGUST 7, 1997
7:32 A.M.

Ian and Angus had returned to Edinburgh the previous day, after being gone for nearly three weeks. Angus was delighted to see his wife. He had missed her terribly. He had slept soundly after a warm evening of intimacy with Kathleen.

Ian, on the other hand, had not slept well. Elated with the DNA results of the Shroud testing and content that he had said everything he could possibly have said to the Pope to encourage him to proceed with the project, he should have rested peacefully. His tours of ancient Rome and the Vatican were amazing as was his new friendship with Cardinal Jaropelk. Still, his sleep was fitful as his thoughts dwelled on the implications of the Shroud testing results.

His mind kept racing over the change he was undergoing, and he kept wondering where it would lead. Might there actually be a higher power and all of this didn't just "happen"? Could the Shroud be real and actually hold the image of the resurrected Jesus? He really wanted to be able to continue with the project, but now it was for an added reason. Of course, he would like to be the first person to clone a human being. But now, there was an additional and maybe even more important reason. What would the cloned Jesus be like? It would be fascinating to watch him grow and to ask him questions. The cloning might be the proof that Jesus was indeed the Son of God.

Ian resigned himself to the fact that the Pope would not allow the project to proceed. John Paul had as much as said that at their last meeting. So, a different approach to discovering his spirituality would be needed. Oleg suggested he begin his quest with a book written by an American titled *The Case for Christ*.

For the first time since his personal tragedy he felt lonely, even though he had so much. His work was fascinating and rewarding. His cottage was extremely comfortable. There was his best friend, Angus, and his loyal dog, MacDuff, to love. He relished his passion for hiking in his beloved Scottish Highlands. And now, this new adventure, discovering his spirituality, and maybe even a further new adventure of continuing the cloning project. Still, something was missing.

When he went to bed and tried to sleep last night, he felt incomplete. Even with all the excitement of the past month, something was missing in his life. He couldn't figure out what it was as he fitfully attempted to sleep.

When he awoke, barely refreshed, he realized what was missing. He was surprised it took an almost sleepless night to figure it out.

People.

Apart from his sister, Kathleen, and Angus, there was no one to love, and no one to love him. And he had certainly never told either that he loved them. When he left the Vatican to return to Edinburgh, Oleg's last works to him were that he loved him. He recalled the last time someone had said those words to him, and a mood of darkness and anger swept over him.

Quickly, he walked to the bathroom, turned on the shower and stood under the cold spray for a moment. Having regained his composure and feeling refreshed, he got ready to return to work.

Even with the lack of sleep, he arrived at the institute in a joyful mood, delighted to be back at work and, surprisingly, delighted to see his coworkers.

———

Ian's secretary, Laura, welcomed him back with a perfunctory greeting. She didn't dislike her boss, but she found him to be cold and insensitive and uncaring about her wants and needs. He always addressed her as "Miss Galbreath," and as a result, she referred to him only as "Dr. McKinney."

She had enjoyed the past several weeks. The office atmosphere was brighter and happier without his dour presence.

When she obtained her job at the Roslin Institute nearly three years ago, she had been overwhelmed with joy. It was a dream-come-true position for her. She hoped she could advance from being a secretary to an assistant for one of the scientists. The salary was good, the working conditions were excellent, and there was an outstanding company pension plan. She wasn't directly involved in the Dolly Project, but she was close enough to share in the excitement. Her job was perfect except that her boss was dull, self-absorbed, and unexciting, albeit very handsome.

Before entering his office, Ian glanced at Laura as she coolly greeted him and said, "Good morning, Laura, it's good to see your smiling face. Is everything fine with you?"

Before she could respond, he continued, "I'll check my mail and messages and then, perhaps, we can sit down, and you can bring me up-to-date on events of the past several weeks." After a contemplative pause, he added, "On second thought, why don't we have lunch at the pub in town, and you can tell me about the recent events."

Her eyes widened as she sucked in a quick breath. Ian smiled at her and disappeared into his office.

After she composed herself, she picked up her telephone and called her best friend at the institute.

"Shannon, you won't believe it, but I think that Dr. McKinney found some female companionship on his holiday. He came back all smiles and he's actually going to take me to lunch."

As she listened to her friend's response, she chuckled and then quipped, "Well, I wouldn't put it quite so crudely, but yes, I would guess that's exactly what he got."

It was nearing noon when Ian finally completed reading all his mail and responding to his messages. Mrs. Morrison had called him earlier and informed him that Dr. Graham would like to meet with him at three o'clock. Ian left his office and greeted his secretary in her reception area. "Laura, would you care to have a bit of lunch?" He quickly added, "May I call you Laura?"

"The answer to both questions is yes, Dr. McKinney. I would enjoy having lunch with you and you may certainly call me by my first name."

"Well, after you, young lady," Ian said as he gently ushered her out of her reception area. As they left the building, she was amazed at his change of attitude; he was like a different person. *I wonder how long this will last*, she thought to herself.

It was a short drive to the town pub, punctuated by some small talk. When they were seated, she began the conversation. "Tell me about your holiday, Dr. McKinney."

He thought for a moment and then responded, "Perhaps we should dispense with the formalities and you should call me Ian."

Further taken aback, she replied, "If it's all the same to you, I'd like to show you the respect you deserve and continue to call you by your title." She noticed his head lowering and quickly added, "At least at the institute. I will be delighted to call you Ian while we have lunch today. So, Ian, tell me about your holiday. Where did you go? What did you do?" She paused and then coaxed, "And, did you meet any interesting people?"

"Well, those are a lot of questions, Laura, and I'll answer them. But first, you must promise me that our conversation must be strictly confidential and will remain between us."

"Yes, of course." She was slightly mystified. She had worked for this man for almost two years and in all that time he had referred to her only as Miss Galbreath. Now, he was suddenly going to tell her some hidden thoughts.

I know he's going to tell me that he met a lady or perhaps that he took a lady with him on his vacation, she thought to herself. She was delighted with the apparent change in her boss, but a part of her was suddenly disappointed. She couldn't understand why that was. Her thoughts were interrupted by the server who took their order and quickly departed.

She snapped her head to attention as Ian said, "In answer to your first question, I went to Italy and I had a fabulous time. In answer to your second question, I did quite a bit of research, but I did manage to see a bit of ancient Rome and a considerable amount of the Vatican as well as some other cities." He paused as he carefully formulated his words. "To answer your third question, I met several extremely interesting people. I think I may well have met the most important person in my life."

"You met a lady," Laura responded in a matter-of-fact tone.

"No, I met a man, Laura," he softly replied.

Oh my gosh, she thought, *he's homosexual.* I guess I shouldn't be surprised. He's never been married, he lives alone, and as far as anyone knows, he doesn't have a social life.

"Ian," she said, "I appreciate your confiding in me, I really do. For two years, you've never asked me a thing about myself or told me anything about yourself. I'm flattered, but I really don't want to know about your personal life."

He looked at her with a puzzled look and after a moment broke out in laughter.

Now, she was the one who didn't understand. This was the first time she had ever heard him laugh.

"You thought that I was going to tell you I was homosexual and met the man of my life."

Laura nodded yes, without saying a word. He laughed again, which put her a little at ease. "Let me assure you, I am not homosexual." She briefly closed her eyes and exhaled a silent breath.

"Before I tell you about it, I'd like to ask you a question, if I may."

"Of course," she answered with raised eyebrows.

"Are you spiritual, Laura?"

Her eyes widened. This was not a question that she anticipated. "Yes, I am. Jesus Christ is an important part of my life. Perhaps he's too important." She lowered her head and looked down at the table with a reflective look on her face. "Why do you ask?"

"I ask," Ian hesitated and then continued, "because I was introduced to Jesus and I feel like I might want to get to know him."

Before either could say a word, their server brought them their lunch. As they were being served, four coworkers from the institute sat down at the table next to them and started a conversation with Ian. They asked about Dolly and how she was faring, and they asked about his holiday. The rest of the lunch was filled with business talk.

They were silent as they drove the short distance back to the institute. As they left his car and walked to the building entrance, Laura said, "Ian, I'd like to hear more about your finding Jesus."

"And I would like to know what you meant when you said that perhaps Jesus is too big a part of your life. Can we continue this conversation at a later date?"

As he held the door open for her, she replied, "Yes, of course we can, Dr. McKinney." He looked in her eyes and they both began to laugh.

It was back to work.

At five minutes to three, Laura knocked on Ian's office door. After walking in, she found him standing, with his back to her, staring out his window looking at the buildings of the institute. "It's time for your meeting, Dr. McKinney."

"Thank you, Laura. Thank you for reminding me," he said as he walked out of the office. As he walked by her, he gave her a warm smile. She was both surprised and elated at the warmth and kindness.

"Welcome home, Ian. How was your holiday?" Duncan Graham asked, as Ian was admitted to his office promptly at three o'clock.

"It was fine, Duncan," Ian responded as he sat down in front of Dr. Graham's large desk.

"You never did tell me where you traveled for your holiday," Duncan inquired.

"I went to Italy," Ian replied with a trace of hesitancy.

Duncan raised his eyebrows as he remained speechless. He rested his elbows on his desk and brought his hands up to his chin with his fingers intertwined. He thought for a moment before asking, "Would you care to tell me about your trip?"

"No, there's really not much to relate. We traveled a bit, toured ancient Roman ruins, and ate a lot of wonderful Italian food."

"Should I take it, Ian, that you simply don't want to discuss your vacation?"

Ian nodded affirmatively and then said, "I'd rather discuss our continued monitoring of Dolly and our further research on animal cloning. I have some catching up to do."

"Yes, well, get to it. I simply wanted to welcome you back, Ian," Duncan said as he stood up to escort him to the door. As they reached the door, Duncan put his hand on Ian's shoulder and commented, "Ian, you seem to be quite chipper. I can see it in your smile and in your eyes."

"I am, Duncan. Thank you. Perhaps someday I'll tell you about it."

As he opened the door for him, Duncan pronounced, "Ian, I'm very fond of you. If ever I may be of assistance or you would like my advice, I will be there for you."

Ian nodded as he walked away.

Instead of returning to his office, Ian walked down to the first floor to the human resources department. "Good afternoon, ladies." he chirped, flashing a bright smile.

The girls that worked there were taken aback. They had rarely seen Dr. McKinney in their department and when they did see him, he had never acknowledged them, and he certainly had never smiled.

"What can we do for you, Dr. McKinney?" asked the department head as she came out from her office to greet him. All other eyes were on Ian.

He walked with her into her office and replied, "Not much really. I'd like to review an employee file."

Being a department head, Ian was allowed access to the employee records. "Fine, Dr. McKinney, one of the scientists in your department?"

"No, I'd like to review the file of my secretary, Laura Galbreath."

She lifted her eyebrows as her eyes widened. "Of course," she sputtered as she retrieved the file and handed it to Ian. "The employee files cannot leave my office, Dr. McKinney. I'm certain you understand. Please, make yourself comfortable on my sofa. I'll return in a few minutes."

She left her office to the inquiring stares of the four ladies who worked for her. "Back to work, girls; it's nothing important." She casually walked around the corner to an empty office and dialed an in-house extension.

Two floors above her, the telephone rang in Dr. Ian McKinney's reception area. "Dr. McKinney's office, this is Laura speaking."

"Laura, this is Shannon. How was your lunch with your stuffy old boss?"

"Well, Shannon," Laura responded with some defensiveness, "He's not so old and he appears to have lost some of his stuffiness."

"Yes, he does seem to be a bit more cheerful, doesn't he?"

"What are you talking about? How would you know that?" Laura queried.

"Because, my dear, he's in my office as we speak, reviewing your personnel file."

Laura was silent. Shannon added, "I must get back to my unexpected visitor. I'll talk to you later, and not a word of this phone call. I'm rather fond of my job here."

As she returned to her office she sat down at her desk and inquired, "Are you finding what you are looking for, Dr. McKinney?"

"Yes, Shannon, I am. I'm simply trying to get to know her. I've been remiss in that aspect of my job. I do have one question, however. I notice that she has received the same two percent salary increase at the beginning of each of the past two years. Isn't that the minimum increase?"

"Yes, Dr. McKinney. That is the minimum."

"Why did she receive only the minimum?"

"Dr. McKinney," she admonished, "she received the minimum because you never returned her evaluation forms on which salary increases are based. Without a request for termination from you and without a returned evaluation form, it is standard to give the minimum increase. That's company policy," she emphasized.

"So, it's my fault?" Ian questioned as his eyes widened.

"Yes, it is if you simply neglected to return the forms."

"Well, let's correct this situation," he replied. "Can we give her a salary increase at this time of the year?"

"Yes, we can," she responded as she reached into a file drawer and handed him an employee evaluation form.

"Fine. Now, can we make it retroactive to the beginning of the year?"

"Yes, we can do that also, but it's a little more complicated. You will have to write me a letter stating because of your intensive involvement in the Dolly Project, you neglected to return the form."

"Good. Good, I'll do that." He thought for a moment and then inquired, "What about last year? I was just as neglectful last year. Can we go back to the beginning of 1996 and give her an increase for all of last year?"

"Dr. McKinney, you are asking for a lot."

"Yes, yes, I know, but I feel terrible," he said with true remorse. "Please call me Ian and tell me if we can do that, Shannon."

She nodded and told him to include last year in his letter.

"Fine, Shannon. Now, I know that two percent is the minimum salary increase. What is the maximum?"

"The maximum is five percent without a change in job title."

"What is her title now?"

"Secretary."

"What is the next highest level?"

"Senior secretary, but she would need two more years of employment at the institute to rise to that level." Shannon replied. She saw the disappointed look on Ian's face. "There is another way. You could request that she be made your personal assistant retroactive to January 1 of this year. She would receive a pay increase for the higher job level as well as the five percent increase for each year. She will receive a hefty check. Is that what you would like, Dr. McKinney?" She corrected herself and said, "I mean Ian. This would require a rather complete explanation detailing how she has been performing that function since January 1 of this year."

"Yes, that is exactly what I would like. Can you tell me what that would amount to? And when can you give her the check."

"Of course, I'll calculate that right now, just give me a few moments." She reached into her files and brought an additional form for him to fill out for the job change. "If you fill out these two forms and bring them back to me this afternoon with your letter of explanation of your omission, I can have a check for her late tomorrow before she goes home for the weekend." She looked at Ian and saw a warm glow spread across his face.

"Let's figure this out." She began to silently calculate.

After several minutes she announced, "Laura Galbreath would receive a check in the amount of twenty-one thousand nine-hundred and seventy-seven pounds." She pursed her lips as she looked at Ian. "Are you certain that you want to do this? You know that it will affect your bonus somewhat?"

"Yes, I'm aware it will affect my bonus and, yes by all means, I want to do this. She has worked hard, and she deserves it. I'm only sorry that I have been so remiss."

"I can't tell you how much this will mean to Laura," Shannon beamed. "She's been living on a very tight budget. She helps to support her parents because her dad is an invalid." She walked around her desk and stood before him and reached out her hand, which he clasped while displaying a genuine smile. "Now, go write that letter and fill out those forms," she playfully instructed him.

"I'll do just that. But you must promise me that you will not tell her about this until the check is delivered. I will have left by then. I would like to avoid a scene."

"I promise," Shannon replied.

As Ian returned to his office and walked past Laura, he said, "Laura, I have some forms to fill out and then I'll be leaving for the day. I didn't sleep well last night, and it has finally caught up with me. Please hold my calls, unless there is one that you think is urgent."

As soon as he had shut his door, Laura called her friend. "Shannon, why was he looking at my employment file?"

"I can't tell you anything, Laura, except that he seems to be a different person. What on earth happened to him?"

Laura thought for a moment and replied, "I'm not sure. I'll talk to you later. On second thought," she quickly added, "why don't we have dinner tonight and talk?"

It took Ian almost forty minutes to fill out the two forms and to write his letters.

As he opened his door to leave, Laura stood and said, "Dr. McKinney, may I speak with you privately for a moment?"

"Of course, you may, Laura," he replied as he ushered her into his office. He sat down behind his desk and asked her to make herself comfortable in one of the guest chairs across his desk.

"Dr. McKinney ..." She paused for a moment. "I've been thinking about our conversation at lunch. I would very much like to continue where we left off. I'd like to hear about your experience."

"Well, Laura, I guess I need someone to confide in. So, I'd be delighted to continue our talk, and I would like to learn what you meant by your comment about Jesus being too big a part of your life. But right now I have to deliver some papers and get home to a good night's sleep."

"I understand. I didn't mean right now," Laura replied. "Dr. McKinney, you will think this awfully forward of me, but perhaps over the weekend we could meet and continue our conversation."

He jerked his head back and she quickly said, "I'm sorry. I'm afraid I've overstepped my bounds.

"No. No, not at all." He smiled, then thought for a moment. "Perhaps we could have dinner Saturday night?"

"I'd like that," she replied with a wide grin. "I'm spending the day with my parents. Would you care to pick me up at their house in Musselburgh in the evening and we could go to a quiet restaurant for dinner?" Before he could respond, she hurriedly added, "Nothing like me making all the plans."

"Please, don't feel embarrassed," he said. "I rather like your spontaneity."

And with that, he left his office.

She sat down at her desk as he departed for the evening. She softly said to herself, "What in God's name is happening. I don't understand this!"

On his way home, Ian drove into Edinburgh and stopped at its largest bookstore. He had called ahead to be certain they had the book he wanted.

When he arrived home, he connected the encryption machine to his telephone and placed a call to Oleg. There was no answer, so Ian left him a message asking him to return the call the following evening.

He started the evening relaxing with Beethoven and a glass of Macallan as he thought about the day's events. He felt an enormous satisfaction with what he had done for Laura, and he wondered why he had been so neglectful to her in the past.

He opened his new book, *The Case for Christ*, and began reading. Later, after ten minutes of reading the same paragraph multiple times, he put the book down, went to bed, and immediately fell into a deep contented sleep.

ROSLIN, SCOTLAND
FRIDAY, AUGUST 8, 1997
7:33 A.M.

As Ian entered his reception area, he found Laura already seated at her desk. "You're in early," he queried. He had never known her to arrive before eight o'clock, her official start time.

"Yes, I know you arrive early, and I thought you might be in need of my assistance as you try to get caught up." She smiled at him, waiting for a reply.

"Well, that's thoughtful of you. I took some work home with me last night, but I didn't begin to touch it. I got caught up in a book that was recommended to me. So, I'll have some work for you in about a half hour."

He started to take a step toward her, then quickly stopped. "Well,

I had better get to work. Don't forget to give me directions to your parents' home." he said as he turned and went into his office.

Laura sensed his wanting to move toward her and she briefly felt an electricity in the air until he had caught himself and went to his office.

Oh my gosh, she thought to herself, *I don't believe what's happening.* She lifted the phone to call her best friend, Shannon, but then thought better of it. If it was simply her imagination running wild, she would look foolish.

About forty-five minutes later, Ian came out with a stack of work for her to do, explaining he would have still more in another hour.

It was shortly after ten o'clock when Ian brought out additional work for her. "I'll be spending the remainder of the day in the labs. You know how to reach me," he said in a matter-of-fact manner.

He paused for a moment. "Perhaps, you'd care to join me for a tour of the labs next week," he stated. He took a step closer to her and gently put his hand on her shoulder. "I think you might be of more help to me there than simply sitting at your desk."

She looked at his hand and he quickly took it away. "I'm sorry, that was forward of me. I apologize." Before she regained her composure and could tell him there was no need for an apology, he had left the room.

She shivered as she thought about his hand on her shoulder. Two days ago, that would have been a shiver of disgust. Now, she felt a heightened attraction to this man and briefly wondered what further touches would feel like. She felt a warm stirring, which she had not felt in quite a while as she sat, staring into space.

Suddenly she got up, went to the ladies' room and doused some paper towels with cold water. She held them against her face and said to herself, "Laura, get ahold of yourself."

Ian left the institute early—around four o'clock, having made certain that Shannon had not yet delivered the good news to Laura.

It was after seven o'clock by the time Ian finished his supper and sat down with his book. The silence was suddenly broken by the ringing of the telephone. It was Oleg.

"How are you, my friend?" Ian inquired. "I don't suppose you have heard anything from His Holiness?"

"Ian, I hope you don't have your hopes up too high."

"I don't. If it's meant to happen, we will continue. If not, then perhaps you have helped me examine my life." Oleg expressed his delight at what he just heard Ian say. Ian told him about purchasing the book and he told him about his lunch with Laura, the pay increase and their meeting tomorrow night.

"It sounds more like a date than a meeting." Oleg humorously chided him. "Be careful of those office romances," he jested.

"We're both single adults, Oleg. I can assure you that our relationship is not going in that direction. I need someone to talk to about my confusion, and I think she may well be the one."

After they chatted for a few more minutes and as they ended their conversation, Ian wondered for a moment about where the relationship with Laura was headed.

He shook himself out of his deep thought and said out loud, "Come on, Duffy, let's go for a long walk. The last thing we need is another woman in our lives."

MUSSELBURGH, SCOTLAND
SATURDAY, AUGUST 9, 1997
6:01 P.M.

After finding a parking space a block away, Ian rang the buzzer to the Galbreath row house. A moment later the door opened, and he was met by a woman who appeared to be in her late sixties with gray hair and an exuberant smile on her face.

"Dr. McKinney, please come in." As he entered the small sitting room, he observed Mr. Galbreath sitting in an easy chair with his legs propped up on an ottoman. A cane was leaning against one side of the chair. Laura sat on the floor, leaning against the other side, tears glistening on her cheeks.

Startled at this scene, Ian protested, "Oh, I must have arrived at a bad time, I apologize. We'll continue our conversation another time."

As he turned to go, Laura sprang up and shouted, "Don't you dare leave this house, Ian McKinney!"

He turned toward her and nearly fell backward as he was met with her full force as she ran to him and threw her arms around his neck. "Thank you, you darling man. Thank you. Thank you." Through the shock and surprise, he could feel her breasts pressed against his chest as she tightly embraced him.

After the feeling of surprise, he began to feel an arousal such as he had not felt in years. He briefly put his arms around her as he breathed in the scent of her perfume. Quickly, he regained his composure and put his hands on her shoulders, gently pushing her away so he could look at her.

"What are you talking about?" he asked in an incredulous voice.

"You ninny! I'm talking about the promotion and the raises and all the back salary!" She again buried her head against his neck, and he could feel her warm tears. He felt embarrassed as he looked at her father and then her mother. He saw nothing but enormous smiles on each of their faces. He momentarily held her as she clung to him. Again, he felt himself being aroused and quickly took her shoulders and gently moved her away. He hoped that she hadn't noticed his physical reaction.

"Laura, that was the least I could do. I apologize for neglecting you for so long."

"And the promotion to be your assistant, I can't believe it. It's a dream come true."

"I'm glad," he responded. "I'm certain you will be an enormous help to me. After all, according to your personnel file, you excelled in math and science in school. Now you're going to have to put them to use." After Laura composed herself, she introduced Ian to her parents, who had thoroughly enjoyed the scene played out before them.

Her father said, "I hope you'll forgive me if I don't get up to shake your hand. It pleases me greatly to know that my daughter is working for such a fine gentleman. Can I offer you something to drink?"

"No, thank you," Ian responded as he walked over and firmly shook his hand. "We'd best be getting along to dinner." He went to Laura's mother, gently took her hand and told her how pleased he was to meet her.

Laura went to her father, bent over and kissed him on the cheek. Then she went to her mother and gave her a hug and a kiss. She looked up at Ian, took hold of his arm and teased, "Well, Dr. Ian McKinney, you've made a suitable impression on my parents. I want you to know they are not easily impressed. You may have to give me another raise the next time you meet them to maintain that good impression."

"Laura, that's a terrible thing to say," her mother chuckled. Laura began laughing at her own joke and she was joined by Ian and then her father.

As they turned to leave, Ian noticed a photograph hanging on the wall next to the doorway. He stood in front and stared at it. "That's Pope John Paul II," Laura's mother interjected.

"Yes, I know. He's a kind man with a warm friendly spirit," Ian quietly said as he reflected on the photograph.

"It sounds as if you know him," Mrs. Galbreath quipped.

"I do," Ian softly said. The room was quiet for a moment, then both parents began to laugh. Ian joined in the light laughter. He looked down at Laura, who was still holding onto his arm. She wasn't laughing as she looked up at him with a puzzled look.

As they walked to his car, he asked if she had driven her car to her parents. She informed him that she had taken the bus so he could properly take her home after dinner.

He appreciated that. He opened the car door for her, then walked around to the right side and slid in behind the steering wheel. He was about to start the car when Laura said, "Ian, I'm an impetuous girl. I hope you don't mind."

"No, on the contrary, I find you …."

Before he could finish his sentence, she exclaimed, "Good!" Then she leaned over, reached up and turned his face toward her and kissed him fully on the lips. "I warned you that I am an impetuous girl," she repeated. "I think you were about to say that you didn't mind."

"Yes, I was about to say, before you accosted me, that I don't mind at all. I find you vibrant and exciting."

"Yes, I noticed that," she said with a sly smile. He didn't respond. "Ian, I'm sorry I said that. I embarrassed you."

"Well, I can feel myself blushing." He paused and then turned to look at her. "Laura, it's been a long time. I'm not sure how to act."

"Ian, just be yourself. But please, be the new Ian, not the old one." They both laughed. "Ian, I do want to tell you something, though. I am an impetuous girl, but only up to a point."

173

He was silent for a moment. He looked at her and thoughtfully said, "I understand. Now, let's go have some dinner."

"That's a wonderful idea, on two conditions."

"And what might they be?" he coaxed with a wide grin.

"Number one, I choose the restaurant." He agreed with that. "And number two, I pay for dinner. It seems as though I recently came into a tidy sum of money."

He laughed and said, "I'll accept that condition as long as it doesn't set a precedent."

"Ian, that implies that there will be another dinner."

"Yes, I guess it does. Would you like that?"

She reached over and put her hand on his and replied, "Yes, I think I would."

"Good. Where are we going to dinner?"

"We're going to the Witchery. I made reservations for eight o'clock. I thought we'd first take a stroll down the Royal Mile and perhaps stop into a pub."

"What a superb idea," he exclaimed. "I could get used to you taking me out on dates."

Laura looked at Ian and smiled.

They both fell silent during the fifteen-minute drive to the restaurant. Their questioning thoughts were similar but remained unspoken.

After arriving at the restaurant and leaving his car with the valet, Ian checked his watch and determined they had more than an hour before their reservation time. They started to walk down High Street toward South Bridge, the center of activity. After walking for several minutes, each being silent and deep in thought, his hand accidentally brushed against hers as they walked. He looked down with a slight blush.

She smiled at him, took his hand and said, "Touches are good, Ian, there's no reason to be embarrassed."

Holding hands, after a few minutes they found themselves in front of St. Giles Cathedral.

She looked up at him and asked, "Ian, have you ever been inside?"

"No, I never have."

"It's the most famous Presbyterian church in the world, you know," she replied.

"Laura, before we go inside, I'd like to say something to you." He paused as she looked up at him. "A lot has happened to me recently that I would like to discuss with you. But I can't."

"Do you mean like seeing the Pope?"

"How did you know that?" he sputtered.

"My parents thought you were joking when you said that you knew him. I thought differently."

"That's just a small part of it."

As they stood outside the medieval cathedral, Laura questioned, "Do you call seeing the Pope a small event?"

"I didn't just see him, Laura. I met with him." Ian paused. "Twice," he added.

"Where did you meet with him?" she gasped.

"In his private apartments."

"You met with Pope John Paul II in his private apartments two times?" she blurted. Ian nodded. "Oh my gosh!" she exclaimed. "Are you serious?" He nodded. "I need to sit down. Let's go inside."

The cathedral was open to the public, even during special events. When they entered, they were surprised to find a wedding in process. He suggested they leave.

"Not on your life," she whispered. "This is my date, remember. The pub can wait."

Later, as they walked back up the hill to the restaurant, he said, "Laura, I don't want you to think that I gave you the promotion and salary increases just to entice you and make you feel beholden."

"Well, Dr. Ian McKinney," she pouted, her tone admonishing. "You are a monster of a man and that is exactly what I think. And do you know what else?" She paused as he gave her a questioning look. "It worked!" As she took his arm, they both laughed.

Located just outside the gates of Edinburgh Castle at the top of the Royal Mile, The Witchery had long been known as one of Edinburgh's better restaurants. They were seated, at Laura's request, at a quiet table at the rear of the main floor dining room.

When the waiter introduced himself, and asked for their drink order, Laura promptly said, "I'm partial to whisky. I would like a Macallan 18."

The waiter then turned to Ian and asked, "And you, sir?"

"That's incredible. I'll have the same." After the waiter left, Ian asked, "Laura, that's my favorite drink. Have you been a Macallan drinker for long?"

"No, it's not in my budget, but tonight's a special occasion. How about you?" she asked.

"It's one of the few luxuries that I afford myself." He took a sip of his drink. "Laura, I've never dined here, have you?"

"Again, it's not in my budget. But I've always longed to. Isn't this room beautiful?" she answered as they both looked at the brick walls, the red leather seating and the painted and gilded ceiling. "Ian, you've made this evening possible; I can't thank you enough. I'm so excited about working as your assistant." They both remained silent for a moment as they sipped their drinks.

"Ian, tell me about your meeting with the Pope. Is that what has changed you and introduced you to your spirituality?"

"I just can't tell you much at this point." Ian paused as he took several sips of his drink. "I met with him twice last week and he's a kind and gentle man. And, no, he's not the reason for my confusion.

Laura, I've been an atheist, or at least an agnostic, all my life. Over the past several weeks, I've come to wonder if there might not be a higher power. But, it's so hard for me to grasp."

He took a sip of his drink as he searched for his feelings. "I guess what I'm really feeling is confusion. This higher power theory just doesn't make sense to me. But I'm reading an interesting book that offers some compelling theories. I just need time to sort it out."

"Would you like to discuss the book?" Laura asked.

"I'd like that very much, but not tonight. I'd like to finish and study the book before discussing it," he stated.

"Was this the same book that you were reading the other night that was so enthralling that it took you away from your work?" she questioned.

"Yes." he responded. "It's written by an American and it's titled *The Case for Christ*, and it is compelling." They were silent for a few moments, each taking several sips of their whisky.

"Ian, can we talk about how I can help you as your assistant?" she added. "And how can I prepare?"

Before he could respond, the waiter appeared and brought them each another drink.

He gave Laura a perplexed look as he thought to himself, *she must have signaled him without me seeing her. This is an intriguing woman.*

Throughout the remainder of the evening, they discussed their childhoods, their youths, and their current lives. They talked extensively about the Dolly Project and where she would fit into the project team. She wanted desperately to know about the circumstances of his meeting with the Pope, but she didn't ask. She assumed he would tell her about it if, and when, he was ready.

It was ten-thirty when they left the restaurant and he retrieved his car to take her home.

She lived in a small flat close to the university, about nine kilometers from her parents' house and less than seven kilometers from the institute.

After he walked her to her door and they stood on the doorstep, she asked, "Ian, I've enjoyed this evening immensely. Might we continue our discussion some evening this coming week?"

He looked down pensively and before he could respond, she quickly added, "I'm sorry, I'm being too forward again aren't I?"

"No. No, you're not." He responded as he reached out and put his comforting hand on her shoulder. With his touch, she moved slightly toward him. He responded by closing the gap between them.

He paused, removed his hand from her shoulder and stammered, "Let me think about that, I'll need to check my schedule. Laura, thank you for the lovely dinner, it was most enjoyable. It's late and I really must be leaving." He turned and rushed to his car.

As she closed the door behind her, she thought, *What was that about? I know he was about to kiss me and then he froze up and fled. That was the fastest mood swing I've ever seen.*

ROSLIN, SCOTLAND
MONDAY, AUGUST 11, 1997
7:32 A.M.

As Ian arrived at his office, he was elated to find Laura seated at her desk. "I'm anxious to start my new job," she said as she greeted him with a smile, her face beaming with enthusiasm.

"Well, let's get started. We'll take a tour of the lab facilities and I'll introduce you to all the people I interact with on the Dolly Project.

Also, I've paid some thought to your suggestion about continuing our discussion. Would you be amenable to spending some evenings together this week? We could work late and then get a bite to eat."

"Yes, Ian, I'd like that. I have so much to learn about the project and I would like to continue our conversation about spirituality. I'm available tomorrow evening."

EDINBURGH, SCOTLAND
SATURDAY, AUGUST 16, 1997
8:08 P.M.

Ian and Laura were seated for dinner after spending the afternoon in the labs. They both had realized how much she had to absorb about the Dolly Project. They had spent the major part of each day together in the labs from Tuesday through Friday and they had worked late in the office each day so they could catch up on their regular duties.

Because of the lateness, he had taken her out for dinner each evening. They had only discussed their work and when they had finished their meals, he had politely escorted her to her car without any expressions of intimacy.

"Ian, how are you doing with your reading of *The Case for Christ*?

He pulled on his collar, looked down at his lap and conceded, "I haven't progressed very far." He looked up. "It seems as though I've been spending day and night with my new assistant."

They were silent for a moment, each taking several bites of their dinners.

"Ian," she asked, "why don't you come to my church with me some day? It's a fun, happy place filled with people who truly care for each other." She reflected, then continued," Our pastor is not speaking tomorrow, would you like to join me the following Sunday?"

179

He thought for a moment and then pronounced, "I'll do that, Laura, but on one condition."

Her head tilted as she looked at him. "And that is?"

"After church, we go to my home, you can meet Duffy and I'll cook you brunch. We can spend the afternoon discussing the book. There's a Beethoven concert being conducted in the early evening at Dalmeny Park. We can pack a picnic dinner, take a couple blankets and sit on the grass. That's my one condition." He paused to watch her reaction. "Now, am I the one being too presumptuous?" he inquired.

"That's a lot more than one condition, or did you forget how to count, Dr. McKinney?" she retorted, emphasizing the word doctor. "And no, you are not being too presumptuous."

"Well, then my one condition is that we spend the day together."

She reached across the table and grasped his hand, gently squeezing it. "If that's what it takes to get you to church, I guess I can force myself to spend the entire day with you," she quipped. "And, who is this Duffy? And do we have to wait a week before we discuss your book?" she asked with mock indignation. "If you will remember, we were interrupted at lunch and I would like to hear more about your holiday in Italy."

"Well, perhaps we can do that next week. Would you care to continue our work and dinner schedule next week?"

Her eyes widened as she smiled with obvious pleasure. "I'd like that, Ian."

EDINBURGH, SCOTLAND
FRIDAY, AUGUST 22, 1997
7:18 P.M.

Laura and Shannon were finally seated at a quiet table at the rear of one of their favorite restaurants after a fifty-minute wait. They spent the time at the bar having a casual conversation.

"All right, Laura, tell me about him." Laura flinched in surprise. "Don't pretend to be surprised, Laura Galbreath. You skipped our normal Wednesday night evenings out the last two weeks, and you've been busy every night both weeks. You obviously have a new man in your life. Who is he and where did you meet him?"

"Shannon, he's not a new man in my life, he's been in my life for the past two years and it's not a romantic relationship. It's strictly work-related."

Shannon's mouth fell open. She stared accusingly at Laura. "You've been seeing Ian McKinney. Laura, what are you doing? You've told me a dozen times you can't stand the man." Her eyes tightened as she admonished, "Laura, you're my best friend. Is he using that raise and promotion to come on to you?"

"No, of course not!" Laura exploded. She described their dinner together at The Witchery, intentionally omitting any mention of the Pope. "Shannon, we've worked into the evenings every day for the past two weeks and he has bought me dinner every evening. Shannon, he never once attempted to even kiss me, but I know he's wanted to."

"And do you want him to?"

Laura looked sheepishly down at her drink.

"Oh my God, Laura, you're falling for a man that you despise. How many times have you complained to me about men, and particularly about Dr. McKinney? How many times have you told me he's boring and cold and unattractive?"

"I never said he's unattractive," Laura defended. "On the contrary, I've always found him to be rather handsome. But he's different now. He's kinder and more attentive. He's a different person."

"I must admit, from what little I've seen, he does seem a bit more outgoing. But remember, a leopard doesn't change his spots."

"Maybe he's not a leopard anymore. Maybe he's a lamb," Laura jested.

Shannon didn't respond. She just stared at her friend. "Be careful, Laura, I don't want to see you hurt again."

"He hasn't expressed the slightest interest in anything other than work," she bemoaned.

EDINBURGH, SCOTLAND
SUNDAY, AUGUST 24, 1997
8:27 A.M.

Laura opened her door for Ian and welcomed him to her flat.

"Excuse me for a minute; I'll be right back." She returned after a moment with an enormous smile on her face and a small overnight case in her hand. "I brought a change of clothes for the picnic," she explained. She noticed him perusing her bookshelves and said, "Do you find anything interesting?"

"Well, I see quite a few science-related books and over here, an equal number dealing with spirituality. Laura, I'm impressed."

"Ian, I guess that shows I love science and I love God." She looked at him with a pert smile and said, "Isn't that what you would want from your new assistant?"

They arrived at her church, the Green Woods Community Church, ten minutes before the service was to begin. As they waited for the start of the service, she told him about the church.

"The Evangelical Presbyterian Church was founded in the United States only seventeen years ago and is known as the EPC. Ian, it's different from any other church I've ever been to. It's fun, it's exciting and it's upbeat. You'll love our pastor. His name is Tim Morton and he has a great sense of humor. This is the first EPC church in Great Britain and was founded less than a year ago."

Ian told her about the mass at St. Peter's Basilica and how uninspiring the service was.

She responded, "There's room for all kinds of services in the Christian world, Ian, just so we recognize God and understand how blessed we are. Personally, I want to spend my Sunday mornings being uplifted, not obligated. You'll see what I mean."

The service opened with music, but not the type of music he had imagined. There were three guitarists, a drummer, a pianist, and four singers and they sang contemporary music. Laura explained that the music came from America and had much more meaning to her than the two-hundred-year-old hymns that were sung in the other churches of Scotland.

After three songs, a woman went to the pulpit and greeted the audience. She spoke for a few minutes, led a prayer and introduced a young married couple who related their spiritual life and how they came to believe in Christ.

Ian listened attentively. After the offering, the pastor went to the pulpit and gave his sermon. Ian found it amazing that he did not refer to notes and that he talked from his heart for thirty-five minutes. The service ended with several more songs, then Laura took Ian to meet Pastor Morton. She addressed him by his first name as she said, "Tim, I'd like you to meet my friend, Ian."

"Ian, it's wonderful to meet you and have you as our guest. I must say, you are indeed a fortunate man, being in the company of such an intelligent and lovely young lady. You are welcome to visit us at any time."

Ian was taken aback by the warmth and sincerity of the minister. He thanked him and told him that he concurred about his good fortune. Laura interjected, "Tim, Ian is in the process of exploring his spirituality."

"That's wonderful, Ian. I'm happy for you and I hope you'll find that you are not alone in your search." He glanced at Laura, observing the sparkle in her eyes and continued, "I think you may have already discovered one of the blessings he has given you." Laura blushed and Ian smiled.

Pastor Tim added, "Ian, if ever you would like to meet and talk, I'm available for you." Ian and Laura both thanked him. As Tim watched them as they walked away, a big smile spread across his face.

They arrived at Ian's cottage in the countryside after a quiet twenty-five minute drive. After he showed her around his home and introduced her to Duffy, he cooked his favorite breakfast, eggs Benedict. As he made the hollandaise sauce, she perused his large library collection.

"Ian, this breakfast is delicious. I've never had eggs Benedict before."

They chatted about the unique church service and how much he enjoyed it. After eating, she insisted, "Ian, you go relax and I will do the dishes and clean up the kitchen."

When she finished, she went to his study and found him listening to classical music while he sat in his chair, apparently deep in thought. Duffy was at his feet.

"Would you like to go to my church again next Sunday?" she asked.

"Yes, I believe I would," he responded. "But only if you'll spend the day with me again." He looked at her hopefully, with a wide smile.

"I think that can be arranged," she replied. "But, before that happens, I'd best get to know your friend here. How old is Duffy?" she asked as she sat on the floor next to the dog.

"Duffy is seven years old and he owns this house. At least he thinks he does."

"Tell me your reaction to the book," she urged as she began rubbing the dog's ears.

"Well, it's a fascinating book. You might want to read it."

"I already have. I agree, it is fascinating, and very convincing, I might add."

His eyes widened as his lips parted and his jaw dropped. "You amaze me, Laura Galbreath. You bought and read the book just for me?"

"I read it so we could discuss it, Ian. I get excited whenever I see someone explore their spirituality."

"Well," he paused as he contemplated his response, "I found it to be persuasive. I think the fact that the author was an atheist who was also an investigative reporter adds credence. The fact that he started investigating the Jesus theory to prove it false, because his wife had become a Christian, is interesting. He certainly makes some compelling points. What did you think?"

"It reconfirmed my beliefs and really made them stronger. But we're here to talk about you. What do you think?"

"I don't know. There's so much to absorb and it's so difficult to imagine. I've seen some things over the past weeks that really make me wonder." He gazed at Laura for a moment. "I will say this, I do feel a kind of inexplicable warmth that I've never felt before. Tell me, Laura, do you ever have doubts?"

"Yes, of course." She paused. "But they don't last long. I've come to accept the fact that my belief in God and my love of science are not opposed to each other." Laura was silent for a moment. "Ian, what happened to you that started this whole thing?"

He looked at Laura sitting on the floor, playing with his dog. It was such a heartwarming scene, her looking up at him with her beautiful blue eyes and her dark blonde hair falling to her shoulders.

Her pure beauty reminded him of the actress Meg Ryan. It dawned on him what was missing in his life. It was sitting right in front of him.

He climbed out of his chair, sat down next to her and cupped her face in both of his hands. "Laura, you are an incredibly wonderful and beautiful person. I so enjoy being with you."

They both leaned forward and their lips nearly met. He quickly pulled away and said, "I'm sorry, that was wrong of me. Let's take Duffy for a walk." As he stood, he saw her eyes start to water and it nearly broke his heart.

As they walked down the country lanes surrounding Ian's cottage, they were silent for nearly ten minutes, each deep in their own thoughts. Finally, Ian stopped walking and broke the silence.

"Laura, I'm not being fair with you. I'm just not able to enter into a romantic relationship at this time and I can't explain it to you." He stared at the ground and shook his head. "I think the world of you, but I just can't move forward." He paused and added, "As much as I would like to."

"Ian, I don't understand," Laura said, her eyes moistening and a tear running down her cheek. "Can we talk about it? Is there anything I can do? If it's physical, I'll understand."

"No Laura, it's not physical. It definitely is not physical," he emphasized. "I just can't talk about it now. Can you be patient with me?" He leaned forward and tenderly kissed away the teardrop.

She nodded and sobbed, "There's another one."

He put his lips to her cheek and kissed it away. Sniffing, she brought her finger up and pointed to her other cheek and said, "There's another one over here." He again kissed her cheek. "Darn it!" she laughingly sobbed. "Those things just keep coming."

After receiving several more tender kisses on her cheeks, she regained her composure and said, "I have an idea. I brought my copy of *The Case for Christ*. Let's go back and read. We'll each read the same chapter separately, then we'll discuss what we read. I think we'll learn a lot." She looked up at him, waiting for a response.

He sighed, then responded, "Let's go."

As they walked back to his cottage, they had no idea they were being watched through high-powered binoculars.

———

The afternoon was spent separately reading and then discussing what they had read. As the hours passed, the depth of their discussion increased, and Ian felt a greater comfort level talking about his spirituality. It was nearing three o'clock when they had read and discussed the first two chapters.

Ian got up and said, "I have to finish preparing our dinner for the concert."

"What are we having?" Laura asked as she followed him into the kitchen.

He opened the refrigerator, pulled out a package and unwrapped it. She looked in amazement at two large lobster tails. He proceeded to clean them and then put some butter on each tail along with paprika and placed them under the broiler. She watched as he gathered together some spices, sour cream, and mayonnaise, and started mixing them together.

"May I ask?" she playfully inquired.

"It's a Cajun rémoulade sauce for our chilled sliced lobster." When the tails were broiled to his satisfaction, he immediately placed them in the refrigerator to chill. "That's it. When the lobster is chilled, I'll slice it. The wine is chilling, and I made the desert last night when I got home."

"And, what might that be, my amazing chef?"

"Oh, I put together a Bavarian cheesecake. We'll take several slices and leave the rest for another time."

"I am incredibly impressed. What other surprises do you have in store for me?" Laura quipped.

"Ian, I want to get out of this skirt and get into something comfortable. I brought a change of clothes. What are you going to wear tonight?"

"It's going to continue to be warm tonight, so I'm going to wear shorts. I have blankets and pillows already packed so we can be comfortable," Ian replied. "I'll show you to the guest bedroom so you can change."

As they entered the bedroom, she turned to him as he glanced over at the bed.

She followed his glaze and coyly said, "Tempting, isn't it?"

He responded with a wide smile.

She kissed him quickly on the cheek and said, "Shoo, go to your room and change. Can't a lady change clothes without being tormented by you?" He laughed and left the room.

He was in the kitchen preparing their meal when she appeared. She had on white sandals, white shorts and a turquoise blue blouse. The blouse was tied in front above her waist, exposing her taut stomach. Her ankles were thin, leading up to well-shaped calves and thighs. Her bare midriff showed no signs of excess weight and her blouse was stretched tight because of her ample breasts. She wore a black baseball cap and her hair was gathered into a ponytail protruding through the opening at the back of her hat.

He stood silently as he absorbed her beauty. "You are absolutely gorgeous," he uttered as his eyes devoured her. "How could I have been so blind?"

"You're not so bad yourself, for an old fuddy-duddy scientist," she replied.

Ian, too, was wearing sandals, along with a pair of tan shorts with a navy blue short-sleeve shirt.

"Ian, your legs are so strong and powerful. That's not from sitting in your favorite chair and listening to Beethoven."

"I do a fair amount of climbing and hiking in the Highlands whenever I get the chance."

"I've never been to the Highlands," Laura remarked as she stared at his well-defined chest and arm muscles.

"Well, perhaps, we'll have to remedy that someday." Ian finished packing the food and wine in a large picnic basket and they left the house for the twenty-minute drive to Dalmeny Park.

It was a warm night as they set up their blanket and food about fifty yards from the orchestra where it was less crowded. They sipped their wine and chatted, as they talked about the events of the day.

Laura looked up at the overcast sky and remarked, "I hope it doesn't rain. This is so lovely being here, especially being with you."

"I don't think it will. Those don't look like storm clouds. Let's eat. I brought some wine and cheese to have with our lobster."

"This is delicious," she exclaimed after taking a bite of lobster tail. "I am very impressed with your cooking skills."

Ian smiled and said, "I'm glad." They finished their meal as the orchestra was warming up.

"Ian, this is heavenly." I'm so happy." He smiled warmly as she continued, "Speaking of heaven, I enjoyed our discussion this afternoon. Do you think you're getting closer?"

"I don't know. A part of me wants to believe in the evidence I've discovered. But another part of me, the scientist part of me, requires proof. I'm not certain what I believe." They cleaned up the remnants of their dinner and put it in the picnic basket just as the orchestra began playing.

They had only played a few notes when Laura exclaimed, "Oh, they're playing 'Pastorale,' his sixth symphony. This is my favorite."

"Laura, I'm astounded. I didn't know you were a fan of Beethoven."

"Beethoven is one of the many things I love in this life. And God keeps bringing me new things to love." Their eyes met briefly before she slightly blushed and said, "I'm sorry, Ian. I've always had the bad habit of saying whatever comes to my mind."

"Don't be sorry, Laura. I love that about you." He held both of her hands with his, looked in her eyes and said, "Now it's time for me to be bold." He paused for a moment. "I want you to know how much I've enjoyed spending time with you over these past weeks. When I'm not with you, I find myself thinking about you."

"But?"

"No buts, I guess I'm just asking you to be patient with me."

She smiled, leaned over and softly kissed him on the cheek. Neither said a word for a moment as they listened to the beautiful orchestral music.

Ian yawned slightly.

"Are you tired?"

"No, I'm just content," he replied.

"Why don't you lie down and rest your head on my lap?"

Ian stretched out and put his head on her lap and looked up at her beautiful face. He smiled deeply as she bent down and kissed his forehead. She cradled his face in her arms and gently rubbed his temples. After several minutes of listening to the music, she brought his head tightly against her stomach and softly purred as she gently stroked his face.

This could have been erotic, with his cheek against the warmth of her bare stomach, but that wasn't what he felt. He felt a deep peacefulness, such as he had never felt before. He felt himself spiraling into deep feelings for this woman that he never believed he could again experience.

Things were happening so fast—the Shroud and the potential cloning of Jesus, his meeting with the Pope and his friendship with Oleg, his confusion over his spirituality—and now, this new relationship with his secretary.

Laura sighed with a deep smile and held his head tightly against her.

Ian looked at the darkening clouds with their varying shades of gray. He thought to himself, *Oh God, I'd like to believe in You. I'd like to believe that You brought this amazing woman into my life, but it's so hard to believe. Please, show me that You exist.*

A moment later, Laura felt him shiver, looked down and saw that his legs and arms were covered in gooseflesh. His eyes were wide open in amazement as he stared at the sky.

"Are you all right?" she asked in a concerned voice. Ian didn't respond, he didn't move a muscle as he barely breathed. Laura slightly shook his head and fretted, "Ian, are you all right?"

He looked up and confided, "Laura, that was the most amazing thing." He sat up and gazed in her eyes. "When I was lying on your lap looking at the clouds, I asked God to show me that He was real. Then, suddenly, the moving clouds formed a face. I could see the eyes and nose and the mouth. There was a dark band across the forehead. It was the same face that I saw on the Shroud."

Laura remained silent, as if she were mesmerized by his words.

He lay back down on her lap, staring at the darkening clouds, and wondered what this meant. After a moment, he regained control of his senses and realized that the face in the clouds was only his imagination. It was his desire to find an answer where there was none. He transposed the face on the Shroud to the clouds. He was satisfied that his imagination had momentarily taken ahold of him.

But what if there is a God? What if He answered me and showed me His face? Okay, if you're there, show me again. Prove it to me, he thought to himself.

After a moment, Laura felt him shiver again. She looked down at him and saw the same gooseflesh on his bare skin. She saw the same look of amazement on his face. She remained silent.

"Laura."

"Yes," she whispered.

"I asked for another sign and I just saw the face of a sheep, a lamb." He sat up and looked into her eyes. "I don't know what to say; I don't know what to think."

"Don't say anything; just think about what you saw." They spent the rest of the evening listening to the concert, each caught up in their own deep thoughts.

During the thirty-minute drive to Laura's home and still deep in thought, Ian did not notice the two cars that were following them.

ROSLIN, SCOTLAND
TUESDAY, SEPTEMBER 2, 1997
10:24 A.M.

After having spent nearly every evening with Ian during the past ten days, Laura reached a decision. Ian was across the campus at one of the labs when she picked up her phone and dialed.

"Angus, this is Laura Galbreath. I'd like to meet with you regarding your brother-in-law."

"What's this about, Laura?"

"I really don't want to talk on the phone. Could we possibly meet privately someplace, after work for a few minutes?" Angus remained silent for a moment and then gave her directions to a pub about three kilometers from the institute and they agreed to meet at six o'clock that evening. "Angus, please don't tell Ian about this."

He agreed.

Later, she informed Ian she was to have dinner with her parents that evening and would have to leave work by 5:30. She noticed his disappointment and inwardly smiled.

She was already seated at a table in the back of the pub, sipping a glass of ale, when Angus arrived shortly before six. He sat down, ordered a glass of ale from the server and said, "How can I help you, Laura?"

She took a swallow of ale, drew in her breath and let it out slowly. "Angus," she declared, "Ian and I have spent almost every evening together for the past three weeks." If Angus was surprised at this revelation, he did not show it. She continued.

"I care for him, Angus, and I'm sure he cares for me. But he won't show it. Several times, he has come close to kissing me, but something holds him back and he pulls away. Angus, I'm frustrated. There's no point in spending all this time together if there's no chance of building a relationship, particularly since we work together during the day. I'm asking for your advice. Is it me? Is it the fact that we work together or is there something about Ian that makes him retreat?"

Angus was silent for over a minute as he drank his ale, deep in thought. "Laura, I agree with you; you cannot go on like this. It's not

193

fair to you and I know it's very painful for Ian. He and I go back a long way, and yes, there is a reason for his restraint."

He took a swallow of his ale. "But Laura, it's not my place to discuss it. He's going to have to tell you about it." He saw the look of frustration cross her face. "Laura, I'll do this. I'll talk to Ian and I'll encourage him to discuss this with you. That's all I can do."

She thanked him and watched as he hurriedly finished his drink. "I can't promise you what he'll do, but I'll try to convince him to talk about it."

He stood up and reached in his pocket for some money to cover the tab. "Come on, I'll walk you to your car."

ROSLIN, SCOTLAND
WEDNESDAY, SEPTEMBER 3, 1997
8:47 A.M.

"Ian," Angus spoke into the telephone, "we need to meet today."

"When and where?" Ian responded, sensing both the urgency and the importance in Angus's voice. Angus directed him to the same pub where he had met with Laura the previous evening and they agreed to meet after work.

It was early evening when they sat down, oddly enough, at the same table at which Angus had sat the previous evening. They each ordered beef pies and ales and after their drinks arrived, Angus began to speak.

"Ian, I met with Laura last night at this very same table."

Ian was taken aback, but not totally surprised.

"This woman has a lot more depth of character than I ever imagined. Ian, she cares for you."

Ian crossed his arms over his chest. "Angus, I'm well aware of that."

194

"I'm telling you this as your best friend, you have to confront your past. You must decide if you are capable of having a relationship and if Laura is that woman. You cannot keep spending all these evenings and weekends with her and not let her know what happened. It's simply not fair to her. She's a good woman, Ian, and I think she might be good for you." Angus took a swallow of his ale and added, "In a lot of ways."

"I hear you," Ian responded. "I'll think about it. Actually, I have been thinking about it," he added. "Angus, I agree with you, she is a wonderful woman. You can't imagine just how amazing she is. Thank you for your advice."

ROSLIN, SCOTLAND
FRIDAY, SEPTEMBER 5, 1997
9:12 A.M.

Ian and Angus met outside one of the lab buildings where they could talk in private.

"Angus, I agree with you. Laura must know everything. Then she can decide if she wants to continue seeing me or even continue working for me. We either have to end this relationship or move forward and see where it goes."

"I agree, my friend. How are you going to tell her? Would you like me to describe to her what happened?"

"I think that would be best. Can you come to my place tomorrow afternoon, say 3:00 o'clock? Laura and I have agreed to spend the day together but haven't made any plans yet."

"I'll be there," Angus replied.

BROXBURN, SCOTLAND
SATURDAY, SEPTEMBER 6, 1997
3:07 P.M.

The always-punctual Angus arrived at Ian's cottage just prior to three o'clock, much to the surprise and delight of Laura. He greeted Laura and made himself comfortable in an easy chair across from the couch where Laura sat fidgeting. Ian excused himself by saying, "I know it's early, but I'm going to have a drink while Angus tells you a story."

After Ian returned and sat in the other easy chair facing the sofa and Laura, Angus began.

"I can't tell you when or where this happened and I can't tell you names, but several years ago Ian and I both worked at SIS. As you may or may not know, SIS stands for Secret Intelligence Service and is also known as MI-6. The official purpose of the SIS is to provide the British government with a global covert capability to promote and defend the national security and economic well-being of the United Kingdom. It operates worldwide to collect secret foreign intelligence in support of our government policies and objectives.

"That is the official and published description. There are other functions and objectives which I won't discuss. Ian worked as an analyst in the scientific arena and I worked in a different department, covert operations. We worked closely together on several assignments and I think it's safe to say that we grew to like and respect each other. Ian introduced me to his sister and now Kathleen is my wife."

Laura was surprised, seemingly enthralled with Ian's background as she rubbed her hands together.

"I had a partner on a number of projects, a young lady who was both intelligent and beautiful. She could be sweet and innocent on one hand, yet cunning and remorseless on the other. To make a long story short, she and Ian fell in love and had planned to marry and build a life together after they left the Service."

Laura glanced at Ian as he stared down at the drink that he cupped in his hands. Ian did not return her gaze.

Angus continued, "Over a period of time, several of our operations failed due to unusual circumstances and several of our field operatives lost their lives. It became obvious there was a mole in the service, and it was not far removed from my sphere of operations. No one was beyond suspicion and eventually I began to suspect that the mole might be my beautiful partner, by then Ian's fiancée. Either I displayed my thoughts or she had great intuitive abilities because one night I let my guard down and had a couple of drinks with her at my apartment.

"We were discussing our current assignment when she put a drug in my drink and I woke up to find myself naked and securely bound and gagged with duct tape, propped up on the floor against a wall. Ian had been out of town and was not scheduled to return for several more days, so he was not a threat to disrupt her plan."

Her eyes wide open, Laura sat speechless.

"Simply, her plan was to extract as much information as possible before she killed me. Fortunately, Ian returned home unexpectedly and had tried to contact her. Failing this, he came to my flat and happened to see her car parked down the street. He became uneasy and unknown to her, he had a key to my flat and silently let himself in. What he found was his naked friend in a drugged stupor, unable to move and unable to utter a sound, with multiple shallow knife slices. She was an expert, cutting me in places intended to cause maximum pain with minimal bleeding. She had repeatedly asked me questions about other operatives and operations. She told me the pain would only get worse and that it would stop if I gave her the information she wanted.

"That's when your friend here surprised us." Angus glanced at Ian. "She made up a quick story about how I was the double agent and that I had confessed. I guess Ian looked at my glazed-over eyes and determined that she was lying. Sensing this, she told him she had proof in her handbag. She put the knife down and went to retrieve her handbag from a nearby table. Now, Ian normally didn't carry a weapon even though he had authorization. It wasn't necessary, being an analyst. But for some reason he had his gun with him, and he brought it out as she turned her back to get her handbag. I watched the scene as she removed her pistol from her bag, turned, and pointed it at Ian. She was shocked to see him pointing a gun at her and was even more shocked when he shot her in the chest. She fell to the floor and she had to know she only had seconds to live. I'll never forget her final words. She whispered, 'Ian, you killed me. I thought you loved me.' Then she died."

Laura's mouth dropped open as she stared at Ian and gasped, "Oh my God!"

After a few seconds, Angus continued, "Later, SIS uncovered the fact that she was a double agent who had a lover in the Soviet KGB. Ian left the Service within weeks. He went back to school and immersed himself in studying for his second advanced degree. He was later hired by the Roslin Institute and brought me over to head up security."

There was total silence until Laura whimpered, "Oh, my gosh! Ian, you've had to live with this all these years, the deceit, the betrayal, the pain. Oh, my gosh!" she repeated. "You had to kill the woman you loved." She stared at him, her eyes moistening.

Finally, he raised his head and looked at her, seeing her distress. He was unable to react, let alone move. Angus knew these were tortuous memories he was reliving.

Suddenly, Laura rose from the couch, came over to Ian and sat on the arm of the chair. She reached out, put one hand on his cheek and brushed his hair back with the other. She looked into his eyes, tears still flowing and murmured, "Darling, I could never hurt you or deceive you. Could you try to trust me? I've opened myself up to you. Can you try to do the same with me? I understand your pain and I'll do whatever it takes to ease your suffering."

He looked deeply into her eyes, his eyes moistening, and gently took her face into his hands. "Oh, Laura, you are so wonderful." He softly kissed her lips.

It was their first kiss.

Angus stood up and said, "I think I'll be leaving. You two have a few things to discuss."

Laura rushed to Angus, stood on her toes and put her arms around his neck. "Thank you, Angus, you dear sweet man. Thank you, thank you."

Angus quickly departed and Laura returned to her spot on the sofa and sank into it, stating, "I'm exhausted. I can't begin to imagine how you feel."

They remained silent, staring at each other, their hearts and minds racing. Finally, after wiping away her tears and with a demure look on her face, she asked, "Did you just kiss me?" She raised her head and looked up at him.

He nodded, smiled and asked, "Did you just call me darling?" She returned both the nod and the smile. He went to her and they fell into a warm, loving embrace.

Their lips softly met with a lingering kiss. His lips moved away from her mouth and explored the rest of her face. Her breathing became deeper as he lowered her on the couch and stretched out next to her.

He looked lovingly into her eyes as she lay on her back, her breathing becoming more rapid. Lowering his head, he kissed her lips again, this time with more passion, more urgency. He lost himself in her warmth as she returned his kisses with equal passion. Their tongues sought each other out as they lay side by side, their bodies pressed against each other. He could feel the beat of her heart as his hands ran over her back and then ventured to her chest. His arousal was full as he pressed against her.

Laura ran her hands over his face and around his back as she was equally aroused. His firmness brought a stimulation to her that she hadn't felt in years. Somehow, this body contact was far more passionate and meaningful to her than the full act had been with Brian.

She wondered to herself, *is this what it could be like?*

Ian's heightened passion was showing, not only physically, but in his breathing. "Laura, I want you so much," he whispered.

"I want you too, darling," she whispered in return, her body pressed against his. They paused, each realizing what was about to happen. Slowly, their bodies started to relax and their hold on each other loosened.

Ian pulled slightly away so he could gaze into her eyes and said, "Laura, we can't do this. Not yet."

She let out a deep breath and said, "I know." Neither said a word, they just stared into each other's eyes, their bodies now several inches apart but their arms still around each other.

"This is the most difficult thing I've ever had to do," Ian stammered. He tried to formulate his words but couldn't do so.

"Ian, I know what you're trying to say. Please, let me say it for both of us. Ian McKinney, I think we're falling in love. It's not going to be easy because of our jobs, because at our stage of life we've become set in our ways, and because we're now working side by side all day long. It's going to be difficult and we can't complicate it more by going to the next level. If this doesn't work, and I hope and pray that's not the case, we couldn't face each other every day if our relationship had become physical. I felt your passion, your strength, and I wanted to hold you and feel complete with you, but it would be a huge mistake. I found myself desperately wanting you, but there's so much more we need to know before we go there. I want this to work. But, if we went there, it could ruin it and I'm going to do everything in my power to make sure this is not ruined." She waited for a moment and then asked, "Is that what you were going to say?"

He looked lovingly at her and whispered, "That is exactly what I'm feeling, but I couldn't have said it nearly as well as you did." They continued to look into each other's eyes. "But I can tell you this," he said softly, "I love you a little bit more because of your strength and understanding."

"Did you just tell me you loved me?"

"Yes, I guess I did," Ian stammered. "Is that all right?"

"Yes, darling, it's definitely all right," she exclaimed. "You make me so happy." He looked at her inquisitively.

She held his face in her hands and whispered, "And I'm falling in love with you, too." She paused, it was difficult for her to say it, but she whispered, "No, I've already fallen, Ian McKinney. I love you."

They were both silent, their words sinking in as they lay on the couch looking at each other, each filled with a level of happiness and contentment that neither had ever felt before.

She broke the silence. "Let's take Duffy for a walk. I think we both need it."

They walked, hand in hand down the surrounding country lanes, for nearly two hours discussing their work, Ian's emerging spirituality, their pasts, and Ian's devastating experience with his fiancée. On several occasions they stopped and embraced with soft lingering kisses.

As they walked back to his cottage, they again did not realize they were being watched through binoculars, this time by two men, one of whom was unaware of the existence of the other.

The man who was watching the less-experienced agent also had a long-range directional microphone pointed at Ian and Laura.

He murmured to himself, "Now that's interesting, our studious scientist was MI-6, and capable of killing."

For the remainder of the afternoon, they read and discussed their book. "Are you going to cook for me tonight, my darling chef, or are you going to let me starve to death?"

Chuckling, he responded, "I didn't know if you'd still be here after hearing what Angus had to say, so I didn't plan anything. Why don't we walk into the village and have dinner at the pub?"

As they were drinking their ales and eating their meat pies, Ian suddenly changed topics and said, "Why don't we go to church tomorrow morning and then drive to Loch Lomond? There are some great hiking trails and I know a quaint little inn that serves a wonderful meal. We could have an early dinner and I could get you back home and to bed so you can get a good night's sleep."

"Now, that's an intriguing idea," she responded with a demure look.

"What's so intriguing?" he questioned. "The hike or the dinner at Loch Lomond?"

"None of the above," she smirked. "I was thinking about you getting me home early and to bed."

"You are obstreperous, young lady!"

"I'm what-aperous?"

"Obstreperous; it means unruly or uncontrollable."

"That's me!" she proudly responded. "And, you had best get used to it."

"I guess maybe I'll have to," Ian chuckled.

BALMAHA, SCOTLAND
SUNDAY, SEPTEMBER 7, 1997
4:57 P.M.

After hiking nearly twelve miles over the past four hours, they felt exhilarated when they sat down for dinner.

The Oak Tree Inn was very rustic with rough-sawn wood walls, smooth wood tables and floor and a large stone fireplace. They sat at a table by the window overlooking Loch Lomond. Laura was transfixed by the beautiful lake. "So, this is the lake of that lovely song. It's a beautiful lake, Ian. I don't know that I've ever seen it before."

"Yes, sweetheart, it is a beautiful lake, but it has a violent history. And the song is really a tragically sad song, although I doubt many of the people know of its history."

"Ian, I love it when you call me *sweetheart*. You can call me that as often as you want."

He smiled.

"Tell me about the history and song," she continued.

After they were served their meal and Ian had a swallow of his ale, he began.

"I'll give you some background. In 1745, Bonne Prince Charlie returned to Scotland from France, gathered many of the clans, and attempted to regain the throne of England for the House of Stewart.

At first, he was successful and won several small battles, defeating the British. His army marched through the English countryside on its way to London."

He paused to let her digest what he said. "Charlie's army made it all the way to Derby, only two hundred kilometers from London, when they turned back. That's a whole other story. When they left Scotland on their way to Derby, they went through the border city of Carlisle where they captured the British garrison without a fight. Now, Charlie was a gentleman, and he let the entire garrison free after relieving them of their weapons. He left a small detachment of highlanders behind to secure the fortress.

"After the battle of Culloden in April of 1746, where Charlie and his army were soundly and unmercifully defeated, his small Carlisle garrison was left unprotected. The English quickly captured the garrison and they tried all the captured Scots as traitors. That, my dear, was the difference between the English and the Scots in those days." He paused to take a bite of his meat pie.

"Ian, did the Scots commit atrocities?"

"Oh, yes, but they were not as severe over the centuries as what the English did. Anyway, legend has it that a lassie from the Loch Lomond area walked all the way to Carlisle to see her lover and plead for his life. That's close to 225 kilometers. Unfortunately, she was unsuccessful, and the sentence of death was carried out. Legend has it that before her lover's execution, he put words to music and a century later Robert Burns immortalized the song. When her lover wrote about her taking the 'high road,' he was referring to her walking back to the Highlands. When he wrote about himself taking the 'low road,' he was referring to his path to the grave. The implication was that his liberated spirit would return to the scene of their lovemaking at Loch Lomond before she got there."

"What a beautiful and sad story, Ian."

Leaning forward, she requested, "You mentioned there is a lot more history to Loch Lomond. Tell me more."

"All right, but are you prepared to hear about the violence while you're eating dinner?"

"I am," she stated as she took a bite of her steak pie.

"Very well. In the fourteenth century, the lands to the west of Loch Lomond were home to the Colquhoun clan, the lands to the north-west were home to the MacFarlanes, the Buchanans occupied the land to the southeast, while the MacGregors roamed over the Trossachs to the north and east. The Colquhouns were constantly feuding with their neighbors, particularly the MacGregors." Ian interrupted his story to take several more bites.

"In the mid-1400s, Sir John, chief of the Colquhouns, was killed on Inchmurrin Island, the biggest island on the loch. He had gone to what he thought was a peaceful meeting of the clans to settle their differences. Thus, the fighting continued for several hundred years. It reached its peak in the late 1500s. Sir Humphrey Colquhoun was married to a daughter of the Marquis of Hamilton. However, he was a handsome young man and he always had an eye for the ladies. At some point he met and was attracted to Agnes, the beautiful wife of Andrew, the chief of Clan MacFarlane.

"The attraction was apparently mutual because she made frequent trips to the western shore, ostensibly to visit a weaver and have her clothes made. In reality, she was having a passionate affair with Sir Humphrey, much of which was conducted in the woods above the shoreline. I believe the affair went on for some time before the cuckolded husband discovered what was taking place and began his revenge. He gathered a group of his clansmen, as well as some MacGregors, who never needed an excuse to fight the Colquhouns, and marched to the village of Luss, directly across the loch from here."

Laura took her eyes off Ian and instinctively looked out the window at the lake. This gave Ian a chance to take several more bites of his dinner. "Tell me if this gets too gruesome," he instructed.

She shrugged her shoulders. "Go on."

"At Luss, a bloody battle took place and Sir Humphrey fled to Bannachra Castle several kilometers away. There, he was safe—or so he thought. The MacFarlanes captured a Colquhoun servant who, after some torture, revealed the location of a secret entrance to the keep. Andrew MacFarlane and his men happily took advantage of this information and Sir Humphrey ended up with an arrow through his heart." Ian paused. "I hope you have a strong stomach for this because it gets brutal."

"Go ahead. I know the ancient days were nasty."

Ian took several more bites of food while he contemplated how to delicately continue. "The humiliation of Sir Humphrey continued. His corpse was beheaded and castrated. His genitals were then cooked, and Sir Humphrey's newly-widowed wife was forced to eat this as Andrew gloated." Ian stared at Laura who was about to take a bite of food.

Holding her fork in the air, she said, "You're right, that's not very pleasant." She promptly put her forkful of meat pie in her mouth and continued with her meal.

Ian looked at her with admiration.

"That's fascinating, Ian. Your knowledge of Scottish history is extraordinary. Tell me about your ancestry."

"Well, McKinney is a sept of Clan Mackenzie. The Mackenzies were once one of the largest and most powerful clans in Scotland. Their history is far too long and detailed to delve into at this time. We need to get you back home."

"Yes, you do. And, to bed early," she replied with a coquettish look.

"Oh, you are exasperating," he exclaimed with mock frustration. "Come on, let's drive you home."

I think I could spend my life with this woman, he thought.

They were both quiet as they drove through the beautiful forested countryside around Loch Lomond. Ian concentrated on his driving and thinking about all the life changes he was undergoing. Laura silently watched the scenery, while softly humming.

Ian parked the car in front of her flat and turned to her. "Laura, so much is happening so fast in my life. Are we moving too quickly? Only a month ago, you were my secretary that I barely noticed. And now we've almost gone to bed, we've used the word love several times, we've discussed intimate and personal parts of our lives, and I've had a spiritual experience with you. What's next?"

"I don't know, darling," she answered. "We're just going to have to wait and see."

They both were silent for a moment.

"Ian," she continued, "You know that I say what I feel." She saw him nod in the dim light from the streetlights that shone through the car windows. "It is fast, maybe too fast. But I can't help it. I've fallen in love with you, but I don't want to get hurt again."

He cupped her face in his hands, kissed her softly and lovingly, and said, "Laura, I'll never hurt you. I'll protect you until the day I die." He felt a tear fall onto his hand. He moved his hand away and moved closer. "I love you," he whispered as he kissed away her tears. They held each other tightly for several minutes until she composed herself.

"You had better take me upstairs. It's been a long day." After they entered her flat, she said, "Darling, would you like a 'wee dram'? I have a bottle of whisky in the kitchen. I don't know if it's any good, though."

"What kind is it?" he inquired. She brought out a bottle of Macallan 18. "Laura, you continually amaze me. You bought that just for me, didn't you?"

"Yes, I did. I like to make you happy."

They each had a small amount of the golden liquid. "You had best go. It's been a long day and you have a long drive home. Please be careful driving, my love. I wouldn't want anything to happen to you now that I've found you."

He again took her face into his hands and softly kissed her moist lips. After a moment they put their arms around each other and held each other tightly as their bodies melted into each other. They kissed long and passionately, his tongue caressing hers.

"I'd best leave before I get too aroused."

"I think it's too late for that." she teased as she looked down at him. He blushed. "Are you getting used to my directness?"

"Yes, but it's hard."

She looked at him with a coy, knowing smile and said, "Yes, I know it is."

He blushed again and replied, "I meant it's difficult."

"Oh!" she said. She took his face in her hands and kissed him quickly. "Now, shoo. Go home and let a girl get some sleep."

After Ian had departed, she went into her bedroom to change clothes and get ready for bed. As she removed her panties, she noticed that they were moist. "It's been a long time since that happened, Laura girl." she said out loud to herself.

ROSLIN, SCOTLAND
MONDAY, SEPTEMBER 8, 1997
7:31 A.M.

When Ian entered his reception area, Laura was already seated at her desk.

"Good morning, Miss Galbreath, you look lovely this fine morning. Did you have an enjoyable weekend?"

"Yes, I did, Dr. McKinney, and how about you. Did you have a pleasant weekend?" She returned the banter.

"Yes, I did, Miss Galbreath. I had the most wonderful weekend."

As he walked into his office, he turned and said, "I'm going to gather together some additional files on the Dolly Project for you to read this morning. This afternoon, we'll go over to the labs and do some more work." He saw her face light up as he continued, "I'll buzz you when the files are ready."

About thirty minutes later, he called her on the intercom and told her that the files were ready for her to take. When she entered his office, she closed the door behind her.

"Here are the files, Laura. Start with the one on top; they're in sequential order. And, Laura," he said as an afterthought, "I'd like to spend some additional time with you this week, discussing the Dolly Project. Are you available for dinner?"

"Hmm, let me think about my schedule. I'm available Monday through Thursday. Does that work?"

"Well, now let me think about my schedule. I could arrange that."

"But what about the weekend—don't we have a lot to discuss, Dr. McKinney?" she teased.

"Yes, we do, and I've already arranged that. If you are available, there is a fantastic inn located in the village of Plockton and I thought we might spend a long weekend there. I'm taking Friday off and I've arranged for you to also have the day off."

"Where is Plockton?" she asked incredulously. "When would we leave?"

"It's a coastal village in the northwest Highlands and it's a fascinating place. There are some beautiful hiking trails in the area and a lot of history. And, believe it or not, there are palm trees growing on the shore."

"Palm trees, in northern Scotland? Are you serious?"

"Yes, I am serious, and we'd leave early Friday morning. We'd have a half day of hiking and a full day on Saturday. Sunday, I'll show you around the area and I'll have you home Sunday evening."

"Dr. McKinney, are you suggesting that you want to take your secretary away for a clandestine weekend? I am a prim and proper young lady," she responded with mock indignation. "I need time to think about this."

"All right, how much time do you need?"

"I've had enough time. What should I pack?"

EDINBURGH, SCOTLAND
SUNDAY, SEPTEMBER 14, 1997
9:48 P.M.

They arrived back at Laura's flat after their weekend of hiking, sightseeing, and a lot of conversation.

They had arrived at Plockton early Friday afternoon after a four and a half-hour drive into the Highlands. During the drive, Ian told her what he knew of his ancestry. He relayed how his knowledge only went back five generations, but he knew prior to that time the family tree was connected to the Mackenzie clan, but he didn't know how.

Laura was captivated by both the history lesson and by the gorgeous mountain scenery during the drive. They had a picnic lunch, which Ian had packed, and they spent the afternoon hiking through the hills above Loch Carron.

When they arrived at the inn, Ian checked in and handed her a key to her room. He noticed a slight look of disappointment.

"Laura," Ian had later remarked while they were dining, "we need to talk about the sleeping arrangements." She was attentive as he continued, "I noticed a momentary look of disappointment when I handed you your room key."

She remained silent. "Laura, I love you and there is nothing more I would rather do than sleep with you. But it's only been five weeks and the surest way to ruin what we have is to have sex prematurely. I want our relationship to last, and in order to make sure it does last, I want it to have a solid foundation." He thought for a moment. "Picture our relationship like a brick wall. If there isn't a concrete foundation underneath, it could topple in a storm. We need to build that foundation before we start piling on the bricks. I want us to be able to weather any storm that comes along."

"Oh, my gosh, Ian you are such a romantic. That is such a wonderful analogy." She added, "You are absolutely right, of course. You always are."

"I'm certainly not always right, and I'm not certain that I am now. My heart and body tell me one thing and my mind tells me another."

"That's why I've fallen so deeply in love with you," she responded with a loving smile. Ian had given her an adoring look for a moment before gazing at people around the dining room.

As he glanced at a handsome, middle-aged blond-haired man across the room, the man suddenly looked away. *It appeared he had been looking at us*, Ian thought. He quickly dismissed the thought and went back to staring at Laura. He had not recognized the man; he appeared to be just another local.

Had Angus been there, he would have recognized him from their encounter in Turin.

Shimon Cohn was in Plockton, Scotland.

ROSLIN, SCOTLAND
MONDAY, SEPTEMBER 15, 1997
7:34 A.M.

When Ian entered his reception area, Laura was again seated at her desk. They went through their now-customary morning banter.

"I have some reports ready for you to study," he remarked as he entered his office.

"Dr. McKinney, may I ask you a question, in private?"

"Yes, of course you may."

She closed his office door behind her and glanced around the room. "Dr. McKinney, do you love me as much today as you did over the weekend?"

He sat behind his desk and feigned a frown. "I've done a lot of thinking this morning. No, I don't, Laura," he answered as he pursed his lips. He saw the questioning look on her face and quickly said, "I love you even more." He displayed a huge, bright smile.

"You are a rogue, Ian McKinney." She picked up the reports, tossed her hair back, turned and pranced out of his office. She immersed herself in reading the material, discovering the repeated failures in the early stages of the Dolly Project.

It was after ten o'clock when she rang Ian on the intercom. "Dr. McKinney, Shannon in the personnel department wants me to come down there and sign some forms. I'll be away from the phone for a few minutes."

"That's fine, Laura. Let me know when you return."

As she entered her office, Shannon looked up and after a moment, said, "Laura, you're glowing. You look absolutely radiant. What's happening to you?"

"Shannon, I had the most marvelous weekend ever."

Shannon thought for a moment and then said, "Laura, I don't

think I want to know about this. Did this involve the 'new' employee that I met with weeks ago?"

"Perhaps," Laura responded with a sly smile on her face.

As she signed the forms and turned to leave, Shannon advised, "Laura, be discreet and be careful."

"I will."

"And Laura, for your sake, I hope it works."

"It will. And for your information, we haven't taken that final step."

It was nearly noon when Ian rang Laura on the intercom and said, "Laura, why don't you have lunch and meet me back here at one o'clock. Then we'll go over to the labs."

"That's fine," Laura said into the speaker phone. "Dr. McKinney, may I come see you for a moment?" When she entered his office, she again closed the door behind her. "I have two questions for you, sir."

He nodded and responded, "Yes?"

"First, may I have a key to your cottage? And second, may I leave at three o'clock for the remainder of the day?" She once again displayed her saucy smile.

"Might I ask your reason for these two rather unusual requests?" Ian asked, feigning a serious professional demeanor.

"Well, Dr. McKinney," she beseeched, with a teasing look, "it seems as though I fell in love with the nicest man over the weekend and he has cooked me several wonderful meals. I think I had best let him know that I am also a pretty good cook, just in case we decide to spend more time together. So, I thought I'd surprise him and have a meal ready for him when he gets home from his work today."

Ian looked up at her lovingly, reached into his coat pocket, brought out his key ring, removed a key and handed it to her.

"That's the answer to your first question. The answer to your second question is yes, but just this one time. This man that you fell in love with can carry on without you for the day. He should be home by about six o'clock. Now, go have some lunch and I'll meet you back here in an hour."

"Yes, Dr. McKinney. I'll do that, Dr. McKinney. Oh, and Dr. McKinney?"

"Yes, Laura?" he said with mocked impatience.

"I love and adore you, Dr. McKinney!" She formed a kiss and blew it to him and then sashayed out the door.

It was almost four o'clock when Laura drove within sight of Ian's cottage, the bag of groceries on the seat next to her. As she got closer, she noticed a utility truck from Scottish Power driving out of Ian's driveway.

Darn, she thought to herself, *I hope there's nothing wrong.* She wanted so much to have this be a perfect evening. As the truck drove past her, she noticed there were two men in the truck cab.

Dinner was well underway and nearly ready to be served when Ian arrived home. She met him at the door with a glass of Macallan and a lingering kiss. He returned the kiss and exclaimed, "I could get used to this."

"Could you now?" she responded, not really looking for an answer.

"Yes, I could," he said as he wrapped his arms around her and tightly held her. "I could get very used to this."

"I'm glad," Laura said. As she left his embrace and walked to the kitchen, she added, "I was afraid for a moment that we might not have dinner, that you might have a power problem."

"Why do you say that?" Ian replied as he followed her into the kitchen and again took her into his arms.

"When I drove up, there was a Scottish Power truck leaving. I thought there might be a problem."

She felt Ian stiffen. He took hold of her shoulders and gently eased her away so he could look at her face. He looked concerned.

Laura was about to say something when Ian put his finger up to his mouth, motioning for her not to speak. He whispered in her ear to shut off the burners and to step outside with him.

They walked out to the back fence and Ian pulled out his cell phone and dialed Angus's home number.

"Angus, I think we might have a problem. Laura is here with me. She arrived earlier and saw a utility truck leaving my driveway. I haven't had any problems with my gas or electric." He listened to Angus's response and then replied, "Good, we'll see you in twenty minutes."

Laura crossed her arms as her shoulders tightened. "Ian, what's going on?" she questioned.

"Laura, I can't tell you anything more now, other than Angus is on his way over. We think that someone may have bugged my house. I'll get Duffy and let's take a short walk."

After walking for several minutes, they were safely away from the cottage. Laura demanded, "Ian, would you please explain?"

"No, not now," he answered, turning her to face him. "But I think I'll have to, soon. I need to talk to Angus first."

"Ian, you're scaring me. What am I getting myself into? Does this have anything to do with your meeting the Pope?"

"I can't answer your question." He realized this was not a good answer and that he owed her an explanation. "Sweetheart, I'll explain everything shortly, but trust me. We are furthering science and we are not doing anything illegal."

She looked up at him with a perplexed look.

Ian sensed her frustration. "Laura, please trust me on this. I love you and would never do anything to hurt you. I'll explain everything as soon as I can, but you're going to have to be patient with me."

Laura gave him a resigned smile. "Ian, of course I trust you. I think I've shown you that over the past month. I've given you my heart and made myself completely vulnerable to you."

Ian looked in her eyes. "Laura, you have done that, and I appreciate it and love you for it. It's a long and complicated story and I promise I'll tell you everything. Soon," he added.

Ian looked up and saw Angus's car approaching and they started to walk back to his cottage.

Angus removed a small case from the trunk of his car and whispered an instruction to both not to speak until he had completed his work.

Angus went to the telephone in the kitchen and held the sweeper up to it. He listened to the signal on the sweeper and then opened the phone, looked at it, and pulled out a tiny microchip. He motioned for both to be silent.

Angus next went to the phone in Ian's bedroom and then to the phone in his study. The results were the same. Ian was about to say something when Angus again motioned for him to be silent. Angus went to the computer and swept the telephone connection. He opened the connection and this time pulled out two tiny microchips.

Next, he walked around the room, sweeping it from floor to ceiling. He reached into the lamp beside Ian's easy chair and pulled out another chip. He proceeded to sweep every room, finding additional listening devices in the kitchen and in Ian's bedroom, in the gathering room and in both guest bedrooms.

Satisfied that he had found all the bugging devices, Angus said, "All right, we can talk now." It was nearly nine o'clock.

Laura stood with her arms crossed over her chest and was the first to speak. With her jaw set, she fumed, "I'm afraid to ask."

Silence.

"I'm sorry, but this is getting complicated and I need to know what I'm getting into," she demanded. Angus looked at Laura, then at Ian with a questioning look.

"Angus," Ian began, as he moved to Laura and put his arm around her, "Laura and I have found something very special. I am in love with her."

Angus turned to Laura. She felt his questioning look and immediately put both arms around Ian's waist. "It's mutual, Angus. I can assure you, I love him deeply." She stepped away from Ian, again folded her arms over her chest, and exploded, "Now, will someone kindly tell me what the hell is going on!"

Angus marveled, "Well, my dear brother-in-law, this new Ian certainly doesn't waste time, does he?"

"Speaking of moving fast, Angus, I owe Laura a full explanation."

"I was going to talk to you tomorrow about that. Kathleen wants an explanation about why you and I were away for three weeks and what we did. And she deserves it," Angus said. "In view of what has happened here tonight, I think the four of us should sit down for a long chat."

"I agree, how about tomorrow evening? Can you and Kathleen make it?" Ian asked. Angus nodded.

Ian turned his face to Laura, who still had her arms crossed over her chest. "How about you, sweetheart?"

Laura seethed for a moment and then huffed, "That's fine. I'll refrigerate tonight's dinner and add to it tomorrow. Ian, would you pour me a drink, please? And make it a double!" she snapped.

After five minutes spent in the kitchen storing her dinner, she returned to the gathering room with her nearly empty glass. She sat down next to Ian and murmured, "Angus, you can judge tomorrow if my cooking will be suitable for your brother-in-law's lifelong culinary tastes."

"Lifelong?" Angus exclaimed, displaying a sly smile. "The new Ian does move quickly. After only a month, you've fallen in love and are using the word lifelong. What will the next several weeks bring?"

"You never know, my dear brother-in-law. You never know," Ian replied. "Laura, let's go to the pub in the village and have dinner. Angus, we'll meet you and Kathleen here tomorrow at six-thirty. That will give me time to pick Laura up and get back here."

They all agreed to the plan.

Ian and Laura had a light meal and a pint of Tennents Lager as they quietly discussed their short tour of the lab that afternoon. Nothing was said of the bugging of Ian's home or Laura's previous anger.

When they returned to Ian's cottage, Laura said, "I can only stay a few minutes. It's late and I have to drive home." They sat down on the couch in the gathering room. Laura continued, "Darling, what did you mean when you answered Angus's question about what might happen over the next few weeks?"

Ian thought for a moment and responded, "Sweetheart, I'm not sure I really meant anything." He looked at her with a sheepish grin and added, "I'm a man. I'm entitled to say dumb things and to say things without meaning."

"Yes, you are. That is a guy thing."

"Seriously, Laura, things have happened so fast with us and in my life, that nothing would surprise me. There could be some major changes taking place soon, which you'll learn about tomorrow night. Whatever happens, I know one thing for certain." She gazed at him with an inquiring look. "I know I would like to have you by my side," he said. After a pause, he continued, "And for the rest of my life."

"What are you saying? Or, is that just another meaningless male comment?" she questioned.

"Laura, it's like we have two separate lives—the one at work and the important one, when we're together. What I'm trying to say is that I want to be with you every evening and I don't want to end the evening with one of us having to make that long drive home."

"You know we just can't live together," she said. "We've discussed this."

"Yes, I know that. I don't want to just live together. I would not dishonor you that way."

"Ian, what are you saying?"

"I'm trying to say that I love you. You'll learn a lot more by tomorrow night, and by Friday night, I'll know a lot more about what direction my life is taking. I think we should continue this conversation after tomorrow night."

"Well, Dr. McKinney," Laura said, her tone light. "you certainly give your secretary and new lab assistant a lot to ponder."

"Did I say too much? Am I being presumptuous?" Ian asked.

Laura paused and then replied, "No, darling. I like your thinking." She kissed him lightly and then said, "Now, I have to leave."

As he walked her out to her car, she said, "You don't have to pick me up tomorrow night. There's no need for you to make that extra trip to take me home."

"No, I'll pick you up. I don't want you driving home alone. When you get home tonight, I want you to call me. I want to know you are safe." As she got in her car, he exclaimed, "As a matter of fact, I'm going to follow you home right now."

"Thank you, darling, for protecting me. I appreciate it." She got in her car, waited for Ian to get into his Land Rover, and they proceeded to her flat.

The men who were watching them were a bit perplexed by all the consternation.

BROXBURN, SCOTLAND
TUESDAY, SEPTEMBER 16, 1997
6:11 P.M.

After Ian and Laura arrived at his cottage, Ian took Duffy for a walk while she began adding to and reheating the dinner. Angus and Kathleen arrived a short time later and Kathleen rushed to Laura, put her arms around her neck and said, "Angus told me the good news. I'm so excited and happy for you both.

"I want you to know that my brother has never been impulsive. He has always thought long and hard about every item of his life. You must be quite the lady for him to move so quickly." Laura felt immediately at ease with Kathleen and told her about their relationship and about the new Ian.

While they were getting acquainted, Angus again swept the cottage for bugs. There were none.

Ian came into the room, poured drinks for everyone, and said, "I think you will all need these tonight." He set the table while the ladies finished preparing the food. When they were seated and the dinner had been served, Laura asked Kathleen, "Are you and Angus spiritual?"

"I'm certainly more spiritual than my brother. At least I believe in God," she replied. "As for Angus, he'll have to answer that for you."

"Kathleen, have you talked to Ian since his return?" Laura asked.

"I have not, but that's not unusual. We normally only see each other on holidays, or," she added with a smirk, "when he picks up Angus for some function or sporting event."

"I think you may be surprised how Ian has changed," Laura advised. "Do you mind if I say a blessing before we eat?" she asked.

After receiving everyone's approval, Laura thanked God for the food, the friendships at the table, and for her relationship with Ian. She asked God to bless everyone at the table with patience and understanding for the evening's discussion.

After she was finished and everyone had started eating, Laura suddenly sat back in her chair and demanded, "Now, Ian McKinney, would you care to tell us what the hell is going on and why someone would put listening devices in your home?"

Ian looked surprised by her change of direction from softly giving thanks for him to making a strong demand. "This is going to be a long and unbelievable story, so please have an open mind. Laura, do you recall when the cardinals came to the institute?"

"I heard about their visit, but I didn't see them."

Ian proceeded to tell them about the meeting with the cardinals and Dr. Graham's negative response. He continued with the description of the following day, paging the cardinals at the airport and bringing them back to his cottage for the day. He related his theory of the energy blast from the resurrection, the solidification of the oils, and the entrapment of Jesus' blood. He had Angus tell them about the man who had followed them to and from the institute and his unfortunate demise in a traffic accident.

The ladies sat enthralled, barely able to eat, although Laura was a bit dismayed about the *accident* and she looked at Ian with a questioning stare.

He looked down at his lap, unable to meet her eyes.

After a moment, he changed the mood. He looked up and stated, "Please, eat your dinner, it's getting cold. Sweetheart, your beef stroganoff is delicious. I could see myself getting fat in my old age, living with you."

Kathleen froze at Ian's words, her fork halfway to her mouth. Her mouth fell open as she looked at her brother and then at Laura to see her reaction. She saw them looking adoringly at each other.

"Well, you two had best get married soon. It looks like you're ready to jump across the table onto each other," Kathleen quipped.

"Kathleen, mind your tongue," Angus playfully admonished. He chuckled, looked at Ian and said, "At least can you wait until after we finish desert."

Ian and Laura both blushed and then followed Angus and Kathleen in laughter.

Finally, Laura said, "Darling, continue with the story. You're getting sidetracked by these two comedians."

Kathleen chuckled, reached over and squeezed Laura's hand and said, "I'm glad you have a good sense of humor. Ian needs that."

"Well, if I may continue with important matters?" Ian said, feigning a look of exasperation.

He proceeded to tell them about their days in Turin, the tedious testing procedures, and the final positive outcome.

Angus interjected and described his encounter with the two men who watched them from across the piazza and that he later determined their identities.

Ian saw that both women had concerned looks on their faces and stated, "Why don't I finish the story and then answer your questions."

He continued by telling them about their stay at the Vatican, their first meeting with the Pope, and the testing for intact DNA. He talked about attending the long mass with Oleg and Joseph and their tours of ancient Rome and the Vatican. He described their anxious moments waiting for the final testing results to come in, their excitement with the results and their final meeting with Pope John Paul II.

Laura was visibly disappointed when Ian described John Paul's strongly negative response to the project. Ian saw her look of disappointment and smiled lovingly at her.

Angus interjected and told the ladies about Ian's talk to John Paul and how he at least convinced the Pope to consider proceeding with the project.

"So, what was his response? Don't keep us in further suspense," Laura urged.

"The Pope said he would consider it and he would advise Oleg and Joseph of his decision this Friday, after he returns from his summer residence," Ian answered.

"Their meeting is at six p.m. their time, which is five o'clock our time. I'm expecting a call sometime after six o'clock," Ian responded. Laura and Kathleen both instinctively looked at their watches.

"Darling, I'm going to be here with you when you receive that call!" Laura firmly stated.

"Of course, I would really like you to be here. As a matter of fact, I think we should all be here since that conversation could affect all our lives."

Kathleen said, "I'll bring dinner this time. Ian, you be sure to have enough whisky. You're either going to be doing a lot of celebrating or you're going to be drowning your sorrows."

After they all cleared the table and the ladies cleaned the dishes, the four went to the gathering room and sat down to discuss the events. Laura sat next to Ian and cuddled up to him, tightly holding his arm as she leaned against him.

Laura spoke first. "If the Pope gives his blessing, what happens next?"

"Well, we'd have to set up a lab and begin work. I haven't thought about details because I honestly don't think that's going to happen. Angus and I would have to leave the institute. I advised the Pope and the cardinals that we would be giving up our careers, so the funding would have to be sufficient to account for that fact."

"I can see why you said that Friday could be a life-changing day for you," Laura said as she gently squeezed his arm.

"That reminds me," Ian said, "I should call Oleg and tell him we've discussed the project with the two of you. We promised him we would tell no one."

Angus explained how the encryption machines worked while Ian was calling Oleg to leave him a message. To Ian's surprise, Oleg answered the call.

"Oleg, my friend, it's Ian. I didn't expect you to answer." He told Oleg about their evening and how they related all the events of the past to Laura and Kathleen. Have you sensed any reaction from John Paul?"

"No, actually I have not seen him since we all met while you were here. Ian, how are you and Laura getting along?"

"We've been reading *The Case for Christ* together." He also told him about what he had seen at the concert picnic.

"My friend," Oleg responded, "That is phenomenal. Truly, God is watching over you. Are you convinced now?"

"No, not yet. I still have a lot of questions. It's still difficult for me to accept."

"Ian, think about the disciples and why they all went out to certain deaths and how they must have seen the resurrected Jesus. That's compelling logic for a scientific brain like yours."

"I often think about that aspect," Ian replied.

"Ian, is Laura there with you, and may I speak with her?" Ian handed the phone to Laura and told her that Cardinal Jaropelk would like to speak with her. "Hello, Laura, I want to thank you for helping guide Ian in his search. From what he tells me you are a remarkable woman. I hope to meet you someday, my dear."

"Thank you, Cardinal Jaropelk, I look forward to meeting you. And, I'm not really guiding him. I'm letting him find his own way. He has to become convinced on his own, otherwise his belief won't be solid."

"I sense that your relationship may become permanent. You have a wonderful man there. Take good care of him."

"I will, and I agree with you on both points. It was a pleasure to talk to you, Cardinal Jaropelk. And thank you for being such a wonderful friend to Ian. Good evening."

She gave the phone back to Ian, who chatted for several more minutes with the cardinal.

Kathleen resumed their conversation. "Ian, you've been my older brother for a long time and I know you well. This project has changed you; you're more outgoing. You're more expressive and you're happier." She looked at Laura and smiled and then added, "You're more loving." She paused and then asked, "What happened?"

"Kathleen, you know how my scientific mind works. Let me ask you a rhetorical question," Ian replied. "If the image on the Shroud is that of Jesus, how did it get there? I have read all the theories and studied all the reports on the authenticity of the Shroud. I've concluded that the image may have been transposed to the linen by an enormous blast of energy. Unless lightning struck the body inside an enclosed tomb, then this blast of energy must have come from the resurrection. And, if there was a resurrection, then Jesus had to have been divine. And, if that's true, then there must be a God. That's the only conclusion that I'm able to come up with. So, I'm reading. I'm learning. I'm searching."

"And, what have you found?" Kathleen asked in a quiet, serious voice.

"I think I'm finding that my life is being directed right now. He brought me Laura and He showed Himself to me the other night in the only way I could see Him." Ian then added, "I'm not sure exactly what to think; it's all so preposterous. But I get the feeling I'm being led somewhere."

Laura remained silent. She let Ian express himself as she tightly held onto his arm. Kathleen turned to her husband and said, "Angus, what about you?"

"I was already a marginal believer, although not a strong one. I've had the same thoughts as Ian. Seeing and studying the Shroud was unbelievable," Angus replied. "Ian, what is the name of that book you are reading?"

Laura quickly inserted, "Angus, I'll pick one up for you and bring it to work."

"Thank you, I'd like that," Angus responded. "Well, Kathleen and I had best be leaving. There's one thing we haven't discussed. Who bugged your house and why? Ian, I'm putting your home under surveillance for the next few days until we know what is happening."

"Thank you, Angus," Laura said. "I thought I might have to move in to protect him." They all laughed.

Angus offered, "Laura, we'll drive you home."

Laura turned to Ian, kissed him and whispered in his ear that she loved him. "Darling, we have more studying to do. Let's spend the next two evenings at my home."

"That's a good idea," he replied as he walked them out to Angus's car. After the ladies were seated and Ian had walked back into his house, Angus stood by his car and breathed in the crisp night air. When he finally climbed into the car, Kathleen asked if he had seen something.

"No," he replied. "I didn't see anything."

But I sure felt something.

THE VATICAN
FRIDAY, SEPTEMBER 19, 1997
5:58 P.M.

As Oleg and Joseph entered the Pope's study, they once again found John Paul II standing at his favorite window staring out at the piazza. He did not turn around to greet them.

"Please," he finally spoke, still with his back toward them, "sit down and be comfortable. We have a lot to talk about." After a brief pause, John Paul turned around, greeted the two cardinals, and sat down in his favorite chair.

"Gentlemen, I've thought long and hard and prayed constantly about this. To proceed with your outlandish project goes against everything in which I believe. You are asking me to condone an act that is immoral, ungodly and perhaps illegal." He had a sad expression and he lifted his hands, with his palms up, as if he were pleading.

"I am a mere human and you are asking me to act like God. You are asking me to take on a responsibility heavier than any man has ever been asked to assume. This venture of yours is so fraught with danger that it frightens me. If we were to proceed with your scheme and it were discovered, it could be the ruination of the Church. Still, I can't get Dr. McKinney out of my mind, an atheist who is coming to find God because of the Shroud."

John Paul fell silent for a moment. "If the Shroud can do this to an atheist scientist, what might it do to the hungry masses that believe in Christ and are searching for meaning in their lives?" He again paused while looking down with his head resting in his hands.

Finally, he lifted his head and looked first at Joseph and then at Oleg. Oleg immediately saw the pain and trepidation in his expression and felt a huge sorrow for the hurt he had inflicted on this wonderful man.

"I've made my decision," John Paul quietly said. "I've decided to proceed with the project."

The cardinals were stunned. They did not anticipate the papal approval and were speechless.

"I have some terms and conditions that you must follow and agree to, in order to proceed." John Paul observed the shocked looks on the cardinals' faces as they remained silent. He continued, "First, this project must be totally secret. If word gets out to the public, I will immediately abandon the project, and I mean immediately," he emphasized. "Second, I want the mother to be an American and I want the baby to be born in America."

This took the cardinals by surprise.

"Third, I want the mother to be a Messianic Jew. Fourth, I want her to be incurably infertile. If she becomes pregnant, I want there to be no doubt the baby is a product of the Shroud. Fifth, if the project is successful, I want to see the baby. And lastly, if the project is successful, there will be no further contact with the baby after we see him. We will have done our part. The rest of his development will then be in the hands of God."

The cardinals were delighted but still shocked. Oleg stated, "Loleck, we most certainly agree to your terms. But, might I ask why you want the mother and baby to be American?"

"Oleg, I've thought and prayed long and hard about this. The United States was founded on the principle of religious freedom. It was, and still is, a gathering place for oppressed people from all over the world. Its strength is in its diversity and its tolerance, both religious and cultural. For all its many faults, the United States remains the greatest bastion of freedom in the world. If the project is successful, it is critical that the baby be in a country of safety where the people would be amenable to his message. The United States has a large and strong Christian population. The Church is strong, as are the many Protestant denominations. There are more freedoms there than in most any other country. Perhaps of even greater importance is the fact that the United States has the largest and most unrestricted communications industry in the world. The television, radio, and newspaper industries are the largest in the world and will be accessible to a new ministry. Add to that the fact that the United States is the most secure and stable country in the world from an economic and political perspective. This means it would be the safest location for the Messiah to spread his word."

Gently nodding his head, Oleg offered, "Loleck, you are correct. I never really focused on where the project would take place."

"I, too, agree with your logic, Your Holiness," added Joseph.

"Well, my friends, I suggest you set up extremely secure communications with Dr. McKinney and instruct him to proceed. The costs that he proposed are workable. We'll fund the project through my personal Vatican accounts, and only I have access and accountability to these accounts. I would like to receive monthly verbal progress reports and would like to be advised of any important developments as these occur. Please let me know how he reacts to moving to the United States." The Pope thought for a moment and inquired, "How is he doing with his science-versus-religion dilemma?"

Oleg responded, "He seems to be a changed man and appears to be falling in love with a young lady who is assisting him with his spiritual quest."

"I would like to visit with him again. See to it he comes here one more time. And tell him, apart from funding, I will be unable to assist him in any manner whatsoever. Joseph, you will oversee the monetary aspects of the project along with any security measures you deem necessary. Oleg, you will be responsible for all other aspects of the project. You are relieved of your regular duties and will concentrate full-time on the project. Joseph, you will not have that luxury. Your duties on this project must be in addition to your regular functions. You are too visible and prominent to have a schedule change. Remember, there is to be nothing in writing; everything is to be verbal. Good luck, my friends. I sincerely hope the project is successful."

Both cardinals were amazed at this comment. Oleg asked in an incredulous tone, "Loleck, what has changed your mind on the project?"

"Let's just say that I was told to move forward with the endeavor."

———

Ian and Laura, and Angus and Kathleen were nervously seated in Ian's gathering room each with a glass of whisky, anxiously awaiting the telephone call. Ian was seated next to the phone, with a pen and pad of paper at the ready.

It was precisely twelve minutes after six o'clock when the phone rang.

Ian looked across at Angus and the two ladies sitting on the sofa. "This is it." he said quietly. He answered the phone and heard Oleg's soothing voice. He listened, without expression, writing notes on his pad, as Oleg told him of the Pope's approval and described his conditions.

Ian stood up as he spoke into the receiver, "Oleg, we both have a lot to think about. Let's talk tomorrow at noon, my time. Good night, my friend." Ian ended the call.

He hung up the phone and looked at his guests. A wide smile broke across his face.

"The Pope gave his approval!"

———

The sniper lay on the ground within a small clump of trees, his high-powered rifle set up on a tripod.

Salam had received basic training in the use of firearms, so he was familiar with this weapon, but he had received only minimal training as an agent. He was a minor operative with only one kill on his record. The settings were adjusted for the correct distance and the lack of wind. He had a clear and easy shot; he just needed the target to appear at the large window.

There he is, Salam thought, as the target stood up with a telephone to his ear.

The sniper took a deep breath and put his finger on the trigger.

Laura immediately leaped up off the sofa, ran to Ian, and threw her arms around his neck. "Congratulations, darling, I'm so happy for you!"

Kathleen suggested they eat dinner and discuss the ramifications of the Pope's decision. Laura was giddy with excitement.

Damn, he thought, as the girl suddenly rushed to the target and threw her arms around him. *She was in the way. I hate to kill her, too. But he must die. If I hit her, so be it.*

He momentarily took his eye off the scope and put his hand to his mouth to stifle a slight sneeze. The sound was minimal. He went back to the scope to discover that the target and the woman had left the scene.

He brought out his binoculars and watched the door, but there was no activity.

———

After they sat down and after Laura again said a blessing, Ian quietly said, with a trace of reluctance in his voice, "There are conditions."

He told them about the mother having to be a messianic Jew and explained to Angus and Kathleen that meant a Jewish woman who believed that Jesus was indeed the Messiah. He went on to say she had to be incurably infertile so there would be no question the baby was the product of the Shroud. He told about the complete funding of the project and the requirement for total secrecy.

Deep in thought, he looked down at his food as he slowly took a bite.

Laura's forehead wrinkled as she squinted her eyes and questioned, "There's more, isn't there, Ian?"

Ian glanced at Angus and Kathleen, then looked at Laura and softly said, "Yes there is. The Pope wants the baby to be born in the United States and the mother to be an American." He paused and then continued, "The project has to be done in the United States."

"Why?" Kathleen immediately exclaimed.

Angus was expressionless. Laura, with a shocked look on her face, gasped, "Yes, why, Ian?" Ian explained all the reasons that Oleg had related.

No one spoke for a few minutes until Angus said, "Well, I think it would be fun to live in the States for three or four years."

"Sure, why not?" Kathleen responded. "I've always wanted to see the United States. If we lived there for a while, we could see the entire country."

Laura's mouth fell open and her body stiffened. "Three or four years," she gasped. "Will it take that long?"

"It will take at least that long," Ian conceded.

232

Where are they? Salam wondered as he rubbed the back of his neck. His hands were sweating as the inexperienced sniper waited.

Laura grimaced as she gently set her knife and fork down on her plate. "I'm sorry. I'm not hungry anymore." The others rushed through their meals in silence.

Angus interjected, "Would you ladies mind cleaning up the dishes? I'd like to talk to Ian alone for a few minutes. Let's go into the gathering room where we can talk, Ian."

There he is, the sniper murmured as he watched through his binoculars. Salam switched to the rifle scope as he waited for Ian to appear in the crosshairs.

Suddenly, there was a loud noise in the brush to his left. Startled, he looked up.

Angus's cell phone rang. He listened for a minute and said, "Where are you? I'll be right there."

He stood up and announced, "I've had several friends of mine watching your house every night, ever since we found the bugs. It appears that we have a visitor. I'll be back shortly. Ian, go in the kitchen with the girls," he ordered.

He left the cottage, got in his car, and drove to a dirt road a quarter mile across the street from the cottage. He found three men, one with his mouth gagged and his wrists and ankles securely bound with duct tape.

Angus went up to him as one of his friends shined a flashlight into his face. "Well, well, what do we have here?" Angus scowled. "I haven't seen you since Turin. Salam, isn't it?" Angus tore the tape from his mouth and jerked his head back from the fetid breath.

"Now, let me explain something to you and please listen closely. I have friends waiting for me, so I don't have a lot of time. My friends are very close to me and I don't like to see them being followed. And I don't like my friend having his house bugged." Angus noticed a slight look of surprise on the man's face at this statement. "I only have time to ask you this once. Who do you work for?"

Salam snarled, "Go to hell," and spat in Angus's face.

Angus wiped the spittle off his face. "Put his gag back on." After Salam's mouth was tightly wrapped, Angus said, "Wrong answer."

Angus lifted his leg and smashed his heel down on the man's instep. He heard the crack of several delicate bones being broken. As the man sank to the ground in agony, Angus said, "Lift him up and remove the gag." The man was whimpering. "Now, I have to get back to my friends. Would you like to tell me now who you work for?"

The man shook his head no.

"Put the gag back on and hold on to him."

Angus took a step away, then suddenly lashed out with a side kick to the man's knee, dislocating his kneecap and ripping tendons. He heard the muffled scream of pain.

"Do you have an answer for me now? Before you shake your head again, allow me to tell you what will happen next. My friends are going to lift you up by your wrists until they are straight above your head and your arms will pull out of their sockets. Would you like to tell me who you work for?"

"The Director," Salam whimpered. "But I never met him, and I don't even know who he is."

"What should we do with him?" asked one of Angus's friends, the same man who drove the Hummer more than a month ago.

"Let him go," Angus responded. "He's not worth bothering with. He's no threat." The men half-carried and half-dragged him back to his car, opened the front door, and threw him in.

Suddenly, one of the men exclaimed, "Angus, come here and look at this."

Angus walked over to the rental car and asked if there was a problem. "Look on the front seat," the man said. "There is an open box of rifle shells."

Angus thought for a moment and said, "Where exactly was he when you first spotted him?"

"Over there about fifty yards, near the clump of trees. He was running this direction."

"Describe exactly what you saw."

One of his men spoke up. "I heard a thumping noise followed by a gasping sound. Then suddenly, I saw him running to his car."

"Let's go have a look," Angus said. He directed the second of his men to watch their captive. When they got to the clump of trees, Angus noticed they had a clear view of the window to Ian's gathering room. He suddenly felt unnerved. The two men searched the area with their flashlights, looking for anything out of the ordinary.

"Over here," his friend said after searching the area for several minutes. He pointed next to a large tree and Angus walked over. His flashlight shone on a high-powered rifle with a scope mounted on a tripod. Angus lay down on the ground and looked through the scope. He felt a shudder go through his body as he looked at Ian's front window.

After searching the area to make certain nothing was left behind, they returned to the gunman's car with the rifle and tripod.

"It appears you spotted him just in time, my friends. Now, we must have a change in plans. I can't let a killer walk around loose, particularly one who wants to kill my brother-in-law. I think he needs to join his friend who had the car accident last month." Angus shook his head. "I wonder what spooked him. Why he was running to his car? And he left his rifle behind?"

Angus's friends looked at him for direction. "We have no choice, dispose of him. Remove all his identification and get his fingerprints. One of you drive his car. Drive over toward Stirling and make sure you don't leave any prints in the car. Make sure his accident is at least fifty kilometers away."

Angus looked at the man, saw the terrified look in his eyes, and said, "I don't like you threatening the lives of my sister and brother-in-law." With that, he gave him a short hard upward chop to the nose, with enough force to drive the cartilage through his sinus cavity and into his brain.

Angus got into his car and drove back to Ian's cottage.

As Angus walked into the kitchen, he saw worried looks on everyone's face. "What was it?" Ian quickly asked.

"False alarm," Angus replied while rubbing his hand. "But it's good to know that my men are on top of the situation." Laura let out a sigh of relief, Kathleen gave him a questioning look, and Ian immediately knew he was lying.

"Thank goodness," Laura exclaimed as she let out a large breath and wiped away her tears.

Ian couldn't tell if they were tears of relief or tears of worry. He looked at Kathleen and realized they were probably tears of worry.

"Angus, we should leave, these two have a lot to talk about," Kathleen urged.

"We're staying," Angus ordered.

"Well, can we at least go for a walk, so they can be alone?" Kathleen demanded. On the way out, Kathleen said, "We'll be back in a while, we're going to take Duffy for a short walk." As Angus left the room, he closed the curtains over the front window

Laura and Ian were silent for a moment, then Laura looked up at him and said, "Ian, I don't know what to make of all this, what does it all mean? What are you going to do?"

It took a moment for Ian to respond. He looked at Laura, straightened his shoulders, took a deep breath and declared, "I'm going to resign my position at the institute, move to the United States, set up a lab and attempt to clone Jesus."

With tears continuing to flow, Laura sobbed, "You'll be gone for three or four years."

"I know," he whispered, "but I'd like you to be with me. I'd like you to assist me with the entire project."

Her mouth fell open as she sputtered, "Where would I live? What would I do? What about my parents? What about my friends? her questions came in rapid succession. "I just can't pack up and move."

"Sweetheart, in answer to your first question, I'd like you to live with me," he murmured as he sat down next to her.

"You know I can't do that. It's against all my principles and beliefs. That's the quickest way to end a relationship, to live together."

"What if we made it so that it wasn't against your principles?"

Startled, she looked up at him and said, "What are you saying?"

"I'm saying that I love you. I've never known such happiness as I've had since I found you."

"Ian, what are you saying?" Laura repeated, still with a look of shock and disbelief.

"I'm saying that I want to spend the rest of my life with you."

She looked up at him without saying a word. She didn't have to; her questioning eyes told him that she didn't understand. "I'm saying that I want to live with you …" he paused and then added, "… as my wife."

After a thoughtful pause, she exclaimed, "Wow! And, I thought I was the impetuous one. Are you sure about this?"

"I'm absolutely certain," he replied.

He got off the sofa and got down on one knee. He took her hands and looked up into her eyes. "Laura Galbreath, will you please do me the honor of becoming my wife and making me the happiest man in Scotland?"

"Just Scotland?" she chirped.

"No, the whole damn world! Please tell me yes," he beseeched as he sat down beside her.

"I need some time to think about it," she said with a gleam in her eyes.

"Of course. How much time do you need?" Ian asked with a concerned look.

Tears flowing, she looked at him and spoke through her sobs, "About ten seconds."

He held her face, kissing away her tears. "Your ten seconds are up."

"Yes, darling, I will marry you," she cried as she clung to him. She didn't see it until she pulled her face away to look at him, but his tears were mixing with hers. She reached up and held his face and whispered, "I love you, Ian McKinney. I truly do." They tenderly kissed.

With an inquisitive look, she tilted her head. "Laura McKinney. Hmm, it doesn't sound bad. I think I can get used to it."

They both laughed and Ian said, "Good, because that will become your name very soon."

"How soon?" she purred.

"Well, I haven't thought this out, so tell me if you think this will work. I have a friend, Jared, who has a family diamond importing business. I'll call him tomorrow morning and we'll set an appointment. You can design the ring." He rubbed his chin and smiled. "Let's have the wedding in two weeks.

"Two weeks!" she shouted.

"Yes, two weeks from tomorrow. That will be October 4." He thought for a moment and then asked, "How important is it that you have Pastor Morton perform the ceremony?"

"Well, I'd certainly like him to do it. Why do you ask?"

"Now, I'm just offering this as a possibility, so think about it. Your parents are strong Catholics. What if we took your parents and Angus and Kathleen to Rome and we had the Pope marry us in St. Peter's Basilica? You could meet Cardinal Oleg and Cardinal Joseph and we could honeymoon in Italy."

She thought for a moment. "I think Tim would certainly understand. Would the Pope do that if we're not Catholic?"

"I think he might. I'll call Oleg tomorrow, tell him the good news and ask him."

"Ian, darling, that would be fantastic, being married by the Pope at St. Peter's."

"Yes, it would."

"Ian?" Laura asked with a demure look, "I have a favor to ask you. Can we have a baby?"

He thought for a moment. "No."

He saw her look of surprise and hurt. Then he added, "We can't have a baby." He emphasized the word a. "But we can have three or four."

They embraced as he again kissed away her tears.

The door opened and Kathleen and Angus walked into the room.

"I hope we're not interrupting," Kathleen queried as she observed Laura's joyful tears.

Laura looked at Ian with a questioning look. He nodded to her to go ahead.

"Kathleen and Angus, we have a surprise for you," Laura bubbled. "We're getting married!" She put her arms around Ian's waist and tightly held him.

A bright smile formed on Kathleen's face as she rushed to Laura and hugged her. "I'm so thrilled for both of you. I don't know if I can take many more surprises," she said with a laugh. "It's a shock that my stuffy brother even has a date. First, he's dating you, then he finds God after doing scientific research on the Shroud of Turin, then he tells us he's going to bring about the second coming of Jesus Christ, and now he's getting married. Please tell me that's all the surprises for tonight."

"Well, we do have another surprise for you. We're getting married two weeks from tomorrow."

"Two weeks!" Kathleen exclaimed. "What have you done to my deliberate, conservative brother?" she teased.

"It's his timetable, Kathleen. But there is another surprise."

Kathleen gave her a mock exasperated look, as if to ask what now.

"We're getting married in Rome." She paused for effect. "At St. Peter's Basilica." She paused again for further effect. "Pope John Paul II will perform the ceremony." She paused again, looking at the shocked looks on Kathleen's and Angus's faces. "And ..." she drew this out for further effect, "... we'd like both of you to stand up for us."

"Laura, is that it for tonight? Are there any more surprises?"

"Oh yes, I almost forgot. We're going to have a baby."

Kathleen's expression changed from amusement to shock. Laura suddenly realized what she had said and quickly added, "Oh, I don't mean now. I'm not pregnant," she stammered. "We haven't even … what I mean is … after we're married, we're going to try and have babies."

Ian started laughing at Laura and how she dug her way out of the hole she had put herself into.

"Now you see why I love her so much. Angus, I'm going to call Oleg tomorrow and see if the Pope might officiate the ceremony for us. Laura's parents are strong Catholics and it would be a thrill for them." Then he added, "As well as for us. And yes, we'd like you two to stand up for us."

Angus walked over to Ian, wrapped his burly arms around him and said, "Of course, we'll be there. We wouldn't miss it for the world."

"Now can we go home, Angus?" Kathleen jested. "I can't take all the drama in this house." They all bid their farewells with hugs and kisses.

After Angus left the cottage and he and Kathleen climbed into his car, he dialed a number on his cell phone.

After several rings, he said, "I want all four of you to continue to watch the house until daybreak. There will be extra pay for you. I'll meet you tomorrow at your place at four o'clock to make further plans. Let's arrange for some added help for the next several weeks."

———

Back in the house, Laura said, "Everything is so sudden, darling. I'm overwhelmed. What's your next step?"

Ian poured himself a large glass of Macallan and a smaller one for Laura.

"We'll spend tomorrow and Sunday formulating a plan for the project and for our ceremony after we talk to Oleg. We should go see your parents tomorrow so that I can ask your father's permission. There's a lot to do."

"You said 'we.' Would you like me to be there?"

"Absolutely I would, Laura. I want to be with you every minute." They sat on the sofa, snuggled next to each other for several hours, talking about the future and about all the things that had to be done over the next two weeks.

Ian was finishing his glass of Macallan when Laura suddenly blurted out, "Can we name our first son Andrew? I love the name. We can call him Andy."

"Yes, of course we can. You can be in charge of naming our children." Ian replied with a yawn. "It's been a long day. I'd best get you home."

"You are in no condition to drive, my dear. I'm spending the night here." She saw a sly smile creep across his face and added, "In your guest bedroom." She kissed him lightly and asked, "I'd like to take a warm shower. Do you have a long shirt I can use as a nightgown?"

"Yes, of course," he replied.

He went to his bedroom, got her a shirt, and escorted her to one of the guest bedrooms and showed her the attached bathroom. As she stood in the doorway, he kissed her goodnight and walked away to his room. As he left, he said, "I'll be dreaming about you tonight."

He, too, took a warm shower. He dried off, brushed his teeth, climbed into his bed and turned the light off. His mind raced over the day's events as he began drifting off to sleep.

He was not quite asleep when he heard his bedroom door open and he heard the soft padding of feet moving toward his queen-size bed. He felt the covers lift on the other side of the bed as he breathed in Laura's fresh scent.

She leaned against him and purred, "I was afraid in that strange room all by myself. Would you protect me?"

He responded by putting his arms around her and drawing her close. Their lips softly met, and he gently caressed her entire face. His breathing became deeper as he felt her breasts pressing against his chest through her shirt. She moved closer to him and pressed against him as her tongue sought his. Her breathing became more rapid as their passion grew. She removed her lips from his and whispered, "Darling, do you always sleep naked?"

"Yes," he responded, his warm breath softly caressing her cheek. "Could you tell?"

"Oh yes, I can tell." She paused and whispered, "Darling, can I ask a big favor of you. Can we wait for two weeks? Can we hold that final part back until we're married?"

He slowly replied after taking a deep breath, "Yes, we'll do whatever you want. I love you so much. I would never do anything to dishonor your wishes." He relaxed his hold on her and said, "But it'll be hard."

Before he could clarify his meaning, she whispered, "Darling, it already is. Maybe we can do something about that." She pulled slightly away and began unbuttoning and removing her shirt.

BROXBURN, SCOTLAND
SATURDAY, SEPTEMBER 20, 1997
7:23 A.M.

The morning sunlight was barely entering the room through the closed draperies, when Laura got out of bed, and went to the bathroom to brush her teeth.

Ian watched her as she returned to the bedroom, the soft morning sunlight dimly illuminating her lovely body. He took a deep breath as he felt enraptured by his love for her. As she crawled in next to him, he whispered, "You are incredibly beautiful. I never thought love could be so wonderful."

As their hands began seeking each other, she said, "Ian, your fingers are so gentle and loving. I've never felt such warmth and love as last night." She kissed him and softly said, "Do you have to call Oleg right away?"

"No," he said.

"Good," she said as her hand moved down his chest.

Later, after they had showered and dressed, he made breakfast. Ian gazed at her across the table.

"Why are you staring at me?" she asked.

"I didn't think it was possible, but I love you more today than I did yesterday. I feel like my heart is going to burst, just looking at you. I'm going to love spending the rest of my life with you."

"Darling, you make me so happy. Last night was wonderful, holding onto you all night and waking up next to you. I can't wait until we're married, and we can start making babies."

Beaming, Ian got up, kissed her and began to clear the dishes. "Now let's get to work. I'll call Oleg."

As expected, Oleg did not answer. Ian left a message that he had something extremely important to discuss with him and to please call him back as soon as possible. After hanging up, he went to his study and shortly returned with an armfull of files and reports.

"Since you're going to be my valued assistant for the attempted cloning, you need to read everything I've gathered on the Shroud. Start here with the history files and then you can move on to all the reports on the results from the different tests that have been conducted over the years. You can finish with the results from the tests that Angus and I ran several weeks ago. I'm going to prepare an inventory and budget of all the items we'll require, along with a budget for payroll and expenses. Also, why don't you call your parents and tell them that we'll take them out to dinner tonight. Let's pick them up at seven and you select the restaurant and make reservations."

As he set the files down on the table next to the sofa, he kissed her and said with a gentle smile, "Now get busy and earn that big salary. You've wasted half the morning."

"Once we're married, I can think of even better ways to waste half the mornings."

"Hmm, that sounds intriguing, but we'd have to work into the evenings to make up for that wasted time." He emphasized the word wasted with a sly smile.

"Done!" she pertly replied.

Shortly before noon, Oleg called. Ian informed him of their marriage plans and asked about the possibility of the Pope performing the marriage ceremony. "I am elated for you, my dear friend," Oleg congratulated. "Loleck is at the summer residence, but I'll call him immediately and call you back."

Laura was fascinated with the history of the Shroud and with the test results. "Darling, I'd like to see it. Do you think that could be possible?"

"I was thinking the same thing. I'll ask Oleg when he calls back." Ian responded. They spent the next several hours with their work until Oleg called. It was nearly four o'clock.

"His Holiness said he'd be delighted. The ceremony will be abbreviated, because you are not Catholics and will have to be performed in the evening after the Basilica is closed to the public."

"That's wonderful!" Ian exclaimed. He then told Oleg of their desire to see the Shroud and they made plans for Ian, Laura, Angus, and Kathleen to meet Oleg and Joseph at the cathedral in Turin to view the Shroud on Thursday morning before the wedding and then take an afternoon train to Rome. Laura's parents could fly in on Friday morning and everyone would meet with the Pope in his study on Friday evening.

Laura was thrilled with the plans. She got on the phone and profusely thanked Oleg, telling him she was extremely excited to meet him. After ending the call, Laura suggested, "Let's take Duffy for a long walk, before we pick up my parents."

During the ninety-minute walk, they talked about the Shroud and Ian explained the details of his testing. He was delighted with the enthusiasm that she had for the project.

As they walked along the quiet country lanes, they were blissfully unaware of the many sets of eyes observing them.

Angus's men were watching them while they surveyed the surrounding countryside, looking for any abnormal activity.

Unfortunately, none of Angus's four men were aware of the fifth pair of eyes that was watching Ian and Laura through powerful binoculars while their owner directed a long-range directional microphone toward the lovers. This man was a professional, unlike the other Middle Eastern man who had recently met his demise in a traffic accident east of Stirling. He smiled as he listened to bits and pieces of their conversation about the Shroud and about cloning. His superiors would find this information very interesting.

He felt certain it would not be long before he would be called upon to use his true skills.

———

After they returned to his cottage, Ian said, "We have a lot more planning and studying to do tomorrow and Angus and Kathleen want to meet with us. It's nearly time to leave for your parents. I'm going to quickly wash up."

Laura went to the guest bathroom and also washed up to get ready for the evening.

When they each returned to the gathering room, Laura put her arms around his neck and said, "Darling, why don't you bring a change of clothes and some toiletries and spend the night at my flat? We can go to church in the morning and then come back here to make plans."

"How could I say no to such a beautiful lady?" Ian said with a wide smile. "I'll call Angus and let him know of our plans."

———

They arrived at the Galbreaths' row house shortly before seven o'clock. "This is certainly kind of you to take us out to dinner, Dr. McKinney. Is there a special occasion?"

"Please, call me Ian. And I'd like to call you Alastair if I may."

Alastair responded that he certainly could do so.

"Yes, it is a special occasion, sir." Ian paused for a few seconds as he looked over at Laura's mother, Meg. She had a wide smile on her face as she eagerly waited for Ian to continue. "I'd like to ask you for permission to marry your daughter."

Alastair Galbreath stared at Ian with a serious expression. "You said that you'd like to ask. Well, for God's sake, man, go ahead and ask me."

Alastair broke out in a wide smile as Ian said, "May I have your permission to marry your daughter?"

Alastair looked at Meg, who had her hands up to her mouth, her eyes starting to moisten. Then he looked at Laura, who never looked happier and more beautiful to him. "That is fine, Ian, you have my permission. We're tired of her hanging around here all of the time," he said with a twinkle in his eyes. "But I need to ask you a question. Will you be making me a grandfather? This lassie is not getting any younger, you know."

"Yes, we will tend to that matter as soon as we're married."

"And when might that be?"

After Ian told him, he exclaimed, "Two weeks, you say." He thought for a moment and then followed, "That is fine. Meg, go get that bottle of whisky that Laura brought over. This calls for a celebration drink."

Meg brought out an unopened bottle of Macallan 18.

Ian looked at Laura with love in his eyes. "You continue to amaze me, Laura Galbreath."

"In two weeks, I'll be promising to take care of you. I thought I'd get a head start." Laura looked at her dad and said, "We have a lot more to tell you, but we'll save that for dinner."

After finishing their drinks, they left the house and drove to Alastair's favorite restaurant. While at dinner Laura told her parents about the wedding plans for Rome and how the ceremony would be performed by the Pope. Meg almost fainted when she realized this was not in jest.

"There's one other thing," Laura said. "We'll be moving to the United States within the next several months and we'll be there for several years. But we'd love to have you visit."

Meg's hands flew to her chest as she exclaimed, "Is this necessary?!"

Laura explained, "Ian will be doing some top-secret scientific research for the British and American governments with the blessing of the Vatican. That's all we can tell you, except that our wedding location at the Vatican and our move to America must remain private. No one must know. It's a matter of national security and if word were to get out, our lives and the lives of your future grandchildren would be at risk."

"Aye, we'll keep your secret as long as we can come see my grandson next year at this time," Alistair admonished.

Later, when Ian and Laura returned to her flat, she said, "Darling, I'm exhausted. Can we go right to bed?"

"I can think of nothing I'd rather do," he replied with a loving smile. She used the bathroom first, emerging after several minutes in a long soft flannel nightgown. She went straight to her large bed, crawled in and turned the light off.

"The bathroom is all yours, Dr. McKinney." After several minutes he walked through the darkness to her bed, pulled back the sheet, and crawled in. She snuggled up against him.

"I'm going to have to get used to you sleeping naked, my darling."

"I can put on shorts, if you would like," he said.

She was quiet for a moment and then said, "No, I think I like you the way you are. I'm the one that will have to change." She sat up and pulled her nightgown over her head. As she rested in his arms, she softly said, "Ian, I adore you." Her eyes closed as she drifted off to sleep.

He held her in the darkness, listening to her soft breathing, and whispered, "Thank you, God, for coming into my life and for bringing her to me."

She smiled and then fell asleep.

He soon followed.

TEL AVIV, ISRAEL
SUNDAY, SEPTEMBER 21, 1997
8:03 A.M.

"Here are the most recent developments from Scotland," the director informed Fox as they entered Danny Yatom's office. "Viper had an agent come up from London and they planted bugs in McKinney's house. Unfortunately, the bugs were immediately discovered, so they were useless. The next day, Viper found another Arab agent watching McKinney's house. From the description, it might have been your *friend* from Turin.

"On Friday night he observed the Arab while the Arab was surveilling the McKinney house. Viper discovered him setting up a high-powered rifle and it appeared that he was about to assassinate McKinney. The Roslin security man had some men watching the house, so Viper had to be careful. He didn't want to blow his cover, but he didn't want to allow the Arab to kill McKinney. So, he kept his cover and threw a large rock toward the assassin. Apparently, the Arab thought he was discovered and fled. This brought the security men quickly down on him. It was certainly fast thinking on Viper's part."

"What happened to the Arab?" Fox asked.

"Apparently, the security men killed him, put his body in his rental car and drove off. The next day, a fatal accident was reported about sixty miles away. Guess who the accident victim was." Yatom looked down as he folded his hands in his lap. "Viper is coming home tonight."

He looked straight at Fox and stated, "I'm bringing Research into this. I'm meeting with Avi Gur at 8:00 tomorrow morning. I'm going to introduce him to both you and Viper. Be here promptly at 8:15," he ordered.

EDINBURGH, SCOTLAND
SUNDAY, SEPTMEBER 21, 1997
10:16 A.M.

After the church service ended, Laura and Ian walked up to Pastor Morton and Laura said, "Tim, can we talk to you for a bit, in private?"

After he was finished greeting his parishioners, they went to his office. Tim had them comfortably seated and asked Laura what he could do for them.

"Tim, we're getting married in two weeks in Italy," Laura bubbled. "And we would like to have you give us premarriage counseling."

Tim was surprised and a little hurt over their wedding plans. But after he thought about it, he told them, "Of course, you must do that, what a thrill. I will be delighted to give you counseling, but it seems as though you will be pressed for time for the next ten days. I have a better idea," he said as he walked over to his bookshelf.

He pulled out a book, handed it to them and said, "Here, take this and read it together. It's called *The Five Love Languages*. It's written by an American, and a book that every couple should read. If they did, the divorce rate would be drastically reduced. You read it and discuss it together. It's better than any counseling I could give you in such a short period of time." He gave them each a hug as they left and said, "God bless you, Ian."

"He already has, Tim. He already has."

Ian and Laura returned to his cottage where she spent the afternoon reading the last of the Shroud reports. Ian finished his plans for the design of the laboratory at about the same time.

They began reading the book that Pastor Tim had given them. They read and discussed the first two love languages, *words of affirmation* and *quality time.*

Angus had called earlier and told Ian that they all had some important matters to discuss. They agreed to meet at the cottage at six o'clock and Kathleen would bring dinner.

As soon as they arrived, Angus pulled the drapes to the front window and swept the cottage for bugs. The house was clean. Ian poured a glass of whisky for everyone and asked Angus to begin the discussion.

Angus proclaimed, "The project has been compromised and I'm concerned for your safety."

Ian and Laura both looked startled and became more attentive.

Angus stood up and began pacing. "I'm going to tell you what really happened on Friday night. First, my men discovered a man across from your cottage. He was the same man who was watching us in Turin. He told us who he was working for, the same people that our friend from last July worked for. Like the first one, he was not very professional. However—and this is what worries me—he had a high-powered rifle set up on a tripod when my men found him. The rifle was aimed directly at your front window. I believe he was getting ready to kill you."

"Oh my God!" Laura exclaimed. No one spoke for a minute. "Where is he now?" Laura pleaded as her lips began to tremble.

Ian nodded with a knowing smile. "Who was he, Angus?"

"He worked for a Middle East group headed by a man referred to as The Director. We have no idea who this Director is."

"Laura, in answer to your question, we let him go," Angus replied. "But shortly after he left, he was in an unfortunate automobile accident over by Stirling. He didn't make it. I won't feel comfortable until we get you two married and we're all off to the United States. There's something else," he continued. "I'm quite certain this man acted alone. Laura said she saw two men getting into the utility truck when the house got bugged. And there was no trace of bugging equipment on this guy. He wasn't sophisticated enough to obtain a utility truck, let alone bug your house. Someone else did the bugging. I think there are at least two different groups interested in our project and at least one of them is deadly."

He paused to let his words sink in. "Laura, I want you to know I have teams of four men watching the cottage twenty-four hours a day. I also have a team watching your flat. There are no concerns while you are at work. It's the nights I'm worried about. From now on, I want to know each of your schedules, day and night. I'll have someone watching you every night. I know you've spent the last two nights together and I think that should continue. It will make our job much easier if you are together. It will also be much safer. At the first sign of an intruder, both of you will have to stay at the clinic in the guest quarters. Before Kathleen and I leave tonight, I want you both to write out your anticipated schedules for the next ten days until we all leave for Turin."

After Angus and Kathleen left, Laura asked Ian if he was worried. "No, Angus will protect us. Are you all right?"

"Yes, darling. I feel totally safe with you." She paused and then said with a sly grin, "On second thought, I am really scared. I'd like to go hide in bed where it's safe."

"That's an excellent idea, I'm a wee bit frightened myself," he murmured with a grin.

ROSLIN, SCOTLAND
MONDAY, SEPTEMBER 22, 1997
6:43 A.M.

They arrived at Laura's flat at daybreak so she could change clothes and drive to work. He watched her as she dressed, feeling an immense love that he never imagined could exist.

"Darling," she confessed, "I never thought I could feel so comfortable having a man watch me get dressed. Your eyes show so much love; I am so comfortable." She went to him, kissed him softly and gushed, "I love you so much and I'm so incredibly happy."

He was in his office for ten minutes before she arrived. "Good morning, Miss Galbreath," he said when she peeked into his office.

"Good morning, Dr. McKinney, did you have a nice weekend?" Before he could respond, she asked, "What do we have planned for today?"

"We're going to spend most of the next ten days in the laboratory getting you up to speed on the entire cloning process." He whispered to her, "I'll let you know when we have the meeting with my friend Jared. That takes precedence over anything."

They met with Jared at his shop in Edinburgh and spent nearly two hours learning about diamond clarity and quality. Finally, they selected a stone in excess of two carats and a beautiful setting with six baguette diamonds.

Ian told him they had to have the ring in three days. After some consternation, Jared promised that he would have the ring ready for them by the close of business on Thursday.

TEL AVIV, ISRAEL
MONDAY, SEPTEMBER 22, 1997
8:01 A.M.

Director Yatom welcomed the head of the research division of Mossad, Avi Gur, to his office and ushered him to his seating area.

After describing the Roslin File events of the past month, he instructed, "I'm having the two agents involved meet us here in a few minutes. As you are aware, the identity of our agents is highly classified. But I think it's important that you hear their report firsthand." Unsmiling, he added, "And, I know I can trust your discretion, Avi."

"Of course. That goes without saying."

"I will not disclose their names, as I will address them by their code names. The older is Fox while the younger is Viper."

"I've heard of the Fox; he's legendary."

"Yes, he is," Yatom responded. "He had a large role in the assassinations of most of the Palestinians responsible for the Munich Olympics massacre. You will remember too some of his other assignments: Yahya al-Mashad, Khalil Wazsir, and Gerald Bull among others. All these men had one thing in common, either they were murderers or were designing mass destruction weapons to be used against Israel."

Yatom reflected, "If only Metsada had been in existence in 1936, World War II might have been avoided with the assassination of Hitler."

"Why are you making this introduction?"

"I want you to meet with these two men and get a sense of what they experienced and what they learned. I have no idea what is going on, but I think it could be big. Incidentally, the younger agent, code name Viper, was responsible for the assignments on Salah Khalaf in 1991 and Yahya Ayyash last year. As you know, we had an extensive manhunt for years for that mass murderer of women and children."

After Yatom admitted Fox and Viper to his office and made the code name introductions to Avi Gur, he had them both relate their experiences with the Roslin project. Several times Avi interrupted to ask them about their impressions of the people they observed. When the agents were finished with their report, Avi concluded, "Danny, we'll research everyone involved as well as the Roslin Institute. That's about all we can do at this point. There just isn't much to go on."

Yatom noticed Fox rubbing his chin. "Do you have something to add, Fox?"

"Director, I have a theory. It's not very plausible, but it is a theory."

"Go on," Yatom directed.

"The cathedral in Turin where the cardinals and scientists met for five days is temporarily housing the Shroud of Turin. The Shroud of Turin is supposedly the death shroud of Jesus and has his image on it. It was proven to be a fake several years ago. What if it's not a fake? These scientists just got finished with cloning a sheep. What if they're searching for blood samples and are trying to clone the man on the shroud?"

"That's preposterous," Yatom exclaimed.

"I know it is. But give me another explanation that makes more sense."

DAMASCUS, SYRIA
TUESDAY, SEPTEMBER 23, 1997
3:44 P.M.

The leader, as always, sat at the head of the table. He addressed his four friends with flaring nostrils, "Salam is dead." After silencing the room, he continued.

"He was killed in a car crash. I'm getting tired of these car crashes and I'm tired of my friends being killed. I'm contacting Nasrallah and asking him to reach out to The Director. I want this McKinney dead," he stated grimly.

EDINBURGH, SCOTLAND
WEDNESDAY, SEPTEMBER 24, 1997
7:12 P.M.

Ian had arranged a dinner meeting with Dr. Graham, having told him there were some serious items he'd like to discuss in private and in confidence. They decided on drinks and dinner at the Doric. Located on Market Street, across from Waverly Station, The Doric had been one of Edinburgh's finest restaurants for more than thirty-five years.

Seated in a private room off the main dining room, Duncan and Ian enjoyed their drinks. Angus sat at a table in a corner of the dining room where he silently watched the other diners.

After they placed their dinner orders, Ian confided, "Duncan, you've been wonderful to me over the years, and what I'm about to do is extremely difficult for me. I have loved my work at the institute, and I've been extremely satisfied, but I have to submit my resignation."

Dr. Graham slowly nodded and said, "I'm not totally surprised by this, Ian. Tell me about events since the cardinals left."

Ian's eyes widened, but then he smiled. He knew Duncan to be a man of great insight. He proceeded throughout dinner to describe everything that had occurred, except for his relationship with Laura. He'd get to that later.

"Duncan," he concluded, "I have to pursue this. It's not just a scientific breakthrough for me now. It's a major part of my personal discovery quest. I've seen the face of Jesus and he has come into my life. I must continue to seek him."

"I'll miss you both, but it's good that Angus is going with you. You may need the protection. There are different factions out in this world that would stop at nothing to see that your project fails. You've already experienced a near-assassination." Duncan reflected for a moment. "Ian, do the good cardinals know you are confiding in me?"

"Yes, they do, Duncan. We all thought it best that you be made aware of the project."

"Hmm, I guess that's for the best, Ian."

"Duncan, there's one other important matter that requires my explanation. Laura Galbreath and I are going to be married in ten days."

"Now, that is a surprise," Duncan responded with genuine astonishment.

"I want to assure you that the retroactive raise and promotion that I gave her occurred before I had any thought of starting a relationship with her."

He proceeded to tell Duncan about the development of their relationship, its suddenness, and its depth. When he described his vision at their picnic, Duncan became enthralled. Ian went on to describe the wedding and security plans and informed Duncan that he and Laura would like to tender their resignations after they returned from their honeymoon. Duncan agreed to the schedule.

"We'll work with whatever schedule best suits you, my friend," Duncan said as he started laughing. "Forgive me, Ian, but it's all so humorous. I'm the devout Catholic head of a scientific institute who declines to break any moral or religious boundaries. And, you are the atheist scientist who befriends the Pope and his two highest-ranking cardinals and agrees to push science over the limits of propriety. And to top it off, the Pope is personally going to marry you and your fiancée of only several weeks. This is quite astounding."

They both laughed as they raised their glasses and clinked them together.

"Ian, of a serious nature, I will assist you in whatever way possible over the next months as long as we do not compromise the institute. I wish you happiness in your marriage. I am delighted to see that you are finding God, and I wish you safety in your endeavors. Once you leave, you can have no more contact with the institute. I will pray for you, my friend."

ROSLIN, SCOTLAND
FRIDAY, SEPTEMBER 26, 1997
8:18 A.M.

Ian and Laura went downstairs to the human resources department and walked straight into Shannon's office without being announced. Laura stood before her and lifted her left hand in front of her, flashing her new ring.

Shannon screamed in excitement. "Have you set a wedding date yet?"

"Yes, a week from tomorrow," Laura answered.

"A week from tomorrow!" Shannon burst out.

"Yes, in Rome. We leave on Wednesday."

"I'm so thrilled for both of you."

It didn't take long for word to spread throughout the institute. Ian and Laura received well wishes throughout the day from countless coworkers, including Duncan Graham.

DAMASCUS, SYRIA
MONDAY, SEPTEMBER 29, 1997
8:38 P.M.

The leader declared, "I learned this afternoon that Nasrallah received approval from The Director to kill McKinney. However, it's now out of our hands." His shoulders slumped as he sighed. "He wants us out of it."

After a long exhale, he muttered, "He's having Nasrallah hire a professional. This kind of man does not come cheap, but The Director agreed to pay for it. That's all I know at this time."

EDINBURGH, SCOTLAND
WEDNESDAY, OCTOBER 1, 1997
11:16 A.M.

As Ian sat at their departure gate with Laura, Angus, and Kathleen, he reflected on the past five days.

Laura read every bit of material Ian had given her regarding the Shroud, as well as every article on the internet that dealt with the subject. She then finished studying all the files and reports that the institute had produced on the Dolly Project.

Ian also had used the time to his advantage. He completed his design of the laboratory and clinic as well as the budget for its completion and ongoing operation, including the compensation costs for Laura and himself as well as Angus and Kathleen. These were generous amounts that would comfortably take care of all of them for life. He budgeted a large amount for the anticipated expenses of finding doctors who would refer their patients and the associated costs of childbirth along with a sizeable amount to take care of the family after the birth.

Laura, at one point, asked, "Where do you think we'll live in the States?"

"I haven't given that a lot of thought yet. Where would you like to live?"

Laura thought for a moment and then exulted, "I don't care, as long as I'm with you."

During the past five days Ian and Laura finished reading and discussing *The Case for Christ*. Ian felt that it brought out a lot of strong points which he had never considered, while Laura felt even more confirmed in her faith.

They also finished reading and discussing *The Five Love Languages*, the book Pastor Tim had given them. Ian had concluded, "Laura, I can see why Pastor Tim gave us this book. It makes so much sense how we need to recognize each other's needs and how to fulfill them. It's amazing that our two love languages are the same."

There was an air of excitement as the four of them sat waiting to board the plane for the flight to Turin. Laura and Kathleen were going to see the Shroud, Angus and Kathleen were going to participate in the wedding ceremony, and Laura and Ian were on their way to the official start of their married life together.

Kathleen leaned over to Ian and said, "Ian, there is something I want to say to you. I've always admired you for your accomplishments and I've always loved you because you're my brother. But now, I also love you for the person that you've become. You two really do deserve each other. I'm so incredibly happy for both of you, and I'm so excited about being able to be so close to you over the next few years."

"I love you, too, Kathleen." He reached for her hand and smiled. "I don't think I've ever told you that." He looked down at his lap and mumbled, "I'm sorry."

"There's nothing to be sorry about, Ian."

Laura overheard their conversation and beamed.

TURIN, ITALY
THURSDAY, OCTOBER 2, 1997
8:02 A.M.

Angus made certain they were not followed as they took a taxi to the cathedral. He had the driver drop him off three blocks away before continuing with Ian, Laura, and Kathleen. He waited for several minutes as he closely observed the ongoing traffic and the pedestrians. As he walked to the piazza, he continued to study his surroundings and the activity.

Moments later, the cardinals arrived. Ian started to make introductions, but Angus quickly interrupted him and suggested they immediately go into the cathedral and make the greetings.

———

Once inside, Ian introduced Kathleen and Laura to Cardinal Ratzinger who kindly greeted each lady. He then introduced them to Cardinal Jaropelk.

Oleg warmly greeted Kathleen and then turned to Laura and took her hands, "Ian understated your beauty, my child. I am so thrilled to meet you and I am so happy for the both of you. I truly believe that God has brought you two together."

Oleg turned to Ian, gave him a strong hug, and said, "It's wonderful to see you, my friend. So much has happened to you since our last meeting. I'm anxious to hear the details. I've made the arrangements for the six of us to have a private compartment on the train to Rome this afternoon. The train departs at 12:45 p.m. so we need to leave here by eleven o'clock to gather everyone's luggage and get to the station. We'll have five hours to talk in privacy on the train. Now, if I may be so fortunate as to escort these two lovely ladies downstairs to your workroom, let's show them the Shroud." Oleg reached out each arm for Kathleen and Laura to grasp as he led the way.

Laura looked up at him and said with a warm smile, "I can see why Ian loves you, Oleg."

Oleg stopped walking and stood still as a bright smile lit up his entire face. He warmly replied, "Thank you, my child. That warms my heart."

As they approached the door to their former lab where they had spent five days working, Oleg explained, "We have the Shroud displayed just as Ian and Angus first saw it. You are free to examine it, but I ask you to be careful."

The guards opened the door and admitted them. The room was dimly lit except for the lights shining on the display on the far side of the room. Laura gasped as she slowly walked up to the Shroud, not taking her eyes off the image.

As she stood before it, she sank to her knees and asked Oleg if she could touch it. He gave his permission and she leaned forward and lightly kissed the linen. "This covered the body of our Savior," she said as tears began streaming down her face. She stood up and went to Ian and hugged him. "Thank you, darling, for letting us see this."

She turned to Oleg, the tears still flowing and said, "I've never hugged a cardinal, may I?"

"Of course, my dear. I would be honored."

She put her arms around his neck and held her cheek next to his. "Thank you so much, Oleg, for letting us see this. It brings a whole new meaning to the work we'll be doing." She moved away and saw that her tears had dampened his cheeks. "I'm sorry," she said as she reached into her purse, brought out a tissue and wiped his cheek.

"Think nothing of it, my child. I love tears of happiness and joy. It's the tears of sadness that I find difficult."

They spent the morning looking at and discussing the Shroud. Oleg related its history as Kathleen and Laura asked him questions. Laura already knew the answers, but she wanted to make Oleg feel good about his history lesson.

As it was time to leave, Laura said, "This is the most spectacular thing I have ever seen." She again went up to the Shroud, knelt before it and kissed it.

"It has this effect on many people," Oleg said. "I believe it to be the most holy relic known to man."

As they walked through the cathedral, Laura turned to face the altar, then knelt and genuflected. As she stood up, she saw a surprised expression on Oleg's face. "I was raised Catholic," she said to Oleg. "I'm sorry."

"There's nothing to be sorry about, Laura. What is important is that you are a Christian and you know Jesus. What is also important is you are there for Ian as he finds his way and makes his discoveries."

Oleg glanced at Cardinal Ratzinger and noted his frown at what he had said.

Oleg and Joseph had many discussions over the years on Christianity and had several divergent opinions. Oleg believed what was of paramount importance was that a person believe in God first and secondly, believe in Christ as the Savior. He also believed, contrary to orthodox Christian belief, that one need not be a Christian to reach Heaven and that being a Christian did not automatically enable one to gain entry.

Joseph believed that the Catholic Church was the true Church, that one had to be a Christian to gain entrance to Heaven, and that non-Catholics were misled and were almost to be considered heretics. Despite these differences, they had become and remained close friends.

Once on the train and in their comfortable compartment, Angus swept the area for bugs, finding nothing. He excused himself and went for a walk through the cars observing the passengers. There was nothing alarming. When he returned, he suggested that Ian tell the cardinals of their plans about moving to the States and getting started on their search for a building and homes to purchase.

After relating the details of their plans, Ian gave Oleg an itemized budget, in code, of the proposed expenses. "As soon as you get situated, you can set up the encryption machine at your end and we can talk. Once you have the lab set up, we can ship you the blood and DNA samples."

Angus interjected, "I think you should ship them in separate shipments at different times. And, just to be absolutely safe, I think you should keep some at the Vatican in total security and protection."

"I totally agree," Joseph concurred.

After their lengthy discussion, Oleg said, "Now, let's talk about wedding plans. Angus, we have a suite at the Vatican for you and Kathleen. Ian, we have a room for you and a room for Laura. Laura, we'll have a driver take you to the airport tomorrow to pick up your parents. We also have a suite for your parents. On Saturday night, I've arranged for you to have the bridal suite at the Grand Hotel de la Minerve in Rome. I didn't think you would want to spend your wedding night at the Vatican," he said with a sly smile.

He continued, "Also, I have brochures for several resorts that you might want to consider for your honeymoon. They all have space available for you." Oleg paused as Laura told him how kind he was to do that. "I have another little surprise for you two. Your entire honeymoon stay will be paid for in advance. That is Loleck's, Giuseppe's, and my wedding present for you."

"You two are such wonderful men," Laura gushed. "I can't thank you enough." She thought deeply for a moment and then said, "Oleg, your real first name is Aleksandr, isn't it?" He nodded. "Well, we've already named our first boy Andrew. I've always loved your name. If we have a girl, I'd like to name her Alexandra, after you. Would you mind?"

"Would I mind?" he enthused. "I'd be thrilled and honored!"

"Fine," she bubbled. "Andrew and Alexandra it is. We'll begin to tend to that matter on Saturday night." Oleg lightly chuckled as Joseph blushed.

"I told you she was impetuous, Oleg," Ian said, "and that she might surprise you."

"No, Ian, I find her delightfully refreshing. I'm just glad that I didn't meet her fifty years ago, otherwise I might not have gone into the priesthood."

"Fine, then that's settled." Laura said through the laughter as she stood up and went and sat down next to Oleg. She put her arm through his and said, "Our first girl will be named Alexandra and I can't wait for you to meet her."

She continued to hold Oleg's arm as she rested her head back and closed her eyes. Oleg looked at Ian, sitting across from him with a fulfilled deeply happy look on his face.

"I'm so happy for you my friend; I'm so happy for you."

THE VATICAN
FRIDAY, OCTOBER 3, 1997
6:00 P.M.

Ian and Laura, Angus and Kathleen, Alastair and Meg Galbreath, together with Oleg and Joseph, were ushered through the Papal apartments to John Paul's study.

Meg was incredibly nervous as she walked up to the Pontiff and kissed his ring. She was followed by her husband and Laura.

John Paul graciously welcomed them and said to Laura, "I'm so delighted to meet you, my child. I greatly admire Ian and I am thrilled for his recent discoveries."

Laura wasn't sure if he meant Ian's discoveries concerning the Shroud or his personal spiritual discoveries. After spending the next thirty minutes getting acquainted, Oleg informed John Paul that he and Joseph, Ian and Laura, along with Angus and Kathleen, needed a few more minutes with him.

The Pope concluded the meeting with a short prayer, blessing tomorrow's wedding and their project. Joseph escorted Laura's parents back to their suite and returned to John Paul's office.

What was to be a few short minutes turned into a meeting lasting more than an hour.

GENEVA, SWITZERLAND
FRIDAY, OCTOBER 3, 1997
7:00 P.M.

The twelve formally dressed men and two women, all from different countries, sat at their customary chairs around the horseshoe-shaped table in the formal banquet room.

The host greeted them. "I welcome you again to my chalet and I apologize for the urgency of our meeting. I realize this summons is an inconvenience and that most of you have traveled a great distance to be here. I trust that you are all comfortable in your usual suites. As is customary, I will pass out a package detailing the issue before us while my staff takes drink orders. After we discuss the issue, I will collect your packages and we will proceed to the dining room for dinner where all discussion of the issue will cease until we meet tomorrow evening at this time. As usual, following dinner Cuban cigars and brandy will be served after which I invite you to take advantage of my home and its facilities."

After passing out the envelopes, the host waited for ten minutes while his fellow members of The Alliance read and digested the contents while their drinks were served. "Members, the situation before us is unprecedented. In my opinion, this cloning project must be stopped immediately. The question before us is, do we issue a sanction and, if so, on whom. I will open discussion and take questions."

The ninety-minute discussion centered on the future ramifications of the project and the implications of sanctions placed on cardinals of the Church, as well as the Pope.

THE VATICAN
SATURDAY, OCTOBER 4, 1997
6:02 P.M.

The day was spent touring St. Peter's Basilica and the Sistine Chapel with Oleg and Joseph acting as tour guides. Ian and Angus were amazed, even though this was their second visit in a matter of months.

Laura's parents were in awe; this was a dream come true for them. Kathleen repeatedly commented on the wonderous works of art while Laura was nearly speechless throughout the tour.

At one point, as they stood in front of the baldachin in St. Peter's, Laura looked up at the cupola, tightly holding Ian's arm and said, "God has answered all of my prayers."

"This is an amazing structure," Ian responded.

"That isn't what I meant, darling," she replied. "I'm talking about you. Tonight, I will become Mrs. Laura McKinney. I am so incredibly blessed." She sparkled as Ian held her tightly.

Oleg noticed her smile and walked over to her. "I'm so happy for the two of you. I truly believe that God has brought you together and I'm so looking forward to becoming a part of your lives over the years." This brought wide smiles to both Ian and Laura. "As a matter of fact," he added, "I can picture this beautiful little girl named Alexandra sitting on my lap, calling me Uncle Oleg."

Pope John Paul II conducted the wedding ceremony in English for the benefit of the participants. It was a short ceremony, conducted without a mass. The surroundings, the participants, and especially the Pope conducting the event made it a memorable occasion. Laura, of course, had tears in her eyes, as did Kathleen and Meg Galbreath. Ian, Angus, and Oleg bore wide smiles, while Joseph and Alastair sported stoic looks of pride.

After the ceremony, they all walked across the piazza to the Pope's private apartments for a small reception. Appetizers and wine were served before they sat down to a sumptuous dinner. After dinner, everyone toasted the new bride and groom.

John Paul announced, "I would like to salute this lovely couple, however, I've been told that I don't have the proper material." One of the waitstaff, on cue, brought in a bottle of Macallan 25.

John Paul added, "I limit my alcohol consumption to an occasional glass of wine, but Oleg tells me that I must try a, what do you call it, a wee dram."

After their glasses were filled, the Pope toasted Ian and Laura McKinney, wishing them a lifetime of happiness. He concluded by saying, "And, may your lives be filled with the sound of many happy and healthy children." He added, with a twinkle in his eyes, "And, may some of them become Catholic." This brought smiles and warm laughter to the room.

As the festivities ended, the Galbreaths and the MacGregors paid their respects to John Paul and were escorted to their accommodations by Joseph and Oleg. As Oleg departed, he hugged both Ian and Laura, and said, "I will see you both back here in ten days. Have a wonderful time and don't think about business."

Ian and Laura spent a last moment with John Paul, who said, "It's been decades since I've performed a marriage ceremony. Laura, my child, you bring much joy to this old man."

"You're not old," she gently replied. "You're beautiful." She reached up and kissed him on the cheek. A warm smile crossed his face as he bid them farewell.

———————

It was nearly ten o'clock when they arrived at the Grand Hotel de la Minerve and were shown to the honeymoon suite.

As they entered the suite, Laura became mesmerized by the scene before her. Their luggage had been delivered and they found a large bouquet of fresh flowers and a chilled bottle of Dom Perignon awaiting them. The lights were dim, casting a soft glow throughout the living room. Laura quickly counted twelve candles burning throughout the suite, emitting a sweet jasmine scent. Soft romantic music was playing through the television system.

"Oh, Ian," she said, "this is so perfect." She went to the windows and looked out at the evening lights of Rome. "This is such a gorgeous city. We have to come back here some day and really get to know it."

Before he could reply, she rushed to the bedroom and then the bathroom and marveled, "Darling, look at this."

As he joined her, he found an enormous bathroom with the focal point being the largest bathtub he had ever seen. The entire room was done in white marble including the tub. Placed on the ledge next to the tub were several scented bath oils, bubble bath mixture, bathing sponges, shaving equipment and six more scented candles.

"Well, Miss Galbreath, this is the night we've been waiting for," Ian said as he took her hands and looked lovingly into her eyes.

"Yes, it is, Dr. McKinney. But my name isn't Miss Galbreath any longer. It's Mrs. McKinney, Mrs. Laura McKinney, so I am all yours," she purred. "Darling, I'd like to freshen up by taking a hot bubble bath.

That tub looks so inviting." She looked up at him with an alluring smile. "But, it's so big for just me, I'm afraid I might slip under and drown. Do you suppose you might join me and protect me?" Before he could respond, she gushed, "Good, I'll prepare the tub."

She turned on the water and started filling the tub, adding the bubble bath mixture and scented oils. After several minutes the tub was filled and covered with a thick layer of glistening scented bubbles. Laura murmured, "Why don't you get out of that business suit and climb in, I'll be back in a few minutes. I'm going to make myself beautiful for you."

She kissed him softly. "See you soon."

"It's impossible for you to be any more beautiful, Mrs. McKinney," Ian said as he started to remove his clothes. He climbed in the tub and felt his muscles immediately relax.

After several minutes Laura appeared in the doorway, wearing a sheer white nightgown with a low-cut front. The soft lights behind her silhouetted the soft curves of her body as she slowly walked toward him. He caught his breath as he watched her approach the tub and slowly remove the nightgown. She stood in front of him for a moment before climbing into the tub.

As she sat in front of him, she leaned back against him, and rested her head on his shoulder. Amazingly, she shivered in the hot water as the sensuality of the moment engulfed her senses. He put his arms around her and gently cupped her breasts as he whispered, "I never thought it was possible to love someone as much as I love you."

"Ian, I never want this feeling to end."

She laid her head back on his shoulder and lost herself in splendor as he softly caressed her with his fingertips. They changed positions several times as they kissed and expressed their love with soft touches and gentle strokes.

At one point as she caressed his face, she reached for the razor and said, "I'd like to shave you." With careful strokes, she began to tenderly shave what little growth there was since his morning shave. She leaned against him, her chest pressing against his as she moved her lips over each area of his face that she had finished shaving. After several minutes she completed her task and whispered, "Now you're totally smooth."

As she sat back and lovingly looked at him, he took the razor from her, lifted her right leg, put it on his shoulder and kissed her toes. With loving tenderness, he gently stroked her leg with slow deliberate strokes of the razor. After each stroke, he moved his fingertips over her leg to make sure he had not missed even the smallest area.

"Oh my…" she moaned. "That is the most sensuous feeling I could ever imagine." She closed her eyes and said, "Can we make this a habit?" After several minutes she purred, "Darling, I think we've had enough bubbles for the evening." He readily agreed as they both stood up in the tub. He reached for a towel and began drying her off. Again, she shivered as he tenderly dried off her entire body.

When he was finished, she reached for another towel and began to dry him off. Her eyes never left his as she gently dried him. As she brought the towel around to the front, she displayed a tenderness that made him suck in his breath. Stepping out of the tub they finished drying each other. They put the towels down and walked hand in hand into the bedroom and to the king-size bed that awaited them.

As they stood before the bed, Ian tenderly held her face in both of his hands, gazed into her eyes, and softly kissed her lips. The kiss became longer and more passionate and they sank onto the bed, their bodies seeming to melt together. His eyes never left hers as he stroked her cheeks, their bodies pressed together. His fingertips left her cheeks, making soft circles down her neck to her shoulders and onto her back.

As his warm, loving hands moved around to her front, she lay back with her head on the pillow and her eyes closed. He gently stroked her breasts, drawing circles with his fingertips. Moving his hand down her side to her stomach, he continuously caressed her skin with his soft fingertips. He moved his hands over to her hips as he kissed her breasts. He brought his lips slowly down to her navel as his fingers kept making small circles down the outside of her thighs to her calves. As his fingers moved to the inside of her calves, and then to her inner thighs, he brought his lips down and softly kissed her. Her entire body shuddered as she experienced an ecstasy that was previously unimaginable.

"Darling, please," she panted as she reached the height of rapture. As he entered her, he felt a warmth and closeness to her that he never imagined possible. They were still for several moments, remaining in that position, savoring the euphoric and spiritual feeling that engulfed their senses. As they consummated their love for the first time, a rich feeling of loving fulfillment swept over them.

They had no way of knowing that the love they had so beautifully expressed for each other had just created new life.

GENEVA, SWITZERLAND
SATURDAY, OCTOBER 4, 1997
7:14 P.M.

After drinks were served and the wait staff dismissed, the host began, "I open the floor to discussion before I put forward a motion for a vote."

The discussion was brief. The host continued, "Gentlemen and ladies, in my opinion we cannot issue a sanction on cardinals of the Church at this time. However, I am putting forward a motion that we issue sanctions on Dr. McKinney and his new wife. We cannot allow the wife to live as she has undoubtedly participated in the cloning project."

After several questions about the timing and the method, the host replied, "The sanctions must be made to look like accidents and must be conducted as soon as possible. Should you vote to authorize these sanctions, I will contact our serpent friend and have him gather his forces to complete the task. Of course, he knows nothing of The Alliance or its fifteen members. Are you prepared to mark the ballot placed in front of you?"

They were.

The host got up from his chair at the center of the head table and walked around to each member and collected the ballots. The host counted the ballots and then handed them to the member to his right to validate the results.

"Gentlemen and ladies, the vote is all fourteen of you voted for sanction. I will commence with the operation. Are there any final questions?"

A member from the Far East stood. "What do we know of this assassin? We don't even know his code name, other than it's a poisonous snake. What does he know of our organization? Is there any way he can be traced to us?"

"I know nothing of this man other than his code name, although I suspect he might be from Central or South America. He knows nothing of me or The Alliance. His fee is wired to his account in the Cayman Islands. I have attempted to trace the funds from there but lost it after its third transfer. We go through a series of six fund transfers before his fee reaches the Cayman Islands. Now, let us proceed to the dining room for dinner and no more will be spoken of this operation."

ISCHIA, ITALY
SUNDAY, OCTOBER 5, 1997
2:14 P.M.

Ian and Laura arrived at the Hotel Mezzatorre Resort and Spa and were led to the honeymoon suite. Once again, they found flowers waiting for them along with several bottles of Macallan 25.

As they entered their suite, they were amazed by the accommodations. In addition to their large bedroom and luxurious bathroom, they had a large living room and a private garden with a small private pool and Jacuzzi. From their garden, they enjoyed a superb view of the Gulf of Naples and the Isle of Capri.

They spent the next eight days in splendor, not only in the surroundings but in each other. They visited Capri and the Blue Grotto. They spent an entire day with a private tour of Pompeii and spent another day in the beautiful town of Sorrento. They swam and hiked, took thermal baths, had several massages and savored the elegant dining. For eight wonderful days, they luxuriated in their love of the area and in their love for each other.

DAMASCUS, SYRIA
WEDNESDAY, OCTOBER 8, 1997
7:49 P.M.

Once again, the leader brought his four remaining men up-to-date. "I've been told this is the last information I will receive about this matter. A professional has been hired and he went to Scotland, only to find that McKinney has again traveled to Rome. He learned that McKinney and his wife are spending time at an island resort near Naples. Apparently, the assassin doesn't like the island location for his assignment, so he's returning to Scotland where he will prepare for their return."

"What do you know of this assassin?" inquired one of his men.

"I only know that he's very thorough and professional and that he knows nothing of the reason for his assignment. Oh, yes, I also know he has the code name of a deadly snake."

TEL AVIV, ISRAEL
SATURDAY, OCTOBER 11, 1997
3:12 P.M.

"Gentlemen," Yatom seethed, "our sources tell us that a professional assassin has been sent to Edinburgh. This Shroud matter is getting out of hand. McKinney and his new wife are due back in Edinburgh next week. I'm sending you both there to end this matter. You know what you must do. Gather as many men as you think you'll need from our London office."

THE VATICAN
TUESDAY, OCTOBER 14, 1997
3:51 P.M.

Ian and Laura were warmly greeted by Oleg and Joseph as they returned to the Vatican from their unforgettable honeymoon. They had an early dinner and spent the evening discussing last-minute details of the project and their pending move to the United States.

TEL AVIV, ISRAEL
TUESDAY, OCTOBER 17, 1997
4.23 P.M.

"Viper," Director Yatom spoke on the telephone on their secured line. "I'm sending some men up from London. We're hearing noise that Nasrallah has called for a professional. We're also hearing noise about another group but don't know who they are."

LONDON, ENGLAND
WEDNESDAY, OCTOBER 15, 1997
7:33 A.M.

The team of six men were given instructions for their travel to Edinburgh. Two were to depart immediately for their four-hundred-mile drive while the other four would travel by train, seated in separate cars. They were given directions to the safe house where they were to meet and await further instructions.

ROSLIN, SCOTLAND
THURSDAY, OCTOBER 16, 1997
8:07 A.M.

As they drove past the security gate of the Roslin Institute, Ian and Laura saw a large banner spread across the front of the main building, stating *Welcome back, Ian and Laura.* A wide smile came to her face as she held onto his arm.

When they entered the building, they were met by dozens of their fellow employees who greeted them with hugs and kisses. During the day they had a lengthy meeting with Dr. Graham and Angus. They caught up on telephone messages and correspondence and what little work that awaited them.

LINLITHGOW, SCOTLAND
SUNDAY, OCTOBER 19, 1997
2:16 P.M.

The newlyweds arrived at the ruins of Linlithgow Palace at the end of a busy weekend. They had spent Friday at the institute catching up on their work and most of Saturday with Laura's parents. Meg and Alastair were still excited about their visit to the Vatican and all the surrounding events.

Sunday morning Ian and Laura attended church, followed by a meeting with Pastor Tim. They discussed the book he had given them and how they discovered their love languages were identical. They described their wedding ceremony, omitting the fact that the Pope was the officiant, their tour of the Vatican, and their wondrous honeymoon.

After leaving the church, they drove back to the cottage to change clothes and pack a lunch. They had decided to spend the afternoon having a picnic.

Looking up at the ruins of the massive four-story castle, Laura marveled, "Ian, I've never been here; this is amazing."

"Darling, if you're going to be married to me, you're going to learn more of your country's history." As they entered the massive courtyard and walked through the structure, he described its history. "The palace was once the most magnificent castle in all of Scotland. It was home to many of the kings and queens and was the birthplace of Mary, Queen of Scots."

Laura listened with rapt attention. "I'm amazed by your knowledge of Scottish history. But why is it a ruin? Why wasn't it maintained?"

"That's a wonderful question. Sadly, the British troops gutted it and set it on fire in their search for Bonnie Prince Charlie after his defeat at Culloden in 1746."

She winced. "Such a waste."

"Yes, it is," he grimaced.

After completing their tour, he turned to her. "Let's walk out to the lake and have our picnic and talk about happier thoughts." They spent the afternoon playing with Duffy, talking about the future of the project and their future together.

As the sun started to lower and the fall temperature dropped, Laura felt a slight chill as the sun ducked behind a large cloud. "We should be going," Laura suggested.

After gathering their picnic supplies, they stood gazing at the awesome castle across the green expanse of lawn, oblivious to everything but themselves. Suddenly, she reached up, threw her arms around his neck and kissed him lovingly.

"What was that for, Mrs. McKinney?" he asked.

"It's been such a perfect day and I love you so much."

Hand in hand, they walked across the lawn to their car. Ian carried the picnic basket and blanket while Laura led Duffy on his leash.

"Let's drive back a different way," Ian remarked as they climbed in his Land Rover. "There's a little used country road that goes through some lovely countryside."

As they drove out of the parking lot and turned south into the town of Linlithgow, two cars followed them.

After driving through the town, they entered the pastoral countryside. "This is a pleasant drive," Laura remarked, gazing at the passing hedgerows.

Ian was silent.

She glanced at Ian and saw a concerned look on his face. "Are you all right?" she questioned. He was staring into the rearview mirror.

Instinctively, she turned around. Eyes widening, she saw a large black sedan behind them.

Turning to Ian, she saw him transfixed on his driving on the narrow road. Looking behind at the black sedan again, her face turned ashen as she saw it rapidly gaining on them.

Ian slowed down and pulled as far to the left as he could to let the car pass them. As the car pulled alongside, Laura looked over and gasped as she saw four men staring at them. The car stayed even with them for a moment and then sped ahead.

A bolt of fear flashed through her as she tightly gripped her knees.

When the black sedan was about ten meters in front of them, the driver suddenly slammed on his brakes and swerved sideways, totally blocking the road. Her hands lurched for the dashboard as Ian slammed on his brakes. When he thrust the gears into reverse, she turned to look behind.

She cried out as she saw a second car blocking the road from behind. They had no room to maneuver.

Things were happening so quickly.

Four men rushed out of the first car followed by two men from the second car. As they approached Ian's Land Rover, Laura exclaimed, "They're carrying guns."

Laura grabbed hold of Ian's arm as he looked down at her. "Stay here!" he ordered as he opened his door to confront the men.

Less than an hour later, darkness was falling when the owner of a distant farmhouse happened to be outside and saw smoke and the glow of flames over by the country road leading from Linlithgow.

ROSLIN, SCOTLAND
MONDAY, OCTOBER 20, 1997
1:41 P.M.

Duncan Graham was working at his desk when Mrs. Morrison knocked on his office door and nudged it open.

"Dr. Graham, you have a couple of visitors." He looked up with an inquisitive look. "There are two policemen here to see you," she continued.

"By all means, show them in," he responded as he wrinkled his forehead.

They walked in and introduced themselves as Inspector Douglas and Lieutenant Armstrong of the Edinburgh Police Department.

"How can I assist you gentlemen?" Duncan questioned. He noticed that Mrs. Morrison was standing by the door. "But, first, may I offer you some coffee or tea?"

"No, thank you, sir. I'll get right to the point," replied the inspector. "You have an Ian McKinney working at the institute?"

"Yes."

"I'm afraid there's been an accident, Dr. Graham."

"What kind of accident? Is he all right?"

"I'm afraid not, sir," the inspector replied. Standing at the doorway, Mrs. Morrison let out an audible gasp.

"There was an automobile accident late yesterday afternoon, west of the city near Linlithgow. I'm sorry to have to tell you that it was a fatal accident involving two people, and, oh yes, a dog."

Duncan sank into his chair while Mrs. Morrison began sobbing. "We were able to get the VIN number of the automobile although it took some doing." The inspector paused as he watched Duncan's reaction of grief.

"The automobile was engulfed in flames and the bodies were burned beyond recognition. We do know that we have the bodies of a man, a woman, and a small dog. We were able to retrieve several personal items, watches, and rings that were not destroyed in the flames. We understand that Dr. McKinney recently got married. Do you have anyone here at the institute that knew either of them well enough that could identify these items?"

Dr. Graham rested his head in his hands and mumbled, "Yes, Ian's brother-in-law is head of security for the institute. He could probably help you." He looked up at Mrs. Morrison. He was about to ask her to call Angus MacGregor, but he saw her crying uncontrollably.

Visibly distraught, he gulped. "Would you like me to call him? This will be very hard on him."

"Yes, I would. I've brought the items with me. Also, would your human resources department know who their dentists were? We'd like to get their dental records for further identification."

"Yes, of course." Duncan looked at his employee directory, picked up his phone and dialed the human resources department. "Shannon, this is Duncan Graham. Would you please look in the files of Ian and Laura McKinney and give me the names and telephone numbers of both of their dentists? Yes, I'll hold on."

He waited for a few minutes, wrote down the information and thanked her. Next, he called Angus and asked him to immediately come to his office. He called both dental offices and asked them to immediately courier the dental records to Inspector Douglas. They promised they'd have them there by the end of the day.

"Dr. Graham," Inspector Douglas began. He glanced over at Mrs. Morrison.

"Mrs. Morrison, why don't you go and compose yourself?" Duncan said. "Let's keep this quiet for the time being, until we know for certain." She left the room sobbing.

"Dr. Graham, I want you to know that I work in the homicide department," the inspector said as he waited for the desired effect. "It's difficult to know for certain until the full autopsy is completed, but it appears there may have been foul play involved. We'll have the results of the autopsy by tomorrow. Can you tell me why someone might want to kill your employees?"

Before he could respond, Angus walked into the office.

"Angus, sit down. I have some tragic news for you." Duncan introduced the inspector and the lieutenant to Angus. "The inspector has just informed me it appears that Ian and Laura were in an automobile accident yesterday afternoon. It appears they were killed." The room was totally silent for a moment. Duncan continued, "The inspector has some personal items that were removed from the bodies. He'd like you to look at them."

"Oh my God! Where? When? How did this happen?" Angus stammered as he collapsed onto one of the visitor chairs in front of Duncan's desk.

Inspector Douglas closely watched his reaction for a few moments before saying, "I have some items I'd like you to look at." He reached into the pocket of his jacket and brought out a small cloth bag. "May I use your desk?" he asked Dr. Graham.

"Of course," Graham replied as the inspector was already emptying the contents. There were two watches, a pair of earrings, a silver cross on a chain, a man's wedding band and a woman's engagement ring and wedding band.

"Mr. MacGregor, can you identify any of these items?' the inspector asked.

"Is this necessary? Can't you just take fingerprints?" Duncan blurted out.

"I'm afraid not," the inspector responded. "As I said, the bodies were burned beyond recognition."

Angus got up and came over to the desk and looked at the items. "That looks like Ian's watch and that looks like Laura's engagement ring, but it's difficult to be certain. They're so charred," he sniffled.

"I'm sorry to have to put you through this," the inspector said. "but we have to identify the bodies. Do you know who their jeweler was and who else might identify these items? Also, I'd like to look at their employment records if I may." In response to Duncan's surprised look, he added, "If there was foul play, we need to get to the bottom of it."

Duncan picked up his phone and again dialed the human resources department. "Shannon, would you please come to my office right away, and bring the employee files of Ian and Laura McKinney." He sat still for a moment, then mumbled to no one in particular, "They got married only two weeks ago. They just got back from their honeymoon." He shook his head in resignation. "What makes you think there might have been foul play?"

"Quite frankly, Dr. Graham, over the past several months there have been two fatal automobile accidents that were very suspicious. They might have been homicides that were made to look like accidents. This may only be a coincidence, but I have to look at all of the possibilities."

They all looked up as the door to Duncan's office opened and an attractive young woman entered carrying several files. She had a concerned look as she took in the scene before her and walked to Duncan's desk, handing him the files.

She looked down at the items spread out on the desk and exclaimed, "Those are Laura's rings and watch!" Her concerned look turned to a look of shock and then to a look of fright. "Oh my God! What's going on?"

Angus got up and took her by the shoulders, directing her to the chair he had just left. "Sit down, Shannon. There was an automobile accident yesterday. It was Ian's Land Rover. It appears that Ian and Laura were killed."

"No!" she screamed. She began crying uncontrollably. "It can't be. They were so happy."

"Inspector, how can I help you with these files? I can't let them leave my office. What is it that you're looking for?" Duncan asked. "I'd like to end this meeting as quickly as possible." After a slight pause, he added, "For obvious reasons," as he looked compassionately at Shannon.

"I'll be but a few minutes. I'm looking for addresses of the next of kin. Also, Mr. MacGregor, can you give me the name and address of their jeweler?" the inspector replied, this being more of a statement than a question. He spent several minutes writing down information from the files while Angus looked up the address of Ian's jeweler friend, Jared.

Duncan glanced at his watch and looked over at Mrs. Morrison, who was standing by the door, crying.

"Mrs. Morrison, this is difficult for all of us, but would you please announce an assembly of all employees in the conference center for three o'clock. I want all employees to attend and there will be no exceptions for any reason. Say that there will be an important announcement to be made."

As Duncan watched her stumbling out of his office, he lamented, "On second thought, I'll make the announcement. Angus, leave the security men at the gate. You can tell them personally after the assembly."

The inspector finished his writing and closed the files. "I have everything that I need for the time being," he announced. "I'd like to meet with you and Mr. MacGregor personally tomorrow, Dr. Graham. We should have the autopsies and the identification complete and I'd like to discuss other matters with you."

"We will make ourselves available," Duncan murmured.

"I'll send someone to notify her parents," the inspector continued.

"Inspector," Angus sniffled, "I know her parents. They're elderly and this will be devastating to them. I'd like to do that myself if it's all right with you."

"Of course. I'll see you gentlemen sometime tomorrow afternoon," Inspector Douglas responded as he and the lieutenant left the room. Angus escorted them to their automobile.

Duncan glanced at Shannon and then at Mrs. Morrison. "Ladies, please wait here in my office for the next half hour until the assembly. You're in no condition to return to your work. Try and make yourselves comfortable in the sitting area and help yourselves to tea."

TEL AVIV, ISRAEL
TUESDAY, OCTOBER 21, 1997
11:03 A.M.

"I have an update for you, Fox," Danny Yatom said as he ushered him into his office. "Viper informed me that Dr. McKinney and his new wife were killed in an automobile accident two days ago. Our mission is over."

ROSLIN, SCOTLAND
TUESDAY, OCTOBER 21, 1997
1:41 P.M.

Duncan Graham and Angus MacGregor were waiting in Duncan's office as Inspector Douglas and Lieutenant Armstrong were shown in.

The inspector began, "Gentlemen, I'm sorry to report that the bodies have been positively identified as Ian and Laura McKinney.

Their jeweler identified their rings and the dental records are a match. The official conclusion is that their car overturned and caught fire, killing them and their dog. We did a quick check on his credit cards and he filled his car up with petrol in Linlithgow in the late afternoon. This explains the incineration."

"I see," Duncan said with a resigned look. After a pause, he said, "You don't seem convinced."

"I have no doubt the bodies are those of the McKinneys. The jewelry and the dental records are conclusive, but I'm not comfortable with the official explanation of it being an accident. There are too many coincidences and I don't believe in coincidences. I'll ask you again. Can you think of any reason why someone would want to have killed Dr. McKinney?"

Duncan looked straight into his eyes and replied, "No, I cannot think of any plausible reason for his death."

GENEVA, SWITZERLAND
TUESDAY, OCTOBER 21, 1997
6:18 P.M.

Secured instructions were sent to the fourteen members of The Alliance, suggesting they access today's copy of the *Edinburgh Evening News* and read about a tragic automobile accident.

DAMASCUS, SYRIA
THURSDAY, OCTOBER 23, 1997
6:34 P.M.

The Leader jutted his chin and thrust out his chest as he bragged, "Shakar and Salam have been avenged." After quieting down the celebration, he cackled, "McKinney and his wife are dead. I don't know what Nasrallah and The Director want to do about MacGregor. But I want him killed, too."

EDINBURGH, SCOTLAND
SATURDAY, OCTOBER 25, 1997
2:00 P.M.

Angus and Kathleen made the funeral arrangements. They were the only members of the family who had the strength to do the task.

They dispensed with the traditional Friday night wake because there could not be open caskets and because they, themselves, could not handle the massive outpouring of grief.

Pastor Tim conducted the memorial service at his small church, welcoming an overflow crowd. He talked about the meaning of life, how death is of the body, not of the soul. He talked about the lives of Ian and Laura, Ian's greatness in the scientific arena and Laura's greatness as a warm, caring person who had an extreme passion for life, for Christ, for her parents and for her new husband. As he gave his emotional talk from his heart, there wasn't a dry eye in the gathering of nearly three hundred people.

He then talked about the celebration of life, what these two people meant to other people and to each other. He talked about his personal conversations with Ian, how Ian had come to discover Christ and how it had changed his life. He concluded by asking friends and family to come forward and relate their love and admiration for Laura and Ian. He was amazed that more than twenty people came forward and that a memorial service that normally would last for an hour, lasted more than two hours. The service ended with instructions to proceed to the cemetery for the internment.

The sky was gray and overcast with no sign of the sun as the mourners arrived at the cemetery. The autumn chill only served to further dampen the spirits of those in attendance. When everyone had gathered, Pastor Tim read the Twenty-Third Psalm.

Angus proceeded to gather a handful of soil and threw it on the lowered casket of Ian. Kathleen did the same for Laura. The only departure from tradition occurred when the cemetery employees placed a small casket containing the remains of McDuff alongside Ian's casket.

When the service was completed, most everyone asked about the well-being of Laura's parents because they were noticeably absent from the service. Angus explained they were devastated by the death of their only child, were under physician-prescribed medication, and could not bear to attend the funeral.

With the large turnout, only Angus noticed there were several men in attendance who were total strangers. None of these men realized they were having their pictures taken, apart from one. He didn't really care. He had accomplished his task.

TEL AVIV, ISRAEL
SUNDAY, OCTOBER 26, 1997
6:43 P.M.

"Fox," Danny Yatom advised, "McKinney and his wife are definitely dead and the official report states that it was an accident. Viper read the autopsy report and the dental records match, right down to the gold fillings. Even their dog was killed in the accident. The funeral was held last Friday, and it was attended by several hundred people, including the director of the Roslin Institute. Viper attended the funeral and there was heartfelt grief on the part of all the mourners. We're going to use all of our resources to find out what the Vatican is doing now."

ROSLIN, SCOTLAND
MONDAY, OCTOBER 27, 1997
8:31 A.M.

Angus was promptly admitted to Duncan Graham's office. At the funeral, he had told Duncan, through his grief, that he needed to meet with him as early as possible on Monday.

"Duncan, I'm sure this won't come as a surprise, but I need to tender my resignation. My life has totally changed. I need to track down those people who were responsible for what happened to Ian and Laura."

"I understand. Please, be careful," the director responded. "I wish you well, Angus. Do you have any idea who these people are?"

"There were several strangers at the memorial service and funeral. I have their pictures and that should help determine who they are," Angus answered. "I'll start there."

"What will you do next?"

"Kathleen and I have to go through all of Ian and Laura's belongings, pack things up that we want to keep and sell the rest. I'll sell Ian's cottage and I have a lot of work to do on their finances. Kathleen, being the next of kin, will receive the proceeds from the sale of Ian's assets."

"What will you do after all this work is done?" Duncan asked.

"We're not absolutely certain, but Kathleen wants to leave the area. It should take several months to clean up Ian's affairs. After that's done, we'll probably go on an extended trip, perhaps to New Zealand and Australia. We may decide to stay if we find a place we like. I know we won't be coming back here for quite a while—too many memories to confront."

"And, what do you hear from the cardinals?" Duncan asked.

"Cardinal Jaropelk was devastated, but he extended his best wishes to you. In view of what has happened, they have officially abandoned the project."

They bid each other farewell and Angus proceeded to his office to remove his personal belongings.

TEL AVIV, ISRAEL
FRIDAY, OCTOBER 31, 1997
8:23 A.M.

"Fox," Director Yatom advised, "our sources tell us the Vatican had some kind of secret project going, but it has been abandoned. It appears this assignment is over and we're putting the file into *inactive*. Should something else develop, I'll let you know."

PART THREE

THE NEWCOMERS

DUBLIN, IRELAND
THURSDAY, NOVEMBER 20, 1997
8:23 A.M.

Sean and Lauren Murphy checked in for their Aer Lingus flight to Boston with a continuing flight to Orlando. Sean was being sent to the United States by his company to set up its first overseas operation and they decided to arrive early and vacation in Orlando. They had long wanted to see Disney World. They showed their tickets, passports, and permanent resident alien cards to the ticket agent and again to security.

Security was extremely thorough for flights departing Ireland for the United States. The security agent had to flip through most of the pages of Lauren's passport to find a blank page to stamp. He remarked, "I see you've traveled throughout the Middle East, Africa, Asia, and Europe. I don't recall ever having seen so much travel in such a short time."

"I'm a freelance photojournalist and I'm under contract with four different publications," she advised, looking directly into his eyes.

He observed the two expensive cameras she carried over her shoulder. He examined her papers and noted she was born in the country town of Kilkenny on June 8, 1966, making her thirty-one years old. He checked to make certain that her description on her papers matched her photograph and her appearance. She was five feet six inches in height, weighed a trim one hundred and thirty pounds and had green eyes and red hair. Her maiden name was O'Donnell. She was married in June 1993 and had the name change recorded on her passport that same month. *She was obviously of good Irish stock,* he thought.

"How long do you anticipate living in the United States?" he inquired.

She looked at Sean and replied with a lovely Irish accent, "Sean has committed to open up the operation and remain for five years."

"And, where will you be residing?"

Sean replied, "We'll be living in Chicago, although we could possibly expand our business and relocate to a different city."

"I see," the agent said as he handed Lauren her papers and picked up Sean's. He noted that Sean was born in Galway on May 5, 1960. He stood six feet three inches in height with a listed weight of one hundred ninety-five pounds. He had blue eyes with dark hair, a short, neatly trimmed beard and wore glasses. The description and photo matched his person. "What type of work will you be doing, Mr. Murphy?" the agent inquired.

"I'm a principal of a company called Eradex. Our company has developed a chemical application that eradicates mold. The product is far superior to anything else on the market and is about half of the cost of other products and is faster and safer. Mold has become a major issue in the United States. When a house is sold, which happens a lot more frequently than in Ireland and the UK, they have inspectors test for mold. It's a natural market for us."

The agent noticed that Sean's passport was only three years old and that he had done far less traveling than his wife. "Enjoy your stay in the States, Mister and Mrs. Murphy. I wish you success." He added with a bright smile. "And, do come back to Ireland. We don't want to lose our fine citizens."

"Thank you. That is certainly our intent," Sean replied as he and his wife left to board the plane.

As they settled into their comfortable first-class seats, Lauren took his arm and said, "Well, my dear, we're off to a new life. I do hope we can return someday. I already miss our friends and families."

ORLANDO, FLORIDA
MONDAY, DECEMBER 1, 1997
9:08 A.M.

Sean and Lauren Murphy boarded the United flight to Chicago after having spent a wonderful week seeing the tourist sights of Orlando. They had also flown to Nassau and spent three days enjoying the warm water and white sand beaches of the Bahamas.

Their vacation wasn't all play. Sean had set up an appointment for Tuesday with a commercial real estate broker to look at buildings for purchase. He called and talked to the branch manager and they discussed the Eradex space requirements.

The branch manager rearranged several appointments and agreed to spend the day with Sean and Lauren showing them all available industrial buildings between fifteen and twenty thousand square feet in the northwest suburban market. Sean told him they wanted to act quickly and if they found a suitable building, they were prepared to make a cash offer with an immediate closing.

They arrived in Chicago in the late morning and took the courtesy shuttle to the Marriott Suites Hotel. When they left Orlando, it was nearly eighty degrees and sunny. When they arrived at their hotel it was overcast and a frigid twenty-two degrees.

"This reminds me of home," Lauren shuddered.

ROSEMONT, ILLINOIS
TUESDAY, DECEMBER 2, 1997
7:54 A.M.

Douglas Wulf, the branch manager of Cushman Wakefield, met Sean and Lauren in the lobby of their hotel. He was tall, nearly Sean's height, and had thinning dark blond hair with a reddish tint. He appeared to be in his midforties and his professional manner and gentlemanly approach quickly made Sean and Lauren feel at ease.

They walked to the dining room where Wulf requested a quiet table in the rear of the room so they could talk privately. When they were seated, he showed them a map of Elk Grove Village where he had circled the locations of the ten buildings he had arranged to show them. He presented each of them with a bound copy of demographic information of the area with a listing and description of each building.

"This is quite thorough, Mr. Wulf. I'm impressed," Sean remarked.

"Please call me Doug. You will notice that the price per square foot ranges from ninety-five to one hundred and twelve dollars per square foot. If you pay cash for the building and close quickly, we have the leverage to negotiate a price reduction of perhaps as much as ten percent."

"As I told you when we spoke on the telephone, that is our intent," Sean responded. "We'd like to act swiftly, perhaps even make a decision this week. I'll need to open several bank accounts tomorrow and get funds wired in. There's another way you might be of assistance to us, Doug. We would like to purchase a home. Can you assist us with this?"

"Of course. You will need a good residential realtor and I have just the person for you. Her name is Lyn Drake. She's with RE/Max and she is as good as they get. We can call her and you can tell her what you're looking for."

It was early evening by the time they had visited and inspected all ten buildings. Sean narrowed his choices down to three and they agreed to revisit them the next morning. Sean spoke with Lyn Drake and set up a meeting for Thursday morning to begin looking at houses.

At dinner, while they enjoyed their steaks, Doug offered, "I'll pick you up at 8:30 tomorrow morning and we'll inspect your three choices.

Then we can analyze them and make your offer. After that, I'll take you to US Bank and you can open your accounts."

"Sean, I must say, you certainly move quickly," Doug commented over dinner. "How many employees do you anticipate having?"

"Before I answer that, I must tell you, this is the best steak I've ever had. We don't get beef like this in the U.K." Sean glanced at his wife, seeking her response.

Lauren agreed, "It's incredibly tender and juicy. As we say back home, it's smashing."

After savoring several more bites, Sean stated, "In response to your question, we want to get our business started before we expand. First, we'd like to select a home by the weekend and complete both purchases within the next several weeks. We'd also like to get your recommendations on a company to make alterations to the interior of the building we select, as well as furniture stores for our home and workplace. In answer to your other question, I have an associate from Ireland joining us in several weeks. He and his wife will be assisting Lauren and me in running the business. I'll hire others as they are needed."

ELK GROVE VILLAGE, ILLINOIS
WEDNESDAY, DECEMBER 3, 1997
11:57 A.M.

After thoroughly inspecting the three buildings, Sean and Lauren made their selection.

"Doug, you do the negotiating for us. We trust you to obtain the best price possible. When that's accomplished and after you take us to the bank, I have another favor to ask of you."

"I'm at your service," Doug replied.

"We both need driving lessons. It seems that you folks tend to drive on the wrong side of the street over here. Would you be so kind as to let us gain some experience with you and could you take us to obtain operating licenses? Lauren and I would be most appreciative."

By two o'clock, Doug had made an offer, received a counteroffer, and informed the listing broker of his client's final offer. He told him they required an acceptance by five o'clock, otherwise they would begin negotiations on their second-choice building.

While they were waiting, Doug took them to the nearest branch of US Bank. He escorted them in, introduced himself and his clients, and asked for the branch manager, saying that they would like to open an account.

The young banker, who appeared to be fresh out of college, said, "Have a seat, please. I'll see if Mr. Jennings is available." He returned several minutes later. "Mr. Jennings is in a meeting and requested that I assist you."

"That's unfortunate," Doug said. "The Murphys want to open a business account and have four million dollars wired into it." He paused for effect. "It's too bad that your Mr. Jennings can't take the time. Can you tell me where the nearest Wells Fargo branch is?"

Doug displayed no emotion as he watched the shocked expression on the young man's face. He turned and headed toward the door, escorting Lauren and Sean ahead of him.

"Wait! Please wait. Let me tell Mr. Jennings what you need. I'm sure he'll end his meeting." He was almost in tears as he ran to the corner office at the rear of the bank. Doug looked at Sean and Lauren and gave them a knowing, satisfied smile.

"I like the way you operate, Doug," Lauren said. "We may call on you for additional advice over the next several weeks."

They turned to see the young nervous banker rushing toward them, followed by a composed and smiling man. "Good afternoon,

I'm Steve Jennings. Let me assure you, I wasn't putting you off. I really was in a meeting. Shall we go to my office where we can discuss your needs and requirements?"

Sean acted quickly. It took less than thirty minutes to open a business account for Eradex with instructions to wire in two million dollars from The Bank of England. "Doug, how much do you think we'll require for the purchase and furnishing of our house plus the house of my associate?"

Doug thought for a moment and then responded. "I'm not sure where and what you'll buy, but I would guess at least a million for yourself and nearly the same for your associate."

Sean responded in a businesslike fashion, "Mr. Jennings, let's transfer in an additional three million into the business account and a hundred thousand into Lauren's and my personal account. I also want to set up a joint account for my associate and his wife who'll be joining us in several weeks. Their names are Scott and Judith Williams. We'll transfer a hundred thousand dollars into their account also."

"Do you need financing for your homes?" Mr. Jennings asked. "We have some excellent interest rates for our preferred customers."

"No thank you, sir. We'll pay cash," Sean responded. "Please let me know what additional paperwork you will need from us," he offered. "Now, let's go have that driving lesson, Doug."

Doug looked up the address of the nearest licensing bureau and said, "Let's go get copies of the *Rules of the Road* booklets for you to study tonight and then we'll go driving."

By five o'clock, they had obtained the driving regulations booklets and had been practicing driving for an hour when Doug's cell phone rang. He answered and listened for a moment. "That works. Draw up the contract and we'll meet at three o'clock at my office."

He looked at Sean. "We got it for ninety-three dollars a foot. You just bought yourself a building for one million eight hundred and fifty-six thousand dollars. We sign the purchase agreement tomorrow and I already have an inspecting engineer scheduled for tomorrow morning. Assuming he doesn't find any structural or mechanical problems with the building, we'll close the transaction mid-next week. I have to tell you, this is the fastest transaction I've ever done."

Doug watched the delighted looks on their faces. "Lyn Drake is picking you up at your hotel at eight in the morning. Have her bring you to my office no later than three o'clock and we'll sign the purchase contract."

"That's fine, Doug. Lauren and I would like to get your opinion on the homes that we investigate. Would you be so kind?"

"Of course, I'll be happy to help. As a matter of fact, if you don't mind, I'll bring my wife, Maureen. She'd be of more help to you in that regard than I would."

"That would be wonderful. Perhaps we could plan on Saturday afternoon if that fits your schedule. We could all go to dinner that evening. You select the restaurant and Eradex will cover the cost."

ROSEMONT, ILLINOIS
THURSDAY, DECEMBER 4, 1997
7:57 A.M.

Sean and Lauren were waiting in the lobby when Lyn Drake arrived.

As she walked toward them, Lauren immediately knew she would like her. Lyn was several inches taller than Lauren, wore an attractive business skirt and blazer, and had brunette hair cut medium-length. As she greeted them with a soft but firm voice, her infectious smile exuded a feeling of sincerity and trust. They had previously discussed

Lauren and Sean's tastes and desires on the telephone, and the suburbs that they would consider.

After being seated for breakfast, Lyn began, "I have compiled thirty listings on the North Shore that fit your requirements."

Sean emphasized, "We're looking for two homes in close proximity, that are in a high-demand area and we'd like to finalize both purchases within the next several weeks."

"I've set aside the rest of the day as well as tomorrow and the entire weekend," Lyn advised. "I suggest we visit as many homes as possible so you can become familiar with the neighborhoods as well as the styles in the area. Coming from Ireland, I'm sure you will find housing to be a lot different here."

They agreed to spend the remainder of the day looking at homes until the time for the contract signing for their industrial building.

WINNETKA, ILLINOIS
SUNDAY, DECEMBER 7, 1997
4:03 P.M.

Lauren, Sean, and Lyn returned to her office to write the offers on the two homes they had selected. Since Thursday, they had looked at nearly forty homes and they had Doug and his wife inspect and approve their final choices late Saturday afternoon.

Lyn faxed the offers to the two listing realtors stipulating a closing date of Wednesday, December 17.

Sean advised, "Lyn, we would like to close both homes in the afternoon because my employee Scott Williams and his wife Judith will arrive that morning from Dublin."

Lyn drove them back to their hotel, ending an exhausting four days of looking at real estate properties.

303

CHICAGO, ILLINOIS
WEDNESDAY, DECEMBER 17, 1997
11:37 A.M.

As Sean and Lauren drove the short distance to the airport, both were enthusiastic about the events of the past ten days.

"Lauren, we've certainly accomplished a lot in a short period of time," Sean exclaimed. "We've purchased a building for our company and selected the contractor for the interior construction. We've opened the bank accounts, obtained our driver's licenses and purchased two new Land Rovers as well as furniture for the two homes. And now, we're going to welcome Scott and Judith and purchase houses today."

They had enjoyed exploring their new neighborhood in Winnetka as well as downtown Chicago. Sean was enthralled with the Museum of Science and Industry, while Lauren fell in love with the North Michigan Avenue district.

Lauren remarked, "Sean, our clothes are so British-looking. Do you suppose your company could cover the cost of some new clothes so we fit in with the American culture?"

"I think we can do that. Let's see if Scott and Judith need to do some shopping with us. We'll have some free time while we wait for the construction to be completed."

They waited in the terminal for Scott and Judith to clear customs and retrieve their bags. Lauren saw them first. She did not know Judith very well. They had only met several times. But Sean had worked with Scott for several years and the men had become good friends.

Scott was tall, with an athletic build. He had dark hair with medium-length sideburns and a full mustache. His tweed jacket, British hat, and black-rimmed glasses gave him a studious appearance.

"Sean, it's wonderful to see you," Scott said as he reached out his hand. "You remember Judith."

"Yes, of course. Judith, we're looking forward to working closely with both of you. Judith, you know Lauren."

"Sean, you needn't be so formal," Judith replied. "I've met your lovely Irish lassie on several occasions. How are you, my dear?" she said as she gave her a quick kiss on the cheek.

Before Lauren could respond, Sean interjected, "We'll help you with your luggage and bring you up-to-date on our accomplishments here in Chicago. You'll be happy to know we purchased two homes in the village of Winnetka, and we finalize their purchase this afternoon. They are only two blocks apart, which will make it convenient for commuting to work.

"We'll take you to the hotel first, so you can freshen up and then we'll go to the real estate closings. Your suite connects to ours, so we can have some privacy for the next several days. The building won't be ready for occupancy for about two weeks and we won't have furniture delivered to our homes for at least another week, so we'll have to stay at our hotel for about a week."

When they arrived at the hotel, Sean and Lauren escorted them to their suite and they agreed to meet in thirty minutes to drive to the closings.

It was shortly after two o'clock when all parties were seated at the closing table at the title company. The sellers for the Williams' house were present and warmly greeted Scott and Judith. It took nearly an hour to sign the paperwork, none of which meant anything to Scott. They then closed the purchase of the new Murphy house.

Lyn Drake was extremely helpful in explaining the procedures to them. "Congratulations," Lyn said after they signed the last of the documents. "I think you'll love your new homes."

"As a matter of fact, as soon as we're finished here, let's go look at them. Is that all right with you folks?" Lyn asked of the sellers. They replied that it was, and they agreed to go see both homes.

After visiting their new homes, the two couples drove back to their hotel and immediately went to their suites. After entering their room, Sean opened their connecting door. He found Scott holding a small piece of equipment sweeping their rooms for listening devices.

When Scott was satisfied that it was clean, he went to the Murphys' suite and went through the same procedure. When he was certain that both suites were clean, he put down the equipment and both couples embraced each other. With tears in her eyes, Kathleen said, "Laura, I've missed you both so much. It's so wonderful to see you."

"We've missed you, too. How was our funeral?" Laura asked. "I'm certainly glad I missed it."

"It was the most difficult thing I've ever done. There wasn't a dry eye in the church or at the burial. I felt so guilty, bringing such sadness to all those people," Kathleen replied.

"We've discussed this matter a dozen times," Angus instructed. "We had to do this to protect your lives," Angus said to Ian and Laura. He changed subjects. "I'm starved. Let's order room service and eat here. We can fill each other in about the last two months of our lives."

"That's a fine idea," Ian said as he retrieved the room service menu. "The food here is quite good." They made their dinner selections and Ian called them in.

"I have several things to say," Laura offered. "First, I think we should call each other by our new names, so that you can get used to them. You slipped up once today, Scott. It really won't take you long to get used to it."

"It will take me longer to get used to Sean's dark hair and beard and your flaming red hair and green eyes," Judith said. "Continue on, Lauren. What else did you want to say?"

"I have some questions," she replied. "First, when does Duffy get out of quarantine?"

"He's here in Chicago and I can pick him up on Monday," Scott replied, much to Sean's delight.

Lauren continued, "How many people know of this deception and did the fake teeth work as well as you thought?"

"The only people who know are Duncan Graham, your parents, the four of us, and my men who 'killed you' almost two months ago. Of course, the cardinals and the Pope know, since we planned this with them the day before your wedding. The teeth worked perfectly. The coroner and the chief detectives believed them. It's amazing what modem science can do with a molding of your actual teeth," Scott answered.

"Do you know whose bodies were used? And, how are my parents?" Lauren asked.

"The bodies came from the morgue in Birmingham, England. They were homeless people and the bodies were unclaimed. Your parents are doing fine. They didn't come to the funeral service. I thought it would be too difficult for them and I wasn't sure if they were very good actors. I told people they were overcome with grief and their physician would not allow them to attend."

They spent the next several hours discussing events of the past two months back in Scotland and at the institute.

Sean and Lauren relayed their experiences living in London for nearly a month while they waited for their new identities to be completed and for his beard to grow.

"I set up accounts with the Bank of England and ordered all the laboratory equipment we will need. Some of it has already arrived. I've contacted the two doctors who will refer their patients and they already have some potential hosts. Once we have our facility completed, and secure, we can begin that phase of the project," Sean told them.

"Speaking of bank accounts," Sean added, "we have an appointment at US Bank for you two tomorrow morning, to sign some forms for your personal accounts that I opened up for you. After that I thought we'd take you on a furniture and clothing-buying excursion. I'm not spending John Paul's funds recklessly, however, we do have to fit into this culture and not stand out."

"I absolutely agree," Scott concurred.

"Speaking of which, what did you and Judith do for the past two months and what did you learn of our adversaries?"

"After the funeral, I turned in my resignation as planned and listed both yours and our houses for sale. Neither have sold yet but there has been some interest. After taking care of that business, we traveled New Zealand and Australia, as would be expected."

"What did you learn of our enemies?"

"There were some new faces at your funeral but MI-6 hasn't been able to identify them. They thought they spotted Mossad, but there were two others that could not be identified. They believe they might have been professionals. I can picture the Arabs going professional, but I have no idea who could have hired a second one."

Scott noticed Lauren's worried look. "The two men left Edinburgh, the Mossad recalled their team and the Vatican quietly let it be known that they had abandoned some sort of project." He sat back with a smile. "As far as the world is concerned, you two are dead, and it is moving on without you." He added, "Sad, but true."

The room was silent for a moment before Lauren interjected, "We've also found an excellent OB-GYN for me. I have an appointment in a week." She paused as Judith stared at her with sudden excitement and anticipation.

"Are you?" Judith asked.

"Yes, I believe so. Obviously, that timid scientist brother of yours wasn't quite so timid on our honeymoon. He wanted to have a child as soon as possible and he did everything he could and as often as he could to make certain it happened immediately."

"Lauren, stop that! You're terrible," Sean jested, with fake indignation.

"You told me I was wonderful. That's why you kept coming back for more every day," Lauren teased.

"What am I going to do with her?" he asked with exasperation.

"You know exactly what you're doing with me, Sean Murphy, or whatever your name is. You're turning me into a baby machine." She looked at Judith and gushed, "He wants four or five. We even tried when we spent the night at the Vatican after our honeymoon. I bet there hasn't been a baby conceived in that place in a good long time." This brought laughter to everyone and an endearing kiss from her husband.

"I don't know how we're going to name all these children when we don't even know our own names?" Lauren joked.

"It's so wonderful to see you two, and how happy you are," Judith exulted. After several hours of talking, the Williams returned to their suite.

As Sean closed the door behind them, Lauren said, "Don't you think it might be a good idea to try again, just in case those store-bought tests are wrong?"

"That's a wonderful idea, Mrs. Murphy. And I think we should continue that procedure indefinitely, don't you?"

"Most definitely!"

CHICAGO, ILLINOIS
WEDNESDAY, DECEMBER 24, 1997
8:37 P.M.

The two couples decided to go downtown for dinner and celebrate Christmas Eve.

They were finishing their appetizers when Sean remarked, "This certainly is a night for celebration, isn't it, being the eve of the birth of Jesus?" They all agreed and toasted the evening with their glasses of Scotch. Lauren was drinking water.

"We have another reason for celebration tonight, darling," Lauren remarked. "It's not quite like the eve of the Christ childbirth, but we are on the verge of another birth." They were silent for a moment and then Sean's mouth fell open before forming a wide smile. He shivered with excitement. "Are you?"

"You forgot, but I had my doctor appointment this morning. I'm due in early July." After a round of excited congratulations and warm hugs, Lauren bubbled, "It happened on our honeymoon, you rascal. I think it was on our wedding night; I thought so at the time."

"Where will you have the baby?" Judith asked.

"My doctor practices at Evanston Hospital."

ELK GROVE VILLAGE, ILLINOIS
THURSDAY, FEBRUARY 19, 1998
1:34 P.M.

"Oleg," Sean said on the secure phone line to Cardinal Jaropelk's office, "the lab is completed and all of the equipment is installed. We're ready for you to send us the first fifteen samples."

"I'll have a courier bring them to you."

"Be careful and be discreet. You never know who might be watching."

"I've already planned for that. As far as anyone knows, we're sending some frozen blood samples of the Holy Father for analysis at the University of Chicago Medical Center. There will be instructions that a local courier be sent by a Mr. Sean Murphy who will pick them up. That way no one will see you." Cardinal Jaropelk paused to clear his throat. "Ian, what's the status of finding the host mother?"

"We're looking at several potentials. We have quite a bit of further analysis to do. And, that brings up a subject we need to discuss."

"Go ahead," Oleg responded with a touch of hesitation.

"I know His Holiness insists there be absolutely no possibility the host mother can conceive in any manner other than through the cloning. Oleg, that may not be possible."

"Why not?" Oleg implored.

"Because any woman with a uterus can conceivably get pregnant."

"I'm sorry, I don't understand, Ian."

"I'll give you the science. The first 'test tube baby' was born in England twenty-one years ago. Since then, thousands of babies have been conceived through in vitro fertilization. The concept is simple, but the process is complex. Under normal circumstances, conception occurs when an egg cell in a woman is released from an ovary, travels through the fallopian tube, and is fertilized by the man's sperm. The fertilized egg continues to travel through the fallopian tube while it undergoes numerous cell divisions. It then adheres to the uterus and begins to grow."

"I understand that," Oleg stated.

"Good. A problem arises with a woman with blocked fallopian tubes. She cannot conceive because her eggs cannot travel through the fallopian tubes to become fertilized. There are probably millions of women around the world who have this or a similar problem. Oleg, please understand the problem has been solved over the past twenty years. Doctors are now able to remove healthy eggs from the woman and then mix an egg with sperm from the man. After the egg is fertilized, it's placed in a special solution that nurtures the egg as it divides. It is then placed back in the woman's uterus and nine months later, you have a baby. Thousands of these operations have been done over the past two decades."

"All right, Sean, what does that mean for us?" Oleg asked.

"That in and of itself does not affect us, but here's what does. When a doctor performs in vitro fertilization, he removes as many as fifty or sixty eggs from the woman and they all become fertilized. They usually insert two healthy fertilized eggs into the woman's uterus, hoping that one survives. Often, it results in twins. Here's the problem. What happens to all the other fertilized eggs that have not been implanted? I'll tell you what happens, Oleg. Couples want them frozen for later use in case the first attempt isn't successful. Right now, in the United States, there are estimated to be fifty thousand fertilized eggs in storage."

"I didn't realize. You understand, this is not my area of expertise."

Sean continued, "There is a Christian organization called Focus on the Family that has started an embryo adoption program. It matches donor embryos to infertile women. If this is successful, and there's absolutely no reason why it won't be, then any woman with a healthy uterus can have a baby. Oleg, we cannot guarantee when we implant a fertilized cloned egg into a woman, that she doesn't go out and have a frozen embryo adoption. It's highly unlikely, but it remains a possibility. Oleg, our lab and clinic have been designed with excellent protection and security, but we cannot control what our host mother does once she leaves the premises. But there's one other aspect, my friend. Why would an infertile woman use our procedure when there is an embryo adoption program where she can learn about the donor's heritage and family?"

"Hmm, I see the problem."

"Oleg, I'm very worried that John Paul is putting too many constraints on the project and making it near impossible."

"I'll speak to Loleck tomorrow and I'll call you back at this same time."

———

"Laura, I need to talk to you," Ian implored after he helped clear the dinner table and fill the dishwasher.

"This must be serious, because you're using my real name," she questioned. "Why don't you fill up one of your pipes and I'll pour you a glass of Macallan. You can relax and let's talk about it. Whatever it is, it's been bothering you for days."

After sitting down in his recliner and lighting his pipe, he confessed, "I'm worried that the Pope will halt the program. You've seen the data on in vitro fertilization. I don't see how we can proceed with all his constraints."

"Darling, I've been concerned about that, too. We've discussed many times just how fragile our lives are with this program and that it could end at any time. We'll just have to see what he comes back with tomorrow."

ELK GROVE VILLAGE, ILLINOIS
FRIDAY, FEBRUARY 20, 1998
1:10 P.M.

When the secure telephone rang, Sean anxiously picked it up. "Hello, Oleg."

"Hello, my friend," he said with obvious disappointment. "His Holiness wants to be one hundred percent certain that any conception is from the Shroud DNA. Either you find a way to give him that assurance or we'll have to abandon the program. I'm sorry to have to tell you this."

After a long pause, Sean sighed, "Oleg, let me call you back tomorrow at this time. I have to really do some thinking about this."

ELK GROVE VILLAGE, ILLINOIS
SATURDAY, FEBRUARY 21, 1998
1:16 P.M.

"Oleg, allow me to summarize the problem. We must find a Messianic Jewish woman who has had her uterus removed, but still has her ovaries intact and who would volunteer to undergo the first uterus transplant in history. The transplant would have to not only be successful, but the woman would have to agree to accept cloned DNA from the Shroud of Turin rather than her husband's sperm. Not only that, but the uterus would have to be transplanted and the fertilized egg inserted at the same time."

"That's rather an impossibility, isn't it, Ian?"

"Yes, it is. I'll working on it, Oleg. If she's out there, we'll find her. But, if we do find her, we'd be looking at a far greater cost than we anticipated, probably many millions of dollars."

"Ian, you find her and we'll cover the cost. Good luck, my friend. Do you think there's much of a chance?"

"Unfortunately, I don't," he bemoaned. "We're not very optimistic, but I'll keep up the search," he assured Oleg.

"Speaking of pregnancies, how is Laura doing?"

"She is doing quite well, Oleg. We have less than five months to go."

ELK GROVE VILLAGE, ILLINOIS
FRIDAY, JUNE 19, 1998
11:07 A.M.

"Oleg, we've done the impossible; we've located the perfect woman. She lives in Wauwautosa, Wisconsin, about ninety miles north of here. Her name is Rachael Grossman and she fits the description. We've arranged for the doctors and for the procedure."

"That's amazing! Tell me, when do you plan on doing the surgery?"

"The surgeons tell me it will be probably five or six months. They have an enormous amount of preparation to do. Oleg, in the 1960s, scientists conducted several uterine transplants in dogs and even achieved pregnancies afterward. But little has been done in this field since then. They intend to practice on baboons and goats to perfect blood vessel attachment techniques."

"I don't understand."

"The main difficulty with a uterine transplant is that the uterus is fed, not by a few major blood vessels, but by many smaller ones," Ian explained. "Each one must be reattached with microsurgical techniques. They will have to use extra lengths of blood vessel that will be removed from her leg to help span the distance between the vessel stumps on the uterus and those in her body. So, they need to practice."

"Ian, how trustworthy are the doctors and why would they do this without publicizing it?"

"That's an excellent question. The doctors are sworn to secrecy, but if word got out, we would simply deny this preposterous story. The doctors can use the knowledge and experience they learn from this in the future when the procedure can be made public. They'll be able to gain the notoriety and fortune later."

"So, you're saying they'll be using Rachael Grossman as a test case?"

"Yes, that's right. She'll essentially be an experiment. But we've known that all along. I'll keep you advised. Goodbye, Oleg."

EVANSTON, ILLINOIS
SUNDAY, JULY 5, 1998
11:58 A.M.

Ian McKinney, alias Sean Murphy, watched as his wife Laura, alias Lauren, gave birth to an eight-pound four-ounce baby boy, named Andrew Oleg Murphy. They would worry about a legal change of the last name someday when the project was completed and they returned to Scotland.

Mother and child came through the birthing in perfect health.

Sean sat in a chair next to Lauren's bed, holding her hand as she lightly dozed. He whispered, "There are three of us now, my love, I am so incredibly happy."

ELK GROVE VILLAGE, ILLINOIS
THURSDAY, DECEMBER 3, 1998
6:41 P.M.

The uterus transplant surgery lasted nearly nine hours. Rachael was wheeled from the operating room to her comfortable room. The surgeons were optimistic for the operation's success, but transplant rejection could occur at any time.

During the operation, they removed forty-seven healthy eggs from her ovaries, which were quickly frozen. If all went well, shortly after the New Year, Dr. McKinney would fertilize an egg and implant it into Rachael's new uterus. All they could do now was watch and wait. Rachael would be staying in the clinic for two months.

"Darling, you must be exhausted after the surgery. Let's stop and get a quick dinner and then go home. Scott and Judith are watching Andy at their house for the night. I have the perfect way to relax you when we get home."

"Oh, and what might that be, Mrs. Murphy?"

"Remember that bubble bath we took together on our wedding night? I think a repeat performance of that entire evening might well be in order."

"Including getting pregnant?"

"I'm fertile this week and I'm ready if you are. We're not getting any younger, are we?"

"No, we're not. Let's hurry and get something to eat. I'm famished."

Later that night, Laura McKinney, alias Lauren Murphy, became pregnant for the second time.

ELK GROVE VILLAGE, ILLINOIS
TUESDAY, JANUARY 5, 1999
3.13 P.M.

Ian personally inserted one of Rachael's eggs, that had been fertilized with the cloned DNA, into her uterus and attached it to the uterine wall. Since the uterine transplant operation, she had shown several signs of transplant rejection, but this had been dealt with using immune system suppressing drugs.

Later that evening, Sean remarked, "Lauren, you were fantastic during the surgery."

"Are you sure I wasn't in the way?"

"Absolutely not. You assisted us with the instruments like a pro. You have learned so much over the past year. I'm so proud of you."

"Thank you. I've had an incredible instructor." She smiled with softening eyes.

"We've done everything we can. Now we just have to wait another month to see if the pregnancy will hold."

WINNETKA, ILLINOIS
SATURDAY, JANUARY 9, 1999
5:21 A.M.

Sean received a phone call at home that woke him from a deep sleep. Worried, he quickly answered. His fears were realized when he was told that Rachael had not only miscarried, but her body had rejected the uterine transplant and it would immediately need to be removed. He and Lauren dressed and silently drove to their clinic.

"I'm so sorry, Rachael," Sean said, attempting to comfort her. "You rest easy. The surgeons are going to remove the uterus and we'll send you home in a week. We'll analyze the results of the exam and we may be able to attempt the procedure again, at a later date. That is, if you're willing."

"I'm willing, Doctor Murphy. As you know, my husband is infertile and I've had a partial hysterectomy, so this is our only chance to have a baby. At least it would be half mine. Please, find out what went wrong and let's try again."

ELK GROVE VILLAGE, ILLINOIS
WEDNESDAY, JANUARY 20, 1999
10:46 A.M.

It was a cold bleak day as Rachael left the facility with her husband, Sidney. She gave hugs to all of the medical staff, walked up to Sean and Lauren and said, "I'll be back, Doctor Murphy. With your help and the blessing of Lord Jesus, I'll be back." She reached up and kissed him on the cheek, said goodbye to Lauren and climbed into her car.

"What a wonderful, Godly woman," Lauren softly said as she watched them drive away. "Do you think you can make this happen for her?"

"I'm certainly going to try, darling. I have some ideas that I need to talk to the surgeon about. We have a lot of work ahead of us. Let's get back inside, it's freezing."

ELK GROVE VILLAGE, ILLINOIS
THURSDAY, FEBRUARY 4, 1999
2:22 P.M.

Lauren sat at her desk in the reception area and answered the phone while Sean and Scott were busy in the lab. She entered the lab, closed the door behind her and stood facing her husband, her face ashen.

Sean looked up just as tears started pouring from her eyes and she emitted a low moan. Sean dropped his work, rushed to her and grasped her upper arms to hold her steady. "Lauren, what happened?"

It took several moments for her to recover. "The phone call was from Rachael's doctor in Wauwautosa. There was a gas leak at Rachael's house last night. The furnace exploded and the entire house was engulfed in flames. Rachael and Sidney died in their bed. Ian, it happened at three in the morning and apparently one of the neighbors heard a car drive away shortly before the explosion."

Sean's eyes widened as he ran his hands through his hair. "No..." he exclaimed. He turned away, covering his mouth, as he stumbled to the nearest chair and fell into it. "Oh my God!" he stuttered. "Tell me it's not happening again."

Scott squeezed his eyes shut and his strong shoulders slumped as he stepped to Lauren to comfort her.

There was silence as they pondered the implications.

ELK GROVE VILLAGE, ILLINOIS
MONDAY, FEBRUARY 8, 1999
10:03 A.M.

"Ian, we have a major problem. His Holiness is extremely concerned about security and has decided to abandon the project," Oleg declared on the secure and scrambled telephone line.

Ian had anticipated this, but it was still shocking. His eyes reddened as he mumbled, "I understand, Oleg." He hung up the phone.

Scott pinched his lips together as he watched Sean.

Lauren stood still, unblinking.

"John Paul is canceling the project." Sean sighed. "It's over."

Lauren looked at Sean as he sunk into his chair. She glanced at Scott and saw the defeat on his face.

She took a step toward Sean with her jaw set. "No, it's not, Ian McKinney," she shouted. "We've come too far and worked too hard for this to end. There's a reason why we altered our lives. There's a reason why we are here in this bleak industrial park in the middle of a snowstorm. We're not giving up."

She turned and glared at Scott. "And you, Angus MacGregor, stand up straight. You have a lot of work to do. I want you to find out what happened and who killed Rachael. We owe it to her. Quit acting like a couple of spoiled babies. Now get busy and start planning."

She turned and stormed out of the room and slammed the door behind her.

ELK GROVE VILLAGE, ILLINOIS
TUESDAY, FEBRUARY 9, 1999
9:08 A.M.

Sean placed a call to Cardinal Jaropelk on the secure line.

"Oleg, would you please ask John Paul for some time? Angus is going to investigate the circumstances of Rachael's death, but he must be discreet. It will take some time."

After a contemplative pause, Oleg responded, "I will inform His Holiness that the project has been halted pending Angus's investigation. Good luck, my friend, and keep me advised."

ELK GROVE VILLAGE, ILLINOIS
TUESDAY, MARCH 30, 1999
11:41 A.M.

"Oleg, I have some news. Perhaps we won't have to abandon the project. Angus has completed his investigation. We learned that Rachael told her best friend she had undergone a uterus transplant and a clone implant. She made a stupid mistake in telling her friend about it, but she was smart enough to lie about the location. She told her it had taken place in New York City.

"Well, her friend mentioned it to her hairdresser and the hairdresser at the next chair couldn't help but hear. She apparently told her husband what she had overheard but the trail ends there. But, here's the important part, Oleg. Whoever killed Rachael—and we have to assume that it was not an accident—thinks that the operation took place in New York City. We're safe, Oleg. Angus went to New York and found that there have been a series of recent inquiries into specialized surgical facilities and uterine transplants throughout the city."

"I'll tell Loleck immediately. Perhaps he'll change his mind about canceling the project. He was mainly concerned about Laura's and your safety. I'll try and convince him. But, how long will it take to find another perfect match to bear the child?"

"Oleg, I didn't tell you this, but I've had a backup candidate for the past several months. Miriam Netzer and her husband Jozsi live a short distance from here in Skokie. She's anxious to begin the procedure."

"Assuming Loleck gives his approval, when would you do the procedure?"

"Not for at least six months. Both the surgeons and I have a lot of work to do. They need to practice more on baboons and goats, and I need to work on a safe way to attach the fertilized egg to the uterus wall. Also, I think this time we'll do the uterus transplant several months ahead of the in vitro operation."

"I'll call you as soon as the Pope makes his decision. Knowing him as well as I do, I can assure you that he will think and pray on the matter for at least a week. Why don't you proceed under the assumption that he will give his approval. And Ian—or Sean—please be careful."

ELK GROVE VILLAGE, ILLINOIS
MONDAY, APRIL 5, 1999
12:32 P.M.

The secure phone rang. Sean answered and listened. After several moments he said, "Thank you, my friend, and give our best to His Holiness."

He let out a huge breath as he hung up the phone. Covering his mouth with a trembling hand, he exclaimed to Lauren, Scott, and Judith, "We have a lot of work to do. We have permission to move forward. At the first sign of trouble, we're to permanently abandon the project."

ELK GROVE VILLAGE, ILLINOIS
TUESDAY, AUGUST 3, 1999
6:41P.M.

It was a scorching hot and humid day.

The exhausting nine-hour uterus transplant operation was completed. Ian and the surgeons were cautious about the success of the operation, but they would not feel comfortable until Miriam's body held her new uterus for a hundred and twenty days.

As with the previous attempted transplant, they removed almost thirty healthy eggs from her fully functioning ovaries and immediately froze them. Lauren observed throughout the entire surgery.

———

Back at the Murphy house, after a hearty dinner, and after Andy had been put to bed, the four gathered together to discuss their future. "Sean, tell us your thoughts on the surgery today," Judith requested.

"We won't know for a while. With poor Rachael, we discovered she developed a yeast infection by candida albicans that caused damage to a local artery. That, in turn, limited the blood support of her new uterus. That's why it had to be removed. It's all so experimental.

"I do know this, if she does conceive, the baby will have to be delivered by C-section. Eventually she will have to have a hysterectomy."

"Oh my gosh!" Judith exclaimed. "Why will she have to go through all that?"

Judith and Scott anxiously looked at Sean, awaiting his response.

"She will be on immune-suppressive therapy during her entire pregnancy. She cannot be on these drugs long past her delivery. This has to be her one and only chance at having a baby."

EVANSTON, ILLINOIS
SUNDAY, SEPTEMBER 19, 1999
5:31 P.M.

Once again, Ian McKinney, alias Sean Murphy, watched as his wife Laura, alias Lauren, gave birth. They were ecstatic to welcome a seven-pound seven-ounce baby girl named Alexandra Ceilidh Murphy. Again, they would worry about a legal last name change when they returned to Scotland.

Mother and child came through the birthing in perfect health. Shortly after, Sean explained for the first of countless times the meaning of the unusual name.

"Ceilidh is pronounced Kay-lee and derives from the Gaelic word meaning 'a visit.' It has evolved to mean a concert or an evening of informal Scottish traditional dancing to informal music."

———

Sean placed a phone call to Cardinal Jaropelk. "Hello, Oleg, we wanted to call and give you the good news. I'm going to hand the phone to Lauren."

"I apologize for making this call so late, but we want you to know we just had a baby daughter. Yes, I'm doing just fine, thank you. Oleg, we named her Alexandra after you." She quietly listened, then whispered to Sean, "He's crying, Sean."

After several minutes of conversation, she told the cardinal she loved him and handed the phone to Sean.

After listening for a moment, Sean effused, "I agree, Oleg. I am very blessed. We now have two children who are named after you. We can't wait for you to meet them."

After ending the call, Sean held Lauren's hand. "We have made a wonderful man very happy. And, darling, you have made this man extremely happy. We are now a family of four."

ELK GROVE VILLAGE, ILLINOIS
MONDAY, DECEMBER 5, 1999
10:41 A.M.

Sean implanted a fertilized egg into Miriam's healthy transplanted uterus. It would take fifteen days to determine if the procedure would be successful.

It was not.

ELK GROVE VILLAGE, ILLINOIS
TUESDAY, JANUARY 4, 2000
8:52 A.M.

Sean made the difficult phone call to Cardinal Jaropelk.

"Oleg, I'm afraid the second one also didn't take. After the first implant, the egg stopped dividing within hours. We determined that the uterus was healthy. The problem was with the cloned egg. I used a different chemical solution for the second implant, but it didn't change the outcome."

He listened for a moment, then responded, "Yes, it is disappointing. We'll keep trying."

———

Sean responded to Lauren, "Yes, darling, it is discouraging. But you must remember five years ago we went through the same multiple procedures with Dolly. There's been a lot of progress in the science of genetics since then. I'm confident we will eventually be successful."

However, there was one major concern that was constantly in the back of his mind. He wasn't dealing with the cloning of a sheep. He was attempting to clone a human being.

And it wasn't just any human being; he was attempting to clone Jesus from a two-thousand-year-old blood sample.

WINNETKA, ILLINOIS
TUESDAY, JULY 11, 2000
8:16 P.M.

Lauren came downstairs after putting the babies to bed to find Sean sitting in his recliner cupping a glass of whisky in his hands.

"Sean, you've been depressed for the past three days. Would you care to discuss it?"

"It's nothing."

"Ian McKinney, talk to me, you stubborn Scotsman," she demanded.

Clenching his jaw, he admitted, "This just isn't working." He lowered his head and mumbled, "And I don't think it will."

After a moment of silence, Lauren pulled a chair up in front of him and sat down. She took his glass of whisky from his hands and set it down on the table next to them. Reaching out, she grasped both of his hands and coaxed, "Tell me what you're thinking."

"I'm afraid the DNA is too old, and we've wasted three years of our lives."

"Ian McKinney," she admonished, "we're not wasting time when we follow our dreams. We waste time when we are complacent and let our dreams pass us by without attempting to pursue them."

"I fear I've led you astray and brought you to America to chase a worthless cause. And now we can't go back to the institute and the work we both loved."

"My darling, I don't care where we live or what we do, as long as I'm with you. You've given me Andy and Alexandra. And, more important, you've given me you. No matter what happens, I will always consider myself to be blessed to have our lives together."

She tightly held his hands, their knees touching as she looked deeply into his eyes. "Ian, I love and adore you and I will be with you wherever this road takes us. Think about John Paul, and Oleg and Joseph. With a team like that, something wonderful is bound to happen. We need to just keep trying."

"You're right, Laura." He smiled and confided, "I've missed calling you Laura."

"Let's go upstairs. The kids are asleep and I can think of something better to do than sitting here sulking."

WINNETKA, ILLINOIS
SATURDAY, SEPTEMBER 2, 2000
7:28 P.M.

Scott, Judith, Sean, and Lauren were seated at the dining room table at the Murphy house. Sean spent the day preparing one of his gourmet meals and was about to pour the wine. A melancholy mood pervaded the evening.

Everyone was despondent about the lack of success with Miriam. It had been nearly a year since her new uterus had been successfully transplanted. She was healthy; she was happy; and she and her husband desperately wanted a child. Jozsi was wounded while serving in the Army during Operation Desert Storm and was rendered impotent from his groin wounds. Sean had performed a total of thirteen fertilized egg implants since the first attempt nine months earlier. All had met with failure. He knew that the problem rested with the age of the DNA samples and not with the uterus or the process.

After pouring wine for Scott and Judith, Sean approached Lauren to fill her glass. She held her hand up, signaling that she didn't care for any. "No wine tonight, darling?" Sean asked in a surprised tone. "Are you feeling all right?"

"Yes, I feel wonderful. I just won't be drinking any alcohol for the next seven and a half months," she responded as she looked up at her husband with a wide smile.

"That's wonderful!" Sean exclaimed as he lifted her out of her chair to embrace her. "When did you find out?"

"Yesterday. I thought I might be pregnant again, so I visited the doctor. You're quite the prolific man, Doctor Murphy. We're well on the way to having the five children you wanted."

"Lauren, that's wonderful. When are you due?" Judith exclaimed with a wide grin.

"Early April."

"Evanston Hospital again?" Judith asked.

"No, as a matter of fact, my doctor changed hospitals and I'll be having the baby at Chicago Metropolitan Hospital, downtown near Water Tower Place."

WINNETKA, ILLINOIS
WEDNESDAY, SEPTEMBER 6, 2000
7:23 P.M.

"Doctor Murphy, I don't like to bother you at home, but I think I should see you tomorrow," Miriam said on the telephone.

"Are you all right, Miriam?" Sean asked with obvious concern.

"Yes, I'm fine. I think I might be pregnant."

Sean was dumbstruck and couldn't utter a word. Finally, he was able to speak.

"Miriam, I'll have Scott pick you up at 8:30. I'll have one of the OB-GYNs at the facility at nine o'clock and he'll do a quick exam. Meanwhile, you get a good night's sleep."

"Dr. Murphy, Jozsi and I are so excited."

"Miriam, don't get too excited. Honestly, it's not very likely. You go get some sleep; we'll know tomorrow." Sean quickly walked upstairs where Lauren was softly singing Andy to sleep. Sean started to speak, but Lauren held her finger up to her lips. He walked over to the cribs and softly kissed Alexandra and Andy on their foreheads.

When Lauren came downstairs, Sean was finishing a telephone conversation with Scott.

"What happened? You look like you've just seen a ghost."

"I might have," Sean sputtered. "Miriam thinks she might be pregnant."

Lauren shuddered and whispered, "Oh my God!"

ELK GROVE VILLAGE, ILLINOIS
THURSDAY, SEPTEMBER 7, 2000
10:03 A.M.

Sean, Lauren, and Scott were stunned as the OB-GYN proudly declared, "Well, Doctor Murphy, you have a very pregnant patient."

Lauren's hand flew to her chest and her mouth fell open as she turned to Sean.

Scott stiffened and his eyes widened as he, too, looked at Sean for direction.

"Do you know what this means?" Lauren stammered.

"Yes, I think I do," Sean mumbled with his heart racing and his stomach clenching. His body erupted in gooseflesh.

CHICAGO, ILLINOIS
MONDAY, APRIL 9, 2001
9:13 A.M.

Miriam Netzer gave birth to an eight-pound six-ounce boy in the maternity ward on the fourth floor of Chicago Metropolitan Hospital.

She had been admitted the previous evening under the name of Melanie Miller. For security reasons, Scott thought a change of identity would be prudent. Both Sean and Lauren were present for the birth as was Miriam's husband, Jozsi, alias Daniel Miller. Lauren could not stand for long in the delivery room as she was due any day.

The mother and father were ecstatic with joy with their healthy baby.

"Thank you so much, Sean, for everything you've done. It's a miracle, isn't it?" Miriam said.

"Yes, Miriam, it truly is." He shivered and his eyes began to moisten.

Over the past seven months, Sean had spent most of the time helping Lauren with their two children and monitoring the health of Miriam. He kept conducting experiments and doing research in the event the birth was not successful. Oleg, of course, had been constantly advised of all developments.

The nurses in the delivery room appeared to think it unusual to have another couple in the delivery room and they also appeared to be surprised over the amount of adoration given to the newborn baby.

It was almost reverential.

The baby was scored, weighed, bathed, and wrapped before he was given to the mother to hold. After thirty minutes of having the baby lie on Miriam's stomach, the nurses took the baby down the hall to the newborn nursery.

An orderly wheeled Miriam up to her two-bedroom and living room suite on the eleventh floor. The second bedroom was for Scott Williams, her bodyguard. Sean drove Lauren home, where she could rest and where Sean could make a secure telephone call to the Vatican.

It was shortly after noon in Chicago and seven o'clock in the evening in Rome when Sean informed Oleg that the baby had been born and was healthy.

"Not only is he healthy," Sean said, "he is almost charismatic."

"Ian, don't leave your telephone. I need to advise His Holiness. I'll call you back within an hour," Oleg instructed.

Almost an hour later to the minute, the secure telephone rang. "Get ready for some visitors, my friend. Loleck, Joseph and I will arrive in Chicago the day after tomorrow. We will travel as ordinary citizens, but we'll be in disguise. No one must know we are coming. Do you possibly have room at your house for three guests for several nights? It's too dangerous for His Holiness to appear in public, but he insists on seeing the baby."

"Of course, we can accommodate you. I can't promise you that Laura will be home. She's due any day now."

"That's very gracious of you, Ian. We are looking forward to seeing you and your family. We're scheduled to arrive by private jet at Palwaukee airport on Wednesday afternoon."

"It will be great to see you, Oleg. Angus will meet you after you clear customs and retrieve your luggage. Oh, and Oleg, please remember that my name is Sean."

TEL AVIV, ISRAEL
TUESDAY, APRIL 10, 2001
8:02 A.M.

Mossad Director Ephraim Halevy called Fox and Viper into his office. Also joining them was Meir Dagan, who was reputed to be ready to take Halevy's place when he retired. Fox knew this must be a critically important assignment to involve both men.

Halevy made the introductions. "Meir, I want you to meet Fox. You know of his heroic exploits over the past twenty years. I want you to also meet Viper. He was responsible for the assignments on Salah Khalif in Tunis and Yahya Aryyash in Palestine."

"It's a great pleasure. I know of your services, but I only know of you by your code name. I also know you have two bullet wounds to show for it. Your serpent code name serves you well," Dagan said, his tone filled with admiration.

"Gentlemen, we have a very unusual situation," Halevy instructed. "You have no time to prepare for this assignment. Viper, you're to leave shortly for Chicago. You will hopefully have a quick termination, which may well have to become multiple because of the lack of preparation time. Fox, you will follow him on a different flight and be there to clean up anything that might go wrong."

Halevy and Dagan spent the next thirty minutes explaining what they had learned.

"My God!" Fox exclaimed. "The McKinney deaths were staged to throw us off track. That was brilliant." He squeezed his eyes shut before he proclaimed, "And now, you're again asking us to take steps where only God was meant to walk."

"Yes, we are. But now it's different. Four years ago, it was only theory. Now it has happened," Halevy asserted. "Israel's survival could depend on your success."

After letting his words sink in, he continued, "Viper, take the rest of the afternoon and prepare your identity. You have a late-night flight to Chicago, and you arrive in the early morning. Fox, we'll have a final briefing this evening and then you have a late flight to Frankfurt and then on to Chicago. May God go with you both."

"Ephraim, in twenty years of service I've never questioned my assignments. Are you certain we need to do this?"

"Absolutely."

REMOTE AFGHANISTAN
TUESDAY, APRIL 10, 2001
5:04 A.M.

The assassin with a deadly snake code name had arrived in Kabul late the previous night.

He had received a round trip ticket from Frankfurt to Kabul, together with a deposit of one million euros into one of his accounts. The one million euros would be his simply for attending the meeting.

He was picked up at the airport and escorted to a waiting car where he was frisked, searched, and blindfolded. He was not spoken to, nor did he speak during the five-hour drive over bumpy roads. He sensed he had been driven east into the barren mountains of eastern Afghanistan and western Pakistan.

When they finally came to a stop, he was removed from the car, again frisked and searched, and had his blindfold removed. Disoriented, he glanced around at the barren mountainous terrain hollowed out by a series of large caves. He quickly estimated several hundred heavily armed men standing around the entrances.

Turning around, he looked over dozens of makeshift huts and cooking fires to the distant valley below. His keen senses quickly returned as he studied the surroundings. He noticed some women tending the cooking fires, but he was struck by the silence. There were no children.

As he faced the large caves, he noticed to his left a caravan of heavily-laden pack animals being unloaded. He was stunned by the primitive surroundings.

Silently wincing, he was pushed forward by a rifle butt to his back. His arms still tied, he was led to a large cave entrance, surrounded by nearly fifty armed men and roughly pushed inside.

A man, obviously the leader, stood up, walked up to him and gave him a warm greeting. With a long beard and dressed in plain robes, he was slightly taller than the assassin. He was very thin but appeared to have a gentle demeanor as he spoke in Arabic. He did not offer his name.

"Please, be seated, I have an assignment for you that is immediate and of major importance."

"I want my arms untied," the assassin demanded.

"Of course," he responded as he nodded to one of his men. "We do not have much time. If you accept this assignment, you will fly from Kabul to London in less than seven hours, where you will take an evening flight and arrive in Chicago in the morning. Once there, you are to kill a baby at a hospital. You may not be able to identify the baby, in which case, you must kill all the babies to be certain you have eliminated the target. For this, you will have two million additional euros wired to your account."

"Excuse me, I don't kill babies, at least not intentionally."

"Allow me to tell you the background and then you can make up your mind."

"I will listen to what you have to say after you tell me what I should call you?"

"You can call me The Director."

The Director spent the next twenty minutes describing the circumstances of the assignment. When he was finished, the assassin immediately accepted, even declining to take the fee.

"No, you will earn this fee. We have access to ample funds; what is important is success. Very few of our people are trained in this type of operation and those that are trained are already in place for a major operation late this summer. I apologize for the urgency, but we just found out the details early yesterday. This Netzer Jew baby cannot be allowed to live."

"Thank you, Director. May I ask a personal question?" The Director nodded. "What is your name?"

"Why do you ask?"

"I normally don't care who is using my services, but there is something about you. You have an aura of greatness. I might make myself more available to you should you again need my expertise."

The Director thought for a moment and then said, "My name is Osama Bin Laden. May Allah go with you."

AUSTIN, TEXAS
TUESDAY, APRIL 10, 2001
8:47 A.M.

The professional killer received instructions from The Alliance on Saturday requesting him to immediately come to Austin and wait for instructions for what might be an urgent assignment of critical importance. A reservation was made for him at the Crowne Plaza Hotel under one of his alias names, Matthew Wiens.

Shortly after his early Sunday afternoon arrival, he received a phone call from an unidentified caller. "Please enjoy yourself in Austin, Mr. Wiens. But, please do not venture away from your telephone."

On Monday night at 9:15, he received a telephone call with his instructions. "Mr. Wiens, please immediately walk over to Palm Park and sit down at the picnic table on the south side of the swimming pool. I will approach you from behind and sit behind you at the table. Do not turn around, I don't want you to see my face. The park will be empty and no one can overhear what I have to tell you."

The killer had listened intently as the faceless voice told him a preposterous story about the cloning of Jesus and that the baby had been born that morning in Chicago.

"We don't yet know all of the details, but I will know them by tomorrow morning. Unless you hear differently, I'll meet you here tomorrow morning at 8:30. I will again approach you from behind, so don't be startled. I'll give you the final details then. And, Mr. Wiens, please respect my privacy and don't turn around to look at me."

The killer assured him he would not.

"One more thing, Mr. Wiens, I want you to make flight reservations to Chicago for tomorrow night. This assignment must be carried out on Wednesday. We cannot allow this baby to live. If he lives, it could ruin everything we've worked so hard to achieve."

The mysterious man turned and walked away into the trees.

The assassin with the deadly snake code name did not turn around.

There was a slight chill in the air as he sat at the picnic table facing the pool. He glanced at his watch and noted it was a few minutes before 8:30 a.m. He heard the man approaching well before he heard his voice.

"The baby is in the newborn nursery at Chicago Metropolitan Hospital. He was born yesterday morning to Miriam Netzer. Mr. Wiens, I don't care how you do it, but this baby must die, and it must happen tomorrow before he is taken from the hospital." The faceless man pushed a sealed envelope across the table. "Your customary fee is tripled for this assignment. Good luck, Mr. Wiens."

The enforcer heard him walk away. He sat for a few minutes, thinking about what lay before him, then quickly walked back to the hotel, gathered his belongings, and drove to his home in Plano. He had a lot of work to do before his early morning flight.

SANTA MONICA, CALIFORNIA
TUESDAY, APRIL 10, 2001
4:22 A.M.

Bryson Finch, the titular head of the radical Christian Identity Movement, had met and recruited the assassin seven years ago, in 1994.

Because of his past experiences, the assassin was attracted to the white supremacy, anti-Semitic, anti-Negro and anti-Asian aspects of this philosophy. When the 'minister' explained the biblical history of the races and how the white race was descended from the true Israelites, not the current-day Jews, the killer was infatuated.

Finch had frantically called the enforcer the previous afternoon from Kingman, Arizona. He told him he had an urgent matter to discuss and that he would drive overnight to meet him.

They were alone at the end of the Santa Monica pier in the early morning misty moonlight. "Bryson, what's so important that you would break cover and drive all the way here?"

Finch addressed him by his deadly snake code name. "I've learned of an unbelievable event. It appears some British scientists have actually cloned a human being from the Shroud of Turin. The baby was born yesterday morning to a Jewish mother named Netzer in a hospital in Chicago. Do you realize what this means?"

Before he could respond, Finch excitedly went on.

"This baby is the anti-Christ and has come to lead the Jews and their allies against the white race. That means that Christ is either back here on earth or shortly will be. We're within thirty years of Armageddon and the ultimate confrontation between good and evil. After the final battle is ended and God's kingdom is established here on earth, the Aryan people will be recognized as the one and true Israel.

"You have been sent by God to secure that victory. You must go to Chicago and kill the Jewish anti-Christ at any cost. Your success means victory, your failure will mean defeat of the Aryan race. I don't care what it takes; I don't care who you eliminate. You have got to be successful. I suggest you do your research and plan your strategy. I have booked you on a flight that gets you into Chicago in the morning."

CHICAGO, ILLINOIS
WEDNESDAY, APRIL 11, 2001
5:04 P.M.

Miriam sat up in bed holding the baby, as her husband Jozsi sat in a chair at her side. Sean and Lauren sat on the sofa, staring hypnotically at the baby.

There was a soft knock on the door. Scott entered the room and quickly surveyed the surroundings.

Assured that everything was in order, he ushered in three older gentlemen who were wearing overcoats with the collars pulled up and fedora hats. Sean, Lauren, and Jozsi immediately stood up.

Lauren rushed up to Oleg and threw her arms around him. "Oleg, it's so wonderful to see you," she cried, "especially, under these circumstances."

Cardinal Jaropelk beamed as a tear rolled down his cheek. He turned to Sean and gave him an effusive hug. No words were necessary.

Lauren turned to Pope John Paul II and warmly greeted him, burying her head in his chest. He gave her a wide smile and kissed her on the cheek. He greeted Sean with a firm handshake, then dropped the handshake and put his arms around his shoulders and hugged him tightly.

The Pope turned and smiled. "Ah, you must be Jozsi Netzer. Congratulations, my son. You have a huge responsibility ahead of you," the Pope exulted as he warmly grasped Jozsi's hand with both of his hands.

"I know that, Your Holiness. My son is truly a gift from God."

"Yes, he is, Jozsi," John Paul said as he went to the bedside. "Yes, he is," he repeated.

With some difficulty, he bent over and tenderly placed his hands on Miriam's cheeks. He kissed her forehead. "Bless you, my child." He looked at the baby, who seemed to look straight into the eyes of the Pope. "May I hold him?"

Miriam smiled as John Paul picked up the baby. "What are you naming him?" he inquired.

"Jason," Miriam answered. "Your Holiness, may I ask a favor of you?" John Paul nodded, not taking his eyes off the child he was holding. "Would you baptize him?"

Pope John Paul II looked at Miriam with moistening eyes. He struggled to articulate his words. "My child, it will be the most important event of my entire life. I am honored to be able to do so."

He looked at Cardinal Ratzinger, who produced a vial of holy water. Cardinal Jaropelk leaned over to look at the newborn. The baby appeared to turn his head toward Oleg and seemed to give him a slight smile. The baby's eyes went back to staring at the man who was tenderly holding him.

As the Pope administered the baptism, Sean looked around the room. He looked at the mother and father, at Scott and Judith, and at the three blessed men who had traveled all the way from Rome. His attention went back to the baby and as it did so, he shivered, looked at Lauren, who was standing next to him, and whispered, "Do you realize what we're watching?"

Tears were rolling down her cheeks as she whispered, "Yes, I do."

When the baptism was completed, John Paul said to the others in the room, "Let us move to the other room where we can talk."

With reluctance, he handed the baby back to Miriam.

———

When the door was closed and the six men and Lauren and Judith were seated in the living room, John Paul instructed, "Oleg and Joseph, would you kindly bring everyone up-to-date." He contemplated for a moment and added, "Can we please dispense with the false names, please, for this conversation? It's too confusing for this old man."

"Certainly," Oleg replied. "We fear that news of this event may have gotten out. Mr. Netzer, we want you and your wife to remain here at the hospital for the next several days, where you and the baby will be safe. We ask that you not return to your home for any reason. You will fly to Ixtapa, Mexico, on Friday morning, the day after tomorrow, as Daniel and Melanie Miller with your son, Jason. You will live in the village of Zihuantanejo until it is safe for you to return."

He glanced at Angus and added, "You know them as Scott and Judith Williams. Their real names are Angus and Kathleen MacGregor. They will accompany you and will also live there until Angus believes it to be secure."

"How long do you think we will be there? And, what will we do there?" Jozsi exclaimed as his hand flew to his chest.

"It will probably be for several years. I understand that you have a small construction business, building homes," Joseph stated.

Jozsi nodded.

"You will build homes for the poor of that village. We have your new identities already made up. Angus and Kathleen will go shopping for you tomorrow and bring you back all the clothes and personal items you will require for your journey."

"Jozsi," Cardinal Ratzinger continued, "Angus does not want you to leave the hospital until he takes you to Mexico. Bank accounts will be opened for you in your new names, Melanie and Daniel Miller, and we already have a nice home under lease for you. You can live comfortably, help the poor in that area, and raise that little miracle of yours."

"This is a lot to absorb, Cardinal Ratzinger," Jozsi exclaimed.

"We know it is, Jozsi," Oleg interjected. "Keep in mind the enormous responsibility you now have. Your safety and the safety of your family is of critical importance, not only to us, but to the entire world." He turned to Angus and asked, "Angus, will you describe the details to Mr. Netzer?"

"Now, here's the difficult part," Angus began. "If there are any personal items that you want to save in your current house, you need to make a list of them and their location. I will retrieve them. Ian and Kathleen will return to your house late at night on Friday, driving your van, posing as you and Miriam. They will be carrying a small bundle with them, so anyone observing will think that you are returning home from the hospital with your new baby. In the back of your van will be three cadavers, an adult male, an adult female and a small infant male.

"Ian and Kathleen will place the cadavers in your bed and in the crib in your bedroom. I will pick up Ian and Kathleen at about one in the morning and will take them back to their homes. Then I will return at about three in the morning and cause your furnace to explode and quickly incinerate the entire house. As far as anyone will know, you and Miriam and your new baby will have perished in the accident. Neither of you has any living relatives, and your friends will, unfortunately, have to deal with their grief. The safety of you and Miriam and the child is of paramount importance."

John Paul lamented, "Once again, we need to fake some deaths to prevent these evil forces from seeking you. They must be convinced that the project has been totally abandoned."

Jozsi repeated, "Wow … That's a lot to absorb. I'll explain it to Miriam and we'll make a list of items we'd like to have saved from our house."

"Mister Netzer—Jozsi—I know this is a lot to ask," John Paul proclaimed. "But you must always remember one thing. You are raising the Christ child. You now have the most important job of any man on Earth."

Everyone, except Laura, got up to embrace Jozsi. As Ian started to return to the sofa where Laura was seated, he immediately noticed that she was ashen faced.

"Ian, my water just broke and I don't feel well. Something's not right."

Ian hurried to her side as Angus pulled out his cell phone and quickly dialed the number of Laura's doctor. He left a message and rushed downstairs to the fourth-floor delivery rooms. He asked for the senior OB-GYN on duty and together they raced to the elevators and returned up to the eleventh-floor suite.

The physician quickly examined Laura and saw that she was having difficulty breathing. He took her blood pressure and found it to be 210 over 167. He immediately called the delivery room and ordered, "We have an emergency C-section; I will be performing it in ten minutes!" He quickly listed the items he would need. "I'm afraid we might have an AFE."

Several minutes later, the door to the room suddenly opened and two attendants and a physician rushed in and assisted Laura onto a gurney. Within five minutes, she was in the fourth-floor operating room, being administered anesthesia. On the way down the elevator, Ian frantically beseeched the doctor for an explanation of what was happening.

After Laura was prepped and ready for surgery, the surgeon returned to Ian and Angus. "We are going to do everything possible to save the lives of your wife and baby, but it's extremely serious." He looked over at one of his fellow physicians and said, "Ron, it looks like we have an AFE. Would you escort these gentlemen back to their suite and tell them what is happening."

He swung open the doors and rushed into the operating room.

As they returned to the suite, they found the three men from the Vatican with worried looks on their faces.

"Would everyone please sit down, and I'll explain what's happening as best I can. I'm Doctor Post, and we think your wife has an Amniotic Fluid Embolism. The outlook is not good. This is a rare obstetric emergency where amniotic fluid, fetal cells, hair, or other debris enters the mother's blood stream via the placenta and trigger an allergic reaction. The reaction can result in heart and lung collapse. After being anesthetized, your wife was immediately given oxygen to prevent lung collapse and drugs to keep her heart pumping. They are trying to save the baby. I must tell you that sixty percent of the women do not survive this first phase that I just described. There is, however, a good chance that your wife will survive this phase because of the rapid attention she's receiving."

"And what about the next phase?" Ian beseeched, his chin and lips trembling.

"The second phase is called the hemorrhagic phase and is usually accompanied by severe shivering, coughing, vomiting and excessive bleeding as the blood loses its ability to clot." The doctor paused and looked at Ian. "Only about fifteen percent of the women who make it to the hemorrhagic phase survive."

There was silence in the room as everyone grasped the realization of what was happening.

"You're saying she has less than a ten-percent chance of survival?" Ian pleaded, his breath bursting in and out.

"I'm afraid so. I also have to tell you that of the women that do survive, most have permanent brain damage."

Ian collapsed on the sofa, tears pouring from his eyes. The room became silent as everyone tried to grasp the situation.

The silence was pierced by the ringing of the telephone.

Doctor Post quickly answered it and listened. "Well, I have some good news. You have a son and he is alive and healthy. All vital signs are strong." He again looked at Ian. "Your wife will be on the operating table for at least another hour. I'll leave you alone now. Would you like me to come get you so you can look at your new son?"

Ian nodded. Doctor Post looked at his watch. "It's almost a quarter of eight, I'm going to go check on your wife and I'll come back in a few minutes and escort you down to the viewing windows to see your new son."

Twenty minutes later, Dr. Post returned. "Your wife is stable and there's a team of doctors doing everything they can to keep her that way. It's too early to know much. She'll be in ICU for the next several hours, then she'll be moved to a special suite on the tenth floor where you can all spend time with her. It is one floor directly below the suite where we are now. It will probably be five or six hours before she is awake. But I must warn you, she won't be very alert."

"Thank you, doctor," Ian mumbled.

"Let's go look at your new son," the doctor said as he ushered Ian and Angus to the door.

The assassin with the code name Adder reported for his ten-hour shift at 8:04 p.m.

He wore a nurse's uniform which he had earlier obtained from a storage closet and he introduced himself to the two surprised nurses who were waiting for their teammate.

"I was called over from Northwestern Memorial to fill in for Kristi Raschen," he explained to the surprised girls. "I guess she had a last-minute family emergency and they probably called me because I only live a few minutes away." He let the words sink in and gave them a warm smile. "You'll have to forgive me, but I've never worked in a newborn nursery. You just tell me what to do and I'll do it."

Adder silently went about the work that was assigned to him by the head nurse. Several times she tried to call her friend Kristi on her cell phone. Each time it went to voice mail.

The nurse had no way of knowing that her friend lay dead in a storage closet around the corner not more than fifty feet away, strangled fifteen minutes earlier by this handsome male nurse. They also had no way of knowing that their new associate had a gun with a silencer taped to his lower back.

Adder found it difficult to read the names of the babies on the front of the bassinets. There had to be a list in the office. He would bide his time and get the nurses comfortable with his presence.

Viper knew how critically important this assignment was. He had posed as a doctor several times in his career of assassinations, so he was comfortable as he walked the floors of the hospital to familiarize himself with his surroundings.

He would not have felt so comfortable had he known how many other assassins were in the hospital.

Rattler stood in front of the mirror in the fourth-floor men's room, sizing up his uniform. He had watched the security guard off and on for nearly thirty minutes and had waited until shortly before visiting hours were over before striking.

Appearing as a normal hospital visitor, he had stopped the guard just as he walked by the previously locked door to a storage closet, around the corner from the newborn nursery. The lightning-fast chopping blow to the front of the throat had instantly and silently killed the guard.

Earlier, the assassin had easily picked the lock. He quickly dragged the body into the storage room and closed and locked the door behind him. He stripped the body and put on the uniform. When he dragged the dead security guard to the back of the room, he was dumbfounded to find another body, that of a young female nurse.

The security guard's uniform wasn't a perfect fit, but it would have to do. The pants were a little short and the waist was a little big for Rattler. All the better to conceal his revolver with its silencer, he thought.

The hospital corridors were mostly empty as visiting hours were nearly over when he came upon a maintenance man mopping the floor. Rattler nodded as he walked by him and continued formulating his plan to find the baby.

The Fox was mopping the fifth floor of Chicago Metropolitan Hospital. His role was to make sure the assignment was successful and that Mossad was not linked to the events of the night. As usual, he had full authority from the Mossad to kill.

His disguise as a maintenance man worked well as he pushed his bucket and mop around the different floors of the hospital. Unlike the others, he did not have to kill to obtain his equipment. It was not necessary. A syringe sufficed. The maintenance man would wake up in about ten hours. If necessary, Shimon would give him another shot later.

He was mopping the floor of the B wing on the fourth floor, when the security guard walked past him and nodded. He felt uncomfortable, but wasn't sure why.

His vibrating pager, his only contact with Viper, remained still.

It was nearly eight-fifteen when Doctor Post, Ian, and Angus approached the viewing area of the newborn nursery.

As they entered the observation area, they walked past two couples and a single man viewing the babies. A young attractive nurse brought Ian's newly born son to the window.

"I know this is difficult for you, but you have a good-looking healthy son," Doctor Post gently said.

"Thank you. Can we take my son back up to the tenth floor suite, so he, so he can be with his mother when she wakes up?"

"Yes, of course, I'll see that he is brought up."

None of the three men took notice of the man standing alone at the observation window about twenty-five feet away.

Cobra, however, was keenly aware of them.

CHICAGO, ILLINOIS
THURSDAY, APRIL 12, 2001
2:06 A.M.

As Laura awoke, the effects of the anesthesia were almost totally over, but she felt deathly sick. She was shivering, vomiting, and complaining of a bad taste in her mouth as she lay in bed in the tenth-floor suite.

The doctors had stopped most of the bleeding, but there was still some minor hemorrhaging around her weakened heart. Ian and the others had been told that she didn't have long. She pulled the oxygen mouthpiece away so she could talk.

Struggling, and with pain in her throat, she whispered, "Ian, I'm dying, aren't I?"

He couldn't respond, but she knew the answer by looking at his tearful face. "Ian, take care of our children and always let them know how much their mother adored them and their father."

She looked around the room and saw Angus and Kathleen, the Pope, Oleg, Joseph Ratzinger, Miriam and Jozsi Netzer, and the doctor. She slipped into unconsciousness as the monitor reflected weakening vital signs.

Her eyes flickered open and with an unsteady hand, she pushed aside the oxygen mask. "Ian, bring me the baby," she said in a feeble voice.

"Certainly, darling, he's right here."

"I don't mean our baby. I mean Miriam's baby." Speaking those few words exhausted her. "Please hurry," she pleaded in a whisper. Ian looked at the doctor.

"He's down in the fourth-floor newborn nursery," Doctor Post offered. "I'll have to go with you." Ian, Angus, and the doctor immediately left the hospital room and rushed to the elevator and proceeded down to the fourth floor.

After softly knocking on the office door to the nursing station, they were admitted by a young nurse. "Hello, Doctor Post. What are you doing here at this hour?"

"We've come for the Netzer baby. It's important and we're in a big hurry."

She looked at the bassinet location chart and blurted, "We don't have a baby with the name Netzer."

Adder's eyes widened.

Angus interjected, "I'm sorry, we meant the Miller baby, Jason Miller."

She quickly walked into the nursery and returned a moment later, pushing a bassinet containing a tightly wrapped baby. In her haste, she dropped the chart. Unnoticed, it fell to the floor behind her desk.

"Doctor, it's a regulation that one of the pediatric nurses has to accompany any baby that is taken from the nursery." She paused and then stated, more as a directive than a question. "Perhaps our temporary staff member can assist you," she instructed.

"I'd be delighted to," Adder quickly replied, as he moved behind the bassinet and started to introduce himself.

"Thank you, nurse," the doctor said as he signed a departure sheet and they rapidly walked out the door to the waiting elevator. "We don't have time for introductions. Let's go!"

As he pushed the bassinet down the hall to the elevator, Adder looked down at his prey.

He could try to kill him now, but the big guy was walking behind him and he had looked at him suspiciously when they left the nursery.

I'll wait till we get to the room and they're all in front of me, he thought.

Dressed as a doctor, from the end of a darkened hallway, Viper silently observed the two men, the doctor and the male nurse enter the elevator with the baby. He rushed to the nursery.

"Nurse, this is an emergency. Was that the Netzer baby?" Viper demanded.

Puzzled, she replied, "We don't have a Netzer baby. That was the Miller baby."

The security guard—Rattler—also silently observed the four men removing the baby from the nursery, shortly followed by another doctor. He knocked on the door to the nurse's office and inquired, "There's a lot of activity around here tonight. Is everything all right?"

The nurse explained what had happened.

"I'd better check it out," the security guard said with a yawn. "What room did they go to?"

The nurse looked at the form that Doctor Post had hurriedly scribbled and replied.

Rattler thanked the nurse and walked to the elevators, feigning a casualness that he certainly didn't feel.

Fox, at the end of the corridor with his bucket and mop, discreetly followed him to the elevator.

———————

Ian rushed to the door of their tenth-floor room followed by the doctor and Angus. He immediately saw that Laura's eyes were closed. "Is she…"

"No," Doctor Post said, looking at the monitor. "But her vital signs are extremely weak."

Ian rushed to Laura's side, dropped to his knees and took her hand. Angus stood next to him and rested his comforting hand on Ian's shoulder, their backs to the door. The doctor stood on the far side of her bed as the three visitors from the Vatican stood at the back of the room with Miriam and Jozsi Netzer, all with mournful looks.

Adder, the nurse, stood in the doorway, still holding the bassinet. He reached behind him and brought out his pistol and pointed it at the baby.

Oleg was the first to see it. "Your Holiness, he's got a gun!" Oleg shouted.

Momentarily stunned, Adder looked up at the man who had shouted and then at the man standing next to him. John Paul still wore his topcoat and hat.

Adder quickly recognized him. "You're the Pope!" he stated incredulously.

"Yes, my son," he softly responded. He looked straight into the eyes of the assassin and said, "Think about what you are doing. You are about to commit the gravest mistake that any man has made since Judas. I don't know who hired you, but no amount of money is worth what you're thinking of doing."

Adder was speechless as he was momentarily stunned by the development. He raised up his gun and pointed it at the Pope as a look of abject hatred crossed his face.

"You are the reason for all of the problems in the world. You're the reason my family was murdered. This is too good to be true. Now I can rid the world of its biggest tyrant and this false idol. I'm going to kill you, but before I do, I'm going to enjoy the look on your face as you watch this clone's head blasted apart."

He pointed the gun at the baby's head.

The spitting sound of the silenced gunshot was barely audible, but the sound of the splattering blood and bone and brain matter could be heard throughout the room.

Appearing to be a doctor, Viper stepped fully into the room, after having shot the assassin in the back of the head. He pointed his gun directly at Angus.

"Angus MacGregor, we finally meet. I'm certain you are armed. Kindly remove your weapon and put it on the bed with Mrs. McKinney." With his gun still pointed at Angus, he moved his eyes to Ian, saying, "Dr. McKinney, it is also good to finally meet you."

As Ian looked across Laura's bed at the nearly headless body of the male nurse lying on the floor, he had a blank look on his face.

Viper announced, "You might be interested to know that I saved your life several years ago."

This still didn't register with Ian. With everything that was happening and with his beloved wife dying, his brain was not fully functioning.

Viper continued, "Your friend Angus remembers the night when I threw a rock at the sniper outside your front window."

Angus gave a small smile with a slight nod. "Who are you and why are you here to kill this baby? And, who is that?" he asked, glancing across the bed at the lifeless body on the floor.

"Agent MacGregor, I'm not here to kill the clone baby. I'm here to protect him. And I have no idea who that man was. But it's obvious that he came here to kill the baby."

Sighs of relief came from the men from the Vatican and the Netzers while Laura slipped in and out of consciousness. "Allow me to introduce myself. I know that none of this will ever be repeated because you all have your own secret, lying right here, that you can't possibly make public."

Everyone barely breathed as they waited for him to continue.

"My code name is Viper, and I'm with the Special Operations Division of the Mossad."

"Ah, Metsada," Angus mumbled. Viper nodded.

"But why are you here to protect the baby?" Angus asked.

"I don't know the answer. I simply follow instructions." He paused for a moment. "It could be that we just don't want to again be blamed for the next two thousand years for a killing that we're not responsible for."

"Whatever the reason, I thank you," Angus responded, reaching out his hand.

Rattler, the security guard, got off the elevator on the tenth floor and quietly walked toward the room.

As Viper stepped forward around the bassinet, he put his gun on the bed to grasp Angus's hand with both of his hands. As their hands grasped, they heard the ominous words from the doorway.

"Thank you for putting your weapons down. Now back away with no sudden moves."

Rattler stepped into the room and hissed, "Unfortunately, Mr. Viper, it appears I'll have to kill you along with the devil clone."

Viper quickly anticipated that the gunman would shoot him through the back. A kill shot that would exit his chest after ripping through his heart and strike the baby.

He was right.

With his back to the gunman, he picked up the baby and reached out to hand the bundle to Angus. He bent over, slightly turned and lowered his knees as he thrust the baby out, hoping the shot would go through his upper chest and miss his heart and the baby.

Again, the spitting sound of the silenced gunshot pierced the silent room.

Viper pitched across the bed, cradling the baby in his outstretched hands as he landed on Laura's lower legs. Blood spurted from the exit wound on the left side of his upper chest as a pool of crimson spread over the bed sheets.

———

Fox, with his bucket and mop, stood at the fourth-floor elevators and watched the floor indicator until the cab stopped at the tenth floor. He didn't know what he would find, so he decided to ride the elevator to the ninth floor, get off and climb up the remaining flight of stairs.

It was a mistake.

It was 3:31 a.m. when he entered the elevator.

As the elevator door closed behind him, the door to the stairway at the far end of the long hallway, past the newborn nursery, silently opened.

Cobra slid into the darkened hallway after his long wait in the stairwell.

Fox had just exited the stairway when he heard the spitting sound of a silenced pistol, followed by a female scream. *Oh my God,* he thought, *I should have taken the elevator.*

He rushed to the room.

As Fox crouched at the open doorway with his gun raised, everyone heard the spitting sound of two more gunshots. Again, Miriam screamed as Rattler pitched sideways on top of the body of the assassin know as Adder.

Fox stood up, took several steps over to the man he had just shot in the throat and kicked his gun away. He immediately saw that the assassin was trying to talk as he was taking his last breaths.

Fox bent over the body. With a shocked look, Rattler gurgled, "I killed Arabs for you. Why did you kill me?" He died.

Doctor Post quickly paged the emergency room, rushed over to Viper and put compresses on the exit wound.

"Will my son live?"

"It's serious, but it doesn't look like he hit any vital organs in the upper chest," the doctor replied. "We'll do everything we can to save him."

Angus stared at Fox and asked with a knowing look, "We meet again, my mysterious friend. I assume you are also Metsada?"

Everyone's attention turned to Ian as he put Miriam's baby down next to Laura. He gently moved her arm away from her side to grasp the baby. Her eyes flickered open and she slowly focused on the baby.

"Ian, hold him up so I can look in his eyes."

The baby was wide awake as Ian picked him up and set him in Laura's outstretched arms. The baby appeared to stare straight into Laura's eyes.

She smiled and said, "Put him next to me." She lay with the baby, moving in and out of consciousness. Each time she awoke, she looked at the baby and then at Ian.

A serene look of contentment slowly spread across her face and her eyes closed just before a loud buzzer sounded on the monitor. The screen showed flat lines.

Doctor Post picked up the baby and held him in his arms.

"May I hold him?" John Paul asked.

The doctor looked at his watch and noted that it was 3:59 a.m. Ian bent over Laura's body and softly kissed her on the lips, then turned to the others with tears running down his face.

The silence was broken as the loudspeaker emitted three loud chimes followed by the announcement: *Mr. McRoberts, fourth floor, Pod A. I repeat, Mr. McRoberts, fourth floor Pod A. I repeat again, Mr. McRoberts, fourth floor, Pod A. The message was repeated two more times.*

the loud announcement covered up a slight beep from Laura's monitor

TEL AVIV, ISRAEL
WEDNESDAY, APRIL 26, 2001
2:45 P.M.

Newly elected prime minister Ariel Sharon welcomed Fox together with Mossad director Ephraim Halevy and Meir Dagan to his office.

"Fox, we are thankful that your son is recovering," the prime minister offered after his three visitors were seated in front of his desk.

"Thank you, Sir. He arrived home just yesterday from his hospital stay at Walter Reed." Fox gave a crisp nod to Halevy and confided, "Thank you for arranging his quick departure from Chicago."

Ariel Sharon responded, "I must say, we had some interesting conversations with President Bush and Ephraim had a lot of explaining to do on this matter."

The prime minister sat back in his chair with a contemplative look on his face. "I've only occupied this office for a month and you gentlemen have certainly made it challenging. I also had a conversation with the Pope through our intermediary, Jerzy Kluger. Officially, the Pope doesn't recall meeting you and trusts that your memory is the same."

The prime minister stared at Fox and declared, "I called you here to tell you that this entire matter has been buried. The 'clone' baby is deceased, as is the McKinney baby. They were officially in the nursery along with thirty-five other babies at the time of the fire. And you never met the Pope or the two cardinals." He placed his elbows on his desk and intertwined his fingers. "Is that understood?" he ordered.

"Absolutely," Fox affirmed.

Halevy added, "We were hoping you would uncover the Cobra. But whoever he is, he's still out there."

Ariel Sharon's fingers formed a steeple as he praised Fox. "You did your country proud, my friend. And you did your amazing and wonderful mother proud. Now, this matter is over."

Shimon Cohn, alias Fox, bowed his head as he thought about his mother and thought to himself, *I wonder if it is?*

THE END

GLOSSARY OF CHARACTERS

Many of the characters in this story did, or do, exist. I have attempted to weave real people and real events into this work of fiction. All characters and events, other than the obvious historical ones, are fictitious, except for the following people listed in their order of appearance:

Jerzy Kluger was born in Krakow, Poland, in 1921 and raised in Wadowice where his family were leading members of the Jewish community. He met and befriended Karol Wojtyla, who later became Pope John Paul II. They were best of friends throughout their childhood, but lost touch during the war years. After the German invasion in 1939, Jerzy and his father were sent to a Russian work camp before joining the Polish Free Army. His father was sent to Palestine while Jerzy served in Egypt, Iraq, and finally, Italy. His mother and sister remained behind to care for his elderly grandmother. They were taken by the Nazis and all three perished in the concentration camps.

While serving in Africa, Jerzy met his future wife, Irene White, who was Catholic and was a driver for the British army. After the war he married, studied engineering in England, and moved to Rome. In 1965 he heard a news report about a Polish archbishop name Wojtyla speaking at the Second Vatican Council. He left a phone message and received an immediate response. After Cardinal Karol Wojtyla became Pope John Paul II in 1978, he granted his first audience to Mr. Kluger and his family. They became close confidants throughout the remainder of their lives and Jerzy Kluger became a channel of communication between the Israeli government and the Vatican. The last picture taken of the Pope dining before his death was with Mr. Kluger. Kluger died on December 31, 2011, in Rome of Alzheimer's disease.

Ian Wilmut was born in 1944. He is a British embryologist and was Chair of the Scottish Centre for Regenerative Medicine. After receiving his PhD at the University of Cambridge with a thesis on semen cryo-preservation, he focused on gametes and embryogenesis including working at the Roslin Institute. He was the leader of the research group that first cloned a mammal, a lamb named Dolly. Dolly died of a respiratory disease in 2003 and in 2008, the brilliant Dr. Wilmut announced he would abandon the technique of somatic cell nuclear transfer and concentrate on an alternative method. This method derives pluripotent stem cells from differentiated adult skin cells. Dr. Wilmut believes this method holds greater potential for the degenerative diseases such as Parkinson's and to treat stroke and heart attack patients. He is now Emeritus Professor at the Scottish Centre for Regenerative Medicine at the University of Edinburgh and in 2008 was knighted for his service to science.

Keith O'Brien was born in 1938 and became the Archbishop of Saint Andrews and Edinburgh in 1985. In 2003, he was created cardinal by Pope John Paul II. He resigned as archbishop in February 2013 following publication of allegations of inappropriate and predatory sexual conduct. In March 2015 the Vatican announced, though he remained a member of the College of Cardinals, he would not exercise his rights or duties as a cardinal. He spent his later years living in seclusion and died in March 2018 from complications resulting from a fall.

Joseph Ratzinger was born in Bavaria, Germany on April 16, 1927. He was ordained a priest on June 29, 1951. In 1953 he obtained a doctorate in theology. Four years later he qualified as a university professor and subsequently taught at several universities. From 1969 he was a professor at the University of Regensburg and vice president of the university. He was a prolific writer and had numerous essays and sermons published. In March 1977, Pope Paul VI elected him Archbishop of Munich and Freising. Within three months, he was proclaimed cardinal. Pope John Paul II named him prefect of the Congregation for the Doctrine of Faith in 1981. He was elected Vice-Dean of the College of Cardinals in 1998 and in 2002 he became Dean of the College of Cardinals and a member of the order of cardinal bishops. On April 19, 2005, he was elected Pope and took the name Benedict XVI. Prior to his election as Pope, he had hoped to retire because of age-related health issues as well as wanting to have the freedom to write. He served as Pope until February 28, 2013, when he retired, because of his advanced age. At the age of 85 years and 318 days, Benedict XVI was the fourth oldest person to hold the office of Pope.

Pope John Paul II was born Karol Jozef Wojtyla on May 18, 1920. His accomplishments are too numerous to relate. Suffice it to say that he is thought by many to have been the greatest of the 265 Popes throughout history.

Danny Yatom was born in 1945 in Netanya, Israel, and served in the IDF from 1963 to 1996, rising to the rank of Major General. He served as head of the Mossad from 1996 to 1998. He then served as Chief of Staff for Prime Minister Ehud Barak before being elected to the Knesset from 2003 to 2008, when he resigned and retired from politics. He made headlines in May 2018 when he urged the United States to not leave the Iran Nuclear agreement, but to fix it.

Hassan Nasrallah was born in 1960 in East Beirut, Lebanon, and was the oldest of nine children. He became obsessed with Islam fundamentalism while a teenager. His youth, charisma and oratory skills appealed to many young Shiites and he gained a substantial number of devout followers.

In 1985, Hezbollah (party of God) officially announced its existence with Nasrallah as a military commander. In 1989, Hezbollah broke into two factions. The first was moderate as it advocated acceptance of the Taif Accord, demanded the release of Western hostages, and had a narrower focus on combating Israel. The second faction was headed by Nasrallah and advocated rejection of the Taif Accord and unrelenting hostility toward the United States. President Rafsanjani of Iran, who strove to project a more moderate image for his country, assured the victory of the moderate faction at a September 1989 meeting of Hezbollah leaders in Tehran. Nasrallah was called back to Iran in what appeared to be an effort to sideline him.

In October 1990, Syrian forces invaded Lebanon and swept away the last remnants of a democratic government. Syria successfully requested the return of Nasrallah and after Musawi was killed by the Israelis in 1992, Nasrallah became Secretary-General of the Hezbollah after he began professing more "moderate" political views. His first order of business was to exact retribution for the assassination of Musawi. On March 17, a car bomb was detonated at the Israeli embassy in Buenos Aires, Argentina, killing 29 people. This act communicated to the Israeli government that the assassination of Hezbollah leaders would result in the murder of Jews overseas. Although Israel had a plan in place for his assassination, the order was never carried out and Nasrallah was able to travel and speak in public without fear.

After eight years of combat attrition, Israel pulled out of southern Lebanon, resulting in tremendous prestige for Nasrallah throughout the Arab world. Hezbollah was initially excluded from the U.S. "war on terror" in the aftermath of 9/11 as the Bush administration tried to garner Arab support for the war in Afghanistan. This exclusion was conditioned upon Hezbollah ceasing its border attacks on Israel. However, when Hezbollah resumed its border attacks, President Bush declared Hezbollah to be a terrorist group. In 2003 and 2004, Hezbollah, under the leadership of Hassan Nasrallah, sent militants to the Shiite community of Iraq inciting insurgency. He remains as Secretary-General of Hezbollah at the time of this writing.

Yahya al-Mashad was an Egyptian nuclear scientist, born in 1932. He was educated at Alexandria University and received his doctorate in 1956 in London. He continued his studies in the Soviet Union where he spent six years before returning to Egypt. He worked as a nuclear engineer with the Egyptian Atomic Energy Authority until it was frozen following the Six-Day War in 1967. He then traveled to Iraq where he became known as the "brain" behind the Iran nuclear reactor. In 1980, he refused a shipment of uranium from France as it did not meet agreed upon specifications. The French insisted he travel to Paris to receive the shipment. He was assassinated in his Paris hotel room in June 1980.

Khalil El-Wazir was a founding member of the Palestinian armed group, Fatah, and was later a top aide to Yasser Arafat. He was the mastermind behind several high-profile terrorist operations and was assassinated at his home in Tunis on April 16, 1988.

Gerald Bull was born in 1928 and was a brilliant Canadian engineer who developed long range artillery of a scope never before designed. He was a driven but tactless, largely despised and unscrupulous man. His dream was to launch a satellite using a huge artillery piece. He moved from project to project, working for different governments including Canada, the United States, South Africa, China and Iraq. He was working for Saddam Hussein developing their SCUD-based missile project when he was assassinated outside his home in Brussels, Belgium on March 22, 1990.

Ephraim Halevy was born in London in 1934 to an established orthodox Jewish family and he emigrated to Israel in 1948. He attended high school and university in Israel and began work in the Mossad in 1961. He remained in the Mossad for the next twenty-eight years and became the director in 1998 following the resignation of Danny Yatom. He served in the position until 2002. As an elder statesman, he is a pragmatist and has claimed, "Israel will never have peace unless Palestinians are treated as equals."

Meir Dagan was born on a train on the outskirts of Kherson between the Soviet Union and Poland to parents who were fleeing Poland to escape the holocaust. They survived the holocaust and made it to Israel in 1950. Meir was conscripted into the Israel Defense Forces (IDF) in 1963. He completed his compulsory service in 1966 but was called up as a reservist in 1967 for the Six-Day War where he commanded a paratrooper platoon on the Sinai front. He remained in the service, reaching the rank of Major General before retiring in 1995. He served as a counterterrorism advisor to several prime ministers before being appointed to Director of the Mossad in 2002 replacing Efrain Halevy. He served as director until 2011. He was diagnosed with liver cancer in 2012 and died in 2016.

Salah Khalaf was born in 1933 and was the deputy chief and head of intelligence for the Palestine Liberation Organization and the second-ranking official of Fatah after Yasser Arafat. He was a founder of the terrorist Black September organization that was responsible for the Munich Olympics massacre. He was assassinated in Tunis in 1991 by an Abu Nidal operative.

Yahya Ayyash was born in 1966. He was the chief bombmaker of the Hamas terrorist organization and is credited with advancing the techniques of suicide bombing. Known as "The Engineer," the bombings he orchestrated caused the deaths of more than seventy Israelis, many of them civilian women and children. After a massive manhunt, he was assassinated in January 1996.

Osama Bin Laden needs no description, nor does he warrant one.

Ariel Sharon was born in Kfar Malal, Palestine, in 1928 and became a commander in the Israeli Army from its creation in 1948. He was instrumental in the formation of Unit 101 and its reprisal operations. He also participated in the 1956 Suez Crises, the Six-Day War of 1967, the War of Attrition and the Yom-Kippur War in 1973. Yitzhak Rabin referred to him as being "the greatest field commander in our history." After retiring from the military, he entered politics. As the minister of defense, he directed the Lebanon War in 1982 and had personal responsibility for the Sabra massacre for which he became a very controversial figure. From the 1970s through the 1990s, he championed construction of Israeli settlements in the West Bank as well as the Gaza Strip. He served as prime minister from March 2001 to 2006. However, in his later years, as prime minister he championed Israel's unilateral withdrawal from the West Bank and the Gaza Strip, much to the consternation of his Likud Party. Before he could enact these policies, he suffered a stroke on January 4, 2006, and remained in a permanent vegetative state until his death in January 2014.

IN GRATITUDE

First, I want to thank my amazing wife, Joneen, for her encouragement and support. I especially want to thank her for her understanding and patience for all the nights when she went to bed alone as I was typing away on my keyboard.

Before I started writing, Peg and Marc Johnson listened to my story one afternoon and encouraged me to start the journey of becoming an author. Melissa McCullough listened to my story over dinner one evening and also offered great encouragement. Gary Oberg gave me the idea for the time-delayed fuses for the arsonist, while the late Rory Raschen suggested the concept of using solidified aloes and oils to trap and preserve DNA. Special thanks go to my wonderful friends John Yallop, Tom Mathews and my pastor, Tom Melton, who put up with me as I incessantly talked about my plot development, yet they all still offered constant encouragement over the years. A big thank you goes to Tyler Johnson who provided some great insights that will become central to the sequel, *The Shroud Verdict*.

In the fall of 2005, I flew from Denver to Chicago to watch the White Sox win their first World Series since 1919. I stayed with my wonderful friends, Andy and Laura Vogl, and they provided me with a quiet space to type away at my story. They were two of my biggest boosters, and three of my characters are named after them and one of their daughters.

Finally, I finished the first stab at a manuscript, but without an ending. I was stymied. I made copies for my poker buddies, Scott Williams, Ben Vagher, Dan Norblom, Brent Evans, Dan Murphy, Dave Bishop, and Jeff and Brad Kirkendall. They were amazed; however, I think their amazement was more about my being able to put together two consecutive cohesive paragraphs than about the story line. Nevertheless, over the next ten years, they constantly badgered me about finishing the "book" at our monthly poker nights. In hindsight, I think they were trying to distract me, but they were with me all the way.

I received special encouragement and support over the years of this authoring endeavor from two wonderful co-workers, Yvette Youngs and Shannon Fengler, in addition to another amazing friend for over fifty years, Nanci Hartwick. A special thank you goes to my children and especially to my nephew, Doug Wulf. During the writing process, he did several edits and made numerous suggestions including the title change. He has been one of my biggest fans.

More than a few years ago, my wife heard a promotion on the radio for a writing and publishing extravaganza. I enrolled, attended this three-day seminar, and discovered that I knew a lot about real estate financing, but next to nothing about writing, publishing and book marketing. It was more than daunting; it was downright scary. Enter Judith Briles, The Book Shepherd. Over the next five years, I kept attending her monthly programs and recommended webinars. Slowly, I became more confident as time went by. Finally, the time was right with my work life, my home life and my travel schedule, and I succumbed to Judith's less-than-gentle prodding. I completed and edited the entire manuscript. Enter Terry Johnson and Kate Hall who were my first Beta readers and who offered countless important suggestions.

Enter Barb Wilson, Judith's recommended content editor. I didn't know how big the darn book was: "Bruce, you wrote 172,000 words. You need to cut out 50,000 of them." With the amazing tutelage of Barb and Judith, I was able to do this editing over the next nine months. It went back to Barb for a second edit before going to Judith and her editor, Peggie Ireland, for a third and final edit. Enter Kelly Johnson, Judith's virtual assistant expert, who handled designing and maintaining my website, getting the required ISBN numbers, setting up social media and the seemingly hundreds of additional book-related details that had to be done, none of which I knew anything about. It's a good thing I'm not a male chauvinist because my recent life has been centered around these four talented women plus my wife, Joneen, and my mortgage business partner, Shannon. Add to these six, my four daughters-in-law who live close by, and I realized my life is dominated by lovely and talented women. Judith gave me two choices for a graphic artist for interior and cover design—one female and one male. Enter Nick Zelinger. His graphics and layout work have been superb. Of equal value, he brings some testosterone to the team. And what a team it is!

Thank you to everyone who gave encouragement along the way, and a special huge thank you to my amazing team.

About the AUTHOR

BRUCE MACKENZIE is a proud member of the Mackenzie Clan, having researched his family's ancestry back twenty-three generations to its beginnings in the mid-1200's. As an avid student of Scottish history and through his ancestral research, Bruce has discovered great men of renown, honor and achievement in his exciting history along with fabulous historical events, instances of intrigue and, of course, betrayal.

Bruce is an avid collector of all things Scottish. His personal library includes every issue of five different Scottish history magazines dating back dozens of years. He has personally indexed all major articles of this library, which is nearly 100 pages in length.

As Bruce steps into this second career of writing, he looks forward to bringing joy to those who follow his writing with the publication of his debut novel, *The Shroud Solution* and its sequels, *The Shroud Assassins* and *The Shroud Verdict*.

In addition, a future book will gather all the personalities of his historical Clan as he intends to write the Scottish version of *Roots*.

Originally brought up in an idyllic suburban neighborhood of Chicago, he has called Colorado home since 1981. He writes in the wee hours of the night surrounded by his family tartan, expansive gardens and waterfalls along with a good Scotch.

Connect with the Author

www.BruceMackenzieAuthor.com

https://www.linkedin.com/in/bruce-mackenzie-8285542a/

https://www.instagram.com/brucemackenzieauthor

https://www.facebook.com/BruceMackenzieAuthor

https://twitter.com/kbrucemackenzie

CPSIA information can be obtained
at www.ICGtesting.com
Printed in the USA
BVHW031731150820
586522BV00002B/133